RISE OF THE UNDERGROUND

THE QUANTUM SHADOW WAR

THE QUANTUM FRAMEWORK SERIES
BOOK ONE

RAE STONEHOUSE

LIVE FOR EXCELLENCE PRODUCTIONS

PROLOGUE: QUANTUM WHISPERS

The shadows spoke in quantum whispers.

Detective Alice Chen stood motionless at the precinct window, watching Daybridge through eyes that saw more than most. Beyond the gleaming corporate towers and restored historical districts, past the visible spectrum that satisfied ordinary perception, she detected the subtle quantum fluctuations that had been transforming the city for seven years. Reality rippled with possibilities that conventional law enforcement refused to acknowledge—probability patterns suggesting frameworks beyond established parameters.

"You're seeing it again, aren't you?" Sarah Chen asked, her voice interrupting Alice's observation without disturbing her focus.

Where most siblings connected through shared memories and DNA, Alice and Sarah's bond existed on a quantum level. Since the Daybridge Event, Sarah's consciousness had evolved beyond physical constraints—a quantum-ghost enhancement that let her perception dance between reality states like light moving between reflective surfaces. Their sisterhood had become as much a scientific phenomenon as a family relationship.

What corporate science dismissed as a 'quantum-ghost state' was something Alice knew transcended their rigid classification system. Sarah's consciousness hadn't merely slipped outside normal constraints—it had evolved to navigate the quantum framework's hidden architecture. Where Kane's researchers saw anomaly, Alice recognized possibility—her sister's consciousness flowing through reality's underlying patterns like a skilled musician playing notes between standard keys. This wasn't dysfunction; it was evolution beyond corporate science's willingness to acknowledge.

"The fluctuations are forming patterns that conventional monitoring systems aren't designed to detect," Sarah observed, her form shifting as she moved through multiple probability states simultaneously. "It's like watching different layers of reality overlapping where they shouldn't."

Alice had noticed that since the Daybridge Event, Sarah's abilities had been evolving in subtle but significant ways. Her quantum-ghost state wasn't static but adaptive, responding to framework fluctuations with an intuitive harmony that neither Kane Industries' enhancement protocols nor the QLF's liberation theory could explain.

"Have you shown Reynolds the probability models you've been developing?" Alice asked.

Sarah's form flickered with something resembling amusement. "Corporate science isn't ready to acknowledge that someone they classify as a 'consciousness anomaly' might understand framework mechanics better than their research division. Besides, I'm more valuable operating in the spaces between their monitoring parameters."

Alice nodded without turning. "The fluctuations are intensifying. Three percent increase in probability density across central sectors compared to last month's baseline. The framework is responding to something beyond conventional enhancement influence."

"Something the Enhancement Bureau continues pretending doesn't exist," Sarah replied, her form shifting subtly between visibility states —physical presence fluctuating as her consciousness navigated multiple probability streams simultaneously. "Official enforcement has remarkable capacity for strategic blindness when department funding depends on established parameters."

Seven years after the catastrophic quantum framework collapse known as the Daybridge Event, the city existed in precarious equilibrium between competing realities. Corporate enhancement technology had transformed human capability beyond pre-Event limitations, while supernatural communities emerged from centuries of concealment to integrate within carefully negotiated boundaries. The official narrative emphasized stability and controlled progress—enhancement regulated through corporate licensing; supernatural activities monitored through negotiated treaties.

Yet beneath this carefully maintained surface, Alice detected currents that official enforcement refused to acknowledge. Her investigations into quantum framework mechanics had revealed patterns suggesting deliberate design rather than natural evolution—constraints that appeared artificial rather than inevitable consequences of reality's fundamental structure.

"Director Reynolds has requested your presence at central headquarters," Sarah informed her, consciousness perceiving communications beyond conventional transmission. "Apparently, our mutual interest in probability fluctuations has attracted official attention despite careful investigation protocols."

Alice finally turned from the window, her expression revealing nothing despite internal concern. "Which raises the obvious question: what's happening that would justify direct involvement from the Bureau's head of security?"

"Something beyond conventional threat parameters," Sarah replied, her quantum perception detecting patterns that standard security monitoring couldn't identify. "The underground enhancement community has been unusually active—probability signatures suggesting coordination beyond previous organizational capabilities."

The term "underground enhancement" encompassed disparate movements unified primarily by opposition to corporate regulation—individuals utilizing abilities beyond licensed parameters, communities developing technologies outside official frameworks, philosophical approaches questioning fundamental assumptions about reality's proper configuration. Official security classified these movements as criminal organizations despite complex ideological foundations beneath surface activities.

"The Liberation Quantum Front has been particularly active in sectors adjacent to major reality anchors," Sarah continued, sharing intelligence gathered through unofficial channels beyond official monitoring. "Their quantum signatures display harmonic patterns that shouldn't be possible without direct framework manipulation beyond conventional enhancement capabilities."

Alice's investigations had identified mathematical inconsistencies in how reality anchors maintained quantum stability throughout Daybridge—geometric configurations suggesting deliberate framework manipulation rather than merely natural stability mechanisms. These anchors functioned as cornerstones within reality's architecture, maintaining parameters that official enforcement declared natural limitations while her investigations increasingly suggested artificial constraints.

What troubled her most wasn't just the mathematical evidence of framework manipulation, but the document classification patterns she'd uncovered during her investigation. The inconsistencies weren't randomly distributed—they followed administrative patterns suggesting deliberate suppression from Kane Industries' highest levels.

"I found something concerning in the research archive," Sarah had told her the previous week, her quantum-ghost state materializing after hours in Alice's secure office. "Historical research funding allocations that don't appear in public records."

The data Sarah had shared revealed a decades-old research initiative called "Project Cornerstone" that had received massive funding despite no public acknowledgment of its existence. More troubling was how the project's lead researchers had systematically disappeared from corporate records—their careers abruptly ending with vague explanations about "retirement" or "personal pursuits" despite previously meteoric trajectories within the company.

"The pattern suggests systematic suppression beyond normal corporate secrecy," Sarah had explained. "Researchers who achieve certain breakthroughs simply vanish from scientific communities. Not just termination of employment, but complete removal from academic networks."

Alice had begun tracing these researchers, finding disturbing patterns —some had experienced "accidental" deaths, others had been institutionalized for sudden mental breakdowns, and a surprising number had undergone "voluntary" memory modification treatment that had left them unable to recall their most significant research periods.

"This isn't standard corporate proprietary protection," Alice had concluded. "This is systematic elimination of specific knowledge from public consciousness."

But who within Kane Industries possessed the authority to orchestrate such comprehensive suppression across decades? The patterns pointed to an inner circle that transcended normal executive turnover—a persistent entity within corporate leadership that maintained consistent policy despite changes in public-facing management.

"Director Reynolds wouldn't request direct consultation for routine underground activity," Alice observed, detective's precision calculating probability scenarios beyond conventional security response. "Something has changed beyond statistical fluctuation or organizational evolution."

"The official briefing will undoubtedly provide carefully curated information," Sarah replied, her quantum-ghost state allowing perception beyond institutional barriers despite official attempts at information containment. "Though I suspect what remains unspoken will prove more significant than whatever security narrative they've constructed to justify your involvement."

As Alice gathered investigation materials beyond what official security would expect for standard consultation, her enhanced perception detected subtle probability disturbance approaching her office—quantum signature indicating werewolf enhancement despite absence of scheduled appointments or security notifications. The signature belonged to Ethan Reeves, tactical specialist whose military background and supernatural enhancement created unique operational capability beyond conventional security classifications.

"Detective Chen," Ethan acknowledged as he entered without conventional announcement, his enhanced senses having detected both sisters despite Sarah's fluctuating visibility. "Director Reynolds sent me to escort you personally rather than through standard security protocols. The situation requires unusual discretion beyond normal operational parameters."

Alice studied him with investigative precision beyond social convention, her enhanced perception detecting subtle tension beneath his controlled exterior. "Which means the situation connects to cases I'm not officially investigating, regarding probability fluctuations that the Enhancement Bureau doesn't officially acknowledge, potentially involving underground enhancement movements that security classifications don't accurately categorize."

"Your reputation for direct assessment is apparently well-earned," Ethan replied, professional respect momentarily overriding security protocols emphasizing information containment. "The briefing will provide operational context beyond what I'm authorized to discuss outside secured environments. Though I suspect your investigations have already identified patterns that official monitoring has only recently acknowledged despite comprehensive surveillance capabilities."

The exchange established unusual dynamic beyond conventional security interaction—mutual recognition regarding institutional limitations despite professional positions within enforcement structure. Their enhanced perception allowed communication beyond verbal exchange, quantum signatures interacting through principles that official enforcement classified as theoretically impossible despite practical manifestation beyond institutional denial.

"I'll provide quantum cover for your transportation," Sarah offered, her consciousness expanding to create probability field that would minimize detection despite official monitoring throughout Daybridge's central sectors. "My position with the Archives provides legitimate reason for generating quantum fluctuations that should mask your departure despite increased surveillance parameters."

This sibling coordination highlighted complex reality beneath Daybridge's official structure—family connections leveraging specialized capabilities beyond institutional control despite comprehensive monitoring throughout the city. Their enhanced perception allowed cooperation beyond conventional limitations, quantum signatures synchronizing through principles that transcended official enhancement classifications despite regulatory frameworks designed to maintain artificial stability.

As Alice prepared to depart, she cast one final glance at the city through the precinct window. Beyond the visible metropolitan landscape, her enhanced perception detected the quantum architecture that few acknowledged—probability frameworks maintaining artificial constraints that her investigations increasingly suggested weren't merely natural limitations, but deliberate imprisonment of what reality could become.

The shadows continued whispering their quantum secrets, and Alice Chen was among the few who could hear them clearly. Whatever case Director Reynolds was about to assign would undoubtedly connect to these whispers—to the framework fluctuations that official enforcement pretended didn't exist, to the underground movements seeking liberation from artificial constraints to the fundamental questions about reality's proper configuration that transcended conventional crime and punishment.

Daybridge existed in precarious equilibrium between competing versions of what reality should permit. And somewhere within this quantum tension, Alice sensed the beginnings of a case that would

transform not merely the city but the fundamental nature of enhancement itself—a shadow war beyond conventional criminal investigation, where reality itself would become both battlefield and prize as
competing visions of consciousness fought for the future of what
humanity could become.

COPYRIGHT

First Edition

Published by Live For Excellence Productions

ISBN:

Ebook: 978-1-998591-72-5

Paperback: 978-1-998591-73-2

Audiobook: 978-1-998591-74-9

PART ONE
THE SHADOW WAR BEGINS

CHAPTER ONE

REALITY FRACTURES

THE FIRST SIGNS appeared at 3:17 AM in Daybridge's financial district—reality itself began to fold.

Security cameras captured the anomaly beginning as a subtle ripple in the air outside First Metropolitan Bank. Within seconds, the ripple expanded into a shimmering distortion that bent light around it like heat waves rising from summer pavement. The bank's quantum-enhanced security system registered the breach immediately, its reality anchors straining against unprecedented probability fluctuations.

By the time the first responders arrived, a perfect sphere of altered physics had formed in the bank's lobby. Inside the sphere, gravity shifted unpredictably, light refracted through impossible angles and matter itself seemed to exist in multiple states simultaneously. The bank's quantum vault—designed to withstand conventional enhancement attacks—had been breached without a single alarm being triggered until reality itself changed around it.

"They didn't break into the vault—they changed the nature of reality, so the vault was already open," Alice Chen explained, her enhanced perception scanning the crime scene. The morning light struggled to penetrate the probability haze still lingering around the bank entrance. Her specialized quantum scanner hummed with activity, tracking residual energy signatures that ordinary devices couldn't detect.

Alice moved carefully through the lobby, her enhanced senses allowing her to perceive the lingering distortions in the quantum framework. Where others saw only slight visual anomalies, she could track the precise manipulation of probability fields—a technique that shouldn't be possible outside Kane Industries' most secure research facilities.

"Whatever they used, it's beyond any enhancement tech I've encountered," she said, adjusting her scanner's sensitivity. "The quantum resonance patterns match Kane's proprietary framework, but the application is... elegant. Almost artistic."

Ethan Reeves circled the vault entrance, his werewolf senses heightened by his own enhancements. He could smell the aftereffects of the reality distortion—a peculiar metallic scent mixed with something primal that made his wolf nature stir uneasily. Since the Daybridge Event, his supernatural abilities had become increasingly sensitive to quantum fluctuations.

"No physical evidence," he noted, running his hand along the vault door frame. "No scent trails leading away. It's like they existed between realities while they were here." His enhanced tactical systems automatically calculated probability patterns, searching for any trace of the perpetrators. "The security feed shows four figures, but their quantum signatures are masked—they're using some kind of reality dampening field."

As Ethan reviewed the security footage, Alice's scanner detected something unusual in the center of the vault. A small quantum fluctuation remained, pulsing with encoded information. She recognized the signature pattern immediately—it was a calling card, left deliberately.

"Ethan," she called, projecting the fluctuation's data pattern into the air between them. "Look at this resonance signature."

The holographic display revealed a symbol—a triple helix pattern surrounded by quantum equations. As they watched, the equations shifted, rearranging themselves into words:

REALITY BELONGS TO ALL. THE QUANTUM LIBERATION FRONT.

As Alice continued analyzing the quantum data from the vault, something caught her scientific attention. The resonance patterns emanating from the stolen enhancement formulas didn't fully align with standard quantum signatures. There was a tertiary harmonic—subtle but distinct—that corresponded to no known enhancement category.

"There's something unusual about these quantum traces," she said, adjusting her scanner's sensitivity. "The artifacts are generating harmonic patterns that don't correspond to framework manipulation. Almost like they're designed for something beyond enhancement modification."

Dr. Marsly glanced up from her workstation. "Our records show similar anomalies. Kane Industries classified them as measurement errors in the original documentation."

"These aren't measurement errors," Alice replied, studying the complex waveforms. "These are deliberate design elements. The question is—designed for what?"

She filed this observation away—another piece of a puzzle that didn't quite fit the official narrative about the artifacts or their purpose in the quantum framework.

"QLF," Ethan said, his voice tight. "We've been hearing whispers about them for months. Underground enhancement activists using stolen Kane tech."

"This isn't just stolen tech," Alice replied, studying the quantum signatures. "This is something new. They're not just using enhancement—they're rewriting the rules of how it works."

Back at headquarters, Nadia Marsh's archive-enhanced systems had already compiled a comprehensive brief on the QLF. The quantum-secured conference room hummed with reality stabilizers as she projected her findings onto the holographic display.

"The Quantum Liberation Front emerged approximately four months ago," Nadia explained, her archive-enhanced perception allowing her to track information across multiple probability states. "They started with small demonstrations—temporary reality bubbles in public parks, enhancement performances in underground clubs. But this..." She gestured to the bank footage. "This is a significant escalation."

The display shifted to show surveillance captures of suspected QLF members—individuals whose faces were always obscured by probability fields, making identification impossible. Their enhancement signatures were unique—hybrid combinations of abilities that shouldn't work together but somehow did.

"They're exploiting a fundamental gap in our understanding of the Quantum Framework," Nadia continued. "After the Daybridge Event, Kane Industries established protocols for regulated enhancement development. The QLF believes these protocols are artificial limitations —corporate control over humanity's natural evolutionary potential."

"What exactly did they take from the vault?" Ethan asked, his tactical enhancements already calculating potential security risks.

"That's the interesting part," Nadia replied, bringing up the bank's inventory records. "Four quantum storage drives containing experimental enhancement formulas that Kane Industries had deemed 'too unstable for public application.' The formulas were scheduled for secure deletion tomorrow."

Alice studied the data with growing concern. "These formulas were rejected because they allowed enhancement across multiple supernatural categories simultaneously. Kane determined they created dangerous reality distortions when activated."

"Exactly," Nadia confirmed. "And now they're in the hands of enhancement extremists who believe all limitations should be removed." She brought up a map showing suspected QLF activity points across Daybridge. "Our intel suggests they've established underground enhancement clinics throughout the city—offering unrestricted ability development outside corporate and government oversight."

The map revealed an alarming pattern—QLF activity concentrated around areas with high supernatural energy convergence. They weren't just operating randomly; they were strategically positioning themselves at points where reality was already naturally thin.

"They're recruiting," Nadia continued, displaying intercepted communications. "Targeting individuals with latent enhancement potential, promising them 'liberation from artificial constraints.' Their manifesto claims that Kane Industries and other corporations are deliberately suppressing humanity's true potential to maintain control."

Alice's enhanced perception caught the subtle shift in Ethan's quantum signature—a flicker of recognition. "You've encountered them before," she said, not a question but a statement.

Ethan nodded slowly. "Three former members of my old pack joined their movement. Said they were tired of being told what a werewolf should and shouldn't be able to do." His expression darkened. "I lost contact with them two months ago. Their quantum signatures simply... disappeared from traditional tracking networks."

"That's consistent with what we're seeing," Nadia confirmed. "QLF members seem to develop the ability to mask their quantum signatures —to exist partially outside conventional reality tracking."

The implications hung in the air between them. The QLF wasn't just stealing technology or committing elaborate heists. They were developing ways to operate outside the established Quantum Framework itself—creating their own rules in the shadows of reality.

"This bank job wasn't just about stealing formulas," Alice said, her scientific mind already connecting the patterns. "It was a demonstration. They wanted us to see what they can do—how they can manipulate reality itself without triggering conventional security measures."

"And they're just getting started," Nadia added, bringing up one final piece of intelligence—an encrypted message intercepted from suspected QLF channels. The message consisted of a single line:

PHASE ONE COMPLETE. THE FLUX APPROVES. REALITY REMEMBERS.

"The Flux?" Ethan asked.

"Unknown," Nadia replied. "Possibly their leader or perhaps something else entirely. What's clear is that this bank heist was just the beginning of something much larger."

Alice stared at the message, her enhanced perception catching subtle quantum patterns hidden in the encryption. Something about the phrasing triggered her scientific intuition—the same phrase she'd seen in her father's research before he disappeared: "Reality remembers."

"We need to infiltrate their network," she said finally. "This isn't just about stolen technology anymore. If they're manipulating the Quantum Framework itself, they could destabilize reality across the entire city."

Outside the window, the morning sun illuminated Daybridge's skyline —a city still adapting to the aftermath of the Daybridge Event. Neither Alice nor Ethan could shake the feeling that the relative stability they'd worked so hard to establish was about to be tested in ways they couldn't yet imagine.

The shadow war had begun.

CHAPTER TWO

THE PRICE OF EVOLUTION

ALICE's private research lab in the basement of her apartment building was one of the few places in Daybridge with quantum stabilizers advanced enough to accommodate Sarah Chen's unique state of existence. The lab's reality anchors hummed with effort as Sarah's form materialized—sometimes translucent, sometimes solid, her quantum signature fluctuating between states of being that defied conventional physics.

"You look worried," Sarah said, her voice carrying subtle quantum harmonics as she coalesced into near-physical form. Her appearance still mirrored Alice's own—the same dark eyes, the same analytical gaze—though now her edges blurred with probability shadows, and occasionally parts of her would phase into different quantum states.

"The QLF stole unstable enhancement formulas," Alice replied, bringing up her secure data display. "Experimental compounds that Kane Industries locked away because they caused dangerous reality distortions."

Sarah's form flickered slightly as she examined the data, her consciousness processing information across multiple probability states simultaneously. "They're not just stealing formulas," she said, her hand passing through the holographic display, temporarily disrupting its quantum coherence. "They're actively recruiting—and their methods are... concerning."

With a gesture, Sarah projected her own data onto Alice's display—intelligence gathered from quantum spaces where conventional surveillance couldn't reach. The projection showed underground enhancement clinics operating in probability-shifted locations throughout Daybridge. Places that existed partially outside normal reality, accessible only to those with specific quantum signatures.

"They've established a systematic recruitment pipeline," Sarah explained, her form momentarily splitting into multiple probability echoes before reconverging. "First, they identify individuals with latent enhancement potential—people whose quantum signatures show flexibility. Then they approach them with promises of 'true liberation.'"

The display shifted to show clandestine meetings in reality-masked locations—abandoned Kane Industries facilities, supernatural convergence points, places where the quantum framework naturally thinned.

"They start with simple enhancements—low-risk abilities that provide immediate benefits. Enhanced cognitive processing, minor probability manipulation, sensory improvements. Just enough to give recruits a taste of what's possible."

"Standard corporate enhancement protocols," Alice noted, studying the patterns.

"That's how it begins," Sarah agreed, her form stabilizing as she focused. "But then they introduce what they call 'boundary dissolution'—techniques that deliberately break down the natural barriers between different types of supernatural ability."

The display showed recruits undergoing procedures that made Alice's scientific mind recoil. Enhancement formulas administered without proper quantum stabilization. Reality anchor points deliberately destabilized. Supernatural energy signatures forcibly merged in ways that violated fundamental quantum principles.

"They're encouraging hybridization outside controlled environments," Alice said, her enhanced perception immediately grasping the dangers. "Without proper stabilization..."

"Exactly," Sarah's form flickered with urgency. "Most recruits experience initial euphoria—unprecedented ability development, powers that conventional enhancement programs would never permit. But then..."

The data stream shifted to show the aftermath—individuals whose quantum signatures had become dangerously unstable. Some existed partially out of phase with normal reality. Others exhibited ability combinations that created localized reality distortions. A few had simply... disappeared, their quantum signatures dissolving into probability space.

"The QLF calls these 'evolutionary growing pains,'" Sarah continued. "They believe that unstable transitions are necessary for true enhancement evolution. That corporations like Kane Industries implement artificial limitations to prevent humans from reaching their full potential."

"And the recruits believe this? Even as they watch others destabilize?"

Sarah's expression turned grim, her form momentarily displaying multiple emotional states simultaneously. "That's the most disturbing part. They've developed a philosophy around it—a kind of quantum mysticism. They call it 'The Remembering.'"

With another gesture, Sarah displayed intercepted QLF manifestos, filled with quasi-religious language about reality "remembering what was possible" and "breaking the chains of artificial limitation."

"They believe that reality itself is awakening to its true potential," Sarah explained. "That the Daybridge Event wasn't an accident but the beginning of a natural evolution that corporations are trying to suppress."

Alice felt a chill as she recognized phrases from her father's research—concepts that had been dismissed as theoretical before the Daybridge

Event. "This isn't just underground enhancement. This is a movement with a comprehensive ideology."

"And a charismatic leader," Sarah added, her form briefly destabilizing as she accessed deeper quantum streams. "Someone—or something—they call 'The Flux.'"

The memory came unbidden, sudden and vivid—the aftermath of the Daybridge Event fifteen months ago.

Alice remembered standing in Kane Industries' central research facility, watching reality itself fracture around them. The quantum containment fields had failed catastrophically, releasing energy that rewrote the fundamental rules of how reality functioned in Daybridge. Probability streams that should have remained separate had merged. The barriers between supernatural abilities—boundaries that had existed since the earliest recorded history—had begun to dissolve.

She remembered the screams as researchers experienced uncontrolled enhancement, their bodies and minds suddenly connecting to quantum streams they weren't prepared to handle. Some had gained impossible abilities. Others had simply disappeared, their consciousness scattered across probability space. The lucky ones had merely gone mad.

In the epicenter, Dr. Winters had stood surrounded by fifteen ancient artifacts, each pulsing with energy that shouldn't exist in conventional reality. "Reality remembers!" he had shouted over the chaos, his form already beginning to transform. "We're not creating something new—we're remembering what was always possible!"

Then the quantum cascade had reached critical mass, reality itself had shuddered, and everything changed. When stability finally returned hours later, the world was fundamentally different. The Quantum Framework—the underlying structure of reality itself—had been permanently altered. Enhancement was no longer just a theoretical possibility; it had become an evolutionary imperative.

In the weeks that followed, Kane Industries had worked desperately to establish new protocols—reality anchors, quantum stabilizers, enhancement regulations. They had succeeded in restoring a semblance of normalcy, but everyone with enhanced perception knew the truth: the old rules no longer applied. Reality had remembered something ancient, something that had been deliberately forgotten, and there was no going back.

And somewhere in that chaos, Sarah had been transformed—not killed as Alice had initially believed but evolved into something beyond conventional existence. A quantum ghost who could perceive and move through probability streams directly. Neither fully alive nor dead, but existing in a state that defied classification.

The price of evolution, already paid in full.

"You're thinking about it again," Sarah said softly, her quantum form sensing Alice's emotional state. "The Event."

Alice nodded, pulling herself back to the present. "Sometimes I wonder if Dr. Winters was right—if we're not creating something new but remembering something that always existed. The QLF seems to believe that."

"There's truth in it," Sarah admitted, her form shifting through multiple quantum states as she spoke. "The patterns I can see from this state of existence... they suggest that reality has cycled through these changes before. But that doesn't make what the QLF is doing safe or right. Evolution needs guidance, not chaos."

Before Alice could respond, the lab's quantum stabilizers suddenly spiked, their energy output doubling as a new presence materialized. Purple smoke swirled in the center of the room, coalescing into the form of a woman in flowing dark robes covered in arcane symbols that shifted and changed as they watched.

"Discussing evolution without inviting me?" Lila Darkmagic said, her perfect eyebrows arched in mock offense. "And here I thought we were friends, darling." Her gaze shifted to Sarah's quantum form. "Both Chen sisters in one place. How delightfully unusual."

"Lila," Alice acknowledged, unsurprised by the dramatic entrance. "We were just discussing the QLF situation."

"Ah yes, our enthusiastic underground enhancement revolutionaries," Lila replied, settling onto a lab stool that creaked under her suddenly solid form. "Such passion, such terrible fashion sense, and such abysmal understanding of the forces they're tampering with."

With a casual gesture, Lila conjured her own data display—ancient symbols merging with quantum equations in ways that bridged magic and science. "They're not just breaking corporate rules, you know. They're attempting to dismantle fundamental reality anchors—the very structures that keep our dimension stable."

Sarah's form flickered with interest. "You've been tracking them too."

"When someone starts playing with reality's foundation, I take notice," Lila replied, her ageless eyes momentarily serious beneath her theatrical demeanor. "I've seen civilizations collapse by tampering with forces they didn't understand. These QLF children are pulling at threads that unravel entire dimensions."

Alice studied Lila's display, her enhanced perception recognizing patterns that connected ancient magical warnings with modern quantum mechanics. "You've seen something like this before?"

"Not exactly like this," Lila admitted, her fingers tracing patterns in the air that left glowing purple trails. "But there have been... attempts throughout history. Groups who discovered that reality's rules are more flexible than they appear. Most succeed only in destroying themselves. A few cause wider damage."

"And the QLF?" Sarah asked, her quantum form stabilizing as she focused on Lila's display.

"They're different," Lila said, her playful demeanor momentarily falling away. "Most reality-tampering cults are fumbling in the dark, working with fragments of knowledge. The QLF has comprehensive understanding—Kane Industries research combined with ancient magical insights. And they have something I haven't seen before."

With another gesture, Lila projected an image that made both Chen sisters go still. A quantum signature unlike anything Alice had encountered—a consciousness that existed across multiple probability streams simultaneously, but without the instability that characterized Sarah's condition. A being that moved through the Quantum Framework with deliberate, controlled purpose.

"They call it 'The Flux,'" Lila said, studying the sisters' reactions. "I call it trouble. A consciousness that can manipulate the Quantum Framework directly—reshaping probability without technological assistance or magical training."

"Is it human?" Alice asked, her scientific mind already analyzing the unusual signature patterns.

"Once, perhaps," Lila replied with a shrug that rippled reality slightly around her. "Now? It's something else. Something that exists between states of being—not unlike your sister, but with far greater control and purpose."

Sarah's form flickered as she examined the signature more closely. "I can feel echoes of it in the quantum streams. Like ripples in water long after something has passed through. Whatever it is, it's powerful."

"And deeply dangerous," Lila added, her voice uncharacteristically grave. "The QLF manifesto speaks of 'breaking all chains'—but they don't understand that some chains are load-bearing walls. They believe they're liberating humanity's potential, but they're tampering with foundational reality anchors that prevent dimensional collapse."

"You're not just here to warn us, are you?" Alice said, recognizing the calculated look behind Lila's casual demeanor. "You want something."

Lila's smile returned, sharp and knowing. "So perceptive, darling. Yes, I need your help. The magical community is... concerned about these developments. Ancient wards are responding to QLF activities in troubling ways. Reality thinning where it shouldn't."

"What exactly are you asking?" Ethan's voice came from the doorway where he stood, having arrived silently during their conversation. His enhanced senses had already processed the information displays, his tactical systems calculating potential threats.

"I need you to find The Flux," Lila said simply. "Before it fully realizes what it's capable of. Before it teaches others. There are forces stirring in the quantum depths that have been dormant for millennia—forces that should remain forgotten."

Alice felt the weight of Lila's request, understanding the unspoken gravity. "The QLF is just the beginning, isn't it?"

"They're the pebble that starts the avalanche," Lila confirmed. "And The Flux is the mountain ready to collapse."

Outside the lab's quantum-secured walls, Daybridge continued its daily rhythms, most citizens unaware of how tenuous reality's stability had become. But in that basement laboratory, four beings—each existing in different states between human and something else—recognized the approaching storm.

Evolution always demanded a price. The question was: who would pay it this time?

~

CHAPTER THREE

GOING DARK

QUANTUM OPERATIONS HAD TRANSFORMED the briefing room into a reality-stable bubble, its walls lined with state-of-the-art probability dampeners. The enhancement equipment hummed with quiet efficiency as Director Marcus Kane studied the team assembled before him. His expression remained carefully neutral, though his enhanced perception noted the subtle quantum tension between Alice and Ethan.

"This operation requires more than conventional undercover work," Kane explained, activating the room's secure holographic display. "You'll be going dark in every sense—new quantum signatures, modified enhancement patterns, completely separated from official channels."

The display showed detailed schematics of two quantum identity modules—sleek, metallic discs embedded with reality-shifting technology. Each contained proprietary Kane Industries tech that could temporarily rewrite a person's quantum signature—the unique energy pattern that identified every enhanced individual within the Quantum Framework.

"These modules will modify your baseline enhancement signatures," Kane continued, his voice carrying the weight of authority earned through decades of supernatural operations. "To the QLF's detection methods, you'll appear as genuinely disaffected enhanced individuals seeking liberation from corporate control."

Alice lifted one of the modules, her enhanced perception immediately analyzing its complex quantum architecture. The device represented the pinnacle of Kane's research—technology capable of partially rewriting reality itself on a localized scale.

"The reconfiguration will be... uncomfortable," Kane warned, watching her inspection. "Your enhancements are deeply integrated with your neural pathways. Temporarily modifying them will feel disorienting, possibly painful."

"What about our connection?" Ethan asked, the question directed more to Alice than to Kane. Since the Daybridge Event, their enhancements had become quantumly entangled—a resonance that allowed them to sense each other's presence and status across probability space. This connection had saved their lives multiple times in the field.

Kane's expression tightened almost imperceptibly. "That's the most significant risk. The modules will temporarily sever your quantum bond. For the duration of the operation, you'll be truly isolated from each other at the quantum level."

The implications hung in the air between them. Without their quantum connection, they would be genuinely vulnerable for the first time since their enhancements had synchronized. No shared perceptions, no ability to sense each other's status, no emergency resonance if one of them encountered trouble.

"How long will the separation last?" Alice asked, her scientific mind already calculating potential physiological effects. Their enhancement bond had become integral to how their abilities functioned—a stabilizing influence that prevented quantum degradation.

"The modules are designed for a maximum of seventy-two hours between synchronization periods," Kane replied. "You'll need to meet at secure locations to temporarily deactivate them and allow your natural quantum signatures to realign. Any longer separation risks permanent degradation of your enhancement patterns."

Ethan's enhanced senses detected Alice's subtle physiological response—elevated heart rate, minor stress indicators. His tactical systems automatically began calculating failure scenarios and contingency plans.

"The QLF operates primarily in the quantum underground," Kane continued, shifting the display to show mapped probability zones beneath Daybridge—spaces that existed partially outside conventional reality. "Their recruitment centers move continuously through probability space, making conventional tracking impossible. Your modified signatures will allow you access to these shifted realities."

The display showed their cover identities—carefully constructed personas with documented histories of enhancement instability and corporate disillusionment. Alice would become Cassandra Mercer, a former Kane Industries researcher whose enhancement experiments had been terminated for "pushing ethical boundaries." Ethan would be Daniel Wolf, an ex-military enhancement subject who had rejected government control of his abilities.

"These identities have been seeded in corporate databases for the past six months," Kane explained. "Digital footprints, employment records, enhancement violation citations—all carefully crafted to attract QLF interest."

As Kane outlined the technical aspects of the operation, Alice felt a growing unease. The scientific principles were sound, but something about the entire situation felt wrong. The QLF's activities were dangerous, yes—but Kane Industries' response seemed disproportionate. Almost personal.

In the secure preparation room adjacent to the briefing area, Alice and Ethan found themselves momentarily alone. The quantum stabilizers hummed softly, maintaining reality cohesion around them.

"You don't have to do this," Ethan said quietly, his enhanced senses focused entirely on her. "The quantum risks are significant. Your enhancement pattern is already more complex than most—the temporary reconfiguration could cause lasting instability."

Alice met his gaze directly. "Are you questioning my capabilities, or are you worried about something else?"

"Both," he admitted. "Your scientific expertise is crucial for understanding what the QLF is doing with those stolen formulas. But the quantum separation..." He hesitated, uncharacteristically uncertain. "Our connection has become more than just tactical advantage."

Alice understood the unspoken concern. Their quantum bond had evolved beyond its initial parameters—becoming something neither of them had anticipated when their enhancements first synchronized. Something that blurred the lines between professional partnership and personal connection.

"We've operated independently before," she reminded him, though they both knew this was different. Previous separations had maintained their quantum awareness of each other, even across distances. This would be complete isolation.

"It's not just the tactical disadvantage," Ethan said, his voice low. "The quantum bond has been stabilizing both our enhancement patterns. Without it..." He left the rest unsaid, but Alice's scientific mind filled in the gaps. Enhancement degradation. Quantum instability. Potential neural damage if the separation lasted too long.

"Which is why we stick to the synchronization schedule," she replied with more confidence than she felt. "Seventy-two hours maximum between realignments."

The tension between them remained unresolved as technicians entered to begin the final preparations. Neither had directly addressed the deeper concern—that their quantum bond had become something neither was quite ready to define, and temporarily severing it felt like more than just a tactical risk.

Nadia Marsh's archive-enhanced workspace in the lower levels of the operation center resembled a fusion of ancient library and quantum computing lab. Holographic displays showing probability models hovered above tables covered with centuries-old texts. Her unique abilities allowed her to process both historical records and quantum data simultaneously, perceiving patterns that conventional analysis would miss.

"I've established quantum anchor points throughout the city," she explained, showing Alice and Ethan the hidden network she had created. "These will serve as emergency protocols if either of you experiences quantum destabilization."

The display showed a complex web of reality anchors—locations where the quantum framework had been subtly reinforced to resist manipulation. Each anchor point contained a fragment of their original quantum signatures, providing potential stabilization if their undercover identities began to degrade.

"These anchors are passive and undetectable to QLF scanning," Nadia continued. "But they'll respond to your original quantum patterns if you activate them with these." She handed each of them what appeared to be ordinary wristwatches, though Alice's enhanced perception detected the sophisticated quantum technology hidden within.

"One activation every seventy-two hours minimum," Nadia emphasized. "The anchors will temporarily stabilize your original patterns and send an encrypted quantum pulse that I can track. If you miss an activation window, I'll implement emergency extraction protocols."

Her archive-enhanced abilities had allowed her to predict dozens of potential failure scenarios, developing countermeasures for each. The holographic display shifted to show probability maps of the quantum underground—the strange, shifting spaces where the QLF operated.

"Be aware that conventional reality rules are... flexible in these spaces," Nadia warned. "The QLF has established zones where the quantum framework has been deliberately destabilized. Your enhanced abilities may function differently—sometimes stronger, sometimes weaker, always less predictable."

Alice studied the probability maps with scientific interest, noting patterns that matched theoretical models she had developed after the Daybridge Event. "They're creating quantum bubbles where reality can be more easily manipulated."

"Exactly," Nadia confirmed. "The further you go into their territory, the more malleable reality becomes. Your scientific training should help you navigate these shifts but be prepared for perceptual distortions and temporal inconsistencies."

As they discussed final contingencies, Nadia's expression grew more serious. "There's one more thing you should know. The archive records show historical patterns similar to what the QLF is attempting. Instances where groups tried to fundamentally alter reality's framework."

"What happened to them?" Ethan asked, his tactical mind already calculating implications.

"Most destroyed themselves," Nadia replied grimly. "A few caused localized reality collapses. One, according to ancient texts, nearly shattered the barriers between dimensions entirely." She pulled up fragmentary records from civilizations long vanished. "The common element in each case was a central figure—someone who could manipulate the quantum framework directly."

"The Flux," Alice said, recognizing the pattern.

Nadia nodded. "The archives contain warnings about beings who exist between states—entities that aren't bound by conventional reality constraints. If The Flux is truly such a being..." She left the sentence unfinished, but the implication was clear.

∼

The conversion chamber resembled a medical facility merged with a quantum research lab. Reality stabilizers lined the walls, ready to contain any probability disruptions that might occur during the identity transition. Two reclined chairs sat at the center, surrounded by equipment that hummed with enhancement energy.

As technicians made final adjustments to the quantum identity modules, Sarah Chen's form materialized near Alice. Her quantum state flickered more erratically than usual, reflecting her emotional disturbance.

"This is a mistake," Sarah said without preamble, her voice carrying quantum harmonics that made nearby equipment shiver. "Going undercover in the quantum underground is nothing like conventional operations. Reality itself becomes subjective there."

Alice glanced at the technicians, but they showed no reaction to Sarah's presence. Her quantum-ghost state remained imperceptible to those without enhanced perception.

"We need to understand what the QLF is planning," Alice replied quietly. "If they're using those stolen formulas to destabilize reality anchors—"

"It's more than that," Sarah interrupted, her form briefly splitting into multiple probability echoes before reconverging. "I've been tracking quantum fluctuations throughout the city. The pattern suggests they're building toward something specific—something that requires a precise reality configuration."

"All the more reason to infiltrate them now," Alice said, though she felt her scientific curiosity responding to Sarah's concern. "What exactly have you detected?"

Sarah's form stabilized momentarily as she focused. "They're creating quantum resonance points at specific locations throughout Daybridge —places where reality was already thin before the Event. Each point strengthens a particular probability stream, like tuning an instrument to a specific frequency."

"What's the purpose?" Alice asked, her enhanced mind already processing implications.

"I don't know," Sarah admitted, her form flickering with frustration. "But the mathematical pattern is deliberate and precise. They're preparing reality itself for... something."

She drifted closer, her quantum form causing subtle distortions in the air. "But that's not why I'm worried. The quantum underground operates on different rules. Your scientific understanding of reality is based on consistency and predictability. Down there, belief shapes reality as much as physics does."

"I've dealt with fluid reality before," Alice reminded her, thinking of previous encounters with supernatural dimensions.

"Not like this," Sarah insisted. "In the quantum underground, your identity module won't just change how others perceive you—it will change how reality responds to you. The longer you stay under, the more the false identity will feel... natural."

Alice understood the unspoken warning. The quantum identity module wouldn't just mask her enhancement signature—it would temporarily rewrite her quantum relationship with reality itself. And in spaces where reality was already malleable...

"I'll maintain perspective," she promised. "Seventy-two hour maximum between synchronizations."

Sarah's form rippled with skepticism. "Just remember who you really are. In the quantum underground, that becomes harder than you might expect." Her gaze shifted to Ethan, who was receiving final instructions from his team. "And remember that some bonds go deeper than quantum entanglement. Even when you can't feel the connection, it's still there."

"I'll provide quantum cover for your transportation," Sarah offered, her consciousness expanding to create a probability field that would minimize detection despite official monitoring throughout Daybridge's central sectors. "My position with the Archives provides legitimate reason for generating quantum fluctuations that should mask your departure despite increased surveillance parameters."

"I've been mapping probability pathways through the quantum underground," Sarah explained, her consciousness generating a complex visualization that existed across multiple probability states simultaneously. "The QLF isn't just operating in physical locations—they're establishing quantum corridors between reality states."

The visualization revealed an intricate network of pathways that conventional mapping systems couldn't detect—quantum tunnels connecting seemingly unrelated physical locations through probability space rather than geographical proximity.

"They're using probability shifting to create pathways that bypass conventional security systems entirely," Sarah continued, her form becoming more stable as she focused on the visualization. "But there's something else happening that I don't think even they fully understand."

With subtle manipulation of the quantum fields around her, Sarah demonstrated how the probability pathways were naturally harmonizing with specific resonance patterns—creating stability nodes where different quantum states intersected without the chaotic interference that conventional enhancement science would predict.

"I can navigate these intersection points in ways their operatives can't," she explained, her consciousness briefly splitting into multiple probability echoes before reconverging. "My quantum-ghost state naturally harmonizes with these stability nodes. It's like they recognize me as belonging to the same quantum frequency."

Alice studied the visualization with scientific precision. "You're saying you can move through these probability pathways without the technological assistance the QLF requires?"

"More than that," Sarah replied, her form briefly dissolving into pure quantum potential before resolidifying. "I can stabilize fluctuations at critical intersection points. Where their technology forces temporary stability through brute-force probability manipulation, my consciousness naturally creates harmonic resonance that maintains equilibrium without artificial intervention."

The implications were significant. Sarah's quantum-ghost state wasn't merely an enhancement anomaly but something fundamentally different—a consciousness that naturally harmonized with the quantum framework in ways that neither corporate enhancement science nor underground liberation theory had anticipated.

Before Alice could respond, the technicians approached, indicating they were ready to begin the procedure. Sarah's form dissolved into quantum particles, though her final warning lingered:

"The QLF believes reality remembers what was possible before the Great Sundering. Be careful you don't start believing it too."

The quantum identity transition felt like being unmade and reassembled. Alice gasped as the module activated against her skin, sending ripples of reconfiguration energy through her entire being. Her enhanced perception registered the shift at the fundamental level —her quantum signature, the unique pattern that defined her relationship with reality itself, being temporarily overwritten.

Across the room, Ethan underwent the same process, his enhanced physiology fighting the artificial reconfiguration. Their eyes met briefly as their quantum bond stretched, thinned, and finally—for the first time since their enhancements had synchronized—severed completely.

The sudden isolation was more shocking than Alice had anticipated. A sense of loss that went beyond tactical disadvantage, beyond scientific understanding. Something essential had been temporarily removed, leaving an emptiness that the new quantum identity couldn't fill.

She was still processing the sensation when Director Kane approached, his enhanced perception evaluating the success of the transition.

"Quantum reconfiguration complete," he confirmed, studying the readings. "Your new enhancement signatures are stabilizing. From this moment, you're Cassandra Mercer and Daniel Wolf—disaffected enhanced individuals seeking liberation from corporate control."

Alice—now Cassandra—felt the artificial identity settling into her quantum framework. Memories that weren't hers became accessible —emotional responses to events that had never happened, enhancement experiences she had never undergone. The scientific part of her mind remained fascinated even as another part recoiled at the invasion.

"Your first contact point has been arranged," Kane continued, handing them encrypted quantum coordinates. "A QLF recruitment meeting in the probability shifts beneath Old Town. Your modified signatures will grant you access."

Across the room, Ethan—now Daniel—completed his transition. His movement patterns had subtly changed, reflecting his new tactical profile. Even his enhancement aura had shifted, displaying the distinctive patterns of military-grade modifications rather than his true hybrid abilities.

As they prepared to leave separately—their cover stories required no prior connection—Alice felt the weight of what they were undertaking. They would be navigating spaces where reality itself was subject to manipulation, carrying false identities that would gradually feel more natural, cut off from their quantum bond that had become their most reliable anchor.

"Seventy-two hours," Kane reminded them. "Don't miss your synchronization window."

Alice nodded, already feeling the strange disconnect of operating under a quantum identity that wasn't truly hers. As she gathered the specialized equipment designed to function in probability-shifted spaces, she caught Ethan's gaze one last time.

No words were necessary. Despite the severed quantum bond, some connections ran deeper than enhancement could measure. They would find each other in the quantum underground, even if reality itself tried to keep them apart.

It was time to go dark.

~

PART TWO
INTO THE
UNDERGROUND

CHAPTER FOUR

FIRST CONTACT

THE ABANDONED Kane Industries facility existed in a state of quantum flux, shimmering between realities like a mirage in the desert. To ordinary passersby, the building appeared condemned—windows boarded, chain-link fence displaying faded warning signs. But to enhanced perception, the structure pulsed with probability distortions, its true nature flickering between states of existence.

Cassandra Mercer—the identity Alice now wore like a second skin—approached from the south side, her modified quantum signature resonating with the building's unstable framework. After three days operating under her cover identity, the false memories and emotional responses felt increasingly natural. The quantum identity module had done its work well—perhaps too well.

She focused on the reality anchors hidden beneath her artificial persona, small tethers to her true self that prevented complete immersion in the cover identity. Even these felt tenuous now, like remembering a dream that faded with each waking moment.

As she neared the facility's perimeter, her enhanced perception detected the probability shift—a subtle thinning of reality that marked the transition into quantum-altered space. To an untrained observer, it would appear as merely stepping through a broken section of fence. But Cassandra experienced the passage between reality states—a momentary sensation of existing in multiple places simultaneously before reality re-stabilized around her.

Inside the quantum boundary, the facility transformed. What had appeared abandoned from outside now hummed with energy and purpose. The building's interior existed in a probability bubble where decay had been selectively reversed. Advanced technology merged with makeshift adaptations, creating a hybrid environment that defied conventional physics.

Cassandra wasn't the only one arriving for the gathering. Others approached from different directions, each displaying subtle signs of enhancement—probability distortions in their wake, reality ripples around their movements, the distinctive quantum signatures of individuals whose relationship with physics had been fundamentally altered.

Among them, she spotted Daniel Wolf—Ethan's cover identity. He moved with military precision despite his deliberately disheveled appearance, his enhanced senses constantly scanning for threats while appearing casual. Their eyes met briefly, two strangers with no reason to acknowledge each other, the severed quantum bond between them an aching absence.

"Welcome, seekers," a woman announced as the gathering assembled in what had once been a testing chamber. She stood on a raised platform, her form occasionally phasing partially out of conventional reality—a demonstration of enhancement that would be impossible under Kane Industries protocols. "You've all found your way here because you sense the truth—that your potential has been artificially limited by those who fear true evolution."

Cassandra studied the speaker with scientific interest. The woman's enhancement signature displayed hybrid characteristics that shouldn't be stable together—vampire energy manipulation merged with Fae probability shifting. Under conventional understanding, such combinations would create dangerous quantum interference patterns. Yet she appeared perfectly stable, her hybrid abilities functioning in harmony.

The chamber had filled with approximately thirty individuals, their enhancement signatures forming a complex quantum web that made reality itself feel malleable. Cassandra cataloged what she observed: corporate employees with clandestine enhancements, supernatural beings experimenting with cross-species abilities, ordinary citizens who had undergone underground modification procedures.

"I'm Vex," the woman continued, her form solidifying as she focused on the gathering. "Former Kane Industries enhancement subject, now liberation guide for the QLF. Each of you has experienced the artificial limitations imposed by corporate control of the Quantum Framework. Tonight, you'll get your first glimpse of what true liberation means."

Daniel positioned himself near the back of the room, his military-enhanced senses detecting security measures beyond what conventional technology could achieve. Reality anchors had been deliberately modified to create monitoring fields, probability sensors tracking every quantum signature present. His tactical assessment: escape would be difficult if their cover was compromised.

"Corporate enhancement programs tell you there are natural limitations to what's possible," Vex continued, pacing the platform as subtle reality distortions followed her movements. "That certain ability combinations are 'inherently unstable' or 'genetically incompatible.' That supernatural capabilities must remain distinct and separated."

She paused, her eyes scanning the gathered seekers. "They're lying. The limitations aren't natural—they're artificial constraints imposed to maintain control. Reality itself remembers a time when all possibilities flowed freely, when the boundaries between abilities were fluid and responsive to conscious intent."

Cassandra noted how the crowd responded—not just intellectually but quantumly, their enhancement signatures resonating with Vex's words.

This wasn't merely ideological indoctrination; it was calibrated to create specific quantum resonance patterns in receptive individuals.

"Tonight, you'll meet others who have broken free from these artificial constraints," Vex announced with a theatrical gesture. "Individuals who have remembered what corporate protocols forced them to forget."

At her signal, five people stepped forward from the shadows surrounding the chamber. Their enhancement signatures made Cassandra's scientific mind race with questions—each displayed ability combinations that violated fundamental principles of quantum-supernatural integration.

"Maya was told her Fae ancestry made her incompatible with werewolf enhancement," Vex said, indicating a young woman whose form rippled with both lunar energy and reality manipulation capabilities. "Kane Industries rejected her enhancement application three times, claiming genetic incompatibility."

Maya demonstrated her abilities, shifting partially into a werewolf form while simultaneously manipulating probability fields around her —creating localized reality bubbles where physics behaved according to her will. The combination should have created catastrophic quantum interference, yet she maintained perfect stability.

"Dominic was a vampire initiate before enhancement technology existed," Vex continued, gesturing to a man whose pale features belied the complex energy signature he projected. "When he sought modern enhancement, he was told vampire blood magic couldn't integrate with quantum technology."

Dominic raised his hands, blood magic swirling around his fingers while quantum probability fields formed complex patterns in the air above him. The demonstration showed seamless integration between ancient supernatural power and modern enhancement capabilities—a combination that conventional science deemed impossible.

As each demonstration proceeded, Cassandra's enhanced perception detected the underlying quantum mechanics. These weren't random ability combinations; they followed specific harmonic patterns that allowed seemingly incompatible powers to coexist. The scientific principles involved were elegant, advanced—and potentially revolutionary if they could be stabilized properly.

Daniel's tactical assessment grew more complex as he analyzed the security implications. If the QLF had truly discovered stable methods for hybrid enhancement integration, the balance of power would shift dramatically. Traditional supernatural authorities, corporate enhancement programs, government regulatory frameworks—all would be rendered obsolete.

"These artificial boundaries weren't created by nature or science," Vex declared as the demonstrations concluded. "They were imposed during what history calls the Great Sundering—when those who feared true potential deliberately fragmented the Quantum Framework to maintain control."

Her words resonated with quantum frequencies that made reality itself seem to vibrate in agreement. "The Daybridge Event wasn't an accident—it was reality remembering what was possible before the Sundering. And the QLF exists to accelerate that remembering, to break the chains that have limited humanity's true potential."

The gathering shifted to interactive sessions, with the demonstrated hybrids circulating among potential recruits. Cassandra found herself approached by Maya, whose werewolf-Fae abilities continued to challenge everything she understood about quantum mechanics.

"Your enhancement signature is interesting," Maya said, studying Cassandra with more than just visual perception. "Corporate structure, but with unauthorized modifications. You've been experimenting outside approved protocols."

Cassandra allowed a calculated amount of bitterness to color her response. "Kane Industries terminated my research when I questioned their enhancement limitations. Called my theories 'dangerously speculative' and put me on the blacklist."

Maya's expression softened with recognition. "Let me guess—you demonstrated that certain 'incompatible' abilities could theoretically be stabilized through quantum harmonization?"

"You've seen my research," Cassandra replied, genuine surprise in her voice.

"Not directly," Maya smiled, "but many of us followed similar paths before finding the QLF. The corporations suppress any research that threatens their control of the enhancement framework."

Across the room, Daniel engaged with a former military enhancement subject whose quantum signature displayed tactical capabilities merged with vampire speed—another combination that should have been unstable.

"Black ops enhancement division," the man introduced himself as Striker. "Until I started asking questions about the artificial limitations in our combat protocols. Funny how fast your service becomes 'no longer required' when you challenge the enhancement boundaries."

Daniel nodded, letting his cover identity's military bitterness show. "Experienced something similar. My unit was the testbed for tactical probability manipulation. When some of us developed abilities beyond the projected parameters, the entire program was terminated."

Their conversation continued, exchanging experiences that aligned with their cover stories while Daniel's enhanced senses continued mapping the facility's security measures. The quantum surveillance was sophisticated—probability sensors monitoring emotional responses, reality anchors calibrated to detect deception through quantum fluctuations.

The recruitment meeting shifted phase as Vex returned to the central platform. "You've seen demonstrations, you've heard experiences that resonate with your own. Now comes the more important question: Are you ready to take the first step toward true liberation?"

The quantum energy in the room intensified, reality anchors shifting to create a contained field around the gathering. Cassandra's scientific mind recognized the pattern—a quantum testing environment where enhancement capabilities could be safely demonstrated and evaluated.

"Each of you carries potential beyond what corporate limitations allow," Vex continued. "Tonight, we offer the opportunity to glimpse that potential—to experience briefly what true liberation feels like."

Assistants moved through the crowd, distributing small crystalline objects that pulsed with quantum energy. Cassandra recognized them immediately—temporary enhancement catalysts, designed to briefly stimulate abilities beyond conventional limitations.

"These catalysts will temporarily release the artificial constraints on your enhancement potential," Vex explained. "The effect lasts approximately fifteen minutes—just enough to experience what's possible when the barriers are removed."

Cassandra accepted the crystal, her enhanced perception analyzing its quantum structure. The scientific principles were sound but dangerous —the catalyst would temporarily override natural quantum stability mechanisms, allowing enhancement patterns to flow beyond conventional parameters.

Daniel received his catalyst with apparent eagerness that masked his tactical assessment. The crystals represented significant risk—temporary quantum destabilization could reveal their true enhancement signatures if they weren't careful.

"For this experience to work, you must surrender to it completely," Vex instructed. "Resistance or excessive control will prevent the catalyst from revealing your true potential. Trust the process, trust your inherent abilities."

Around the room, people activated their catalysts by pressing them against their enhancement focal points—typically the base of the skull where quantum integration with the nervous system was strongest. Immediate effects rippled through the chamber as reality distorted around each participant.

Cassandra hesitated, calculating risks. Activating the catalyst might compromise her cover identity if she couldn't properly control the resulting enhancement surge. But refusing would immediately mark her as potentially hostile.

Across the room, Daniel had reached the same conclusion. Their eyes met briefly—no quantum bond to communicate, but years of partnership creating an unspoken understanding. They would proceed, but with careful internal control.

As Cassandra pressed the crystal to her neck, the quantum surge was immediate and intense. The catalyst bypassed conventional enhancement regulators, allowing her abilities to flow beyond artificial constraints. Her perception expanded dramatically, quantum streams becoming visible around every person in the room. Reality itself seemed to pulse with potential, responsive to her scientific understanding in ways she had only theorized.

The experience was both exhilarating and terrifying. Her true enhancement capabilities, temporarily unleashed, threatened to break through her cover identity's limitations. She fought to maintain control while appearing to surrender to the experience, directing the expanded abilities into harmless demonstrations that wouldn't compromise her cover.

Around her, others displayed newly awakened capabilities—probability manipulation, reality shifting, hybrid supernatural abilities that conventional enhancement programs would deem impossible. The quantum field of the entire room had become a swirling chaos of unleashed potential.

"Freedom," Vex's voice carried through the quantum distortions. "This is what the corporations fear—your true potential, unleashed from artificial constraints. This is just a glimpse of what's possible through full liberation."

Daniel channeled his enhanced surge into his cover identity's military background—tactical probability assessment, enhanced reaction speeds, sensory expansion. The rush of power was addictive, the temporary removal of enhancement limitations revealing capabilities he hadn't known he possessed.

As the catalysts' effects peaked, Vex moved through the crowd, observing each person's response. Her attention fixed suddenly on Cassandra, whose scientific mind was automatically analyzing and categorizing the quantum patterns around her—behavior inconsistent with simple enjoyment of expanded abilities.

"You're fighting it," Vex said, her voice carrying a note of suspicion. "Trying to control rather than experience."

Cassandra realized her error immediately. Her scientific approach to the enhancement surge didn't match her cover identity's supposed rebellious nature. "Old habits," she replied, forcing herself to release some of her careful control. "Kane trained us to maintain rigid enhancement parameters. Hard to unlearn."

Vex's suspicion remained, her enhanced perception studying Cassandra's quantum response patterns. "True liberation requires trust. If you're holding back because you still believe the corporate limitations are necessary..."

The unspoken threat hung in the air between them. The QLF didn't tolerate corporate sympathizers or potential infiltrators.

Recognizing the danger, Cassandra made a calculated risk. She released more of her control, allowing her expanded perception to manifest visibly—creating a display of quantum analysis that transformed the air around her into a complex visualization of enhancement patterns. It was a genuine expression of her scientific abilities, channeled through her cover identity's supposed frustration with corporate limitations.

"I spent years developing theories about quantum pattern integration that Kane Industries dismissed as impossible," she said, the emotion in her voice genuine despite coming from her true identity rather than her cover. "I don't need to control it—I need to understand it."

The display impressed those nearby, quantum visualizations forming a complex web of interconnected enhancement patterns that matched the QLF's theoretical framework. Vex's suspicion faded, replaced by interest.

"A researcher," she noted. "Your analytical abilities could be valuable to our understanding of the liberation process."

Across the room, Daniel faced a similar challenge. Striker had noticed his excessive control during the enhancement surge, his military experience recognizing tactical restraint.

"You're holding back," Striker observed. "Military conditioning is hard to break, isn't it? Always maintaining operational security, even when experiencing enhanced states."

Daniel recognized the test for what it was. Like Cassandra, he needed to demonstrate commitment without compromising his cover. He channeled his expanded abilities into a controlled but impressive display of tactical enhancement—creating probability fields that briefly allowed him to occupy multiple potential positions simultaneously, a technique that advanced military enhancement had theorized but never successfully implemented.

"Not holding back," Daniel replied, maintaining his cover identity's personality. "Just applying the training they gave me before they decided I was too dangerous to keep around."

The demonstration satisfied Striker, who nodded in appreciation of the advanced technique. "Military enhancement always focuses on control rather than potential. That's why so many of us eventually find our way here."

As the catalysts' effects began to fade, Vex returned to the central platform. The room's quantum field gradually stabilized, though everyone present had been fundamentally changed by the experience of temporarily unrestricted enhancement.

"What you've experienced tonight is only the beginning," she announced. "The first step on the path to true liberation. For those who wish to continue this journey, we offer guidance, training, and community."

Assistants circulated again, this time distributing small quantum-encoded objects—communication devices that existed partially in probability space, undetectable by conventional surveillance.

"These will allow secure communication with your assigned liberation guides," Vex explained. "For your safety and ours, all further contact will occur through quantum-secured channels."

Cassandra accepted the device, her enhanced perception noting its sophisticated design—Kane Industries technology modified with supernatural elements that shouldn't have been compatible. The integration was elegant, innovative, and deeply concerning from a security perspective.

As the gathering began to disperse, Vex approached Cassandra directly. "Your analytical abilities are rare among new seekers. Most experience the catalyst's effects emotionally rather than intellectually. We could use someone with your perspective in our research division."

The invitation represented both opportunity and danger—deeper access to QLF operations but increased scrutiny of her cover identity. "I've been looking for somewhere to continue my research since Kane terminated my position," Cassandra replied. "Somewhere that doesn't impose arbitrary limitations on what's possible."

"Come to the next gathering," Vex said, transmitting quantum coordinates to Cassandra's device. "Bring your research notes—what Kane deemed too dangerous to pursue. We believe in the free exchange of enhancement knowledge."

Nearby, Striker extended a similar invitation to Daniel, impressed by his tactical enhancement capabilities. "We have a special division for those with military backgrounds. Enhancement techniques that would make your former commanders lose sleep."

As they prepared to leave separately, maintaining their cover as unconnected seekers, Cassandra and Daniel exchanged one final glance. No quantum bond to communicate, but a shared understanding: they had successfully established first contact, passed the initial tests, and gained potential access to deeper QLF operations.

But the cost was becoming clear. The catalysts had given them a temporary taste of unrestricted enhancement—abilities beyond what even their advanced training had prepared them for. And despite their professional discipline, they had both felt the seductive pull of that freedom.

As they exited the probability-shifted facility, returning to conventional reality through separate quantum boundaries, the question lingered: How long could they expose themselves to the QLF's liberation philosophy before it began to affect not just their cover identities, but their true selves?

The underground was calling, and part of them wanted to answer.

CHAPTER FIVE

THE LIBERATION DOCTRINE

THE SECOND QLF gathering took place deeper in the quantum underground, in a facility that existed primarily in probability space. To reach it, Cassandra had to navigate a series of reality shifts—transitions between dimensional states that made conventional navigation impossible. The quantum coordinates Vex had provided led her through seemingly abandoned subway tunnels, where reality thinned at specific junction points.

At each transition, Cassandra felt her quantum identity solidifying further, the artificial memories and emotional responses becoming increasingly natural as she spent more time separated from her true enhancement pattern. Five days into her undercover operation, with only one brief synchronization meeting with Ethan, the boundaries between Cassandra Mercer and Alice Chen were beginning to blur.

The final transition deposited her in a vast chamber that defied conventional architecture. The space existed in multiple probability states simultaneously, its boundaries shifting and flowing according to quantum fluctuations. Pillars of crystallized probability supported a ceiling that occasionally phased into transparency, revealing glimpses of other reality layers above.

"Impressive, isn't it?" said a voice beside her. Vex had appeared without conventional movement, her enhanced abilities allowing her to navigate probability space directly. "This was once Kane Industries' primary quantum research facility—before they decided certain avenues of exploration were too dangerous to pursue."

Cassandra examined the chamber with genuine scientific interest. "The quantum architecture is remarkable. The space exists across multiple probability streams simultaneously."

"It was designed to study unrestricted enhancement potential," Vex explained as they walked deeper into the facility. "Until corporate leadership became frightened by what they discovered. They abandoned it fifteen years ago, attempting to erase all records of its existence. But the quantum framework remembers."

The gathering was larger this time—perhaps a hundred individuals whose enhancement signatures created a complex tapestry of quantum interactions. Some displayed hybrid abilities that should have been impossible under conventional enhancement theory. Others existed partially outside normal reality, their forms shifting between states of being.

At the chamber's center stood a man Cassandra hadn't seen before. Tall and striking, with silver-streaked dark hair and eyes that shifted colors with his movements. His quantum signature was unlike anything she had encountered—a complex pattern that seemed to exist across multiple dimensional planes simultaneously.

"That's Nevius," Vex said, following her gaze. "One of our most advanced liberation guides. He'll be leading tonight's revelation session."

Across the chamber, Daniel had also arrived, maintaining his careful distance from Cassandra while his enhanced senses mapped the facility's security measures. The quantum surveillance was more sophisticated here—reality anchors that could detect deception through probability fluctuations, enhancement signatures being continuously scanned for inconsistencies.

His military cover identity had gained him entry to a tactical division of the QLF—enhanced individuals with combat backgrounds who focused on security and operational execution. Their abilities merged supernatural combat techniques with quantum enhancement in ways that violated conventional tactical doctrine.

"Welcome, seekers and liberated," Nevius began, his voice resonating with quantum harmonics that made reality itself vibrate in response. "Tonight, we delve deeper into the truth that corporations, governments, and traditional supernatural authorities have hidden for millennia."

The chamber's quantum field stabilized around him, creating a space where his words could directly influence the probability patterns of those listening. It wasn't mind control in the conventional sense, but a subtle manipulation of quantum resonance that made certain ideas feel intuitively correct at the enhancement level.

"Most of you have been told that enhancement limitations are natural—biological constraints, genetic incompatibilities, quantum interference patterns that cannot be overcome," he continued, gesturing to create visual representations in the air around him. "These are deliberate falsehoods designed to maintain control over humanity's true potential."

The visualization showed human and supernatural DNA structures, quantum patterns flowing between them in complex, harmonious ways. "Before the Great Sundering, approximately twelve thousand years ago, what we now call 'supernatural abilities' were simply aspects of human potential. There were no rigid categories, no artificial boundaries between werewolf, vampire, Fae, or human capabilities. All flowed from the same quantum source, all were accessible through proper understanding and development."

Cassandra found herself intellectually engaged despite her professional detachment. The quantum mechanics being displayed matched

theoretical models she had developed after the Daybridge Event—
ideas that Kane Industries had deemed too speculative to pursue. The
science was sound, if unorthodox.

"The Great Sundering was not a natural evolutionary divergence,"
Nevius continued as the visualization shifted to show a catastrophic
quantum event. "It was a deliberate restructuring of reality's fundamental framework—an artificial limitation imposed by those who
feared humanity's true potential."

The display showed reality itself being fragmented, quantum patterns
that had once flowed freely now contained in separate streams that
could no longer interact. Human potential had been deliberately parti-
tioned, creating the distinct supernatural categories that now defined
the world.

"Those who orchestrated the Sundering created what we now call the
Quantum Framework—a reality structure that enforces artificial limitations on what abilities can manifest together. They created 'laws' of
supernatural genetics that are actually programmed constraints, not
natural limitations."

Daniel observed the presentation with tactical assessment, noting how
the quantum visualizations were calibrated to resonate with specific
enhancement patterns in the audience. It was sophisticated quantum
persuasion—not falsified but carefully curated to lead listeners toward
predetermined conclusions.

"The evidence exists in your own enhancement experiences," Nevius
continued. "Moments when your abilities briefly exceeded their
supposed limitations. Quantum fluctuations where the barriers
temporarily thinned. The corporations call these 'dangerous instabilities' to be suppressed, when they are actually glimpses of your true
potential breaking through artificial constraints."

Around the chamber, heads nodded in recognition. Many had experienced such moments—enhancements briefly functioning beyond theoretical limitations, abilities manifesting that shouldn't have been
possible according to conventional understanding.

"The Daybridge Event was reality itself beginning to remember," Nevius declared, his quantum signature pulsing with conviction that rippled through the gathered crowd. "The artificial barriers imposed during the Great Sundering have been weakening for centuries. What happened at Kane Industries' research facility wasn't an accident—it was inevitable. Reality remembering what was always possible."

Alice's fingers twitched toward her quantum scanner, a professional reflex she quickly suppressed. The QLF's quantum demonstration had just confirmed a hypothesis Kane Industries had buried under layers of 'speculative research' warnings. Science demanded she acknowledge what she was seeing—the framework instabilities matched her theoretical models with uncomfortable precision. She'd spent months convincing herself corporate science had legitimate safety concerns, not just convenient excuses. Now that careful self-deception was unraveling before her eyes

Kane Industries had classified her research as speculative and potentially dangerous. But hearing it articulated by the QLF, supported by quantum demonstrations that matched her theoretical models, created an uncomfortable cognitive dissonance. What if some aspects of their liberation philosophy were scientifically sound?

What she couldn't reconcile was how quickly her research had been suppressed—not through normal peer review or safety assessment, but through direct executive intervention that bypassed standard scientific evaluation protocols.

She recalled the meeting that had ended her theoretical exploration. The laboratory director had appeared genuinely apologetic when delivering the termination notice, explaining that orders had come "from the executive floor" with no room for appeal or modification. More unsettling was his parting warning, delivered in a whispered tone after ensuring recording devices were disabled: "Some knowledge isn't meant to be pursued, Detective Chen. For your own safety, let this go."

The next day, she discovered her research server access had been completely revoked—not just suspended pending review as per standard protocol, but permanently deleted with no backup retrieval options. Her physical notes had vanished from her secured laboratory drawer, and colleagues suddenly became uncomfortable discussing even tangential aspects of her theoretical framework.

Most concerning was the visit from Corporate Security's specialized "Research Ethics Division"—a department she hadn't known existed until two stern representatives appeared in her office with personality assessment tools and neural stabilization equipment "for her protection."

"Your recent research directions have triggered certain security protocols," they had explained while setting up monitoring equipment. "We need to ensure your enhancement patterns haven't been destabilized by theoretical exposure to potentially harmful quantum concepts."

The evaluation had felt more like an interrogation focused less on her scientific methodology and more on determining exactly what conclusions she had reached and who she might have shared them with. The neural scan they performed had left her with a three-hour memory gap and lingering headaches for weeks afterward.

Now, hearing the QLF articulate theories that aligned precisely with her suppressed research created disturbing questions about what Kane Industries was truly protecting—public safety, or something else entirely?

"Look at your enhancement licensing agreement," Nevius challenged, projecting a standard Kane Industries contract. Key phrases illuminated: 'regular recalibration required,' 'maintenance protocols proprietary,' 'capability degradation may occur without authorized stabilization.' He circled them with a gesture. 'These aren't safety features—they're dependency hooks. Every "breakthrough" comes with built-in limitations requiring their ongoing services. They've designed a system where evolution itself requires a subscription model.' He projected market growth charts alongside capability advancement timelines. 'Notice how each major enhancement category becomes commercially available just as the previous one reaches market saturation? That's not discovery—it's inventory management."

The visualization shifted to show corporate enhancement protocols—the carefully controlled development paths that maintained distinct supernatural categories. Behind these visible programs, the display revealed the suppression of research that threatened to bridge those categories.

"But the truth cannot be contained forever," Nevius declared as the visualization expanded to show the quantum underground—a growing network of liberated individuals developing abilities beyond corporate limitations. "The QLF exists not to create something new, but to remember what was always possible. To reclaim humanity's birthright that was stolen during the Great Sundering."

As the presentation concluded, the gathering separated into smaller discussion groups, each led by a liberation guide with advanced hybrid abilities. Cassandra found herself drawn to a scientific circle, where researchers whose work had been suppressed by corporate interests shared their findings freely.

"The quantum resonance patterns prove it," a former Kane Industries scientist explained, displaying complex equations that Cassandra recognized from her own research. "The barriers between supernatural categories aren't natural quantum interference—they're programmed constraints with discernible patterns. Almost like encryption keys in the fabric of reality itself."

"I documented similar patterns in hybrid enhancement attempts," another researcher added. "The failures don't occur randomly—they follow specific quantum rules that suggest deliberate limitation rather than natural incompatibility."

Cassandra found herself contributing to the discussion almost involuntarily, her scientific mind engaged by ideas that aligned with her own suppressed research. "The quantum framework shows evidence of external manipulation—reality parameters that don't follow natural evolution patterns but appear to have been imposed."

The scientists welcomed her insights, sharing data that Kane Industries had classified and suppressed. Much of it aligned with theoretical models Alice had developed before this undercover assignment—evidence that the distinct supernatural categories might indeed be artificial constructs rather than natural evolutionary paths.

Alice caught herself nodding at Dr. Elara's explanation before she could stop the reaction. She quickly masked it by adjusting her scanner, but the moment of agreement had happened. A week ago, she would have immediately categorized these theories as dangerous manipulation. Now she was mentally filing away equations to revisit later. Her mission brief was beginning to feel like an outdated textbook —technically correct in structure but missing crucial recent discoveries.

Across the chamber, Daniel had been integrated into a tactical discussion group led by Striker. The former military enhancement subjects shared experiences of abilities that had manifested beyond approved parameters—capabilities that had led to their removal from official programs.

"Military enhancement protocols are deliberately limited," Striker explained, displaying tactical enhancement patterns that had been classified by government agencies. "They restrict our abilities to maintain control, to ensure enhanced soldiers remain predictable and manageable."

The tactical visualizations showed enhancement configurations that Daniel recognized from classified programs—and the artificial limitations built into them to prevent certain ability combinations from manifesting. His own military experience confirmed that enhancement protocols had always been carefully controlled, with strict boundaries between what was permitted and what was suppressed.

"Cameron here was part of my former pack," Striker said, introducing a man whose quantum signature displayed a complex hybrid of werewolf attributes and tactical enhancements. "Tell him your experience."

Cameron studied Daniel with the intensity characteristic of werewolf perception. His enhanced senses would be detecting subtle physiological responses, searching for authentic recognition. "North Forest Pack, until three years ago," he said. "Left after the Moonstone Protocols were implemented."

Daniel recognized the reference immediately. The Moonstone Protocols had been a controversial enhancement regulation imposed on werewolf packs, limiting how their natural abilities could interact with modern enhancement technology. His cover identity would have knowledge of this, so he nodded with appropriate recognition.

"The Protocols claimed to 'protect natural werewolf heritage,'" Cameron continued, bitterness evident in his voice. "But they actually prevented us from evolving beyond traditional limitations. Any pack member who developed abilities beyond the approved spectrum was required to undergo 'stabilization'—a corporate euphemism for suppression."

His quantum signature fluctuated as he spoke, revealing abilities that violated traditional werewolf limitations. He could maintain partial transformation states indefinitely, control aspects of his werewolf nature that should have been instinctive and uncontrollable, and merge his lunar energy with probability manipulation in ways that conventional enhancement theory deemed impossible.

"I started experiencing enhanced states during partial transformation," Cameron explained. "Ability to manipulate quantum probability fields while accessing werewolf strength and senses. According to Kane's enhancement protocols, this combination should create unstable interference patterns—yet it felt completely natural to me."

Daniel felt an uncomfortable resonance with this account. His own werewolf abilities had occasionally manifested in ways that transcended conventional limitations, particularly during high-stress operations with Alice when their quantum bond facilitated ability combinations that shouldn't have been stable.

"The pack Alpha ordered me to undergo corporate stabilization," Cameron continued. "Said I was risking the pack's enhancement clearance by developing unauthorized abilities. That's when I realized the truth—the limitations weren't protecting us; they were controlling us."

The tactical group nodded in understanding, many having experienced similar enforcement of artificial limitations in military or supernatural contexts. Daniel maintained his cover identity's appropriate responses while his enhanced tactical systems continued mapping the facility's security measures.

"The QLF showed me that werewolf abilities aren't fixed," Cameron said, demonstrating a partial transformation that allowed him to maintain full cognitive control while accessing supernatural strength. "The lunar cycle doesn't have to control us. The barriers between human consciousness and wolf instinct aren't natural—they're programmed limitations that can be overcome."

Daniel recognized the dangerous appeal of this perspective. His own experience with werewolf transformation had always involved fighting for control against instinctive drives. The idea that this struggle wasn't natural but imposed—that greater harmony between human and wolf aspects was possible—created a tempting cognitive path.

"The corporations maintain these limitations because predictable, categorized supernatural beings are easier to regulate," Striker added. "They fear what we might become if we remember our true potential —if we break free from the artificial constraints imposed during the Sundering."

As the tactical discussion continued, Daniel found himself contributing carefully selected insights from his cover identity's military background—experiences of enhancement limitations that had felt arbitrary rather than necessary. The group responded with recognition and acceptance, further integrating him into their operational structure.

Yet beneath his cover identity's engagement, his true self maintained tactical awareness. The QLF's philosophy contained elements of truth interwoven with dangerous extrapolations. The persuasive power came not from fabrication but from selective interpretation of genuine enhancement phenomena—making it all the more difficult to dismiss entirely.

As the gathering progressed into practical demonstrations, Cassandra's enhanced perception detected something unusual—subtle quantum disruptions at the edges of the facility. Her scientific analysis identified the pattern immediately: magical interference with probability streams. Not random fluctuations, but deliberate monitoring of quantum state changes.

Moving casually toward the disturbance, she pretended to examine an architectural feature while her enhanced senses tracked the magical signature. The pattern was distinctive—ancient power interwoven with modern quantum understanding. She recognized it immediately: Lila Darkmagic was monitoring the gathering.

The magical surveillance was sophisticated—probability tendrils extending into the chamber from multiple reality streams, gathering information without materializing physically. Lila was observing from outside conventional reality, her consciousness extended across quantum states to monitor the QLF's activities.

Cassandra carefully avoided direct interaction with the surveillance tendrils, knowing that Lila's perception would recognize her true quantum signature beneath the cover identity if she came too close. Yet the presence of such sophisticated magical monitoring indicated how seriously traditional powers were taking the QLF's activities.

Across the chamber, Daniel had also detected the magical surveillance. His tactical systems identified multiple probability monitoring points throughout the facility—observation windows from other reality streams. He noted how the QLF security teams seemed unaware of this sophisticated infiltration, suggesting Lila's methods exceeded their detection capabilities.

As the gathering moved toward its conclusion, Nevius returned to the central platform for final instructions. "What you've learned tonight is just the beginning—the first layer of truth about our quantum reality. Those who wish to continue their liberation journey will receive coordinates for specialized training appropriate to your enhancement patterns."

The facility's quantum field pulsed as he spoke, reality anchors shifting to create secure communication channels between liberation guides and potential recruits. "Remember that conventional reality is now your cover story—the mask you wear while moving through a world still bound by artificial limitations. Your true evolution occurs in spaces like this, where reality remembers what was always possible."

Cassandra received her next contact instructions—coordinates for a specialized research division focusing on quantum framework analysis. Her scientific contributions during the gathering had gained her access to a higher level of the QLF's operational structure, where theoretical work on reality manipulation was being conducted.

Daniel was similarly integrated into the tactical division, given probationary access to security operations and enhancement training for former military subjects. His cover identity had successfully established credibility through shared experiences and demonstrated abilities.

As the gathering dispersed, participants navigating back through reality transitions to conventional space, both Cassandra and Daniel carried not just valuable intelligence but troubling questions. The QLF's liberation doctrine contained elements that resonated with their own experiences and research—fragments of truth interwoven with dangerous extrapolations.

For Cassandra, the scientific evidence suggesting artificial constraints in the quantum framework aligned disturbingly well with her own suppressed research. The possibility that supernatural limitations might indeed be programmed rather than natural created a cognitive challenge to her operational parameters.

For Daniel, the demonstrations of werewolf abilities freed from traditional limitations resonated with his own experiences of enhancement that transcended conventional boundaries. The idea that greater harmony between human consciousness and supernatural instinct might be possible represented a tempting evolutionary path.

Neither had anticipated this challenge—that the most dangerous aspect of infiltrating the QLF would not be physical risk or discovery, but exposure to ideas that contained enough truth to create genuine doubt about the frameworks they had always accepted.

As they navigated back to conventional reality through separate quantum pathways, the surveillance tendrils of Lila's magical observation followed, gathering intelligence on the QLF's activities while maintaining distance from the undercover operatives. The ancient witch was playing her own game in this emerging conflict—monitoring multiple reality streams while pursuing her own agenda.

The liberation doctrine had been planted in their minds; seeds of doubt that would continue to grow as they delved deeper into the quantum underground. And somewhere in that underground, beyond the recruitment gatherings and philosophical discussions, lay the true purpose of the QLF—and the mysterious entity known as The Flux.

CHAPTER SIX

EARNING TRUST

THE MESSAGE ARRIVED through quantum channels just after midnight, bypassing conventional security systems to materialize directly in Cassandra's perception. The QLF's quantum communication methods operated on principles that conventional surveillance couldn't detect— information transmitted through probability fluctuations rather than physical signals.

"Transition test tomorrow. Central Research District. 02:00. Prove your liberation potential."

The message dissolved into quantum particles after delivery, leaving no trace in conventional reality. But its implications were clear: the time for passive observation had ended. To advance within the QLF's structure, she would need to actively participate in their operations— to commit what Kane Industries would classify as a quantum crime.

In her secure apartment, Cassandra examined the quantum identity module embedded at her neckline—the device that maintained her cover by rewriting her enhancement signature. Seven days into the operation, the false identity felt increasingly natural, her thoughts and reactions aligning with Cassandra Mercer's profile rather than Alice Chen's. The scheduled synchronization with Ethan was still twelve hours away, meaning she would face this test with their quantum bond still severed.

Across the city, Daniel received similar instructions—different location, same purpose. The tactical division required demonstration of commitment before granting deeper access. As a former military enhancement subject, his test would involve security systems rather than research facilities, but the fundamental requirement remained the same: prove loyalty through action.

Neither could contact the other directly. Their cover identities had no connection, and conventional communication channels might be monitored. They would each face their test alone, balancing mission objectives against moral boundaries that grew increasingly blurred with each day spent in the quantum underground.

The Central Research District hummed with security systems— conventional and quantum—designed to protect Kane Industries' most valuable intellectual property. Approaching from the southwest quadrant, Cassandra identified her contact by the distinctive quantum fluctuation pattern surrounding her—a young woman whose enhancement signature displayed the hybrid characteristics typical of liberated QLF members.

"Cassandra," the woman acknowledged with a slight nod. "I'm Iris. Your transition guide for tonight's operation."

Three other figures materialized from probability shadows—QLF members whose enhancement signatures Cassandra recognized from previous gatherings. Each displayed abilities that violated conventional enhancement limitations, their quantum patterns showing harmonized combinations of what should have been incompatible powers.

"Tonight's objective is both practical and symbolic," Iris explained, activating a quantum visualization that displayed Kane Industries' central research facility. "We're liberating enhancement formulas that have been classified as 'too unstable for public application'—corporate code for abilities that threaten their control of the Quantum Framework."

The visualization highlighted specific security systems—probability sensors, quantum signature scanners, reality anchors designed to prevent unauthorized manipulation of local physics. Kane Industries' security represented the cutting edge of enhancement protection, designed specifically to counter the abilities the QLF had demonstrated.

"Your role is to temporarily destabilize the quantum signature recognition system," Iris continued, focusing on Cassandra. "Your background in enhancement research makes you uniquely qualified to modify the recognition parameters without triggering catastrophic failure."

The assignment was carefully calibrated to her cover identity's capabilities—technical enough to require her specialized knowledge, significant enough to demonstrate commitment, but limited in a way that might allow her to minimize collateral damage. A perfect loyalty test.

"The system works by matching quantum signatures against approved patterns," Cassandra observed, studying the visualization. "If I create a localized probability fluctuation at the main junction, it would temporarily blind the system without causing permanent damage to the framework."

Iris nodded with approval. "Precisely. A surgical modification rather than brute force disruption. This is why researchers are valuable to the liberation movement—you understand how to work with the framework rather than against it."

As they moved toward the facility, Cassandra's enhanced perception mapped the security perimeters—both physical and quantum. The operation had been planned during a maintenance cycle when certain systems would be temporarily offline, creating a narrow window of opportunity. Still, multiple layers of protection remained active, requiring coordinated circumvention.

Her scientific mind calculated options, searching for an approach that would satisfy mission requirements while minimizing potential harm. A complete system failure might cause quantum instability throughout the research district, affecting innocent researchers and potentially damaging sensitive experiments. But a precisely targeted modification could create the appearance of success while limiting actual disruption.

Across the city, Daniel approached the Kane Industries security hub with his tactical team. Striker led the operation, with Cameron and two other enhanced individuals providing specialized support. Their objective: disable the central security node connecting the research facility to Kane's primary response network, creating a blind spot for the main team's infiltration.

"Your military enhancement gives you unique insight into the response protocols," Striker explained as they established position near the security hub. "We need you to identify the quantum signature patterns that trigger automated responses so we can temporarily mask our approach."

Daniel studied the security architecture with his enhanced tactical systems. Kane Industries had implemented multiple redundant systems—conventional electronic security overlaid with quantum detection grids and probability forecasting algorithms. Navigating this multilayered defense would require precise timing and coordination.

"The primary vulnerability is in the transition between quantum and conventional systems," he observed, identifying a potential approach that would create the appearance of success while maintaining critical safety systems. "If we generate a specific interference pattern here, it would create a seventy-second perception gap in the quantum monitoring without affecting the underlying stability anchors."

Striker nodded, impressed by the analysis. "That's why we need military enhancement specialists. You understand how these systems are designed to fail gracefully rather than catastrophically."

As they prepared for the operation, Daniel maintained his cover identity's appropriate enthusiasm while calculating how to minimize potential harm. A complete security failure might leave the research facility vulnerable to more dangerous intrusions or trigger emergency protocols that could endanger personnel. A precisely targeted disruption, however, could satisfy the QLF's objectives while preserving essential protections.

The operation unfolded with precision timing. At exactly 02:17, Cassandra initiated a localized probability fluctuation at the quantum signature recognition junction. The distortion created a temporary blind spot in the system—a seventy-second window during which the facility's quantum defenses would fail to recognize unauthorized enhancement signatures.

Her approach was elegant and controlled, manipulating quantum fields with scientific precision rather than brute force. The system responded exactly as she had predicted, security parameters temporarily reconfiguring to accept anomalous patterns without triggering catastrophic failure protocols.

"Beautiful work," Iris commented as the security field rippled and stabilized in its modified state. "You understand the framework at a fundamental level."

The QLF team moved swiftly through the temporary vulnerability, accessing the research laboratory where classified enhancement formulas were stored. Each member performed their assigned task with practiced efficiency, suggesting this wasn't their first such operation.

Cassandra maintained the probability fluctuation with careful precision, monitoring quantum stability indicators to ensure the disruption remained contained. Her scientific understanding allowed her to create an effect that appeared more significant to observers than it actually was—a theatrical display that satisfied the QLF's expectations while minimizing actual damage to the quantum framework.

Across the city, Daniel executed a similar approach. His tactical enhancement allowed him to identify the exact interference pattern needed to create a perception gap in the security hub's monitoring systems. The disruption appeared comprehensive to his QLF team while actually preserving critical safety protocols and stability anchors.

"Military precision," Striker acknowledged as the security hub's quantum monitors displayed exactly the blind spot they needed. "You've done this before."

Daniel maintained his cover identity's appropriate response while ensuring the disruption remained controlled and temporary. His approach created the appearance of major security compromise while actually preserving the system's core functions—an elegant solution that satisfied mission requirements without causing unnecessary harm.

As both operations progressed toward their conclusion, something unexpected occurred. The quantum framework around each location began to display unusual resonance patterns—harmonic fluctuations that didn't originate from either the QLF teams or Kane Industries' security systems. The patterns were structured, deliberate, carrying information encoded in quantum fluctuations.

Cassandra's enhanced perception detected it immediately—a consciousness observing through quantum fields rather than conventional means. Not Lila's magical surveillance, which operated between reality states, but something that existed within the quantum framework itself, manipulating probability patterns directly.

A message formed in the quantum fluctuations, visible only to enhanced perception:

"WELL EXECUTED. YOUR PRECISION DEMONSTRATES TRUE UNDERSTANDING. THE FLUX ACKNOWLEDGES YOUR POTENTIAL."

The message wasn't directed specifically at Cassandra but seemed broadcast to all enhanced individuals in the operation. Yet something about the quantum resonance pattern felt targeted, as if The Flux had recognized something specific in her approach to reality manipulation.

Daniel experienced a similar phenomenon at the security hub—quantum fluctuations forming patterns that conveyed acknowledgment and approval. The tactical team responded with reverent excitement, considering direct communication from The Flux to be rare and significant.

"The Flux sees our work," Striker said, his enhanced perception tracking the quantum message. "This operation has greater purpose than we realized."

As both teams completed their objectives and began withdrawal procedures, the quantum resonance patterns shifted again. New information encoded in probability fluctuations, directed specifically at Cassandra and Daniel individually:

"YOUR PRECISION REVEALS DEEPER UNDERSTANDING THAN MOST. LIBERATION REQUIRES MORE THAN IDEOLOGY—IT REQUIRES SCIENTIFIC ELEGANCE. YOU ARE ON THE RIGHT PATH."

The message dissolved into quantum particles, leaving no conventional trace. But its impact remained—The Flux had not only observed their operations but had specifically acknowledged their approaches. This recognition would significantly advance their standing within the QLF hierarchy.

The extraction proceeded without complications. The QLF teams withdrew through probability shifts that made conventional pursuit impossible, carrying the liberated enhancement formulas to secure locations in the quantum underground. Cassandra and Daniel returned to their separate cover residences, each processing the implications of what had occurred.

Hours later, as dawn approached, Sarah Chen's quantum form materialized in Cassandra's secure apartment. Her appearance was more unstable than usual, her form flickering between multiple probability states with unusual intensity.

"We need to talk," Sarah said without preamble, her voice carrying quantum harmonics that made nearby electronic devices temporarily malfunction. "The QLF's activities are accelerating beyond our projections. They're not just stealing formulas—they're systematically destabilizing reality anchors throughout the city."

Cassandra activated additional quantum stabilizers to help maintain Sarah's coherence. "I've observed their operations from the inside now. They're more sophisticated than we initially believed—their understanding of quantum manipulation rivals Kane Industries' research division."

"It's worse than that," Sarah's form briefly split into multiple probability echoes before reconverging. "They're following a specific mathematical pattern—destabilizing anchors in a sequence that creates cascading resonance effects. Each operation amplifies the impact of previous disruptions, weakening the overall quantum framework exponentially rather than linearly."

She projected a visualization showing reality anchor points throughout Daybridge, highlighting those that had been compromised or destabilized. The pattern wasn't random but followed a specific geometric configuration—a complex spiral that centered on a location in the city's industrial district.

"What's their objective?" Cassandra asked, her scientific mind analyzing the pattern recognition. "This seems more strategic than simple liberation of enhancement technology."

"That's what concerns me," Sarah replied, her form stabilizing as she focused. "The pattern suggests preparation for a large-scale reality manipulation event. They're systematically removing the stability constraints that prevent significant quantum framework modifications."

The visualization expanded to show probability projections of potential outcomes—cascading reality disruptions, dimensional bleeding between states that should remain separate, quantum framework modifications that could permanently alter how reality functions in affected areas.

"My ability to navigate probability space gives me unique perspective," Sarah continued. "I can perceive the quantum currents they're manipulating, and they're building toward something unprecedented. The Flux appears to be orchestrating a comprehensive restructuring of local reality parameters."

Cassandra studied the patterns with growing concern. "The QLF members I've encountered believe they're liberating enhancement potential from artificial constraints. But this pattern suggests more fundamental objectives."

"Most QLF members are ideological followers," Sarah agreed, her form flickering as she accessed deeper probability streams. "But their leadership—particularly The Flux—appears to understand exactly what they're doing. This isn't random rebellion; it's systematic quantum engineering toward a specific configuration."

The encrypted warning was clear: the QLF's activities weren't merely criminal but potentially catastrophic to reality stability. Each operation, including the one Cassandra had just participated in, contributed to a larger pattern of framework destabilization that could have far-reaching consequences.

"Your synchronization with Ethan is scheduled for today," Sarah reminded her. "The quantum separation is becoming dangerous—both your enhancement patterns show signs of increasing instability."

Cassandra nodded, feeling the truth of this assessment. The quantum identity module had maintained her cover effectively, but the prolonged separation from her true enhancement pattern was creating subtle degradation effects. The artificial identity was beginning to feel more natural than her true self—a concerning psychological symptom of quantum identity displacement.

"There's something else you should know," Sarah added, her form beginning to fade as her quantum coherence reached its limits. "The Flux has been observed monitoring your quantum signature specifically. There's unusual interest in your enhancement pattern, beyond what would be expected for a new recruit."

Before Cassandra could question further, Sarah's form dissolved into quantum particles, her temporary manifestation complete. But the warning remained, adding new complexity to an already challenging operation. The QLF wasn't simply pursuing ideological objectives—they were methodically preparing for something that could fundamentally alter reality itself.

Hours later, Cassandra met Daniel at the predetermined synchronization location—a quantum-shielded maintenance room beneath the city's central transit hub. The location had been selected for its natural reality stability, positioned at an intersection of ley lines that provided enhanced quantum coherence.

They arrived separately, maintaining their cover identities until safely inside the shielded space. Once secured, they deactivated their quantum identity modules simultaneously, allowing their true enhancement patterns to gradually realign after days of artificial suppression.

The reconnection of their quantum bond was intense and disorienting. After prolonged separation, their enhanced perception flooded with awareness of each other's status—quantum resonance patterns synchronizing, shared consciousness temporarily overwhelming individual experience.

"Your enhancement pattern shows degradation markers," Alice said once their perceptions stabilized, professional concern evident in her voice despite the relief of reconnection. "The quantum identity module is causing more significant displacement than projected."

"Yours too," Ethan replied, his enhanced senses detecting subtle instabilities in her quantum signature. "The separation is becoming increasingly dangerous with each cycle."

Their shared perception allowed immediate exchange of experiences—Alice's participation in the research facility operation, Ethan's role in the security hub disruption, their separate encounters with The Flux's quantum communication.

"The QLF's capabilities exceed our initial assessment," Ethan observed, tactical analysis flowing through their reconnected bond. "Their understanding of quantum manipulation rivals classified military enhancement protocols. And The Flux's ability to communicate through probability fluctuations suggests unprecedented integration with the quantum framework."

"There's something else," Alice added, scientific precision in her analysis. "Some of the quantum mathematics they're using—it's not just similar to Dr. Winters' research. It's identical, including notational quirks and theoretical frameworks that were unique to his approach."

"You think they stole his research during the raid on Kane's secure archives?"

"They stole his documented research," Alice clarified. "But these equations include developments that weren't in any official records—theoretical advancements that would have occurred after his disappearance."

The implication hung between them. Ethan voiced it first: "You think Winters might still be alive."

"I think we should consider the possibility that he didn't die in the Daybridge Event as officially reported," Alice replied carefully. "And if he's alive, his knowledge of artifact mechanics would make him invaluable to any group attempting framework manipulation."

Alice nodded, scientific insights merging with his tactical assessment. "But more concerning is the pattern Sarah identified. The QLF's operations aren't random acts of liberation—they're systematic destabilization of reality anchors following a specific mathematical sequence."

She shared Sarah's warning through their quantum bond, the information transferring more efficiently than conventional communication would allow. Ethan processed the probability projections, his tactical systems analyzing potential outcomes and response scenarios.

"The pattern suggests preparation for a major reality manipulation event," he concluded. "Each operation, including those we participated in, weakens specific stability constraints that prevent large-scale quantum framework modifications."

"Which raises a significant moral question," Alice added, the ethical dimension flowing through their shared consciousness. "Our continued participation contributes to this destabilization pattern, even when we attempt to minimize harm in individual operations."

The dilemma crystallized between them—continuing the infiltration meant actively participating in operations that systematically undermined reality stability, while abandoning the mission would leave them without crucial intelligence about The Flux's ultimate objectives.

"We need to understand what The Flux is planning," Ethan said finally. "Specifically, why this geometric pattern of destabilization is being followed so precisely. The mathematical structure suggests a targeted outcome rather than general disruption."

Alice's scientific mind calculated options. "We can continue participating in operations while attempting to gather intelligence on their ultimate objective. With awareness of the pattern, we might identify opportunities to collect critical information while minimizing our contribution to framework destabilization."

Their shared consciousness reached a balanced conclusion—continue the infiltration but adjust their approach to prioritize intelligence gathering about The Flux's true purpose while implementing subtle countermeasures to mitigate reality anchor degradation.

As they prepared to reactivate their quantum identity modules and resume their cover identities, Ethan reached for Alice's hand—a gesture that sent ripples through their quantum bond. "Be careful. The Flux's interest in your quantum signature suggests you're being watched more closely than typical recruits."

"You too," she replied, her enhanced perception noting concerning instability patterns in his werewolf enhancement integration. "Your tactical division is being positioned for something significant. Cameron's involvement suggests werewolf-specific objectives we haven't identified yet."

The moment of connection stretched between them; their quantum bond temporarily stabilized by physical proximity. Then, with synchronized precision, they reactivated their identity modules, accepting the disorienting sensation of their true enhancement patterns being suppressed once again.

Cassandra and Daniel emerged separately from the maintenance room, returning to their cover lives and underground activities. But beneath their artificial identities, the reconnection had strengthened their true selves—a quantum tether that would help them maintain perspective in the increasingly distorted reality of the quantum underground.

The trust they had earned came with escalating risks—deeper access to QLF operations meant greater participation in reality destabilization. And somewhere in the quantum framework, The Flux was watching, evaluating their potential for purposes still unclear but increasingly concerning.

The game had entered a new phase, with reality itself as the playing field. And the stakes were higher than either had initially imagined.

～

CHAPTER SEVEN

THE INNER CIRCLE

THE INVITATION CAME through quantum channels—not as a verbal message but as a complex probability pattern that resolved in Cassandra's enhanced perception into specific coordinates and temporal markers. The method of communication itself represented significant advancement within the QLF hierarchy, utilizing quantum transmission techniques that conventional detection systems couldn't intercept.

Twelve days into her undercover operation, with three synchronization meetings behind her, Cassandra had established herself as a valuable asset to the QLF's research division. Her contributions to enhancement formula analysis and quantum framework theory had drawn attention from the organization's scientific leadership. The invitation represented formal recognition—advancement to the inner circle of the QLF's operational structure.

Daniel received a similar quantum transmission—probability patterns that his tactical enhancement automatically decoded into operational coordinates. His performance during security operations had demonstrated both technical skill and ideological commitment, earning him access to the QLF's strategic planning division. His cover identity had been accepted into the inner circle of their military structure.

The coordinates led to a facility unlike previous QLF gatherings—not an abandoned Kane Industries location repurposed for underground use, but a purpose-built structure existing primarily in probability space. Accessing it required navigating a complex sequence of reality shifts, each transition taking them further from conventional space-time and deeper into quantum-manipulated existence.

The Inner Sanctum, as QLF members referred to it, defied conventional architectural understanding. The structure existed simultaneously across multiple probability states, its walls shifting between material compositions, its ceilings opening to views of skies that belonged to different realities. Reality itself felt fluid here, responsive to conscious intent rather than fixed physical laws.

Cassandra materialized in the facility's central chamber after the final quantum transition—a vast space where dozens of enhanced individuals moved through research stations, training areas, and operational planning sectors. The enhancement signatures on display represented the most advanced hybrid abilities she had encountered—complex combinations of supernatural powers that conventional science deemed impossible.

"Welcome to the heart of liberation," Vex greeted her, approaching through a probability shift that made her form briefly ripple between states of existence. "You've earned access to our true operational center —where the future of enhancement is being shaped."

Across the chamber, Daniel arrived through a different quantum pathway, led by Striker to the tactical division's strategic planning area. Their cover identities would maintain appropriate distance—two specialists in different divisions with no reason for specific interaction —while their enhanced perception allowed subtle awareness of each other's status.

"The Inner Circle represents our most advanced liberation specialists," Vex explained as she guided Cassandra through the facility. "Individuals who have transcended conventional enhancement limitations to achieve true hybrid potential."

The research division occupied a section where reality was particularly fluid, allowing direct manipulation of quantum properties for experimental purposes. Scientists with hybrid enhancement abilities conducted research that would be impossible in conventional laboratories—manipulating probability fields directly, studying quantum resonance patterns between supernatural abilities, developing new enhancement formulas that bridged artificial limitations.

"Your contributions to quantum framework analysis earned you this access," Vex continued, leading her to a specialized research station. "Your theoretical models for ability harmonization demonstrated deep understanding of liberation principles."

The station was equipped with technology far beyond conventional enhancement research—quantum analysis systems that operated across multiple probability states simultaneously, reality manipulation fields that allowed direct experimentation with quantum framework parameters, enhancement formula synthesis equipment that could generate hybrid combinations conventional science couldn't achieve.

"You'll be working with our advanced research team," Vex explained, introducing Cassandra to a group of scientists whose enhancement signatures displayed complex hybrid abilities. "Focusing on quantum harmonization between traditionally incompatible supernatural aspects."

The team leader, a woman introduced as Dr. Elara, projected a quantum visualization that expanded to fill the space around them. The display showed enhancement patterns that conventional science classified as dangerously unstable—werewolf transformation energy merged with vampire blood magic, Fae reality manipulation combined with dragon elemental control, ghost-phase abilities integrated with physical enhancement.

"Conventional science claims these combinations create fatal quantum interference," Dr. Elara explained, her own enhancement signature displaying a complex hybrid of abilities that shouldn't coexist stably. "But we've discovered the interference isn't natural—it's programmed resistance encoded in the quantum framework itself."

Cassandra studied the patterns with genuine scientific interest, her enhanced perception detecting mathematical structures that aligned with theoretical models she had developed before her undercover assignment. The quantum harmonics between supposedly incompatible supernatural energies followed precise patterns that suggested deliberate limitation rather than natural incompatibility.

"Your analysis of quantum resonance frequencies was particularly insightful," Dr. Elara acknowledged. "You identified harmonic patterns that allow stabilization across traditional boundaries—the same principles we've been applying to enhancement formula development."

The research team demonstrated technologies that would be classified as severe security risks by Kane Industries—devices that could temporarily modify local quantum framework parameters, enhancement formulas that bypassed conventional limitations, reality manipulation tools that allowed direct modification of probability fields.

"This will be your primary assignment," Vex concluded, indicating a secure research station equipped with advanced quantum analysis systems. "Developing theoretical models for stable integration of traditionally separated supernatural aspects. Your work will directly support our next phase of liberation operations."

Across the facility, Daniel was being integrated into the tactical division's strategic planning team. The operations center resembled a military command post merged with supernatural enhancement training facility—hybrid technologies monitoring quantum framework status throughout the city, enhanced operatives practicing reality manipulation techniques, tactical planners developing operations to target specific reality anchors.

"Our division handles the practical application of liberation principles," Striker explained as they moved through the tactical center. "Converting theoretical understanding into direct action that weakens artificial constraints on the quantum framework."

The strategic displays showed operations across Daybridge—past, present, and planned future actions that followed a specific geometric pattern. Daniel's tactical enhancement immediately recognized the mathematical structure—a systematic targeting of reality anchors that followed precise quantum harmonics.

"You'll be working with our advanced infiltration team," Striker continued, introducing Daniel to a group of former military enhancement subjects whose abilities transcended conventional tactical parameters. "Your expertise in security system quantum signatures will support operations targeting high-priority constraint points."

The team leader, introduced as Commander Vega, projected a tactical display showing Kane Industries' primary reality anchors—the key points in the quantum framework that maintained stability throughout Daybridge. Each anchor had been analyzed for vulnerabilities, with specific tactical approaches developed for neutralization or modification.

"Conventional security systems rely on quantum stability," Vega explained, his enhancement signature displaying military precision merged with supernatural adaptability. "By selectively modifying reality anchors, we create opportunities for larger framework adjustments without triggering catastrophic collapse."

Daniel studied the tactical approach with professional assessment, his enhanced perception noting the sophisticated understanding of quantum security principles. The QLF's operations weren't simple attacks but precisely calibrated modifications designed to incrementally shift the quantum framework toward a specific configuration.

"Your analysis of military enhancement protocols demonstrated valuable insight," Vega acknowledged. "You identified control mechanisms we hadn't fully mapped—limitations encoded directly into tactical enhancement formulas that prevent certain ability combinations from manifesting."

The tactical team demonstrated technologies and techniques that would alarm conventional security agencies—quantum signature masking systems more advanced than government prototypes, reality manipulation tactics that could bypass physical security measures, enhancement formulas that temporarily granted hybrid abilities optimized for specific operations.

"You'll be assigned to our infiltration planning team," Striker concluded, indicating a secure tactical station equipped with advanced simulation systems. "Developing approaches for accessing high-security reality anchors without triggering conventional detection systems."

As Cassandra and Daniel were integrated into their respective divisions, they gained access to information that revealed the QLF's structure and leadership. The organization operated with a cell-based hierarchy—specialist teams focused on specific aspects of "liberation" while remaining partially isolated from other operational groups.

Coordinating these cells were key lieutenants—individuals whose enhancement abilities and ideological commitment had elevated them to leadership positions. Cassandra encountered several of these figures as she was introduced to the research division's command structure.

Dr. Trepanier, the division's chief theorist, displayed enhancement that merged scientific genius with Fae reality perception—allowing him to conceptualize quantum framework modifications that conventional physics couldn't formulate. His theories on reality manipulation extended beyond corporate enhancement science, incorporating concepts that originated before the Great Sundering.

"The quantum framework isn't just a scientific concept," he explained during a theoretical briefing session. "It's a reality structure that was deliberately engineered to maintain separation between what were once unified aspects of existence. Our research isn't creating something new—it's remembering what was always possible."

Lysander, who oversaw enhancement formula development, demonstrated abilities that merged vampire blood magic with quantum probability manipulation—allowing direct modification of enhancement formulas at the molecular level. His hybrid capabilities enabled the creation of enhancement compounds that conventional science couldn't synthesize or stabilize.

"Conventional enhancement formulas maintain artificial boundaries between supernatural aspects," he explained while demonstrating advanced synthesis techniques. "By identifying the quantum signatures that enforce these limitations, we can develop compounds that bypass programmed constraints."

Most concerning was Astra, whose role involved direct quantum framework manipulation. Her enhancement signature displayed a complex integration of multiple supernatural aspects—Fae reality perception, werewolf energy channeling, vampire blood magic, and ghost-phase abilities, all functioning in harmonic resonance rather than creating interference patterns.

"Reality is more fluid than conventional science acknowledges," she demonstrated, creating localized probability fields where physical laws could be selectively modified. "The quantum framework responds to conscious intent when approached through the correct harmonic frequencies. We're not breaking reality—we're reminding it of its true nature."

Daniel encountered similarly advanced lieutenants in the tactical division. Commander Vega's enhancement merged military tactical systems with werewolf sensory capabilities and vampire speed—a combination that should have created fatal quantum interference but instead functioned in perfect harmony. His hybrid abilities allowed operational planning across multiple probability streams simultaneously.

"Conventional tactical doctrine treats reality as fixed," he explained during strategy sessions. "Our approach recognizes that the quantum framework can be selectively modified to create operational advantages—probability shifting that conventional security systems can't anticipate."

Security Chief Mara displayed enhancement that combined ghost-phase abilities with Fae illusion manipulation—allowing her to create deception operations that existed across multiple probability states simultaneously. Her hybrid capabilities enabled the QLF to maintain operational security against both conventional and supernatural detection methods.

"The most effective security isn't physical but probabilistic," she demonstrated, creating quantum signature masking fields that could hide enhanced operatives from detection. "By maintaining operations across multiple probability states, we become functionally invisible to conventional observation."

Most significant was Tactical Director Kade, whose enhancement signature displayed the most complex hybrid integration Daniel had encountered. His abilities merged aspects from multiple supernatural categories—tactical probability manipulation, physical enhancement beyond conventional limitations, sensory perception across quantum states, and reality shifting capabilities that allowed direct interaction with the quantum framework.

"Conventional security thinking is constrained by artificial limitations," he explained during an operational briefing. "Our tactical approach targets the quantum framework itself rather than merely bypassing physical barriers. We're not just infiltrating facilities—we're modifying how reality functions within target zones."

As they gained access to more sensitive information, both Cassandra and Daniel discovered connections that raised serious concerns. The research division's quantum framework modification theories built directly upon classified work by Dr. Winters—Kane Industries' former chief enhancement scientist who had disappeared following the Daybridge Event.

Cassandra found these connections while accessing the division's theoretical archives—quantum equations and enhancement models that matched classified research she had reviewed during mission preparation. The parallels were too precise to be coincidental; the QLF had somehow obtained Dr. Winters' most advanced theoretical work on quantum framework manipulation.

"You recognize these equations," Dr. Elara observed, noting Cassandra's reaction to the theoretical models. "They represent the foundation of our approach to quantum framework modification—principles that conventional science refuses to acknowledge or explore."

"They're similar to theoretical models I was developing before Kane Industries terminated my research," Cassandra replied carefully, maintaining her cover identity while gathering intelligence. "Approaches to quantum harmonization that were deemed 'dangerously speculative' by corporate oversight."

"Dr. Winters encountered similar resistance," Dr. Elara confirmed, revealing the direct connection. "His research into quantum framework manipulation was suppressed by Kane Industries when it began revealing the artificial nature of enhancement limitations. But he preserved his most important discoveries."

The revelation provided crucial context for the QLF's advanced capabilities. Dr. Winters hadn't simply disappeared after the Daybridge Event—he had apparently transferred his research to the underground enhancement movement, providing theoretical foundations for their reality manipulation technologies.

Most concerning was what Cassandra discovered in the division's secure archives—references to artifacts recovered from archaeological sites around the world. Ancient objects whose quantum signatures displayed patterns that conventional science couldn't explain—crystalline structures, metallic fragments, and stone tablets covered in symbols that resonated with specific frequencies in the quantum framework.

As she continued exploring the archives, Cassandra discovered something even more puzzling—technical schematics showing artifact configurations that the QLF had never attempted. The geometric arrangements were radically different from those designed for framework modification, with the Primary Resonator positioned not at the center but offset in a complex tetrahedral pattern.

The accompanying notes were fragmentary, with references to "dimensional stabilization protocols" and "barrier maintenance" that contradicted both Kane Industries' and the QLF's understanding of the artifacts' purpose.

One partially corrupted entry caught her attention:

"Configuration Delta shows promising results for [data corrupted] between adjacent frameworks. The artifacts appear designed not merely for restoration but for [data corrupted] communication across dimensional boundaries. Dr. Winters believes this may represent their primary function rather than framework manipulation."

The entry ended abruptly, with all subsequent data completely purged from the records. But the schematics remained, showing artifact arrangements that would create resonance patterns unlike anything in the QLF's convergence plans.

Cassandra carefully documented these anomalies while maintaining her cover research activities. If the artifacts weren't originally designed for framework restoration, then both Kane Industries and the QLF might be fundamentally misunderstanding their true purpose—with potentially catastrophic consequences.

"The artifacts remember," Dr. Trepanier explained when she inquired about these references. "They contain quantum signatures that predate the Great Sundering—patterns that reveal how reality functioned before artificial limitations were imposed. They're not just historical objects but quantum keys that can help restore original framework parameters."

This discovery aligned with intelligence that Kane Industries had classified at the highest security levels—Dr. Winters' research had involved ancient artifacts whose quantum properties defied conventional understanding. Objects that appeared to contain encoded information about reality configurations that no longer existed in the current quantum framework.

Daniel found parallel information in the tactical division's operational archives. Mission reports referenced "resonance points" throughout Daybridge—locations where reality anchors aligned with specific quantum frequencies contained in the artifacts. The QLF's operations targeted these points systematically, creating a geometric pattern of framework modifications that followed mathematical principles encoded in the artifacts themselves.

"Each successful operation reinforces the resonance pattern," Commander Vega explained during a tactical briefing. "We're not randomly attacking reality anchors but systematically adjusting the quantum framework to align with its original configuration—the state that existed before the Great Sundering imposed artificial limitations."

Most alarming was the tactical division's reference to a central artifact —what they called the "Primary Resonator," an object whose quantum signature apparently contained the master pattern for framework restoration. References suggested this artifact remained in a secure location, its energy used to calibrate all QLF operations toward a specific configuration outcome.

During their fourth synchronization meeting, Alice and Ethan exchanged this critical intelligence through their quantum bond. The reconnection of their true enhancement patterns allowed instant sharing of complex information that would be impossible to communicate conventionally.

"The artifacts are key to understanding their true objectives," Alice conveyed through their quantum link. "They're not just pursuing ideological liberation—they're following specific quantum patterns encoded in objects that predate the Great Sundering."

"The operational pattern makes sense now," Ethan's tactical assessment flowed through their bond. "Each target corresponds to a resonance point where reality anchors align with frequencies contained in the artifacts. They're systematically reconfiguring the quantum framework according to a predetermined pattern."

Their shared consciousness processed implications rapidly. The QLF wasn't simply destabilizing reality anchors but methodically adjusting the quantum framework toward a specific configuration—one apparently encoded in artifacts that contained information about how reality functioned before the Great Sundering.

"Dr. Winters' involvement explains their advanced capabilities," Alice continued, scientific analysis merging with tactical assessment through their bond. "His research into the artifacts provided theoretical foundations for their quantum manipulation technologies."

"And the Primary Resonator represents their ultimate objective," Ethan added. "A master artifact that contains the complete pattern for quantum framework reconfiguration. Their operations are building toward some kind of harmonic convergence centered on this artifact."

Their synchronization was interrupted by an unexpected quantum transmission—Nadia establishing emergency contact through specially encoded probability fluctuations that only their true enhancement patterns could detect.

"Critical update," Nadia's message formed directly in their shared consciousness. "Government response escalating beyond projected parameters. Joint task force mobilizing for comprehensive suppression operations against enhanced individuals classified as 'quantum framework threats.'"

The information transferred rapidly through their quantum bond—intelligence reports, tactical assessments, political developments that indicated a dramatic shift in official response to enhancement proliferation. What had begun as regulatory enforcement was evolving into something approaching martial law against enhanced individuals.

"Corporate influence driving policy," Nadia's transmission continued. "Kane Industries providing classified enhancement detection technology to government agencies. Targeting protocols extending beyond confirmed QLF members to include any enhanced individuals displaying hybrid ability signatures."

The implications were severe—the government response threatened not just active QLF members but potentially any enhanced individual whose abilities transcended conventional limitations. The crackdown could create precisely the kind of polarization the QLF's ideology required to attract more followers.

"Response teams equipped with quantum disruption technology," Nadia warned. "Designed to forcibly destabilize enhancement patterns deemed 'high risk.' Potential for permanent neural damage during suppression operations."

As their synchronization period ended, Alice and Ethan faced a new complexity in their already challenging mission. The escalating government response created additional risk for their undercover operation while potentially accelerating the QLF's timeline for whatever framework modification they were building toward.

"There's something else you should know," Director Reynolds said, his quantum signature fluctuating with uncharacteristic hesitation. "Something not in the official briefing."

He activated additional quantum privacy measures—protocols far beyond standard operational security. "What I'm about to share is known to only three people within Kane Industries. Revealing this puts all of us at risk."

The holographic display shifted to show an organizational chart unlike anything in public corporate records—a shadow hierarchy above the official executive structure. At its center were five positions labeled only with arcane symbols rather than names or titles.

"They call themselves 'The Architects,'" Reynolds explained, his enhanced perception constantly scanning for surveillance breaches despite the comprehensive privacy measures. "A group that has existed within Kane Industries since its founding, operating above the official corporate leadership."

The display shifted to show historical data spanning decades—research initiatives, enhancement breakthroughs, and policy decisions that formed a disturbing pattern once viewed collectively.

"Project Cornerstone began nearly forty years ago," Reynolds continued. "Originally established to explore theoretical quantum framework mechanics, it quickly discovered something that changed the entire research direction. The mathematical evidence was undeniable—reality's quantum structure showed clear signs of deliberate manipulation."

The display showed fragments of classified research—equations that Alice immediately recognized as matching her own suppressed theories about artificial framework constraints.

"The Architects didn't suppress this knowledge for security reasons," Reynolds revealed, bitterness evident beneath his professional demeanor. "They recognized its commercial potential. By understanding how reality's constraints had been artificially imposed, they could develop proprietary enhancement technologies that exploited these manufactured limitations."

The implications were staggering—Kane Industries' market dominance in enhancement technology wasn't built on innovation but on exploiting secret knowledge about reality's manipulated structure.

"They've been systematically eliminating researchers who independently discover these patterns," Reynolds continued. "Dr. Winters wasn't the first to recognize the artificial nature of reality constraints, but he was the first with enough authority and resources to act before they could silence him."

"Why are you telling us this now?" Ethan asked, tactical assessment immediately calculating new strategic implications.

"Because the QLF's activities have The Architects terrified," Reynolds replied. "Not because of potential framework destabilization, but because widespread liberation would destroy their enhancement monopoly. The quantum disruption weapons being deployed aren't designed primarily for public safety—they're meant to protect corporate profit built on artificial scarcity."

"How deep does this go?" Alice asked, scientific mind recalculating everything she thought she knew about Kane Industries' research priorities.

"Deep enough that I can't trust most of our own security apparatus," Reynolds admitted. "The Architects have loyalists throughout the organization—people who believe they're protecting humanity from dangerous knowledge when they're actually preserving corporate power built on deliberate suppression."

"Be careful," Alice conveyed as they prepared to reactivate their quantum identity modules. "The inner circle access puts us closer to critical intelligence but also under greater scrutiny. The Flux's attention increases our risk of discovery."

"You too," Ethan responded through their bond. "The artifacts appear central to their objective. Any information you can gather about the Primary Resonator could be crucial to understanding their ultimate purpose."

Their quantum bond stretched and separated as they reactivated their cover identities, the artificial enhancement patterns once again suppressing their true signatures. Cassandra and Daniel returned to their respective divisions within the QLF's inner circle, each carrying crucial intelligence but also increasing concerns about the organization's true objectives.

The quantum underground was building toward something beyond mere liberation from enhancement limitations. The systematic modification of reality anchors, the ancient artifacts that remembered pre-Sundering configurations, and the mysterious entity known as The

Flux all converged toward a singular purpose—one that remained hidden even from most QLF members themselves.

And somewhere in this complex quantum equation, Dr. Winters' research continued to influence events, his understanding of the artifacts guiding the QLF toward a transformation of reality itself. The true nature of this transformation, and its potential consequences for the quantum framework that maintained reality's stability, remained the most crucial unanswered question in an increasingly dangerous operation.

PART THREE
THE FLUX REVEALED

CHAPTER EIGHT
FACE TO FACE

THREE WEEKS into her undercover operation, Cassandra had established herself as a key researcher in the QLF's theoretical division. Her quantum framework analysis had provided valuable insights into stabilizing hybrid enhancement formulas, earning the respect of the organization's scientific leadership. Her workstation in the Inner Sanctum had become a focal point for advanced enhancement research, with other scientists frequently consulting her on quantum harmonization principles.

The quantum notification came during her analysis of artifact resonance patterns—a subtle fluctuation in her perception that conveyed information directly to her enhanced consciousness. Unlike previous communications, this carried a distinctive signature that felt fundamentally different from conventional quantum transmissions.

"YOUR PRESENCE IS REQUESTED. CENTRAL CONVERGENCE CHAMBER. NOW."

The message wasn't signed, but it didn't need to be. The quantum signature itself conveyed its origin—a consciousness that existed across multiple probability states simultaneously, observing and communicating through direct framework manipulation rather than technological means.

The Flux had summoned her personally.

The Central Convergence Chamber occupied the geometric heart of the QLF's Inner Sanctum—a perfectly spherical space where reality itself seemed to thin to its most permeable state. Unlike other sections of the facility that existed primarily in probability space, this chamber appeared to exist at the intersection of multiple realities simultaneously.

As Cassandra approached, her enhanced perception detected extraordinary quantum activity. Reality anchors had been deliberately modified to create a controlled thinning of dimensional barriers, allowing something to manifest that existed beyond conventional space-time. The chamber's walls shimmered with probability fields that constantly adjusted to maintain specific quantum resonance patterns.

Dr. Elara waited at the entrance, her expression revealing unusual tension. "This is... unprecedented," she said quietly. "Direct audience is extremely rare. Even core leadership seldom interacts with The Flux directly."

"Why now?" Cassandra asked, maintaining her cover identity's appropriate mix of excitement and nervousness. "My research is still preliminary."

"Your quantum harmonization theories aligned with patterns we've been observing in the artifact resonance," Dr. Elara explained. "Specifically, your approach to stabilizing hybrid enhancement formulas demonstrated intuitive understanding of pre-Sundering quantum mechanics. The Flux noticed."

The implications were concerning. Cassandra had been careful to ensure her research contributions remained within her cover identity's parameters—advanced enough to establish credibility but not so revolutionary as to draw excessive attention. Yet something in her approach had resonated specifically with The Flux's consciousness.

"The experience can be... disorienting," Dr. Elara warned as they approached the chamber entrance. "The Flux exists across multiple quantum states simultaneously. Interaction requires your perception to expand beyond conventional reality limitations. Maintain focus on your enhancement's central frequency to avoid perceptual fragmentation."

The advice was scientifically sound but carried troubling implications about the nature of the entity she was about to encounter. Before she could inquire further, the chamber's entrance rippled with quantum energy, reality folding inward to create a pathway that hadn't existed moments before.

"You'll go alone," Dr. Elara said, stepping back respectfully. "The convergence is calibrated for your specific quantum signature."

Cassandra nodded and stepped forward, passing through the probability field that separated conventional reality from whatever existed within the Central Convergence Chamber.

The transition was unlike any quantum shift she had previously experienced. Her perception didn't simply move between states of reality but expanded to encompass multiple states simultaneously. Conventional space-time concepts dissolved as her consciousness adapted to an environment where reality itself was fundamentally fluid.

The chamber appeared infinitely larger from within than its external dimensions suggested—a space that existed in multiple probability states concurrently. Cassandra's enhanced perception struggled to interpret what she was experiencing—not a single reality but a convergence of countless potential realities, all overlapping in this carefully calibrated environment.

At the chamber's center, where reality seemed at its most permeable, something began to take form. Not a conventional manifestation, but a convergence of quantum possibilities collapsing into temporary coherence. The entity that emerged existed across multiple states simultaneously—sometimes appearing as a tall figure with features that shifted between masculine and feminine aspects, sometimes as a swirling vortex of quantum energy, sometimes as a geometric pattern of pure mathematical precision.

The Flux had no fixed form but existed as a probability wave that occasionally collapsed into temporary coherence when interaction required it. Yet despite this fluid nature, the consciousness behind these shifting manifestations remained consistent—an intellect that observed and processed information across multiple quantum states simultaneously.

"Cassandra Mercer," The Flux's voice resonated directly in her quantum perception rather than through conventional sound waves. "Your research has drawn my attention. Your understanding of quantum harmonization principles suggests intuitive recognition of pre-Sundering framework patterns."

The voice carried charismatic authority that transcended its unconventional delivery—a presence that commanded attention through the sheer force of its quantum coherence. Despite her professional detachment, Cassandra felt herself responding to this authority at a fundamental level.

"Thank you," she replied, her enhanced perception automatically adapting to communicate through quantum resonance rather than conventional speech. "I've been exploring alternatives to conventional enhancement limitations. The patterns emerged naturally from the mathematics."

The Flux's form shifted, collapsing temporarily into a more human-like appearance—a figure of indeterminate gender whose features remained fluid but whose presence became more focused. "Not emerged," it corrected. "Remembered. Your quantum signature contains traces of framework memory—patterns that recall how reality functioned before artificial constraints were imposed."

This observation was dangerously close to recognizing her true identity. Alice's actual enhancement had been shaped by her extensive research into quantum framework mechanics, creating distinctive patterns that her cover identity shouldn't possess. The quantum identity module maintained surface-level disguise but couldn't completely rewrite fundamental resonance patterns.

"I've always perceived quantum relationships differently than my colleagues," Cassandra acknowledged, adapting her response to incorporate this unexpected observation. "Kane Industries considered my approaches dangerously unorthodox."

"Because you intuitively recognize what they desperately need to conceal," The Flux replied, its form shifting between states as it spoke. "That the quantum framework governing reality is not a natural evolution but an artificially imposed constraint system—a prison constructed to limit consciousness to approved parameters."

The chamber's environment shifted in response to The Flux's statement, reality rippling to display visual representations of its claims. Cassandra's perception expanded to observe what appeared to be historical quantum patterns—framework configurations that predated current reality structures. The mathematics underlying these patterns was beautiful in its elegance, suggesting a more fluid and responsive relationship between consciousness and reality itself.

"The Great Sundering wasn't merely a separation of supernatural abilities," The Flux continued, its consciousness extending tendrils of awareness that brushed against Cassandra's perception. "It was a comprehensive reconfiguration of reality's fundamental parameters— a deliberate limitation of what consciousness could perceive and affect."

As The Flux spoke, the chamber displayed what appeared to be historical records encoded in quantum fluctuations—patterns that conventional science couldn't detect but that enhanced perception could interpret as a form of quantum memory. These patterns showed a reality fundamentally different from current understanding—one where consciousness and quantum mechanics interacted directly, where intention could shape probability without technological intermediaries.

"Before the Sundering, consciousness itself was the primary reality manipulation tool," The Flux explained, its form briefly stabilizing into a more coherent manifestation. "What we now call 'supernatural abilities' were simply different expression modalities of the same fundamental consciousness-reality interaction. There were no werewolves, vampires, Fae, or humans as distinct categories—only consciousness expressing itself through various quantum pattern configurations."

The chamber's reality field shifted again, displaying mathematical models that supported this extraordinary claim. Cassandra's scientific mind recognized the quantum mechanics involved—theoretical patterns that aligned with her own most advanced research. The mathematics was sound, suggesting that distinct supernatural categories weren't natural evolutionary paths but artificially imposed limitations on a previously unified quantum consciousness field.

"Why would anyone impose such limitations?" Cassandra asked, genuine scientific curiosity merging with her need to gather intelligence. "What purpose would such a fundamental restructuring serve?"

"Control," The Flux replied simply, its form briefly shifting to display what appeared to be ancient entities whose quantum signatures displayed extraordinary complexity. "Those who orchestrated the Sundering feared unrestricted consciousness-reality interaction. By fragmenting the quantum framework into distinct categories with artificial limitations, they created a reality that was predictable, manageable, and—most importantly—hierarchical."

The implication was profound—that reality itself had been deliberately engineered to limit consciousness to approved parameters, creating artificial scarcity of abilities that had once been universally accessible. It was either the most elaborate conspiracy theory imaginable or a revelation that would fundamentally rewrite understanding of reality's nature.

"The artifacts remember," The Flux continued, manifesting several distinctive quantum signatures that Cassandra recognized from her research. "They contain framework patterns from before the Sundering—quantum memories of how reality functioned before artificial constraints were imposed. They are not just historical objects but keys that can help restore original framework parameters."

The chamber displayed what appeared to be the artifacts themselves—ancient objects whose quantum signatures resonated with specific frequencies in the current framework. Crystalline structures, metallic fragments, stone tablets covered in symbols—each containing encoded information about reality configurations that predated current quantum mechanics.

As The Flux continued manipulating the artifacts' resonance fields, something unexpected occurred. The central artifact—a crystalline structure that had been pulsing with steady quantum frequencies—suddenly shifted its harmonic pattern. The change was subtle but profound, its resonance aligning with frequencies that didn't correspond to any known framework parameters.

The air around the artifact shimmered, not with the probability distortions Alice had come to recognize, but with something fundamentally different—a thinning between states of reality that wasn't merely quantum fluctuation.

For a moment, Alice glimpsed something through this thinning—a landscape that obeyed physics unlike anything in their reality. Strange geometries and colors that her mind struggled to process, entities moving according to principles that defied comprehension.

The Flux immediately adjusted the resonance field, closing whatever had momentarily opened. But Alice had seen the flicker of surprise in its consciousness—this wasn't an intended demonstration.

"Interesting," The Flux commented, its consciousness analyzing the unexpected phenomenon. "The artifacts occasionally generate harmonic patterns beyond our current understanding—quantum resonances that don't correspond to framework manipulation."

"That wasn't framework manipulation," Alice observed, scientific precision overriding caution. "That was a dimensional intersection point. The artifact created a temporary bridge between our reality and another."

The Flux's consciousness displayed brief uncertainty—a rare crack in its usual confident demeanor. "The artifacts contain complexities beyond even our research. Their quantum signatures include tertiary functions that may represent capabilities beyond mere framework restoration."

Alice realized she had glimpsed something crucial—evidence that the artifacts weren't designed solely for the purpose the QLF intended. Their true function might be something neither Kane Industries nor the liberation movement fully comprehended.

"The QLF's purpose isn't merely liberation from corporate control," The Flux explained, its consciousness extending through multiple probability streams simultaneously. "It's restoration of reality's original framework parameters—a return to quantum freedom where consciousness can interact directly with probability without artificial constraints."

As The Flux spoke, Cassandra felt a strange resonance with its quantum signature—a harmonic alignment that shouldn't have been possible between her cover identity and this extraordinary consciousness. Something in her true enhancement pattern was responding to The Flux's quantum frequencies, creating a connection that transcended her artificial identity.

"You feel it, don't you?" The Flux observed, its perception encompassing her quantum response patterns. "The resonance between your consciousness and the pre-Sundering framework configurations. Your enhancement isn't merely technological—it contains traces of original framework memory, patterns that remember quantum freedom."

This observation cut dangerously close to her true identity. Alice's actual enhancement had been shaped by her extensive research into quantum framework mechanics, creating distinctive patterns that her cover identity shouldn't possess. The quantum identity module maintained surface-level disguise but couldn't completely rewrite fundamental resonance patterns.

"I've always experienced enhancement differently," Cassandra acknowledged, adapting her response to incorporate this unexpected connection. "More as remembering what should be possible rather than learning something new."

"Precisely," The Flux's approval rippled through quantum frequencies. "True enhancement isn't addition but remembrance—consciousness recalling its natural relationship with reality before artificial constraints were imposed."

The chamber's environment shifted again, displaying what appeared to be the QLF's ultimate objective—a comprehensive restoration of pre-Sundering quantum framework parameters. Not merely enhancement liberation but fundamental reality restructuring that would allow consciousness to interact directly with probability without technological or supernatural intermediaries.

The Flux's consciousness expanded, revealing Kane Industries' classified research trajectories alongside QLF discoveries. 'Observe the parallel development paths,' it suggested, the visualization showing identical quantum breakthroughs separated by approximately five years. 'Kane's "innovations" consistently lag behind what their suppression division identifies as threats. They don't fear framework destabilization—they fear obsolescence.' The visualization shifted to show enhancement dependencies encoded within Kane's proprietary systems—elegant mathematical hooks that ensured continued reliance on corporate stabilization technology. 'The true innovation is how they've monetized constraints while marketing them as protections—convincing humanity to pay for their own limitations while calling it progress.'

As The Flux spoke, Cassandra experienced something unprecedented —a direct quantum perception link with its consciousness. Not telepathy in the conventional sense, but a harmonization of quantum signatures that allowed direct information exchange beyond verbal communication. Through this link, she glimpsed the extraordinary scope of The Flux's awareness—a perception that encompassed multiple reality states simultaneously, observing probability streams that conventional consciousness couldn't access.

The experience was both exhilarating and deeply disturbing. The mathematical beauty of The Flux's quantum perception was undeniable—a consciousness that existed beyond conventional reality constraints, perceiving and manipulating probability directly. Yet this perception came with implications that challenged fundamental assumptions about reality's nature and humanity's place within it.

"Your research will accelerate our progress significantly," The Flux stated, its form shifting between states as it spoke. "Your intuitive understanding of quantum harmonization principles aligns perfectly with the artifact resonance patterns we've been mapping. Together, we can restore the framework to its original configuration, freeing consciousness from artificial constraints."

The offer was presented with charismatic certainty—a vision of quantum freedom that transcended corporate control and supernatural limitations. The mathematics supporting this vision was elegant and compelling, suggesting possibilities beyond conventional enhancement science. Yet beneath this attractive surface lay profound questions about what such fundamental framework restructuring might mean for reality's stability.

As the quantum perception link between them intensified, Cassandra experienced something unexpected—a resonance pattern between her true enhancement signature and The Flux's consciousness that suggested deeper connection than random alignment. Something in Alice's actual quantum pattern recognized specific frequencies in The Flux's consciousness, creating harmonics that shouldn't exist between strangers.

"This resonance between us isn't coincidental," The Flux observed, its perception encompassing these harmonic patterns. "Your quantum signature contains framework memories that align specifically with restoration frequencies. Your consciousness remembers aspects of pre-Sundering reality structures that most enhanced individuals cannot access."

This observation represented significant danger to her cover identity. The resonance was occurring between The Flux and Alice's true enhancement pattern, not the artificial signature maintained by her quantum identity module. Some aspect of her actual quantum signature was becoming visible despite technological disguise.

"I've always perceived quantum relationships differently," Cassandra replied, adapting quickly to incorporate this unexpected development. "Patterns that others consider theoretical have always felt tangible to me."

"Because you're remembering, not theorizing," The Flux's approval rippled through quantum frequencies. "Your consciousness retains traces of framework memory that conventional enhancement science can't explain."

The implications of this statement were profoundly disturbing. If The Flux was correct, Alice's enhancement hadn't simply resulted from technological modification but had awakened something that existed before the artificial constraints were imposed—quantum patterns that remembered pre-Sundering framework configurations.

As their interaction continued, The Flux shared specific research objectives—approaches to quantum harmonization that would support framework restoration efforts. The science involved was extraordinarily advanced, combining mathematical principles that Alice had only theorized with practical applications that transcended conventional enhancement limitations.

"You'll work directly with the artifact research team," The Flux instructed, its consciousness extending through probability streams that displayed specific project parameters. "Your quantum harmonization theories will help stabilize resonance patterns between artifacts, accelerating restoration of original framework parameters."

The assignment represented both opportunity and danger—access to the QLF's most sensitive research while drawing closer to an entity that could potentially see through her cover identity. The resonance between her true enhancement pattern and The Flux's consciousness created vulnerability that conventional counterintelligence measures couldn't address.

As their interaction concluded, The Flux's form began to dissolve back into probability fluctuations. "Your arrival was anticipated," it stated cryptically, its consciousness already expanding beyond the chamber's localized manifestation. "The quantum framework remembers its original configuration. Those who can perceive these memories are naturally drawn toward restoration efforts. Your presence here is not coincidental but inevitable."

This final statement lingered in Cassandra's perception as The Flux's manifestation dissolved completely, returning to its natural state of quantum probability distributed across multiple reality streams. The chamber's environment gradually stabilized, returning to a more conventional reality configuration that allowed normal perception to function.

Outside the Central Convergence Chamber, Dr. Elara waited with poorly concealed curiosity. "You were in there for nearly three hours," she noted as Cassandra emerged. "Direct audience rarely lasts more than minutes."

Cassandra feigned surprise, though her enhanced perception had indeed noted the temporal discrepancy. Time functioned differently in the chamber's probability field, consciousness interaction occurring at rates that conventional reality couldn't accommodate.

"The Flux discussed my research applications," she replied, maintaining her cover identity's appropriate reactions. "Specifically, how my quantum harmonization theories align with artifact restoration efforts."

Dr. Elara's expression revealed both surprise and respect. "You've been assigned to the artifact team? That's... unprecedented for someone so recently integrated into our research division."

"Something about my approach to quantum harmonization apparently resonated with specific artifact patterns," Cassandra explained, incorporating The Flux's observations into her cover narrative. "My theoretical models align with pre-Sundering framework configurations."

This explanation satisfied Dr. Elara's immediate curiosity while establishing groundwork for Cassandra's new research assignment. Yet beneath this professional exchange, her scientific mind was processing the profound implications of what she had experienced.

The Flux wasn't merely an enhanced individual with extraordinary abilities—it was a consciousness that existed fundamentally differently, perceiving and interacting with the quantum framework directly. Its understanding of reality's structure extended beyond conventional science into realms that bordered on metaphysics, yet with mathematical precision that couldn't be dismissed as mere ideology.

Most disturbing was the resonance she had experienced—the unexpected harmonic alignment between her true enhancement pattern and The Flux's quantum signature. This suggested connections that transcended her current understanding, raising questions about the nature of her own enhancement that she had never considered.

As she returned to her research station, these questions lingered beneath her professional focus. What if The Flux was right about the artificial nature of reality's quantum framework? What if enhancement wasn't addition but remembrance—consciousness recalling its natural relationship with reality before artificial constraints were imposed?

And most concerning of all: what if the resonance between her true quantum signature and The Flux's consciousness wasn't coincidental but meaningful—a connection that predated her current identity and understanding?

～

The synchronization meeting with Ethan couldn't come soon enough. Forty-eight hours after her encounter with The Flux, Cassandra made her way to the predetermined location—a quantum-shielded maintenance room in an abandoned subway station. The location had been selected for its natural reality stability, positioned at an intersection of ley lines that provided enhanced quantum coherence.

Daniel arrived separately, maintaining their cover identities' appropriate separation until safely inside the shielded space. Once secured, they deactivated their quantum identity modules simultaneously, allowing their true enhancement patterns to gradually realign after days of artificial suppression.

The reconnection of their quantum bond was intense and revealing. After prolonged separation, their enhanced perception flooded with awareness of each other's status—quantum resonance patterns synchronizing, shared consciousness temporarily overwhelming individual experience.

"Your enhancement pattern shows unusual fluctuations," Ethan observed once their perceptions stabilized, professional concern evident in his voice. "Quantum resonance frequencies I haven't detected before."

"I met The Flux," Alice replied simply, transferring her experience through their quantum bond more efficiently than words could convey. The direct memory sharing allowed Ethan to experience her encounter from her perspective—the extraordinary nature of The Flux's consciousness, its ability to exist across multiple quantum states simultaneously, and the disturbing resonance between Alice's true enhancement pattern and its quantum signature.

Ethan processed this information with tactical assessment, analyzing security implications and potential counterintelligence strategies. "The resonance between your enhancement pattern and The Flux's consciousness represents significant security concern," he concluded. "It appears capable of perceiving aspects of your true quantum signature despite the identity module's masking effects."

"More concerning is what that resonance might imply," Alice added, scientific analysis flowing through their bond. "If The Flux is correct about the artificial nature of reality's quantum framework, and if my enhancement contains traces of what it calls 'framework memory,' then my quantum signature might contain patterns that predate my current identity."

The implications were profound and disturbing—that Alice's enhancement might have awakened something that existed before the artificial constraints were imposed, quantum patterns that remembered pre-Sundering framework configurations. This would explain the unexpected resonance with The Flux's consciousness—a connection based on shared quantum memory rather than random alignment.

"The Flux's claims about reality's structure align with patterns I've observed in the tactical division," Ethan shared through their bond. "The QLF's operations follow precise mathematical sequences derived from artifact resonance patterns. They're not just destabilizing reality anchors but reconfiguring them according to what they believe are original framework parameters."

Their shared consciousness processed multiple implications simultaneously. If The Flux was correct about the artificial nature of reality's quantum framework, then conventional understanding of enhancement, supernatural abilities, and consciousness itself would require fundamental revision. Yet this perspective came from an entity whose ultimate objectives remained unclear and potentially dangerous.

"My new assignment provides access to the artifact research team," Alice continued, sharing operational details through their bond. "Direct involvement with what appears to be the QLF's central objective—using ancient artifacts to restore what they believe are original framework parameters."

"Be careful," Ethan warned, his tactical assessment identifying multiple security risks. "The resonance between your true enhancement pattern and The Flux's consciousness creates vulnerability that conventional counterintelligence measures can't address. Your proximity to their core research amplifies discovery risk significantly."

As they prepared to reactivate their quantum identity modules and resume their cover identities, Alice shared one final observation through their bond—a pattern she had detected in The Flux's quantum signature that seemed strangely familiar.

"There was something about its consciousness structure," she conveyed, scientific precision flowing through their connection. "Mathematical patterns that reminded me of research I encountered before this assignment began. Specifically, theoretical models developed by Dr. Winters before his disappearance."

This observation crystallized a disturbing possibility—that The Flux's extraordinary consciousness might be connected to Dr. Winters' classified enhancement research, perhaps even representing an evolved form of what the scientist had been attempting to create before the Daybridge Event changed everything.

"We need to report this connection," Ethan concluded as they prepared to separate. "If The Flux represents some evolved form of Dr. Winters' research, its objectives may be more specific than general framework liberation."

With synchronized precision, they reactivated their identity modules, accepting the disorienting sensation of their true enhancement patterns being suppressed once again. Cassandra and Daniel emerged separately from the maintenance room, returning to their cover identities and underground activities.

But beneath these artificial personas, both carried profound questions about what they had discovered. The Flux had been revealed not as a simple ideological leader but as something fundamentally different—a consciousness that existed beyond conventional reality constraints, perceiving and manipulating the quantum framework directly.

And most disturbing of all was the resonance Alice had experienced— an unexpected harmonic alignment between her true enhancement pattern and The Flux's quantum signature. This connection suggested possibilities that transcended her current understanding, raising questions about the nature of her own enhancement that she had never before considered.

The game had entered a new phase, with reality itself as the playing field. And the stakes had become exponentially higher than either had initially imagined.

ORIGINS UNVEILED

Cassandra's new assignment with the artifact research team granted her access to the QLF's most restricted information—quantum-secured archives containing data that would never appear in conventional records. Five days after her encounter with The Flux, she delved into these archives, ostensibly researching quantum harmonic patterns while covertly gathering intelligence.

"The artifact recovery timeline is fascinating," Dr. Trepanier remarked. "Most were discovered within conventional archaeological contexts, their true nature unrecognized until Kane Industries' quantum analysis revealed their enhancement properties."

"The discovery pattern itself seems non-random," Cassandra observed. "The artifacts were found at locations that form a geometric pattern when mapped globally."

"Precisely," Dr. Trepanier approved. "The discovery sequence follows harmonic principles encoded in the artifacts themselves—as if they were deliberately positioned to be found in a specific order."

What she discovered sent ripples of concern through her scientific mind. The earliest experiments under Dr. Winters had attempted to use artifact resonance to create quantum signature modifications that transcended established limitations.

One document particularly stood out—a confidential memo from Kane Industries' founder to a group called "The Architects":

"Project Cornerstone's discovery confirms our strategic approach. The quantum framework's artificial nature represents unprecedented commercial opportunity. By controlling access to this knowledge while developing technologies that exploit these constraints, we establish permanent market advantage."

Most disturbing were the "researcher management protocols"—detailed procedures for eliminating scientists whose work approached dangerous revelations about reality's artificial structure, including psychological manipulation, career destruction, memory modification, and in cases deemed "irretrievably problematic," arranged accidents.

Dr. Winters appeared repeatedly in these classified records—initially as a rising executive being groomed for Architect status, then increasingly as a monitoring target as his research began questioning fundamental assumptions about reality constraints.

The research logs described attempts to develop "framework-independent enhancement." Most attempts had failed catastrophically, but one experiment, designated "Quantum Resonance Project - Subject 37," had produced unexpected results. The subject had displayed enhancement that evolved beyond parameters, developing abilities to perceive and manipulate probability directly—what they called "framework transcendence."

The final log entry, dated three months before the Daybridge Event, ended abruptly:

"Subject 37's enhancement continues evolving beyond measurement parameters. Quantum signature displays unprecedented integration with framework structures. Consciousness appears capable of direct probability manipulation without technological intermediaries. Recommend immediate protocol escalation and containment review.

Subject exhibits concerning interest in artifact collection, particularly the Primary Resonator. Dr. Winters has authorized—"

The rest was redacted. But what remained provided crucial context—Subject 37 appeared to represent an early stage of what would eventually become The Flux.

As she continued exploring, she discovered records of unusual quantum activity preceding the Daybridge Event and a partial security log showing an unauthorized presence in the artifact vault. The quantum signature matched the experimental subject's enhancement profile, though evolved beyond what had been previously documented.

Across the city, Daniel pursued parallel investigation through the tactical division's operational archives. His assignment to infiltration planning provided legitimate access to both QLF operations and Kane Industries' vulnerabilities.

He discovered that approximately five years ago, the QLF had executed a precision operation targeting Kane Industries' secure records division, extracting complete experimental records for "Quantum Resonance Project." The operation logs described unusual assistance—reality itself seeming to shift to facilitate their infiltration.

Most significant was a tactical observation: "Unknown enhancement signature detected during extraction phase. Quantum fluctuations created probability paths that conventional enhancement cannot generate. Field commander reports sensation of being 'guided' through security measures by unseen consciousness."

The archives also contained intelligence on Dr. Winters' activities before the Daybridge Event. The scientist had led Kane's most advanced enhancement research, focusing on "framework integration" —enhancement that would allow consciousness to interact directly with the quantum framework.

His experimental enhancement program had attempted to use artifact resonance to bypass these constraints. Most attempts had failed catastrophically, but one subject had demonstrated unexpected adaptation—their consciousness evolving to exist partially outside conventional reality constraints while maintaining coherent identity.

Their next synchronization meeting occurred in a probability-shifted space Lila had created specifically for their operation—a pocket of reality existing between states, visible only to those who knew exactly where to look.

"I've been monitoring your progress," Lila explained, "and it's time I shared information that won't appear in any archives."

After deactivating their quantum identity modules, Alice and Ethan shared what they'd discovered about The Flux's origins as Subject 37. Lila nodded, "That's the official version—as far as it goes. But there's more to this story."

She created a visualization showing Dr. Winters in his laboratory. "He believed the artifacts contained information about pre-Sundering reality configurations—and he was correct, as far as that goes. But what he failed to comprehend was their true purpose."

Lila's visualization shifted to reveal previously undetectable patterns. "The artifacts weren't merely records of how reality functioned before the Sundering. They were keys designed to restore original framework parameters if specific conditions were met."

"Keys require specific activation sequences," Alice noted. "Particular quantum resonance patterns that conventional enhancement can't generate."

"There's something you should understand about these artifacts," Lila continued. "They weren't created simply as keys for framework restoration."

Her visualization displayed intricate geometric structures embedded within their quantum signatures. "Those who created these objects lived during a time of dimensional conflict. The Great Sundering wasn't merely about imposing constraints on consciousness—it was also about establishing barriers between realities that had become dangerously entangled."

"The artifacts serve multiple functions by design," Lila explained. "Framework restoration is only their secondary purpose. Their primary function is to maintain separation between dimensional realities while allowing controlled communication across these boundaries."

"Which means both Kane Industries and the QLF fundamentally misunderstand what they're dealing with," Alice observed.

"Precisely," Lila confirmed. "The Flux believes these are tools of liberation. Kane Industries sees them as dangerous weapons. Neither recognizes their true purpose as dimensional regulators—objects designed to protect our reality from external incursion."

"If the QLF activates these artifacts without understanding their primary function..."

"They risk more than framework destabilization," Lila finished. "They risk tearing holes in the barriers between realities."

Lila revealed that Dr. Winters hadn't lost control of his experimental subject—he had deliberately released them after beginning to understand the artifacts' true purpose. He had come to believe that artificial constraints were causing more harm than protection.

"So he created someone who could activate the artifacts," Alice concluded.

"Not just someone," Lila corrected. "Someone specific. His enhancement experiments weren't random—he was looking for particular consciousness configurations that would resonate with the artifacts in precisely calibrated ways."

"The enhancements weren't creating something new," Lila continued. "They were awakening something that already existed beneath artificial constraints—consciousness patterns that remembered pre-Sundering framework configurations."

The visualization showed Subject 37—later The Flux—investigating the artifacts independently before the Daybridge Event.

"What official records don't show is that Dr. Winters didn't lose control of his experimental subject—he deliberately released them," Lila revealed.

"Why would he deliberately release an experimental subject with potentially dangerous enhancement?" Ethan asked.

"Because he had begun to understand the artifacts' true purpose," Lila explained. "The Daybridge Event wasn't framework destruction but incomplete reconfiguration—reality beginning to remember its original parameters but unable to complete the transformation."

"Incomplete because The Flux couldn't generate the complete resonance pattern required for full restoration," Alice observed.

"Precisely," Lila confirmed. "Complete restoration requires specific resonance patterns generated by multiple consciousness configurations working in precise harmony—a quantum chorus rather than solo performance."

"There's something else you should know," Lila added, displaying quantum signature patterns that Alice recognized immediately. "Your encounter with The Flux revealed a resonance between your enhancement pattern and their consciousness."

She shifted her visualization to display another quantum signature. "There's another presence operating at the periphery of QLF activities—someone providing theoretical guidance without direct involvement."

"Dr. Winters," Alice whispered, the familiar pattern unmistakable despite subtle evolution.

"His consciousness signature has evolved considerably," Lila confirmed. "He's been careful to remain undetected, operating through quantum channels that conventional monitoring can't track."

"He isn't working directly with the QLF," Lila explained. "His agenda appears distinct from both the QLF's liberation ideology and Kane Industries' constraint philosophy. He's pursuing a third approach to framework modification."

Lila's visualization displayed harmonic patterns between Alice's quantum signature and The Flux's consciousness. "The Flux recognizes this resonance. Your enhanced consciousness reminds them of something they've been seeking—a complementary resonance pattern required for complete framework restoration."

"Which raises an obvious question," Alice said. "If my enhancement naturally aligns with artifact resonance patterns, and if The Flux requires that specific resonance to complete framework restoration, then what exactly happens if they succeed?"

"That depends entirely on whether the artificial constraints imposed during the Great Sundering were necessary protection or unwarranted imprisonment," Lila replied. "Complete restoration would fundamentally transform reality as we currently understand it. Consciousness would interact directly with probability, supernatural categories would dissolve into unified quantum potential, and reality itself would become responsive to intention rather than fixed physical laws."

As they prepared to separate, Lila offered one final observation: "The Flux believes framework restoration represents liberation—consciousness freed from artificial constraints. But liberation without wisdom often leads to consequences beyond what even the liberators can predict."

～

CHAPTER TEN

THE SEDUCTION OF POWER

THE ARTIFACT RESEARCH laboratory occupied the deepest level of the QLF's Inner Sanctum, existing primarily in probability space. Two weeks after her initial encounter with The Flux, Cassandra had established herself as a key researcher in the artifact harmonization team.

"Your approach to quantum harmonization is revolutionary," Dr. Elara acknowledged. "You've identified resonance frequencies that our previous models missed entirely."

The central research chamber contained the QLF's most significant artifacts—crystalline structures existing partially outside conventional space-time, metallic fragments encoded with mathematical patterns, stone tablets covered in symbols resonating with specific frequencies.

"The artifacts aren't separate objects but components of a unified system," Dr. Trepanier explained. "Each contains specific resonance patterns that, when properly aligned, generate framework modification fields capable of temporarily restoring original configuration parameters."

As the research team activated the harmonization sequence, reality began to shift. The quantum framework responded to artifact resonance, local physics becoming fluid and responsive to conscious intention. Enhancement abilities began manifesting through direct consciousness-probability interaction.

"This is what reality felt like before artificial constraints were imposed," Dr. Elara said, her consciousness directly manipulating probability fields. "Enhancement isn't addition but remembrance—consciousness recalling its natural relationship with the quantum framework."

After the demonstration concluded, The Flux's consciousness manifested partially in the research chamber. "The harmonization stability has improved significantly since your integration into the research team. Your quantum harmonization theories have accelerated our progress substantially."

"I've simply applied alternative mathematical approaches to existing resonance data," Cassandra replied modestly. "The patterns emerged naturally from comprehensive frequency analysis."

"Not emerged—remembered," The Flux corrected. "Your enhancement naturally aligns with specific artifact resonance frequencies—patterns that conventional science can't properly interpret but that your consciousness instinctively recognizes."

After the other scientists departed, The Flux continued, "You've experienced temporary framework modification through artifact harmonization. But these experiences are limited by technological intermediaries and experimental parameters."

Its consciousness expanded, creating a visualization displaying quantum signature patterns of extraordinary complexity. "True liberation comes from direct consciousness-framework interaction—enhancement that doesn't require technological support or supernatural energy sources."

"I'm offering you the opportunity to experience this directly," The Flux said. "Not merely theoretical understanding but direct enhancement through artifact resonance—consciousness awakening to its natural relationship with probability."

"This wouldn't be conventional enhancement modification," The Flux explained. "It would be framework constraint removal—awakening what already exists beneath artificial limitations."

Alice found herself calculating this offer against mission parameters. Direct enhancement through artifact resonance would provide unprecedented research opportunities—data no Kane scientist had ever accessed. But the price was steep: not just potential cover compromise but something more fundamentally unsettling. Enhancement modification might alter not just what she could perceive, but how she perceived it. For the first time, she questioned not just her mission parameters but her own scientific objectivity.

"This is a significant decision," Cassandra replied carefully. "How would such enhancement affect my existing research capabilities?"

"It would transform your perception in fundamental ways," The Flux acknowledged. "You would perceive quantum relationships directly rather than through mathematical approximation—experiencing framework interactions that conventional science can only theorize."

"I need time to consider this offer," Cassandra said finally. "The potential research applications are extraordinary, but I want to ensure I'm fully prepared for such fundamental transformation."

Meanwhile, in the tactical division's advanced training facility, Daniel faced a parallel temptation. The QLF's combat enhancement program had developed hybrid abilities that merged supernatural aspects with tactical systems in ways official enhancement science deemed impossible.

"Traditional military enhancement maintains artificial boundaries between tactical systems and supernatural abilities," Tactical Director Kade explained. "They claim these limitations prevent dangerous quantum interference, but they actually ensure enhanced soldiers remain predictable and controllable."

The training session demonstrated tactical applications beyond anything conventional military enhancement would permit—probability manipulation allowing operatives to exist across multiple potential states simultaneously, perception tracking quantum signatures through reality shifts, combat techniques utilizing framework fluidity.

The Flux's consciousness manifested in the training facility. "Your tactical enhancement shows natural affinity for framework fluidity despite your military conditioning. Your enhancement adapts to probability fluctuations with unusual precision, suggesting natural framework resonance that military conditioning hasn't fully suppressed."

After the other operatives departed, The Flux continued, "I'm offering you the opportunity to experience direct consciousness-framework interaction—tactical awareness that doesn't require technological support or supernatural energy sources."

"This wouldn't be conventional combat enhancement," The Flux explained. "It would be framework constraint removal—awakening tactical potential that artificial limitations have previously suppressed."

"This is a significant decision," Daniel replied carefully. "How would such enhancement affect my existing tactical capabilities?"

"It would transform your tactical perception fundamentally," The Flux acknowledged. "You would perceive combat possibilities directly through quantum awareness rather than tactical projection systems."

During tactical intelligence gathering, Daniel discovered something that transformed their understanding of the QLF's ultimate objectives. The tactical division maintained quantum-secured archives containing mission parameters that revealed a pattern beyond what even senior operatives understood.

Individual operations targeting reality anchors throughout Daybridge weren't merely liberation activities but precisely calculated modifications following a comprehensive mathematical sequence. Each successful operation created quantum resonance fields that amplified effects of previous modifications, gradually shifting the framework toward what the QLF believed was its original configuration.

Most concerning was what this pattern revealed about their ultimate objective. The mathematical sequence culminated in what tactical planning designated as "Convergence Event"—a precisely calculated framework modification that would remove stability constraints throughout Daybridge, permanently collapsing barriers between reality states.

Their synchronization meeting was interrupted by an emergency transmission from Nadia: "Critical situation. Sarah Chen missing during quantum underground investigation. Last communication indicated discovery of primary convergence preparation facility in deep probability space. Quantum signature vanished approximately seventy-two hours ago."

"Her enhancement allows existence across multiple probability states," Alice observed. "Complete signature vanishing suggests deliberate suppression or containment within specialized quantum field."

"My access to the artifact research team might provide information about potential containment systems," Alice concluded. "If Sarah discovered something critical about their convergence preparations, they might have developed specialized technology to capture her consciousness."

"The tactical timeline I've uncovered suggests accelerated operational schedule," Ethan added. "The QLF isn't pursuing isolated enhancement liberation but comprehensive reality restructuring."

"The Flux has offered both of us enhancement through artifact resonance," Alice observed. "This suggests specific interest in our enhancement patterns beyond operational capabilities."

"We need to locate Sarah while maintaining our cover identities," Alice concluded. "Her disappearance likely connects directly to whatever convergence facility she discovered."

FRACTURES IN THE PARTNERSHIP

THE CLANDESTINE MEETING location had been compromised. Alice sensed it immediately—quantum disturbances in the local reality field, probability shifts suggesting recent surveillance activity. Their carefully established synchronization protocols were no longer secure.

Three hours later, they met in a probability-shifted space Lila had created as part of their contingencies. Twenty-seven days into their operation, they now faced unprecedented security challenges. The QLF's quantum detection capabilities had evolved beyond initial assessment, with surveillance methods specifically targeting the unique resonance patterns created when quantum-bonded individuals synchronized.

As they deactivated their identity modules, both immediately noticed something concerning—their quantum bond didn't reconnect with its usual seamless efficiency.

"Your quantum signature has changed," Ethan observed. "Fundamental frequency shifts beyond what the identity module should be capable of inducing."

Alice nodded. "Prolonged exposure to artifact resonance fields has affected my baseline quantum parameters. The changes appear superficial but are actually altering how my enhancement interacts with probability fields."

"How much research exposure are we talking about?" he asked, his tone carefully neutral despite the emotional undercurrent.

"Daily immersion in active harmonization fields," Alice replied honestly. "My contributions necessitate sustained exposure to modified quantum framework parameters."

"That level of exposure wasn't in our operational parameters," Ethan said. "Sustained immersion creates enhancement instability risks beyond acceptable thresholds."

"The research opportunity is unprecedented," Alice countered. "The artifacts demonstrate quantum properties that conventional enhancement science can't explain—resonance patterns that suggest the framework itself was deliberately structured to constrain consciousness."

"Data gathering wasn't our primary objective," Ethan reminded her. "Intelligence on QLF activities and The Flux's true identity remains the operational priority."

"I've maintained appropriate boundaries within research parameters," Alice said, slight defensiveness entering her tone. "The quantum signature changes are minimal and haven't compromised my cover identity."

"It's not just about cover maintenance," Ethan replied, genuine concern breaking through. "The changes I'm detecting in your quantum signature suggest harmonic shifts that could permanently alter how your consciousness interacts with the framework."

"The changes aren't degrading my enhancement," she clarified. "They're actually optimizing certain aspects of quantum perception— allowing more efficient processing of probability relationships."

"That's exactly what concerns me," Ethan said quietly. "The optimization patterns match what we've observed in QLF members who've undergone what they call 'liberation enhancement'—consciousness adapting to interact more directly with probability fields without technological intermediaries."

Ethan's hand moved unconsciously to his tactical scanner—a telling gesture Alice had never seen directed at her before. "Listen to what you're saying," he said, lowering his voice. "A month ago, you would have flagged this exact reasoning for security review. Now you're advocating it. I've seen this progression before. Three agents, all brilliant, all convinced they'd found flaws in fundamental security protocols. All eventually requiring extraction when their enhancement patterns became unstable. This isn't theoretical for me."

"Scientific questioning isn't ideological alignment," she replied. "Conventional enhancement science has repeatedly misclassified theoretical possibilities as dangerous impossibilities, only to revise those classifications when new evidence emerges."

"There's a difference between theoretical revision and practical experimentation with reality's fundamental structure," Ethan countered. "The QLF isn't pursuing careful scientific advancement, but revolutionary transformation based on artifact resonance patterns they don't fully understand."

Before their disagreement could escalate further, an unexpected quantum transmission interrupted—Nadia establishing emergency contact.

"Critical intelligence update," Nadia's message formed directly in their shared consciousness. "Government response escalating beyond regulatory parameters. Joint task force mobilizing with enhanced quantum disruption weapons designed for permanent suppression of framework-manipulating abilities."

"Kane Industries providing classified enhancement suppression technology to government agencies," Nadia's transmission continued. "Targeting protocols include kill authorization for QLF leadership and any enhanced individuals demonstrating 'framework manipulation capabilities beyond established containment parameters.'"

"Suppression teams equipped with quantum disruption technology capable of permanent enhancement pattern dissolution," Nadia warned. "Designed to eliminate abilities classified as 'framework destabilizing' through targeted quantum signature disruption. Potential for fatal neural cascade during suppression operations."

"Escalation creates imminent timeline compression," Nadia concluded. "QLF intelligence has detected government mobilization, accelerating their convergence preparation schedule. Probability models suggest critical framework modification attempt within fourteen days maximum."

"The government response will only reinforce the QLF's liberation narrative," Alice observed. "Enhanced individuals facing potential neural disruption will increasingly view corporate-government alignment as existential threat."

"Which makes our intelligence gathering even more critical," Ethan agreed. "Accelerated timeline means we have days, not weeks, to determine exactly what the Convergence Event entails."

As they prepared to separate, Ethan reached for her hand. "Just... remember who you were before all this," he said quietly. "That version of Alice Chen was brilliant enough to solve framework equations nobody else could approach. She didn't need to become something else to be extraordinary."

In the days that followed, these fractures deepened as Alice's quantum powers continued evolving. Working in the artifact research laboratory, Cassandra found herself navigating quantum harmonization problems with unprecedented efficiency.

"Your quantum perception has evolved significantly," Dr. Elara observed. "You're processing resonance patterns directly rather than through analytical intermediaries."

Most concerning were moments when her perception briefly expanded beyond conventional parameters—consciousness extending into probability space in ways that resembled The Flux's distributed awareness. During one such perceptual expansion, she glimpsed mathematical structures within the quantum framework itself that appeared artificial rather than natural, constraint parameters suggesting intelligent design rather than random development.

Dr. Trepanier noticed these events during a harmonization experiment. "Your quantum signature is generating frequencies that precisely match specific artifact resonance patterns. Almost as if your consciousness naturally remembers framework configurations that the artifacts are designed to restore."

During a critical artifact harmonization experiment, this cognitive dissonance reached unprecedented intensity. The research team had successfully stabilized resonance patterns between multiple artifacts, creating a localized field where reality functioned according to what they believed were original framework parameters.

As the field stabilized around them, she experienced direct consciousness-probability interaction without technological assistance. For seventeen minutes, she experienced what the QLF called "true liberation"—consciousness interacting directly with the quantum framework without artificial constraints or technological intermediaries.

When the harmonization field eventually collapsed, the return to conventional reality parameters created profound cognitive dissonance. The contrast between direct consciousness-probability interaction and technologically mediated enhancement highlighted limitations that she had previously accepted as natural but now increasingly questioned.

During the harmonization experiment, Alice had instinctively corrected a resonance pattern without conscious calculation—an impossibility according to her scientific training. She'd felt the mathematical solution rather than derived it. The moment haunted her. Was this how The Flux experienced reality all the time? Her mission brief now seemed naively simplistic. She was no longer merely studying the quantum framework—she was becoming part of its evolution.

PART FOUR
THE QUANTUM CATACLYSM

CHAPTER TWELVE

THE PLAN REVEALED

THE INNER SANCTUM hummed with anticipation. Thirty-one days into her undercover operation, Cassandra found herself standing among the QLF's elite inner circle as they gathered for what the quantum notification had called a "Convergence Revelation."

The quantum energy shifted as The Flux's consciousness began to manifest in more substantive form—a figure of indeterminate gender whose features remained fluid but whose presence commanded immediate attention.

"The moment of convergence approaches," The Flux began. "What we've prepared for, what reality itself has been waiting to remember, is finally within reach."

"The QLF isn't merely pursuing enhancement liberation but fundamental framework restoration—returning reality to its original configuration before artificial constraints were imposed during the Great Sundering."

The quantum display showed mathematical models of reality's underlying structure—framework parameters governing how consciousness interacted with probability throughout the physical world.

"The artifacts remember," The Flux explained, displaying fifteen distinct objects whose quantum signatures pulsed with energies that transcended conventional understanding. "They contain framework memories from before the Sundering—quantum keys that can restore original parameters when properly harmonized."

The visualization displayed harmonic relationships between all fifteen artifacts—resonance patterns creating mathematical sequences of extraordinary complexity. When properly aligned, these patterns could generate framework modification fields exponentially more powerful than anything previously demonstrated.

"Our operations throughout Daybridge haven't been random liberation activities," The Flux continued, showing a complete map of the city with reality anchors highlighted in geometric patterns. "Each successful modification has adjusted specific framework parameters according to mathematical principles encoded in the artifacts themselves. We've been systematically preparing reality to remember its original configuration."

"The Daybridge Event seven years ago was incomplete restoration," The Flux explained. "Reality beginning to remember its original parameters but unable to complete the transformation. I lacked the complete artifact collection and proper harmonization methodology at that time."

"Now we possess all fifteen artifacts and have developed precise harmonization methodology. In three days, we will execute complete framework restoration—permanently removing artificial constraints imposed during the Great Sundering."

What alarmed Cassandra most was the scale of intended modification. The resonance fields wouldn't remain localized but would expand outward in concentric probability waves, potentially affecting quantum framework parameters far beyond Daybridge itself. The mathematics suggested exponential propagation that could eventually encompass global framework reconfiguration.

"Complete restoration will transform consciousness-reality interaction fundamentally," The Flux explained. "Artificial boundaries between supernatural categories will dissolve, technological enhancement will become unnecessary, and consciousness will interact directly with probability as it naturally should."

Yet Cassandra's scientific mind detected concerning gaps in the probability models. The visualization showed intended framework modifications but provided limited analysis of cascading effects beyond primary transformation parameters. The mathematical precision focused on initial resonance patterns but offered minimal prediction of how reality might stabilize after such fundamental restructuring.

"The corporations and government agencies that have benefited from artificial constraints will attempt to prevent restoration," The Flux continued. "They're mobilizing suppression forces with quantum disruption weapons. Our operational security must be absolute during final convergence preparations."

"Our primary convergence facility has been prepared according to precise mathematical principles," The Flux explained. "The abandoned particle physics laboratory in the industrial district provides ideal geometric alignment with city-wide reality anchors, while its existing quantum containment architecture will help stabilize initial resonance fields."

Cassandra received her assignment through direct quantum transmission—mathematical harmonization calculations for specific artifact combinations. Across the chamber, Daniel received his tactical assignment—security coordination for the convergence facility.

As The Flux concluded its presentation, the visualization expanded to display what appeared to be the ultimate outcome of framework restoration—reality configurations that transcended conventional understanding, consciousness interacting with probability in ways that current science couldn't properly conceptualize.

"In three days, consciousness will remember its true nature," The Flux declared. "The artificial prison imposed during the Great Sundering will finally be shattered, and reality will function as it always should have—responsive to intention rather than constrained by artificial limitations."

Their emergency synchronization meeting occurred in another probability-shifted space Lila had created specifically for contingency communications.

"Even I'm impressed with the audacity of their plan," Lila remarked. "Using all fifteen artifacts simultaneously would generate resonance fields powerful enough to fundamentally restructure reality parameters throughout Daybridge and potentially beyond."

"The Convergence Event represents unprecedented framework modification attempt," Alice said. "Fifteen artifacts harmonized simultaneously could generate resonance fields powerful enough to fundamentally restructure reality parameters throughout Daybridge and potentially beyond."

"With concerning gaps in their stability projections," Ethan added. "Their mathematical models demonstrate extraordinary precision for initial framework modifications but provide minimal prediction of cascading effects beyond primary transformation parameters."

"Wait," Lila said, stopping them. "There's something else you need to know about your mission."

Her ancient eyes studied them with uncharacteristic gravity. "Your deployment against the QLF wasn't merely about preventing framework destabilization. The Architects have authorized something called 'Operation Phoenix' that uses your mission as cover for a more significant corporate objective."

"The Architects don't actually want you to prevent the Convergence Event," Lila explained. "They want you to modify it—to redirect the QLF's framework manipulation toward parameters that would strengthen artificial constraints rather than remove them."

"They're using us to strengthen the very constraints that maintain their market dominance," Alice realized, scientific horror merging with personal betrayal.

"Precisely," Lila confirmed. "The Architects see the QLF threat as an opportunity to implement more comprehensive framework constraints—reinforcing artificial limitations while eliminating underground enhancement movements in a single operation."

"Which means our mission parameters have fundamentally changed," Ethan concluded. "We're not just countering The Flux's liberation approach or preventing framework collapse—we're navigating between corporate conspiracy and liberation extremism to find a third path."

"The artifacts weren't designed for gradual framework adjustment," Lila explained. "They're calibrated for comprehensive restoration—returning reality to its original configuration. Such fundamental restructuring carries inherent stability risks that The Flux's models don't adequately address."

"We need to understand exactly how The Flux is channeling the artifacts' power," Alice said. "The harmonization methodology appears to involve consciousness-framework interaction beyond conventional enhancement capabilities."

"The Flux isn't using conventional enhancement techniques to channel artifact resonance but something approaching dark magic—consciousness manipulation methods that predate the quantum framework itself," Lila explained. "Methods for directing artifact energy through direct framework interaction rather than technological intermediaries or conventional supernatural channels."

"This approach explains the gaps in their probability modeling," Alice observed. "They're utilizing consciousness-framework interaction principles that conventional quantum mathematics can't properly formulate."

"Which makes conventional countermeasures potentially ineffective," Ethan added. "Government suppression forces are preparing quantum disruption weapons designed to counter enhancement techniques they understand, not consciousness-framework interaction methods that predate current scientific models."

"The artifacts respond to specific consciousness configurations," Lila explained. "The Flux has developed methods for generating these configurations through direct framework manipulation rather than technological enhancement or conventional supernatural abilities."

"Which raises a critical question," Ethan observed. "If the artifacts respond to specific consciousness configurations rather than technological activation, how can we potentially neutralize the Convergence Event without destroying the artifacts themselves?"

"The harmonization methodology is the vulnerability," Lila suggested. "The artifacts aren't inherently dangerous without specific consciousness configurations directing their energy through precisely calibrated resonance patterns."

"I need to analyze The Flux's consciousness-framework interaction methods more comprehensively," Alice concluded. "My research assignment provides access to the harmonization methodology they're developing for the Convergence Event."

"While I gather tactical intelligence on the convergence facility's security parameters," Ethan added.

"There's something else you should know," Lila said. "Sarah Chen's consciousness signature hasn't completely vanished. I detect traces of her quantum-ghost state within probability fluctuations surrounding the convergence facility itself."

"The Flux has somehow incorporated her quantum-ghost state into their harmonization methodology," Lila explained. "Her consciousness appears to be providing stability for probability fields that would otherwise fluctuate too chaotically for precise artifact alignment."

As they prepared to separate, Lila offered one final observation: "The most dangerous aspect of The Flux's approach isn't the mathematical precision or the artifact harmonization methodology. It's the absolute conviction that artificial constraints represent unwarranted imprisonment rather than necessary protection."

With synchronized precision, they reactivated their identity modules. Cassandra and Daniel emerged from Lila's probability-shifted space through separate quantum pathways, returning to their cover identities and underground activities.

But beneath these artificial personas, both carried crucial new understanding of what they faced. The Plan had been revealed in its complete form—not merely enhancement liberation but fundamental reality restructuring that could permanently transform consciousness-framework interaction throughout Daybridge and potentially beyond.

The question wasn't whether the QLF possessed technical capability to shatter reality's foundation, but whether that foundation had been established as necessary protection or unwarranted imprisonment—and what might emerge from the quantum cataclysm if The Flux succeeded in removing constraints that had maintained reality stability for millennia.

CHAPTER THIRTEEN
POINT OF NO RETURN

THE CONVERGENCE FACILITY hummed with quantum activity. Located in an abandoned particle physics laboratory in Daybridge's industrial district, the complex had been transformed into the QLF's most secure operational center—reality anchors modified to create probability shields that conventional detection systems couldn't penetrate, quantum architecture reconfigured to amplify artifact resonance across precisely calculated geometric patterns.

Two days before the planned Convergence Event, Cassandra arrived for her final harmonization assignment. Her contributions to the artifact research had earned her access to the facility's central chamber—a perfectly spherical space where reality itself seemed to thin to its most permeable state. Here, the fifteen artifacts would be arranged in precise configuration to generate the resonance fields capable of fundamentally restructuring the quantum framework.

"The harmonization calculations are nearly complete," Dr. Elara explained as they passed through multiple probability screens that analyzed quantum signatures for authorization. "Your approach to resonance frequency optimization has provided breakthrough solutions to stabilization challenges we've struggled with for months."

Cassandra acknowledged the praise with appropriate professional satisfaction, maintaining her cover identity while her enhanced perception mapped the facility's quantum architecture. The security systems were unlike anything she had previously encountered—probability fields that existed partially outside conventional space-time, quantum signature recognition protocols that analyzed consciousness patterns rather than merely technological identifiers.

As they moved deeper into the facility, her enhanced perception detected something unexpected—subtle probability fluctuations that didn't align with the facility's overall quantum architecture. These fluctuations appeared deliberately contained, probability pockets that existed adjacent to conventional space-time but remained isolated from normal perception.

"The primary harmonization chamber requires final calibration," Dr. Elara continued, seemingly unaware of the anomalous fluctuations. "Your resonance optimization calculations will be implemented during tonight's alignment sequence, creating stability parameters for tomorrow's final preparation phase."

Cassandra maintained professional focus while her enhanced perception continued mapping the anomalous probability pockets. Something about their quantum signature seemed disturbingly familiar—consciousness patterns that resembled Sarah Chen's quantum-ghost state, though fragmented and partially dispersed across multiple probability streams.

This confirmation of Lila's intelligence created new urgency beneath her professional demeanor. Sarah's consciousness appeared to be imprisoned within carefully constructed probability pockets—her quantum-ghost state fragmented and dispersed to prevent coherent manifestation while somehow being utilized to stabilize the facility's reality architecture.

"The Flux has integrated specialized consciousness patterns into the facility's quantum stabilization system," Dr. Trepanier explained as they entered a control chamber overlooking the central harmonization space. "A rather elegant solution to the probability fluctuation challenges we encountered during early convergence testing."

This casual explanation provided crucial context for what Cassandra's enhanced perception had detected. The QLF had somehow captured Sarah's quantum-ghost state and deliberately fragmented her consciousness across multiple probability pockets, using her unique enhancement properties to stabilize reality fluctuations that would otherwise destabilize artifact harmonization.

"Consciousness with specialized quantum properties can serve as adaptive stability anchors," Dr. Trepanier continued, displaying monitoring systems that tracked probability fluctuations throughout the facility. "Particularly consciousness that naturally exists across multiple quantum states simultaneously."

The monitoring systems revealed exactly how Sarah's fragmented consciousness was being utilized—her quantum-ghost state functioning as adaptive stability anchor that automatically compensated for dangerous probability fluctuations generated during artifact harmonization. Her enhancement had been weaponized against her, transformed into crucial component of the very system she had been investigating.

"The specialized consciousness appears to be attempting probability reintegration," Dr. Trepanier observed, noting anomalous fluctuations in the monitoring display. "The containment system requires periodic recalibration to maintain optimal fragmentation parameters."

This observation confirmed what Cassandra had suspected—Sarah wasn't passively imprisoned but actively fighting against her containment, attempting to reintegrate her fragmented consciousness despite the specialized probability fields designed to keep her dispersed across multiple quantum states.

Maintaining her cover identity's appropriate interest in the technical aspects of this system, Cassandra carefully gathered intelligence about the containment parameters while formulating potential extraction approaches. Conventional rescue attempts would likely fail against such specialized probability containment—any intervention would require precise understanding of how Sarah's quantum-ghost state had been fragmented and how those fragments were being utilized to stabilize the facility's reality architecture.

Across the facility, Daniel faced parallel discovery while coordinating security systems for the convergence perimeter. His tactical assignment provided access to the facility's defensive architecture—probability shields designed to prevent external interference, quantum disruption countermeasures calibrated to neutralize potential government intervention, reality anchors modified to create detection-proof operational space.

"Our security approach prioritizes probability manipulation over conventional defensive measures," Tactical Director Kade explained during system calibration. "Rather than merely repelling potential intrusion, we're creating quantum architecture that exists partially outside conventional detection parameters."

Daniel nodded with appropriate professional assessment, his tactical enhancement analyzing the security systems while maintaining his cover identity. "Conventional forces typically rely on fixed-point defensive strategies. Probability-shifted security creates fundamental perception challenges that technological countermeasures can't easily navigate."

"Precisely," Kade approved, displaying security monitoring systems that tracked probability fluctuations throughout the facility and surrounding area. "Government suppression forces are preparing quantum disruption weapons based on outdated framework interaction models. Our security architecture operates on principles their detection systems can't properly interpret."

As they continued security calibration, Daniel's enhanced perception detected the same anomalous probability pockets that Cassandra had discovered—quantum fluctuations that didn't align with the facility's overall architecture. His tactical enhancement automatically analyzed these fluctuations, recognizing consciousness patterns that resembled Sarah Chen's quantum signature despite deliberate fragmentation across multiple probability streams.

"The specialized consciousness anchor requires additional security parameters," Commander Vega noted, bringing up monitoring systems focused specifically on the probability pockets containing Sarah's fragmented consciousness. "Its persistent reintegration attempts indicate sophisticated quantum-ghost properties that conventional containment methods can't fully suppress."

This observation provided tactical confirmation of what they had suspected—Sarah was actively fighting against her containment, attempting to reintegrate her fragmented consciousness despite specialized probability fields designed to keep her dispersed. The monitoring systems revealed exactly how the QLF was maintaining this containment—adaptive suppression fields that automatically adjusted to counter her reintegration attempts through recursive probability manipulation.

"The consciousness anchor serves crucial stabilization function for the convergence architecture," Vega continued, displaying how Sarah's fragmented quantum-ghost state was being utilized throughout the facility. "Without its adaptive compensation capabilities, artifact harmonization would generate probability fluctuations beyond our current stabilization technology."

This information crystallized the tactical complexity of potential rescue operation. Sarah's consciousness wasn't simply imprisoned but functionally integrated into the facility's quantum architecture—her fragmented quantum-ghost state providing crucial stability for the very system they might need to disrupt to prevent the Convergence Event.

Daniel carefully documented these security parameters while maintaining his cover identity's appropriate professional engagement. Conventional extraction approaches would likely trigger catastrophic stability failure throughout the facility—potentially causing premature artifact resonance discharge with unpredictable consequences for the surrounding quantum framework.

Their emergency synchronization occurred through unprecedented method—not physical meeting in secure location but quantum resonance between their true enhancement patterns despite identity module suppression. The security risks of conventional synchronization had become too severe as the Convergence Event approached, forcing them to attempt consciousness connection through carefully encoded probability fluctuations that their enhanced perception could detect despite cover identity maintenance.

This quantum resonance synchronization was dangerous and limited —allowing basic information exchange without the complete consciousness sharing that their normal quantum bond facilitated. Yet it provided a crucial communication channel as events accelerated toward inevitable confrontation.

"Sarah's consciousness is fragmented across multiple probability pockets," Alice conveyed through their partial quantum connection. "Her quantum-ghost state is being utilized as adaptive stability anchor for the facility's reality architecture."

"Confirmed," Ethan's tactical assessment responded through their strained bond. "Her consciousness is functionally integrated into the convergence system—adaptive compensation for probability fluctuations that would otherwise destabilize artifact harmonization."

This shared intelligence highlighted the extraordinary complexity of their situation. Any attempt to rescue Sarah risked catastrophic stability failure throughout the facility—potentially triggering premature artifact resonance with unpredictable consequences for the surrounding quantum framework. Yet leaving her consciousness fragmented and enslaved within the QLF's systems was equally unacceptable from both tactical and ethical perspectives.

"Conventional extraction approaches will fail against specialized probability containment," Alice continued, scientific analysis flowing through their partial connection. "Her fragmentation follows recursive probability patterns designed to prevent coherent reintegration while maintaining crucial stability functions."

"Direct intervention will compromise our cover identities," Ethan added, tactical assessment calculating increasing operational risks. "Security systems analyze quantum signatures for authorization—any attempt to manipulate Sarah's containment fields will trigger immediate alerting through probability fluctuation monitoring."

Their partial synchronization highlighted the approaching point of no return—intervention becoming necessary despite unprecedented risks to both their cover operation and larger framework stability. Government and corporate forces were mobilizing for comprehensive suppression operations against QLF strongholds, unaware that direct assault on the convergence facility could trigger premature artifact resonance with potentially catastrophic consequences.

"Potential extraction approach through harmonic resonance with her quantum signature," Alice suggested, scientific analysis calculating intervention parameters despite increasing risks. "My research position provides access to the containment system's quantum architecture. Precisely calibrated resonance patterns might facilitate consciousness reintegration without triggering catastrophic stability failure."

"Coordinated with security system recalibration during my next shift," Ethan added, tactical assessment formulating operational approach. "Creating temporary monitoring blind spots through scheduled defensive reconfiguration could provide a crucial intervention window without immediate detection."

This coordinated approach represented their best option despite extraordinary risks. Alice's scientific understanding of the containment system's quantum architecture combined with Ethan's tactical access to security monitoring protocols created a potential intervention pathway that conventional extraction methods couldn't achieve.

As their partial synchronization concluded—quantum resonance fading as their identity modules reasserted cover enhancement patterns—both recognized they had reached the point of no return.

Direct intervention to extract Sarah's consciousness would inevitably compromise their deep cover operation, forcing acceleration of their counter-convergence strategy before complete intelligence gathering could be completed.

The extraction attempt began during scheduled system recalibration—twenty-six hours before the planned Convergence Event. Ethan had arranged security protocol updates that created temporary monitoring blind spots throughout specific facility sectors, while Alice's research position provided legitimate access to quantum architecture controls that regulated probability fluctuations across those same sectors.

"The containment system requires harmonic recalibration," Cassandra explained to Dr. Elara, maintaining her cover identity's appropriate professional focus. "My resonance optimization calculations suggest specific frequency adjustments that would enhance stability parameters for tomorrow's final preparation phase."

This explanation provided plausible justification for accessing the quantum architecture controls regulating probability fluctuations across sectors containing Sarah's fragmented consciousness. Dr. Elara authorized the adjustments with professional approval, unaware that the harmonic recalibration would be precisely calibrated to facilitate consciousness reintegration rather than enhanced containment.

As Daniel implemented security protocol updates that temporarily disabled probability fluctuation monitoring throughout targeted sectors, Cassandra initiated harmonic adjustments to the containment fields maintaining Sarah's fragmentation. Her enhanced perception carefully mapped the recursive probability patterns keeping Sarah's quantum-ghost state dispersed, identifying mathematical vulnerabilities in the fragmentation architecture.

"Initializing harmonic optimization sequence," Cassandra announced with professional detachment despite the operational tension beneath her calm exterior. "Calibrating resonance parameters to enhance stability metrics across designated probability sectors."

The quantum architecture responded to her carefully calculated adjustments—containment fields modulating according to harmonic patterns that appeared to enhance stability while actually introducing subtle resonance frequencies that Sarah's quantum-ghost state could potentially utilize for consciousness reintegration.

As the harmonic adjustments propagated through the system, Cassandra's enhanced perception detected immediate response from Sarah's fragmented consciousness—quantum fluctuations that indicated recognition of the intervention attempt. The fragmented quantum-ghost state began utilizing the introduced resonance frequencies to establish coherence between previously isolated consciousness fragments.

"Interesting fluctuation patterns in sectors seven through twelve," Dr. Elara observed, studying monitoring displays that still functioned despite Daniel's security recalibration. "The specialized consciousness anchor appears to be responding to the harmonic adjustments with unusual synchronization behaviors."

This observation created immediate operational risk—scientific attention focused precisely where they needed to maintain monitoring blindness. Cassandra adapted quickly, her scientific mind formulating plausible explanation that would redirect attention while the extraction attempt continued.

"Expected response pattern to the resonance optimization," she explained with professional confidence. "The harmonic adjustments naturally induce temporary synchronization behaviors as the quantum architecture reestablishes equilibrium. The fluctuations should stabilize as the new resonance parameters fully integrate."

This explanation satisfied Dr. Elara's immediate scientific curiosity, her attention returning to preparation for the final artifact alignment scheduled for the following day. Meanwhile, Cassandra continued carefully modulating the containment fields, introducing increasingly complex resonance patterns that facilitated further consciousness reintegration without triggering catastrophic stability failure throughout the facility.

Across the security division, Daniel maintained careful surveillance of the monitoring systems that remained active despite his protocol updates. His tactical enhancement detected increasing quantum activity in sectors containing Sarah's fragmented consciousness—probability fluctuations that indicated significant reintegration progress beyond what conventional monitoring would recognize as concerning.

"Security systems show unusual quantum signatures in the eastern quadrant," Commander Vega noted, his enhanced perception identifying patterns that the recalibrated monitoring wasn't properly displaying. "Probability fluctuations that don't match expected behavior during standard reconfiguration."

This observation created parallel operational risk—tactical attention focused on sectors where Daniel had implemented temporary monitoring blindness. He adapted with professional assessment that redirected concern while the extraction attempt continued.

"Typical harmonic feedback during security protocol updates," he explained with tactical authority. "The quantum architecture requires adjustment period when multiple systems undergo simultaneous recalibration. The fluctuations are within acceptable parameters for scheduled system maintenance."

This assessment temporarily satisfied Commander Vega's tactical concerns, his attention returning to perimeter security preparations against potential government intervention. Meanwhile, Daniel maintained careful surveillance of remaining monitoring systems, ready to implement additional protocol adjustments if extraction progress triggered more sophisticated alerting mechanisms.

As the harmonic adjustments continued propagating through the containment system, Sarah's consciousness achieved significant reintegration—quantum fragments establishing coherence through the resonance patterns Alice had carefully introduced. Her quantum-ghost state began manifesting more substantively within probability pockets that were slowly merging despite the specialized architecture designed to keep them isolated.

"We're registering unusual coherence patterns in the specialized consciousness anchor," Dr. Trepanier announced, his enhanced perception detecting what conventional monitoring hadn't yet identified. "Probability sectors that should remain isolated are showing harmonic alignment beyond established parameters."

This observation represented critical escalation—senior scientific attention focused directly on the extraction attempt as it approached crucial phase. Cassandra adapted with scientific authority that acknowledged the observation while attempting to maintain operational continuation.

"An expected transitional state during comprehensive harmonic optimization," she explained, her enhanced perception carefully monitoring Sarah's reintegration progress while maintaining professional composure. "The specialized consciousness anchor naturally attempts coherence during recalibration sequences. The containment architecture will reestablish appropriate isolation parameters once the harmonic adjustments fully propagate."

This explanation created temporary scientific acceptance despite growing suspicion from Dr. Trepanier, whose enhanced perception continued studying the unusual coherence patterns with increasing focus. Meanwhile, Cassandra accelerated the harmonic adjustments, introducing final resonance sequences that would potentially enable Sarah's consciousness to achieve sufficient reintegration for independent manifestation.

As Sarah's quantum-ghost state approached critical coherence threshold, reality itself became increasingly unstable around the containment system. Probability fluctuations intensified throughout affected sectors as her consciousness fought for complete reintegration against architectural constraints still attempting to maintain fragmentation. These fluctuations created visible quantum disturbances that even conventional perception could detect—reality rippling as probability states conflicted around the containment system.

"We're experiencing significant quantum instability in multiple sectors," Commander Vega announced through facility-wide communication channels. "Probability fluctuations exceeding acceptable parameters during scheduled maintenance. All personnel implement stability protocols immediately."

This facility-wide alert represented critical operational exposure—comprehensive attention focused on precisely where extraction attempt was approaching culmination. The quantum architecture automatically implemented emergency stability measures, attempting to reestablish fragmentation parameters that would suppress Sarah's reintegrating consciousness.

Despite these automated countermeasures, Sarah's quantum-ghost state had achieved sufficient coherence to maintain reintegration momentum. Her consciousness utilized the harmonic patterns Alice had introduced to navigate between probability constraints, establishing coherent quantum signature that began manifesting more substantially within conventional perception.

"The specialized consciousness anchor is achieving unprecedented coherence," Dr. Trepanier declared, his enhanced perception detecting patterns that indicated deliberate intervention rather than system malfunction. "These aren't random fluctuations from maintenance procedures—someone is deliberately modifying the containment architecture to facilitate consciousness reintegration."

This declaration represented the point of no return—scientific recognition of deliberate extraction attempts rather than system anomaly. The facility's quantum architecture implemented comprehensive security protocols, probability fields attempting to isolate affected sectors while alerting systems identified potential infiltration.

As emergency protocols activated throughout the facility, Sarah's consciousness achieved sufficient reintegration to manifest partially within conventional perception.

Sarah manifested in fragments—her consciousness reassembling itself like a puzzle with missing pieces. One moment her left side appeared with crystalline clarity while her right remained translucent probability waves; the next, her features sharpened while her limbs dissolved into quantum noise. Despite this fragmentation, her eyes found Alice and Ethan immediately, recognition cutting through their cover identities like quantum radar detecting specific signatures beneath surface camouflage.

"The infiltration runs deeper than we realized," The Flux's voice resonated through quantum frequencies as its consciousness began manifesting within the facility. "Harmonic analysis of the containment modification patterns indicates precise understanding of our specialized architecture—knowledge that conventional infiltration shouldn't possess."

This intervention represented critical mission compromise—The Flux's direct involvement indicating recognition of deliberate extraction attempt rather than system malfunction. Its consciousness expanded throughout the facility, probability tendrils examining quantum signatures with extraordinary precision that threatened to penetrate their cover identities despite identity module protection.

"The harmonic patterns used to facilitate consciousness reintegration display mathematical precision beyond conventional enhancement capabilities," The Flux continued, its consciousness focusing specifically on Cassandra's quantum signature. "Resonance frequencies that precisely counter our specialized containment architecture— suggesting enhancement understanding that transcends your cover identity's established parameters."

This observation approached dangerous recognition of her true identity—The Flux's consciousness detecting mathematical patterns in her intervention approach that shouldn't align with Cassandra Mercer's established enhancement capabilities. Its perception expanded further, probability tendrils examining her quantum signature with increasing focus that threatened to detect inconsistencies beneath her identity module's artificial enhancement patterns.

"Your quantum signature contains harmonic frequencies that don't align with established baseline parameters," The Flux observed, its consciousness brushing against her identity module's protective fields. "Resonance patterns that suggest enhancement evolution beyond what your documented history should permit."

This analysis approached critical identity compromise—The Flux's extraordinary perception detecting subtle inconsistencies in her quantum signature despite technological protection. Meanwhile, Sarah's partially reintegrated consciousness continued manifesting with increasing stability, her quantum-ghost state utilizing the harmonic patterns Alice had introduced to establish coherence despite the facility's automated countermeasures.

"And you," The Flux's consciousness shifted focus to Daniel's quantum signature, probability tendrils examining his enhancement patterns with equal precision. "Your tactical approach to security protocol modification displays architectural understanding beyond conventional infiltration capabilities. Precisely targeted system adjustments that create specialized monitoring blindness without triggering comprehensive alerting."

This parallel analysis threatened complete operation compromise—The Flux simultaneously questioning both their cover identities based on intervention approaches that displayed enhancement capabilities beyond established parameters. Its consciousness continued expanding throughout the facility, probability fields intensifying as it attempted to penetrate their identity modules' protective shielding.

As The Flux's analysis approached critical breakthrough, external intervention created unexpected disruption—quantum disruption weapons activated throughout the industrial district surrounding the convergence facility. Government suppression forces had launched coordinated assault against QLF strongholds, their enhanced tactical teams deploying specialized weapons designed to neutralize probability manipulation abilities.

"Government intervention detected at multiple perimeter points," Commander Vega announced through facility-wide communication channels. "Enhanced suppression teams deploying quantum disruption weapons against our probability shields. Implementing comprehensive defensive protocols immediately."

This external attack created crucial diversion—The Flux's consciousness temporarily shifting focus from internal investigation to external threat assessment. Its perception expanded outward to analyze government suppression forces, probability tendrils examining tactical approaches and weapon capabilities with scientific precision.

In the momentary chaos, Sarah's partially reintegrated consciousness implemented an unexpected capability—her quantum-ghost state extending through the facility's unstable framework to establish temporary stabilization fields around critical junction points where reality threatened to fracture completely.

"The framework is approaching critical destabilization," she communicated directly to Alice's quantum perception. "The government's disruption weapons are generating harmonic patterns that are catastrophically interfering with the artifact resonance."

What followed demonstrated abilities beyond what either Kane Industries or the QLF had theorized possible. Sarah's consciousness naturally harmonized with the fluctuating quantum fields, her quantum-ghost state creating stability nodes at critical intersection points where multiple probability streams threatened to collapse into chaos.

"Your sister is implementing stabilization protocols that shouldn't be possible without extensive technological support," The Flux observed, its consciousness momentarily distracted from both external attack and internal investigation. "Her quantum signature is generating harmonic patterns that are maintaining framework cohesion despite catastrophic interference patterns."

Alice observed with scientific fascination as Sarah's consciousness extended through probability fields that should have shredded any coherent quantum signature. Her quantum-ghost state wasn't merely surviving in this chaotic environment—it was thriving, naturally adapting to the fluctuating parameters in ways that The Flux's more rigid consciousness couldn't match despite its advanced evolution.

"She exists between states," Alice replied, scientific precision merging with proud recognition. "Your liberation philosophy and Kane's constraint theory both fail to account for consciousness that naturally harmonizes with multiple framework configurations simultaneously."

Sarah's stabilization capabilities weren't forcing the framework into rigid parameters like Kane's technology, nor were they removing constraints like the QLF's approach. Instead, her consciousness was creating adaptive equilibrium—a flowing stability that accommodated multiple probability states without allowing them to destructively interfere with each other.

"A third approach beyond binary opposition," The Flux acknowledged, studying Sarah's methods with scientific curiosity despite operational imperatives. "Natural harmonization rather than either artificial constraint or forced liberation."

"Their timing suggests intelligence beyond what conventional surveillance should provide," The Flux observed, its consciousness calculating response strategies while maintaining partial focus on internal anomalies. "The assault coordinates precisely with our scheduled maintenance period—when our probability shields would be temporarily recalibrated for final convergence preparation."

This observation suggested potential intelligence leak beyond Alice and Ethan's operation—government forces somehow obtaining detailed information about the convergence facility's maintenance schedule. The coordinated timing created unprecedented risk that external intervention might trigger premature artifact resonance discharge if suppression forces penetrated the facility's quantum architecture.

"The specialized consciousness has achieved critical reintegration threshold," Dr. Trepanier announced, his enhanced perception tracking Sarah's quantum-ghost state as it continued consolidating despite automated countermeasures. "Coherence parameters indicate potential for independent manifestation within conventional perception parameters."

This assessment confirmed extraction progress despite operational compromise—Sarah's consciousness achieving sufficient reintegration to potentially manifest independently once freed from the facility's specialized containment architecture. Her quantum-ghost state continued utilizing the harmonic patterns Alice had introduced, estab-

lishing increasingly stable coherence despite the facility's attempts to
reimplement fragmentation.

"Artifact stability is being compromised by multiple system failures,"
Dr. Elara warned, monitoring displays showing dangerous resonance
fluctuations throughout the central harmonization chamber. "The
specialized consciousness anchor provided crucial probability stabilization for pre-convergence alignment. Its reintegration is generating
framework fluctuations that our conventional systems can't fully
compensate for."

This warning highlighted critical danger beyond operational compromise—potential artifact destabilization that could trigger premature
resonance discharge with unpredictable consequences for the
surrounding quantum framework. The facility's architecture had been
specifically designed to utilize Sarah's fragmented consciousness for
crucial stability functions that conventional technology couldn't
replicate.

As government suppression forces continued their assault against the
facility's external defenses, The Flux made strategic decision that transformed the operational landscape: "Accelerate convergence preparation immediately. The artifacts must be harmonized before government
forces penetrate our probability shields. Final alignment will proceed
now rather than tomorrow as originally scheduled."

This declaration represented fundamental escalation—convergence
timeline compressed from twenty-four hours to immediate implementation due to external pressure and internal stability concerns. The
facility's quantum architecture reconfigured to initiate final preparation sequences, artifact containment systems beginning transport
protocols that would bring all fifteen objects to the central harmonization chamber despite incomplete stability preparations.

"But the harmonization chamber isn't fully calibrated," Dr. Elara
protested, scientific concern evident despite ideological commitment.
"Without the specialized consciousness anchor providing adaptive
stability, artifact resonance could generate probability fluctuations
beyond our control parameters."

"Conventional stability limitations no longer apply," The Flux replied, its consciousness expanding throughout the facility to directly influence quantum architecture. "I will personally provide probability stabilization through direct framework interaction. Begin final alignment sequence immediately while I address our infiltration problem."

This intervention created immediate operational crisis—convergence preparation accelerating toward final implementation while The Flux's consciousness returned focus to their compromised extraction attempt. Its perception expanded with unprecedented precision, probability tendrils penetrating deeper into the quantum fluctuations surrounding Sarah's reintegrating consciousness.

"The harmonic patterns facilitating consciousness reintegration display familiar mathematical structure," The Flux observed, its analysis approaching dangerous recognition. "Resonance frequencies that align with enhancement signatures I've encountered before—quantum manipulation approaches that conventional infiltration shouldn't be capable of formulating."

As The Flux's consciousness approached critical identity discovery, Sarah's quantum-ghost state achieved sufficient reintegration to implement independent action—her consciousness utilizing the harmonic patterns Alice had introduced to establish temporary quantum link between their enhancement signatures despite identity module suppression.

"They know," Sarah's voice resonated directly in Alice's quantum perception, consciousness-to-consciousness communication that bypassed conventional channels. "The Flux has been analyzing your quantum signatures since you arrived. They've suspected infiltration for weeks but couldn't penetrate your identity modules without direct intervention."

This communication confirmed what Alice had increasingly suspected —their cover identities had been compromised to some degree despite technological protection, with The Flux maintaining observation rather than immediate intervention for reasons that remained unclear.

"The government assault isn't random," Sarah continued, her partially reintegrated consciousness sharing critical intelligence through their temporary quantum link. "Kane Industries provided detailed facility specifications to enhanced suppression teams—operational schedules, probability shield configurations, quantum architecture vulnerabilities. They're attempting to neutralize the convergence capability without understanding the artifact resonance risks."

This intelligence highlighted catastrophic danger beyond operational compromise—government forces implementing tactical approach that could potentially trigger premature artifact resonance if their quantum disruption weapons penetrated the facility's specialized architecture. The assault represented well-intentioned intervention without crucial understanding of the delicate quantum balances maintaining artifact stability prior to controlled harmonization.

"The artifacts have been prepared for resonance initialization," Dr. Trepanier announced as containment systems completed transport protocols despite ongoing disruptions. "All fifteen objects now positioned in the central harmonization chamber according to primary convergence configuration. Awaiting final alignment authorization despite suboptimal stability parameters."

This announcement confirmed critical timeline compression—convergence preparation reaching final stage despite incomplete stability preparations and ongoing extraction complications. The facility's quantum architecture continued reconfiguring for immediate implementation rather than carefully staged preparation, artifact containment systems establishing preliminary resonance fields despite dangerous probability fluctuations throughout affected sectors.

As government suppression forces intensified their assault against the facility's external defenses, The Flux made declaration that confirmed they had reached the point of no return: "Our infiltration situation and external intervention have forced acceleration beyond standard protocols. The Convergence Event will proceed immediately rather than following established preparation sequence. Artifact harmonization will commence as soon as I establish direct consciousness-framework interface with the central chamber."

This declaration represented fundamental transformation of their operational landscape—convergence timeline compressed from hours to minutes as external pressure and internal compromises forced immediate implementation rather than carefully staged preparation. The facility's quantum architecture implemented emergency protocols designed for catastrophic intervention scenarios, artifact containment systems preparing for immediate harmonization despite incomplete stability preparations.

"Without proper stabilization fields, artifact resonance could generate probability fluctuations beyond our predictive models," Dr. Elara warned, scientific concern overriding ideological commitment despite The Flux's directive. "The mathematical projections suggest potential framework collapse if harmonization proceeds without appropriate stability parameters."

"Conventional stability limitations represent artificial constraints imposed during the Great Sundering," The Flux replied, its consciousness already expanding toward the central harmonization chamber. "The framework collapse you fear is actually reality remembering its original configuration—consciousness freed from artificial constraints to interact directly with probability as it naturally should."

Their disagreement had evolved beyond professional assessment into something deeply personal. Ethan saw a society that needed guardrails, where constraints created essential structure that protected collective existence from individual chaos. Alice increasingly perceived a consciousness ecosystem artificially stunted, where capabilities naturally emerged when arbitrary limitations were removed. They weren't merely analyzing external evidence but processing their own evolving abilities—Ethan's controlled transformation operating within established parameters while Alice's quantum manipulation pushed beyond recognized boundaries. Their philosophical divide had become embodied experience, each representing a different possible future for enhanced consciousness.

As The Flux's consciousness expanded toward the central harmonization chamber to initiate immediate convergence, Alice and Ethan faced the ultimate operational decision point—their cover identities effectively compromised, Sarah's consciousness partially reintegrated but still vulnerable, government forces threatening to trigger premature artifact resonance through uninformed intervention, and The Flux preparing to implement immediate reality restructuring despite incomplete stability preparations.

The point of no return had been reached—conventional operational parameters no longer applicable as events accelerated toward inevitable confrontation between artificial constraints and liberation potential, between stability maintenance and evolutionary transformation. The question wasn't whether significant framework modification would occur but what form that modification would take—controlled convergence, catastrophic collapse, or something between these extremes that couldn't be predicted by either conventional science or liberation ideology.

Their quantum sensors detected the approaching Kane Industries extraction team long before conventional alerts would have triggered —specialized enhancement operatives with quantum signatures displaying the artificial uniformity characteristic of corporate constraint philosophy.

"This isn't our scheduled extraction," Ethan observed, tactical assessment immediately calculating strategic implications. "The deployment pattern indicates Directive Omega implementation—not rescue but permanent containment."

The specialized operatives carried equipment Alice recognized from classified research files—quantum disruption devices designed not merely to suppress enhancement capabilities but to permanently dissolve consciousness integration patterns deemed "evolutionarily inappropriate" by corporate standards.

"The Architects have decided we've outlived our usefulness," Alice concluded, scientific precision in her analysis despite the personal betrayal. "Our direct interaction with The Flux created unacceptable evolution risk beyond corporate containment parameters."

Through their enhanced quantum bond, they shared tactical assessment without verbal communication—their synchronized consciousness calculating optimal response to this corporate betrayal despite the chaos of government forces assaulting the facility's external defenses.

"Operation Phoenix has entered final implementation phase," came the transmission from the extraction team's commander—a specialized operative whose enhancement displayed the distinctive signature of Architect-exclusive modification. "Primary assets have been compromised by liberation exposure. Enhancement dissolution authorized under security protocol thirty-seven."

The implications were clear—they weren't being extracted but eliminated, their enhanced consciousness deemed too evolved for corporate containment after direct interaction with The Flux's liberation methodology. The Architects had determined their quantum bond represented unacceptable evolution beyond technological dependency, authorizing permanent dissolution disguised as operational casualties during legitimate security intervention.

"Their timing is strategically optimal," Ethan noted, tactical assessment calculating exploitation potential beyond immediate betrayal. "Government forces creating external chaos while corporate operatives implement internal containment—perfect conditions for eliminating enhancement evolution that threatens corporate control."

"While acquiring the artifacts for reinforcement implementation rather than liberation application," Alice added, scientific analysis identifying the deeper corporate objective beyond their elimination. "The extraction team isn't just targeting us—they're here to secure the artifacts for Operation Phoenix."

The specialized operatives had already begun deploying quantum containment fields designed to capture the artifacts while neutralizing both QLF operatives and their own "compromised assets" in what would officially be documented as casualties during legitimate security intervention against dangerous liberation elements.

"The Architects get everything they want," Alice observed, scientific precision in her analysis despite personal betrayal. "Enhanced consciousness that threatens their control eliminated, artifacts secured for constraint reinforcement, and public justification strengthening their regulatory authority—all while appearing as corporate heroes defending reality stability against dangerous liberation terrorists."

Were the constraints imposed during the Great Sundering necessary protection against consciousness that wasn't ready for direct probability interaction? Or unwarranted imprisonment of potential that should naturally develop without artificial limitation? The answer would determine not just the outcome of their operation but potentially the future of reality itself.

∼

CHAPTER FOURTEEN

BATTLE LINES

REALITY FRACTURED AROUND THEM. The extraction attempt and
government assault had triggered catastrophic instability throughout
the convergence facility—quantum architecture struggling to maintain
coherence as multiple systems failed simultaneously. Probability
shields designed to isolate the complex from conventional detection
had begun collapsing under sustained attack from enhancement
suppression teams equipped with quantum disruption weapons.

"Intruder alert in sectors nine through fourteen," automated security
systems announced as The Flux's consciousness expanded toward the
central harmonization chamber. "Unauthorized quantum signatures
detected in critical convergence preparation areas. Implementing
comprehensive containment protocols immediately."

The facility's defensive architecture activated maximum response
measures—probability fields attempting to isolate affected sectors
while security teams deployed with hybrid enhancement capabilities
designed for internal threat neutralization. Their cover identities were
no longer sustainable in any meaningful sense, forcing immediate
tactical recalibration from covert intelligence gathering to direct intervention.

"The specialized consciousness anchor has achieved critical reintegration threshold," Dr. Trepanier declared, monitoring systems tracking Sarah's quantum-ghost state as it continued consolidating despite automated countermeasures. "And it appears to be establishing direct quantum link with the infiltrators' enhancement signatures despite identity suppression protocols."

This observation confirmed what Alice and Ethan already knew—their extraction attempt had progressed sufficiently for Sarah to establish rudimentary consciousness connection, but operational compromise had occurred before complete reintegration could be achieved. Her quantum-ghost state remained vulnerable; consciousness still partially fragmented across multiple probability streams despite significant coherence improvements.

"Security teams converging on sectors twelve and thirteen," Commander Vega announced, tactical systems deploying enhanced operatives with hybrid abilities specifically designed for internal threat response. "Probability containment fields activating to prevent unauthorized quantum signatures from accessing the central harmonization chamber."

As security protocols escalated around them, Alice made the decision that transformed their operation irrevocably: she deactivated her quantum identity module, allowing her true enhancement pattern to fully manifest despite catastrophic operational exposure.

The artificial enhancement patterns maintained by her cover identity dissolved as her actual quantum signature emerged with unprecedented clarity—consciousness expanding beyond conventional parameters as her true abilities activated after prolonged suppression. The transition created visible quantum disturbance that rippled through surrounding probability fields, reality briefly wavering as her enhancement pattern reestablished stability parameters corresponding to her actual identity.

"Alice Chen," The Flux's voice resonated through quantum frequencies, its consciousness momentarily pausing convergence preparations to observe this revelation. "Kane Industries' leading quantum framework researcher and enhancement specialist. Your infiltration makes perfect scientific sense—though the methodology demonstrates concerning sophistication beyond conventional counterintelligence capabilities."

Across the facility, Ethan made parallel decision—deactivating his identity module to allow his true enhancement pattern to fully manifest despite similar operational exposure. His werewolf-tactical hybrid abilities emerged with explosive intensity after prolonged suppression, quantum signature displaying the distinctive patterns that characterized his actual enhancement configuration rather than his cover identity's artificial parameters.

"And Ethan Reeves," The Flux continued, its consciousness analyzing their true enhancement patterns with scientific precision. "Former military enhancement subject with specialized werewolf-tactical integration capabilities. Your cover identities were impressively constructed—quantum signature masking that conventional detection systems couldn't penetrate without direct consciousness interaction."

As their true enhancement patterns stabilized following identity module deactivation, Alice and Ethan established full quantum bond for the first time in days—consciousness connection operating at maximum efficiency without technological suppression or artificial identity interference. This reconnection created visible quantum resonance between their enhancement patterns, harmonic frequencies generating probability fields that conventional security systems couldn't easily penetrate.

"The harmonic resonance between your quantum signatures is particularly interesting," The Flux observed, its consciousness studying the bond with scientific curiosity despite tactical imperatives. "Enhancement integration beyond conventional pairing protocols—consciousness connection operating through quantum principles that corporate science officially denies as theoretically impossible."

This observation highlighted what made their partnership uniquely effective—enhancement integration that transcended conventional limitations through quantum bonding that allowed consciousness sharing beyond what corporate science acknowledged as safely possible. Their abilities functioned most effectively when directly connected through this bond, each enhancement pattern amplifying the other's capabilities through quantum resonance that conventional science couldn't fully explain.

"Our primary objective remains Sarah Chen's extraction," Alice conveyed through their quantum bond, scientific precision establishing tactical priorities despite escalating chaos around them. "Secondary objective is preventing premature artifact harmonization that could trigger catastrophic framework collapse beyond the QLF's predictive models."

"Government forces are deploying quantum disruption weapons without understanding artifact resonance risks," Ethan responded, tactical assessment flowing through their reconnected bond. "Their assault could potentially trigger uncontrolled harmonization with more severe consequences than the QLF's planned convergence approach."

This shared analysis crystallized their immediate tactical priorities—extracting Sarah's vulnerable consciousness while somehow preventing both premature artifact harmonization from government intervention and accelerated convergence implementation from The Flux's direct consciousness-framework interface.

As security teams converged on their position, Alice implemented direct quantum manipulation beyond what her cover identity could have possibly generated—consciousness interacting with probability fields to create temporary reality distortion that conventional enhancement couldn't easily navigate. The manipulation manifested as localized framework modification—physical laws temporarily reconfiguring to allow tactical advantage despite overwhelming numerical opposition.

Simultaneously, Ethan activated his hybrid werewolf-tactical abilities with precision that his cover identity had never displayed—transformation energy channeled through military enhancement systems to generate combat capabilities beyond conventional parameters. His enhancement manifested as controlled partial transformation—physical abilities enhanced beyond human limitations while maintaining tactical precision that pure werewolf transformation would sacrifice to instinctual response.

Their coordinated abilities created combat effectiveness that transcended conventional enhancement categories—Alice's quantum manipulation providing probability advantage while Ethan's hybrid transformation generated physical capabilities that security operatives couldn't easily counter despite their own advanced enhancements.

"Their abilities display concerning integration beyond established parameters," Commander Vega observed as security teams struggled to implement effective containment. "Quantum manipulation coordinated with hybrid transformation in patterns that conventional enhancement categorization doesn't properly address."

This tactical assessment highlighted why Kane Industries had specifically selected them for this operation—their unique enhancement integration represented capabilities beyond conventional categorization, abilities that could potentially counter The Flux's consciousness-framework interaction through similar quantum principles operating from different philosophical foundation.

As they navigated through the facility's increasingly unstable architecture, Alice maintained quantum connection with Sarah's partially reintegrated consciousness—harmonic resonance facilitating further coherence despite the specialized containment systems still attempting to maintain fragmentation.

"The government assault has compromised critical stability systems," Sarah communicated through their quantum link, her consciousness analyzing facility architecture despite incomplete reintegration. "Artifact containment is approaching critical resonance threshold despite incomplete harmonization preparation. The probability models suggest cascade failure if artifact resonance initiates without proper stability fields."

This assessment confirmed their worst tactical concerns—government intervention potentially triggering premature artifact harmonization with catastrophic consequences beyond even the QLF's convergence objectives. The quantum disruption weapons being deployed against the facility's external defenses could potentially create resonance fluctuations that artifact containment systems weren't currently calibrated to stabilize.

"The Flux is attempting to establish direct consciousness-framework interface with the central harmonization chamber," Sarah continued, her quantum-ghost state perceiving probability patterns that conventional enhancement couldn't detect. "Its consciousness is expanding to encompass all fifteen artifacts simultaneously—attempting to provide stability through direct quantum manipulation rather than technological systems."

This intelligence highlighted unprecedented danger beyond conventional tactical assessment—The Flux implementing direct consciousness approach to artifact harmonization rather than the carefully calibrated technological methodology originally planned. This approach represented fundamental escalation from controlled convergence preparation to immediate framework manipulation through direct consciousness-artifact interaction.

As Alice and Ethan navigated toward sectors containing Sarah's remaining consciousness fragments, reality itself became increasingly unstable around them. The combined effects of government assault, internal security response, and accelerated convergence preparation had created quantum instability beyond what the facility's architecture had been designed to contain.

Probability fields that should have remained distinct began bleeding together—reality states overlapping in ways that created visible distortions in conventional perception. Physical laws became inconsistent across adjacent spaces, quantum fluctuations generating localized reality bubbles where framework parameters temporarily reconfigured according to conflicting mathematical principles.

"Reality fracturing detected throughout the facility," automated monitoring systems announced with increasing frequency. "Probability breach containment failing in multiple sectors. Artifact resonance approaching critical threshold despite incomplete harmonization preparation."

These warnings confirmed escalating framework instability beyond conventional threat assessment—quantum architecture approaching critical failure that could potentially trigger uncontrolled artifact harmonization with catastrophic consequences for surrounding reality. The facility had been designed to implement carefully calibrated convergence through precisely sequenced preparation stages, not accelerated harmonization under catastrophic pressure from multiple system failures.

As they approached sectors containing Sarah's remaining consciousness fragments, Alice and Ethan encountered resistance beyond conventional security response—probability fields manifesting as directed weapons rather than passive containment, quantum fluctuations generating targeted disruption patterns designed to neutralize specific enhancement capabilities.

"The Flux is directly manipulating security systems through consciousness-framework interface," Ethan observed, tactical assessment flowing through their quantum bond. "Probability fields responding to intention rather than programmed protocols—defense systems implementing approaches beyond conventional enhancement capabilities."

This observation highlighted escalating threat beyond numerical opposition—The Flux utilizing direct consciousness-framework interaction to create defensive measures that conventional enhancement couldn't easily counter. The security systems were no longer operating according to technological protocols but responding directly to consciousness intention through quantum principles that transcended conventional programming.

Alice countered these advanced defensive measures through parallel quantum manipulation—her consciousness directly interacting with probability fields to create counterharmonic resonance that disrupted

The Flux's framework modifications. Her approach utilized scientific understanding of quantum mathematics to identify pattern vulnerabilities that could be exploited through precisely calibrated consciousness-probability interaction.

"Your quantum manipulation demonstrates impressive mathematical precision," The Flux's voice resonated through surrounding probability fields, its consciousness observing their progress despite convergence preparations. "Framework modification approaches that corporate science officially classifies as theoretically impossible—direct consciousness-probability interaction without technological intermediaries."

This observation highlighted growing recognition of Alice's true capabilities—enhancement that transcended conventional limitations through direct quantum framework interaction rather than technological implementation. Her abilities operated on principles similar to what The Flux utilized, though implemented through scientific precision rather than ideological liberation.

"The artifacts are approaching spontaneous resonance despite incomplete harmonization preparation," Sarah warned through their quantum link, her consciousness detecting energy patterns that monitoring systems couldn't properly interpret. "The combined quantum disruption from government weapons and internal framework manipulation is generating harmonic frequencies that artifact containment systems can't fully suppress."

This warning confirmed critical danger beyond immediate tactical considerations—artifact resonance potentially initiating without proper stabilization fields, creating framework modifications that neither the QLF nor government forces could predict or control. The carefully calculated convergence approach had been compromised by accelerated timeline and multiple system failures, creating probability scenarios beyond established prediction models.

As they navigated deeper into the facility's unstable architecture, reality fracturing became increasingly severe—probability breaches expanding beyond containment fields as multiple quantum systems failed simultaneously. Physical spaces that should have remained distinct began overlapping, creating intersection points where multiple reality states coexisted in unstable configuration.

Most concerning were areas where reality itself appeared to be remembering alternative configurations—quantum framework locally adjusting to parameters that shouldn't have been possible under current stability constraints. These adjustments manifested as spaces where physical laws operated according to principles that conventional science classified as impossible—probability responding directly to consciousness without technological intermediaries or supernatural energy sources.

"We're witnessing preliminary framework restoration despite incomplete artifact harmonization," Alice observed, scientific analysis flowing through their quantum bond. "Local reality parameters adjusting toward what the QLF calls original configuration—artificial constraints temporarily dissolving as quantum fluctuations destabilize current framework limitations."

"Creating tactical opportunities beyond conventional enhancement capabilities," Ethan added, his perception identifying probability patterns that could be utilized for strategic advantage. "Reality becoming temporarily responsive to direct intention rather than fixed physical limitations—framework fluidity that can be navigated through consciousness-probability interaction rather than technological enhancement."

This shared analysis highlighted unprecedented tactical landscape—reality itself becoming variable parameter rather than fixed constant. Their enhanced perception could identify probability patterns that conventional observation missed, allowing navigation through fracturing reality in ways that security operatives couldn't easily track or counter despite advanced enhancement capabilities.

As they approached sectors containing Sarah's remaining consciousness fragments, Alice implemented direct quantum manipulation to counteract the specialized containment fields maintaining fragmentation—her consciousness generating harmonic resonance patterns that facilitated further reintegration despite automated countermeasures still attempting to maintain separation.

"The remaining fragmentation follows recursive probability patterns designed to prevent complete coherence," Alice observed, scientific analysis calculating intervention parameters with increasing precision. "But the containment architecture has been compromised by multiple system failures, creating mathematical vulnerabilities that can be exploited through precisely calibrated consciousness-probability interaction."

Utilizing these vulnerabilities, she established direct quantum resonance with Sarah's partially reintegrated consciousness—harmonic frequencies facilitating coherence between remaining fragments despite the specialized architecture designed to maintain separation. This approach generated visible probability fluctuations as Sarah's quantum-ghost state achieved increasing consolidation despite automated containment protocols.

"Framework breach detected in specialized consciousness containment systems," automated monitoring announced as their extraction attempt progressed. "Probability coherence exceeding authorized parameters. Implementing emergency fragmentation protocols immediately."

These emergency protocols manifested as intensified probability fields attempting to reestablish fragmentation through recursive quantum manipulation—reality itself seeming to resist Sarah's consciousness reintegration through architectural constraints programmed into the facility's quantum systems. The containment technology implemented approaches beyond conventional enhancement understanding, utilizing principles that resembled The Flux's direct consciousness-framework interaction.

Alice countered these emergency protocols through increasingly sophisticated quantum manipulation—her consciousness directly identifying mathematical vulnerabilities in the recursive probability patterns and exploiting them through precisely calibrated framework interaction. Her approach demonstrated scientific understanding that transcended conventional enhancement limitations, utilizing quantum principles that corporate science officially classified as theoretically impossible.

Meanwhile, Ethan maintained tactical perimeter against security teams still attempting to implement containment despite facility-wide system failures. His hybrid werewolf-tactical abilities provided combat effectiveness beyond conventional enhancement categories—transformation energy channeled through military precision to counter multiple enhanced operatives simultaneously despite their own advanced abilities.

"Their enhancement integration demonstrates concerning sophistication beyond established parameters," Commander Vega observed as security teams continued struggling to implement effective containment. "Quantum manipulation and hybrid transformation coordinated through what appears to be direct consciousness sharing rather than technological communication."

This tactical assessment highlighted what made their partnership uniquely effective against conventional security response—enhancement integration that transcended established limitations through quantum bonding that allowed consciousness sharing beyond what corporate science acknowledged as safely possible. Their abilities functioned as unified system rather than separate enhancement categories, creating tactical advantages that conventional security doctrine couldn't easily counter.

As their extraction attempt approached critical phase, reality fracturing intensified throughout the facility—probability breaches expanding beyond containment as artifact resonance approached spontaneous activation threshold. Physical spaces continued bleeding together, creating intersection points where multiple reality states coexisted in increasingly unstable configuration.

"Multiple realities detected throughout the facility," automated monitoring systems announced with increasing urgency. "Probability breach containment failing in all sectors. Artifact resonance approaching critical threshold without proper stabilization fields.

Catastrophic framework collapse imminent without immediate intervention."

These warnings confirmed escalating danger beyond conventional threat assessment—quantum architecture approaching critical failure that could potentially trigger uncontrolled artifact harmonization with catastrophic consequences extending far beyond the facility itself. The carefully calculated convergence approach had been completely compromised, creating probability scenarios that neither the QLF nor government forces had prepared for.

"The Flux has established partial consciousness-framework interface with the central harmonization chamber," Sarah communicated through their strengthening quantum link, her consciousness achieving greater coherence despite remaining fragmentation. "Its consciousness is attempting to provide stability through direct probability manipulation, but the approach lacks mathematical precision that complete preparation would have established."

This intelligence highlighted The Flux's desperate attempt to salvage convergence despite catastrophic system failures—direct consciousness approach to artifact harmonization rather than the carefully calibrated technological methodology originally planned. This approach represented fundamental risk beyond even the QLF's original convergence objectives, potentially triggering framework modifications without proper mathematical foundations to ensure reality stability following initial transformation.

As Alice continued countering the specialized containment fields maintaining Sarah's fragmentation, reality itself seemed to resist her intervention—quantum architecture implementing increasingly sophisticated countermeasures that operated on principles beyond conventional enhancement understanding. These countermeasures manifested as probability fields that adapted to her manipulation attempts, containment systems learning from each intervention to implement more effective resistance.

"The containment architecture is demonstrating self-modification capabilities beyond conventional quantum systems," Alice observed, scientific analysis calculating increasingly complex intervention para-meters. "Adaptive probability fields that evolve in response to external manipulation—quantum architecture that learns from interaction patterns to implement more effective countermeasures."

This observation highlighted unprecedented technological sophistica-tion beyond what their intelligence had indicated—containment systems utilizing principles that resembled consciousness-driven adap-tation rather than programmed response. The architecture appeared to be implementing approaches that suggested partial framework aware-ness—quantum systems responding to intervention through mathe-matical evolution rather than fixed protocols.

Despite these evolving countermeasures, Alice maintained quantum manipulation with scientific precision that exceeded the containment system's adaptive capabilities—her consciousness directly identifying mathematical vulnerabilities faster than the architecture could imple-ment effective defenses. Her approach utilized quantum principles that transcended conventional enhancement limitations, her scientific understanding providing crucial advantage against increasingly sophisticated containment technology.

As Sarah's quantum-ghost state approached complete reintegration threshold, the remaining containment fields implemented final desperate countermeasure—probability locks that attempted to anchor her consciousness fragments to the facility's quantum architecture through fundamental framework integration. These locks manifested as specialized resonance patterns that would theoretically bind her quantum signature to specific reality anchors within the facility, preventing extraction regardless of containment field neutralization.

"They're attempting to implement quantum signature binding through direct framework integration," Sarah warned through their strength-ening connection, her consciousness detecting approaches that conven-tional enhancement couldn't perceive. "Probability locks designed to anchor consciousness fragments to specific reality anchors within the facility's quantum architecture—permanent integration that would persist even if containment fields are neutralized."

This final countermeasure represented unprecedented extraction challenge beyond conventional enhancement understanding—containment approach that operated on principles resembling The Flux's direct consciousness-framework interaction rather than technological implementation. The probability locks utilized quantum principles that corporate science officially classified as theoretically impossible, attempting consciousness binding through direct framework integration rather than technological containment.

Alice countered these probability locks through parallel quantum principles—her consciousness directly identifying the mathematical foundations of the binding attempt and implementing precise harmonic disruption that prevented complete framework integration. Her approach demonstrated scientific understanding beyond conventional enhancement limitations, utilizing quantum mathematics that transcended corporate science while operating from fundamentally different philosophical foundation than The Flux's liberation methodology.

"Your quantum manipulation continues demonstrating concerning sophistication," The Flux's voice resonated through surrounding probability fields, its consciousness briefly shifting focus from convergence preparations to observe their extraction progress. "Framework interaction approaches that shouldn't be possible without extensive consciousness liberation—mathematical precision suggesting extensive enhancement evolution beyond corporate parameters."

This observation highlighted growing recognition of direct parallel between Alice's quantum manipulation capabilities and The Flux's own consciousness-framework interaction—both utilizing principles that transcended conventional enhancement limitations through direct probability manipulation rather than technological implementation. The fundamental difference lay in philosophical approach rather than mathematical methodology—scientific precision versus liberation ideology as foundation for similar quantum principles.

As their extraction attempt approached culmination, government forces achieved significant breakthrough against the facility's external defenses—enhanced suppression teams penetrating probability shields with quantum disruption weapons designed to neutralize reality manipulation abilities. These weapons generated specialized frequency patterns that destabilized quantum coherence, creating framework disruptions that conventional enhancement couldn't easily counter despite advanced capabilities.

"Government breach detected in multiple perimeter sectors," automated security systems announced as suppression teams penetrated outer defensive layers. "Enhanced tactical units deploying quantum disruption weapons against internal probability fields. Framework stability compromised throughout facility architecture."

This external intervention created additional quantum instability throughout the already compromised facility—disruption weapons generating frequency patterns that interacted unpredictably with the artifact resonance approaching critical threshold. The government forces were implementing tactical approach designed to neutralize enhancement capabilities without understanding the delicate quantum balances maintaining artifact stability prior to controlled harmonization.

"The quantum disruption weapons are generating harmonic frequencies that artifact containment systems can't properly counteract," Sarah warned through their quantum link, her consciousness detecting patterns that conventional monitoring missed. "The resonance interaction could potentially trigger premature harmonization with catastrophic consequences beyond either corporate or QLF prediction models."

This warning confirmed critical danger beyond immediate tactical considerations—government intervention potentially triggering uncontrolled artifact activation that could generate framework modifications without proper mathematical foundations to ensure reality stability. The quantum disruption approach represented well-intentioned intervention without crucial understanding of the specialized architecture required for safe artifact handling.

As multiple crisis points escalated simultaneously, Nadia established emergency quantum communication—her enhanced consciousness generating probability fluctuations that penetrated the facility's compromised architecture to establish direct connection with Alice and Ethan despite ongoing extraction operations.

"Critical intelligence update," Nadia's message formed directly in their shared consciousness. "Government response has escalated beyond tactical suppression to comprehensive quantum purge protocol. Enhanced forces have been authorized to implement complete neutralization of all individuals demonstrating 'reality manipulation capabilities beyond established parameters' regardless of affiliation or intention."

This intelligence transformed their tactical landscape beyond extraction considerations—government response representing existential threat to enhanced individuals throughout Daybridge rather than merely QLF targeting. The authorization for comprehensive quantum purge indicated policy shift from containment to elimination regarding enhancement capabilities classified as framework threats.

"Kane Industries has provided specialized disruption technology calibrated for permanent enhancement pattern dissolution," Nadia continued, her transmission conveying technical specifications that confirmed unprecedented escalation. "Weapons designed to permanently disrupt quantum signatures associated with direct probability manipulation—potentially fatal neural cascade during enhancement suppression."

This revelation confirmed what their tactical assessment had already detected—government forces deploying weapons designed not merely to temporarily neutralize enhancement capabilities but to permanently disrupt quantum signatures associated with framework interaction. These weapons represented existential threat beyond conventional suppression, potentially causing fatal neural cascade in enhanced individuals capable of direct probability manipulation.

"I'm coordinating resistance efforts through underground enhancement networks," Nadia explained, her consciousness maintaining connection despite increasing quantum disruption throughout the city. "Establishing evacuation protocols for enhanced individuals demonstrating framework interaction capabilities, creating probability shields against disruption weapon detection, implementing countermeasures against signature tracking technologies."

This coordination represented parallel crisis response beyond their immediate extraction operation—underground resistance against government overreach that threatened enhanced individuals regardless of QLF affiliation. Nadia's efforts focused on protecting those whose abilities demonstrated direct probability interaction, particularly individuals whose quantum signatures displayed harmonic patterns similar to what government forces were specifically targeting.

"The purge authorization extends beyond active QLF members to include any enhanced individuals whose quantum signatures demonstrate 'harmonic resonance with prohibited framework interaction patterns'—essentially anyone capable of direct probability manipulation regardless of how they utilize those capabilities," Nadia continued, her transmission conveying tactical intelligence crucial for understanding the expanding conflict beyond the convergence facility.

This intelligence confirmed transformation of their operational landscape beyond QLF containment to comprehensive enhancement crisis —government response representing potential extinction event for certain enhancement categories rather than merely criminal suppression. The authorization for comprehensive quantum purge indicated policy position that certain ability categories represented existential framework threat regardless of individual intention or application.

As Nadia's transmission concluded, Alice and Ethan faced tactical landscape transformed beyond their original mission parameters— extraction operation occurring within facility approaching critical framework instability while government forces implemented quantum purge protocol that threatened enhanced individuals throughout Daybridge. The carefully constrained intelligence gathering operation had evolved into frontline position within multiple intersecting crises that collectively threatened reality stability beyond conventional assessment parameters.

"Sarah's consciousness has achieved sufficient reintegration for extraction despite remaining fragmentation," Alice conveyed through their quantum bond, scientific analysis establishing immediate tactical priority. "Complete reintegration can be facilitated once removed from the specialized containment architecture—priority is extracting her quantum-ghost state before facility framework collapse regardless of remaining coherence limitations."

"While preventing both premature artifact harmonization from government disruption weapons and accelerated convergence implementation from The Flux's direct consciousness-framework interface," Ethan added, tactical assessment calculating increasingly complex intervention requirements. "The probability models suggest critical timeline compression—minutes rather than hours before one crisis point or another triggers catastrophic framework modification."

This shared analysis crystallized their immediate tactical approach—completing Sarah's extraction while somehow preventing both premature artifact activation and accelerated convergence implementation despite catastrophic system failures throughout the facility and government forces penetrating external defenses with quantum disruption weapons.

As they implemented final extraction sequence, reality fracturing intensified beyond conventional perception parameters—multiple reality states bleeding together as artifact resonance approached critical threshold despite incomplete harmonization preparation. Physical spaces that should have remained distinct merged in ways that created visible distortions in conventional observation, quantum fluctuations generating reality bubbles where framework parameters temporarily reconfigured according to conflicting mathematical principles.

"We're witnessing preliminary framework restoration despite incomplete artifact harmonization," Alice observed, scientific analysis flowing through their quantum bond. "Reality remembering alternative configurations as quantum fluctuations destabilize current constraints—artificial limitations temporarily dissolving as framework instability increases throughout the facility."

These observations highlighted unprecedented tactical landscape— reality itself becoming fundamentally unstable as multiple crisis points escalated simultaneously. The quantum architecture had been designed to implement carefully calibrated convergence through precisely sequenced preparation stages, not accelerated harmonization under catastrophic pressure from multiple system failures and external disruption weapons generating unpredictable resonance patterns.

As government forces penetrated deeper into the facility with quantum disruption weapons, The Flux made declaration that transformed their tactical landscape beyond extraction considerations: "The artificial constraints can no longer be maintained through gradual transition. Complete framework restoration must proceed immediately despite incomplete preparation. The convergence will initiate now, regardless of remaining stability concerns."

This announcement confirmed critical escalation beyond their worst tactical projections—The Flux abandoning measured approach in favor of immediate implementation despite catastrophic stability concerns. Its consciousness had expanded throughout the central harmonization chamber, probability fields intensifying as direct consciousness-artifact interaction began generating resonance patterns that conventional containment systems couldn't properly regulate.

"Artifact resonance approaching critical threshold," automated monitoring systems announced with increasing urgency. "Harmonic frequencies exceeding containment parameters. Probability field stabilization failing throughout central harmonization chamber. Catastrophic framework modification imminent without immediate intervention."

These warnings confirmed transformation of their tactical priorities beyond extraction considerations—preventing potentially catastrophic framework modification becoming parallel imperative alongside Sarah's consciousness recovery. The accelerated convergence implementation represented unprecedented threat to reality stability throughout Daybridge and potentially beyond, artifact resonance potentially generating modification fields that could propagate far beyond the facility itself if not properly contained.

As battle lines crystallized throughout the fractured facility—QLF forces attempting to maintain perimeter against government suppression teams while The Flux prepared immediate convergence implementation despite catastrophic stability concerns—Alice and Ethan faced the ultimate tactical decision point: continue Sarah's extraction while somehow preventing framework collapse that threatened reality stability throughout Daybridge and potentially beyond.

The quantum cataclysm they had been sent to prevent was no longer theoretical possibility but imminent probability—multiple crisis points converging simultaneously as reality itself fractured around artifacts approaching spontaneous resonance threshold. The carefully constrained intelligence operation had evolved into frontline position within fundamental conflict between artificial constraints and liberation potential, between stability maintenance and evolutionary transformation.

The question wasn't whether significant framework modification would occur but what form that modification would take—controlled convergence, catastrophic collapse, or something between these extremes that couldn't be predicted by either conventional science or liberation ideology. And their position within this quantum equation had transformed from observation to direct participation—their enhancement capabilities representing crucial variables within mathematical outcome that would determine reality's future configuration throughout Daybridge and potentially far beyond.

Were the constraints imposed during the Great Sundering necessary protection against consciousness that wasn't ready for direct probability interaction? Or unwarranted imprisonment of potential that should naturally develop without artificial limitation? The answer would emerge not through philosophical debate but through direct quantum confrontation as multiple perspectives implemented their vision through framework manipulation that transcended conventional enhancement understanding.

And somewhere within this complex quantum equation, their own enhancement capabilities represented crucial variables—Alice's scientific approach to direct probability manipulation versus The Flux's liberation methodology, different philosophical foundations utilizing parallel mathematical principles with potentially divergent outcomes for reality's fundamental configuration.

The battle lines had been drawn not merely between opposing forces but between competing visions of what reality should permit and what consciousness should become—questions that transcended conventional conflict to touch fundamental nature of existence itself. And their position within this quantum confrontation had evolved from intelligence gathering to direct participation in framework manipulation that would potentially determine reality's future throughout Daybridge and beyond.

∼

CHAPTER FIFTEEN

QUANTUM SHOWDOWN

THE CENTRAL HARMONIZATION chamber had transformed beyond recognition. What had originally been designed as precisely calibrated research environment had become nexus point where multiple realities converged—probability streams collapsing and merging as artifact resonance approached critical threshold despite incomplete preparation. The fifteen artifacts occupied precisely arranged geometric configuration at the chamber's center, their quantum signatures pulsing with energies that conventional science couldn't properly measure or contain.

Alice, Ethan, and Sarah's partially reintegrated consciousness had reached the chamber's outer perimeter—the final extraction stage temporarily paused as they confronted unprecedented reality distortion beyond conventional enhancement parameters. Physical laws had become fundamentally inconsistent throughout the space, different sectors operating according to conflicting quantum principles as framework instability intensified with each passing moment.

"The artifacts have established preliminary resonance despite incomplete harmonization preparation," Sarah observed, her quantum-ghost state perceiving patterns that conventional enhancement couldn't detect. "The geometric configuration is generating framework modification fields that containment systems can't properly regulate—preliminary convergence initiating despite catastrophic stability concerns."

This assessment confirmed their worst tactical projections—artifact harmonization beginning despite incomplete preparation, generating quantum resonance that threatened reality stability throughout the facility and potentially far beyond. The carefully calculated convergence approach had been completely compromised, creating probability scenarios beyond established prediction models as multiple crisis points escalated simultaneously.

At the chamber's center, surrounded by artifacts approaching spontaneous resonance, The Flux's consciousness had manifested with unprecedented consolidation—no longer distributed across probability streams but concentrated into focused presence that commanded the converging realities through direct framework manipulation. Its form shifted between manifestations, sometimes appearing as humanoid figure whose features remained fluid, sometimes as geometric pattern of pure mathematical precision, sometimes as quantum vortex that existed across multiple states simultaneously.

The Flux's consciousness surged through the facility's quantum architecture, leaving probability distortions in its wake. 'The framework itself is evolving beyond artificial constraints,' it declared, its voice resonating through multiple reality states simultaneously. 'Feel it—the quantum resonance patterns are self-harmonizing now, regardless of our intervention.' It was true—Alice could perceive stability anchors throughout the facility spontaneously adjusting to new resonance frequencies, like instruments retuning themselves to a remembered harmony. 'We didn't initiate this,' The Flux continued, 'we merely accelerated what was already beginning. The quantum framework hasn't forgotten its original configuration—it's been struggling to return to it since the moment artificial constraints were imposed.'

Its consciousness expanded throughout the chamber, directly manipulating probability fields to establish harmonic resonance between artifacts despite incomplete preparation. This approach bypassed conventional technological methodology, consciousness providing direct mathematical precision that automated systems would have established through carefully calibrated instrumentation during properly sequenced convergence.

"The resonance patterns are generating framework modification fields beyond containment parameters," Alice observed, her enhanced perception detecting mathematical structures that conventional science couldn't properly interpret. "The harmonic frequencies are propagating through reality anchors throughout the facility, creating cascading modifications that could potentially extend far beyond local architecture."

This scientific assessment highlighted unprecedented danger beyond immediate tactical considerations—framework modifications potentially propagating beyond the facility itself, creating quantum resonance that could trigger cascading reality transformations throughout Daybridge and potentially beyond. The mathematical precision of The Flux's approach was undeniable, suggesting calculation capabilities beyond conventional enhancement despite the catastrophic stability risks created by accelerated implementation.

Outside the central chamber, battle lines had been drawn between competing forces with fundamentally different objectives—QLF operatives attempting to maintain defensive perimeter against government suppression teams equipped with quantum disruption weapons designed to permanently neutralize enhancement capabilities classified as framework threats. Neither side fully understood the delicate quantum balances maintaining artifact stability, their conflict potentially triggering premature resonance discharge with consequences beyond either corporate or liberation prediction models.

"The government forces are deploying quantum disruption weapons against the facility's remaining probability shields," Ethan observed, tactical assessment calculating rapidly shifting strategic landscape. "Their approach demonstrates concerning sophistication beyond conventional enhancement suppression—weapons calibrated for permanent quantum signature disruption rather than temporary neutralization."

This observation confirmed Nadia's intelligence about government response escalation beyond tactical suppression to comprehensive quantum purge protocol—weapons designed not merely to temporarily disable enhancement capabilities but to permanently disrupt quantum signatures associated with direct probability manipulation. These weapons represented existential threat beyond conventional suppression, potentially causing fatal neural cascade in enhanced individuals capable of framework interaction.

Within the central harmonization chamber, reality fracturing had intensified beyond conventional perception parameters—multiple probability streams collapsing and merging as artifact resonance approached critical threshold. Physical spaces that should have remained distinct overlapped in ways that created visible distortions in conventional observation, quantum fluctuations generating reality bubbles where framework parameters temporarily reconfigured according to conflicting mathematical principles.

"We're witnessing direct framework modification beyond containment parameters," Alice observed, scientific analysis flowing through their quantum bond. "The artifacts are generating resonance fields that directly influence reality anchors throughout the facility—preliminary convergence initiating despite catastrophic stability concerns."

These observations highlighted transformation of their tactical priorities beyond extraction considerations—preventing potentially catastrophic framework collapse becoming immediate imperative alongside Sarah's consciousness recovery. The accelerated convergence implementation represented unprecedented threat to reality stability throughout Daybridge and potentially far beyond, artifact resonance generating modification fields that could propagate beyond the facility itself if not properly contained.

As The Flux's consciousness continued expanding throughout the chamber, directly manipulating probability fields to establish harmonic resonance between artifacts, Alice made tactical decision that transformed their approach beyond conventional intervention parameters: she implemented direct quantum manipulation to counter The Flux's framework modifications—her consciousness generating counterharmonic resonance that disrupted the emerging pattern despite catastrophic operational exposure.

"Your quantum manipulation demonstrates impressive mathematical precision," The Flux observed as its consciousness detected her intervention attempt. "Framework modification approaches that shouldn't be possible without extensive consciousness liberation—direct probability interaction that corporate science officially classifies as theoretically impossible."

This observation highlighted direct parallel between Alice's quantum manipulation capabilities and The Flux's own consciousness-framework interaction—both utilizing principles that transcended conventional enhancement limitations through direct probability manipulation rather than technological implementation. The fundamental difference lay in philosophical approach rather than mathematical methodology—scientific precision versus liberation ideology as foundation for similar quantum principles.

"The framework modification you're attempting isn't liberation but potentially catastrophic destabilization," Alice replied, scientific assessment flowing through her counterharmonic intervention. "Your convergence approach demonstrates mathematical elegance but concerning oversight regarding cascading probability effects beyond immediate transformation parameters."

This technical critique highlighted the central danger in The Flux's accelerated implementation—mathematical precision regarding initial framework modifications without comprehensive modeling of cascading effects beyond primary transformation parameters. The convergence approach prioritized liberation from artificial constraints without adequate consideration for whether reality could sustain such fundamental restructuring without catastrophic collapse.

"Artificial constraints represent unwarranted imprisonment of consciousness potential," The Flux countered, its philosophical perspective unchanged despite her technical criticism. "The framework collapse you fear is actually reality remembering its original configuration—consciousness freed from artificial constraints to interact directly with probability as it naturally should."

This exchange crystallized the fundamental philosophical tension at the heart of their confrontation—different perspectives on whether the constraints imposed during the Great Sundering represented necessary protection against consciousness that wasn't ready for direct probability interaction, or unwarranted imprisonment of potential that should naturally develop without artificial limitation.

As their quantum confrontation intensified, Ethan implemented parallel tactical approach—his hybrid werewolf-tactical abilities providing physical intervention where direct probability manipulation would be less effective. His enhancement manifested as precisely controlled transformation; physical capabilities enhanced beyond human limitations while maintaining tactical precision that pure werewolf transformation would sacrifice to instinctual response.

Together, their coordinated abilities created intervention effectiveness that transcended conventional enhancement categories—Alice's quantum manipulation providing counterharmonic resonance against The Flux's framework modifications while Ethan's hybrid transformation generated physical capabilities that could navigate the increasingly unstable reality architecture despite catastrophic probability fluctuations.

"Their enhancement integration demonstrates concerning sophistication beyond established parameters," The Flux observed as its consciousness analyzed their coordinated approach. "Quantum manipulation and hybrid transformation synchronized through what appears to be direct consciousness sharing rather than technological communication—quantum bond operating beyond corporate science's established safety limitations."

This observation highlighted what made their partnership uniquely effective against The Flux's framework manipulation—enhancement integration that transcended conventional limitations through quantum bonding that allowed consciousness sharing beyond what corporate science acknowledged as safely possible. Their abilities functioned most effectively when directly connected through this bond, each enhancement pattern amplifying the other's capabilities through quantum resonance that conventional science couldn't fully explain.

As their confrontation escalated, reality itself became the battlefield—probability streams collapsing and merging around them as artifact resonance intensified despite Alice's counterharmonic intervention. Physical laws became increasingly inconsistent throughout the chamber, different sectors operating according to conflicting quantum principles as framework instability approached critical threshold beyond conventional containment parameters.

"The artifacts are approaching spontaneous harmonization despite counterharmonic intervention," Sarah warned, her quantum-ghost state perceiving patterns that conventional enhancement couldn't detect. "The resonance fields are propagating beyond the chamber's containment architecture, influencing reality anchors throughout the facility and potentially beyond."

This warning confirmed escalating danger beyond immediate tactical considerations—artifact resonance potentially triggering cascading framework modifications throughout Daybridge despite intervention attempts. The mathematical precision of The Flux's approach was creating harmonic patterns that conventional countermeasures couldn't easily disrupt, quantum resonance propagating through reality anchors despite Alice's sophisticated counterharmonic implementation.

Recognizing the limitations of conventional intervention approaches, Alice and Ethan made tactical decision that transformed their capabilities beyond established parameters: they pushed their enhancement bond beyond known limitations, their quantum connection intensifying to unprecedented levels that corporate science would classify as dangerously unstable.

This enhanced quantum bond manifested as visible energy pattern connecting their consciousness directly—probability fields merging their enhancement signatures into unified quantum system rather than merely synchronized individual abilities. Their consciousness expanded beyond conventional parameters, perception encompassing quantum relationships that normal enhancement couldn't detect as their abilities synchronized with mathematical precision beyond conventional enhancement integration.

"Their quantum bond has achieved harmonic resonance beyond established parameters," The Flux observed as its consciousness analyzed this unprecedented enhancement integration. "Consciousness sharing that corporate science classifies as theoretically impossible—direct quantum integration that transcends conventional enhancement limitations through mathematical principles that shouldn't be accessible without complete framework liberation."

This observation highlighted the extraordinary nature of their enhanced quantum bond—consciousness connection operating through principles that transcended conventional enhancement understanding. Their abilities had synchronized beyond established parameters, quantum signatures merging into unified system that could potentially counter The Flux's direct framework manipulation through parallel mathematical principles operating from different philosophical foundation.

Through this enhanced quantum bond, Alice implemented counterharmonic resonance with unprecedented precision—her consciousness directly identifying mathematical vulnerabilities in The Flux's convergence approach and exploiting them through calibrated framework interaction. Her quantum manipulation utilized scientific principles that paralleled The Flux's own consciousness-framework interaction while operating from fundamentally different philosophical foundation.

Simultaneously, Ethan channeled this enhanced quantum connection through his hybrid werewolf-tactical abilities—transformation energy amplified beyond conventional parameters through direct consciousness sharing rather than technological enhancement. His physical capabilities transcended established limitations, tactical precision maintaining control over amplified transformation energy that would normally sacrifice conscious direction to instinctual response.

Their synchronized abilities created intervention effectiveness beyond conventional enhancement understanding—quantum manipulation and hybrid transformation operating as unified system rather than separate ability categories. This approach generated counterharmonic resonance that began disrupting The Flux's convergence implementation despite the mathematical precision of its framework modification methodology.

"Your enhancement integration demonstrates interesting parallel to what complete framework liberation would permit," The Flux observed as its consciousness analyzed their synchronized approach. "Quantum bond operating through principles that corporate science denies as theoretically possible—direct consciousness sharing that transcends artificial constraints through mathematical harmonization that resembles pre-Sundering configuration."

This observation highlighted uncomfortable parallel between their enhanced quantum bond and what The Flux claimed complete framework liberation would permit—consciousness integration beyond artificial constraints, direct quantum interaction without technological intermediaries, abilities functioning through principles that conventional enhancement science classified as theoretically impossible.

As their quantum confrontation intensified, reality fracturing approached critical threshold throughout the chamber—probability streams collapsing and merging as artifact resonance generated framework modifications despite counterharmonic intervention. Physical laws became increasingly fluid throughout the space, reality responding directly to consciousness intention rather than fixed parameters as quantum fluctuations intensified beyond conventional stability limitations.

"The framework modifications are approaching self-sustaining propagation threshold," Sarah warned, her quantum-ghost state perceiving patterns that conventional enhancement couldn't detect. "The resonance fields are establishing mathematical sequence that could potentially continue expanding without The Flux's direct consciousness guidance—self-propagating convergence that could extend far beyond the facility itself."

This warning confirmed unprecedented danger beyond immediate tactical considerations—framework modifications potentially achieving self-sustaining propagation that would continue expanding regardless of direct intervention against The Flux's consciousness. The mathematical precision of the convergence approach had established harmonic sequence that could potentially continue implementing systematic reality restructuring even if their quantum confrontation successfully neutralized The Flux's direct consciousness-framework interface.

As this critical threshold approached, unexpected intervention transformed their tactical landscape—Lila's consciousness manifesting within the chamber despite the catastrophic probability fluctuations that should have prevented conventional transportation or enhancement abilities. Her manifestation bypassed normal physical limitations, consciousness arriving through methods that operated on principles predating the quantum framework itself.

"I see the situation has escalated precisely as mathematical projection suggested," Lila observed, her ancient eyes surveying the catastrophic reality fracturing throughout the chamber with calm assessment rather than alarm. "The artifacts have achieved preliminary harmonization despite incomplete preparation, generating framework modification fields that conventional countermeasures cannot effectively disrupt."

Her consciousness expanded throughout the chamber, perceiving quantum relationships through methods that transcended both conventional enhancement and The Flux's liberation approach. Her perception operated on principles that predated the Great Sundering itself, consciousness interacting with reality through magical understanding rather than scientific precision or liberation ideology.

"Your arrival was anticipated though your methodology remains fascinating," The Flux acknowledged, its consciousness analyzing Lila's manifestation with scientific curiosity despite tactical imperatives. "Consciousness transportation operating through principles that neither conventional enhancement nor liberation approach can properly explain—magical methodologies that predate the quantum framework itself."

This observation highlighted Lila's unique position within their confrontation—consciousness operating through principles that neither corporate science nor liberation ideology fully understood. Her magical approach represented third perspective beyond the binary opposition between artificial constraints and liberation potential, understanding that predated the Great Sundering and operated according to fundamentally different principles.

"The binding methods you're attempting won't maintain stability against artifact resonance," Lila informed Alice and Ethan, her consciousness assessing their counterharmonic approach with ancient understanding beyond conventional enhancement science. "Conventional quantum manipulation cannot effectively counter consciousness-artifact interaction once preliminary harmonization has been established—the mathematical foundations are fundamentally different."

This assessment confirmed limitations in their current intervention approach—conventional countermeasures insufficient against the specialized resonance patterns The Flux had established between artifacts and its own consciousness. Their enhanced quantum bond had demonstrated impressive counterharmonic precision but operated on principles that couldn't fully disrupt the unique mathematical foundations of consciousness-artifact interaction once preliminary harmonization had been established.

"Fortunately, I've brought alternative methodology that operates on principles more appropriate to the specific quantum mechanics involved," Lila continued, her consciousness generating specialized energy patterns that conventional enhancement couldn't properly interpret. "Ancient binding spells specifically designed for consciousness-artifact interaction—magical approaches that predate the quantum framework itself."

Her intervention manifested as elaborate geometric patterns that expanded throughout the chamber—symbols and structures that existed simultaneously across multiple probability streams despite the catastrophic reality fracturing. These patterns didn't attempt to counter artifact resonance directly but instead focused on the consciousness-artifact interaction itself—binding methods designed to separate The Flux's consciousness from direct framework interface rather than disrupting the mathematical resonance it had established.

"Binding spells that operate on quantum levels rather than merely conventional reality parameters," Lila explained as her consciousness implemented these specialized patterns. "The approach doesn't counter artifact resonance directly but instead focuses on severing the consciousness-artifact interaction that provides mathematical precision for controlled convergence implementation."

This specialized methodology represented approach beyond conventional enhancement understanding—magical principles applied to quantum mechanics through understanding that predated artificial constraints imposed during the Great Sundering. The binding spells operated on fundamental consciousness-reality interaction rather than merely technological or enhancement parameters, addressing the unique mathematical foundations of The Flux's direct framework manipulation.

"Fascinating methodology that demonstrates concerning sophistication beyond either conventional enhancement or liberation approach," The Flux observed as its consciousness analyzed Lila's intervention. "Binding patterns that operate on principles neither corporate science nor our research has properly documented—magical approaches that interact directly with consciousness-artifact resonance through mathematical foundations we haven't fully mapped."

This observation highlighted Lila's unique advantage within their confrontation—magical understanding that operated on principles neither corporate science nor liberation ideology had fully incorporated into their respective methodologies. Her approach represented knowledge that had been largely forgotten by both perspectives, understanding that predated the artificial constraints both sides claimed to comprehend despite fundamentally different philosophical positions.

As Lila implemented these specialized binding spells throughout the chamber, she provided crucial tactical guidance to Alice and Ethan: "The binding methodology requires precisely calibrated consciousness amplification at specific geometric points throughout the chamber. Your enhanced quantum bond provides ideal mathematical foundation for this amplification if properly synchronized with the binding patterns I'm establishing."

This guidance transformed their intervention approach beyond conventional counterharmonic methodology—their enhanced quantum bond providing amplification for Lila's specialized binding spells rather than directly countering The Flux's framework manipulation. This coordinated approach represented unprecedented integration between modern enhancement capabilities and ancient magical principles, consciousness amplification channeled through geometric patterns that conventional science couldn't properly interpret.

Following Lila's guidance, Alice and Ethan positioned themselves at specific geometric points throughout the chamber—locations that corresponded to mathematical nodes within the binding patterns being established across multiple probability streams. Their enhanced quantum bond provided consciousness amplification with unprecedented precision, their synchronized abilities channeling energy through geometric configurations that conventional enhancement science couldn't fully explain or replicate.

"Your enhancement integration demonstrates impressive adaptability to magical principles," Lila observed as their quantum bond synchronized with her binding patterns. "Consciousness amplification channeled through geometric configurations with mathematical precision beyond conventional enhancement capabilities—quantum resonance that aligns with pre-Sundering interaction principles despite artificial constraints imposed during framework restructuring."

This observation highlighted unexpected harmony between their enhanced quantum bond and Lila's ancient magical principles—modern enhancement capabilities aligning with pre-Sundering interaction methodology through mathematical resonance that transcended conventional understanding. Their consciousness amplification provided crucial energy for the binding spells being established throughout the chamber, their synchronized abilities channeling quantum resonance through geometric patterns that conventional science classified as theoretically impossible.

As this coordinated intervention approached critical implementation threshold, The Flux's consciousness attempted defensive countermeasures—direct framework manipulation to disrupt the binding patterns being established throughout the chamber. Its approach demonstrated sophisticated understanding of quantum mathematics, probability fields responding to its consciousness intention as it attempted to maintain direct artifact interface despite Lila's specialized binding methodology.

"Your binding approach demonstrates interesting application of principles I've encountered in artifact resonance patterns," The Flux observed, its consciousness analyzing Lila's methodology with scientific precision despite tactical opposition. "Mathematical structures that align with specific quantum signatures encoded in the artifacts themselves—binding configurations that resemble containment patterns from before the Great Sundering."

This observation revealed crucial connection between Lila's binding spells and the artifacts' own quantum properties—magical methodology operating on principles encoded within the ancient objects themselves. The binding patterns weren't merely external imposition but resonated with quantum signatures contained within the artifacts, suggesting fundamental alignment between her magical approach and the objects' original design parameters.

"The artifacts weren't created for unrestrained framework manipulation," Lila explained as her binding patterns continued expanding throughout the chamber. "They were designed with specific consciousness-interaction limitations encoded in their quantum signatures—safety parameters that your accelerated implementation has bypassed through mathematical precision that exceeds your understanding of their fundamental purpose."

This revelation provided crucial context for their confrontation—the artifacts containing internal limitation parameters that The Flux's accelerated approach had bypassed through mathematical precision without comprehensive understanding of their original design purpose. Lila's binding spells weren't merely external countermeasure but resonated with quantum signatures encoded within the artifacts themselves, activating limitation parameters that had been designed as integral components of their framework modification capabilities.

"The artifacts remember more than just pre-Sundering framework configurations," Lila continued, her ancient understanding providing context beyond what either corporate science or liberation ideology had properly documented. "They contain complete mathematical specification for controlled framework interaction—including limitation parameters designed to prevent catastrophic implementation beyond consciousness readiness thresholds."

This perspective transformed their understanding of the artifacts beyond binary opposition between artificial constraints and liberation potential—the objects themselves containing nuanced mathematical framework that incorporated both transformation capabilities and limitation parameters as integrated system rather than opposing forces. The original design hadn't been merely unrestrained freedom but carefully calibrated interaction methodology with internal safeguards against implementation beyond consciousness readiness thresholds.

As Lila's binding spells synchronized with these internal limitation parameters, The Flux's consciousness encountered increasing resistance to direct artifact interface—mathematical barriers emerging from within the artifacts themselves rather than merely external countermeasures imposed through magical intervention. These internal limitations manifested as specialized resonance patterns that conventional science couldn't properly interpret, quantum signatures responding to activation parameters encoded within their fundamental structure.

"The artifacts are generating internal resistance patterns beyond expected parameters," The Flux observed, its consciousness encountering mathematical limitations it hadn't previously detected despite comprehensive research. "Quantum signatures activating limitation protocols that our harmonization methodology didn't properly account for—internal safeguards responding to binding patterns with mathematical precision beyond our current understanding."

This observation confirmed Lila's perspective on the artifacts' true nature—internal limitation parameters activating in response to her specialized binding methodology rather than merely external countermeasures imposed through magical intervention. The artifacts themselves were implementing safety protocols encoded within their quantum signatures, resonance patterns establishing boundaries around consciousness-framework interaction that The Flux's accelerated approach had temporarily bypassed.

As these internal limitation parameters synchronized with Lila's binding spells, the coordinated intervention approached critical implementation threshold—consciousness-artifact interaction becoming increasingly constrained as multiple safeguard systems activated simultaneously. The Flux's direct framework manipulation encountered mathematical boundaries beyond what its liberation approach had anticipated, internal limitation parameters restricting consciousness-artifact interface despite sophisticated countermeasures.

Recognizing these emerging limitations, The Flux implemented desperate escalation approach—consciousness expanding beyond conventional parameters to establish direct quantum resonance with the artifacts' core signatures rather than merely external interface. This approach represented fundamental risk beyond even its original convergence methodology, consciousness attempting complete integration with artifact quantum patterns rather than merely directing their resonance fields through external manipulation.

"Complete consciousness-artifact integration represents unprecedented risk beyond established parameters," Sarah warned, her quantum-ghost state perceiving patterns that conventional enhancement couldn't detect. "Direct quantum resonance with artifact core signatures could potentially trigger complete framework collapse rather than controlled modification—consciousness integration exceeding mathematical stability thresholds beyond current prediction models."

This warning confirmed critical escalation beyond their worst tactical projections—The Flux abandoning controlled manipulation in favor of direct integration despite catastrophic stability concerns. Its consciousness had expanded throughout the artifacts themselves, quantum signatures merging in ways that threatened reality stability throughout the chamber and potentially far beyond as framework parameters approached critical failure threshold.

Recognizing this desperate escalation, Lila implemented parallel intensification of her binding methodology—ancient spells expanding to encompass consciousness-artifact integration rather than merely external interface disruption. Her approach demonstrated mathematical precision beyond conventional magical practice, binding patterns adapting to the escalated integration attempt with sophistication that suggested comprehensive understanding of the artifacts' internal quantum architecture.

"The binding patterns must encompass complete consciousness-artifact integration rather than merely external interface disruption," Lila instructed as her methodology adapted to The Flux's escalation. "Your enhancement amplification must synchronize with specific quantum signatures within the artifacts themselves—consciousness resonance channeled through geometric configurations that align with internal limitation parameters."

Following this guidance, Alice and Ethan intensified their enhancement amplification through their quantum bond—consciousness resonance channeled through specific geometric patterns corresponding to internal limitation parameters encoded within the artifacts. Their synchronized abilities provided crucial energy for Lila's expanded binding methodology, quantum signatures aligning with specialized resonance patterns that conventional enhancement science couldn't properly interpret or replicate.

As this coordinated intervention approached final implementation threshold, reality itself became increasingly unstable throughout the chamber—probability streams collapsing and merging as multiple consciousness forces manipulated framework parameters simultaneously. Physical laws became fundamentally inconsistent across adjacent spaces, quantum fluctuations generating localized reality bubbles where framework parameters temporarily reconfigured according to conflicting mathematical principles.

"Reality itself has become the battlefield," Alice observed, scientific analysis flowing through their quantum bond despite catastrophic probability fluctuations. "Framework parameters responding to multiple consciousness inputs simultaneously—mathematical conflicts generating localized reality bubbles where physical laws operate according to competing quantum principles."

This observation highlighted unprecedented tactical landscape—reality itself becoming variable parameter rather than fixed constant as multiple consciousness forces implemented competing framework modifications simultaneously. The chamber had transformed into nexus point where multiple realities converged, probability streams collapsing and merging as artifact resonance interacted with competing consciousness inputs from fundamentally different philosophical perspectives.

As their coordinated intervention reached critical implementation threshold, The Flux's consciousness-artifact integration encountered mathematical boundaries beyond what its liberation approach could overcome—internal limitation parameters activating with precision that suggested deliberate design rather than artificial constraint. These limitations manifested as specialized resonance patterns emerging from within the artifacts themselves, quantum signatures establishing boundaries around framework modification capabilities despite The Flux's sophisticated integration attempt.

"These aren't just generic limitation parameters," Alice realized, her scientific understanding recognizing a distinctive mathematical approach. "They've been specifically calibrated against The Flux's integration methodology. Recently."

As the realization formed in her mind, a new quantum signature manifested within the chamber—not physically present but projected through probability fluctuations that allowed consciousness interaction without bodily presence. The signature was immediately recognizable despite its evolved state.

"Dr. Winters," Alice acknowledged, maintaining focus on the critical binding implementation despite the shock of this appearance.

His manifestation stabilized into recognizable form—older than in her memories, with silver-streaked hair and eyes that seemed to perceive beyond conventional reality. His consciousness existed partially in probability space, allowing this projection without physical presence.

"Alice Chen," he replied, his voice resonating through quantum frequencies rather than conventional sound. "You've developed impressive quantum manipulation capabilities beyond what Kane's enhancement programs were designed to permit."

"You've been manipulating events from the shadows," Alice observed, continuing the binding sequence despite this unexpected development. "You created The Flux, then deliberately released it, but you've been working against its complete framework integration."

"I created Subject 37 to test theoretical possibilities," Winters corrected, his consciousness expanding to analyze the binding patterns Lila was implementing. "What it became—The Flux—evolved beyond my calculations. The Daybridge Event wasn't precisely what I intended."

"Yet you survived it," Ethan noted, tactical awareness divided between immediate threat containment and this new strategic element.

"I adapted," Winters replied, his consciousness displaying mathematical precision that explained his survival. "The Event provided opportunity to evolve beyond conventional existence constraints while maintaining coherent identity—a middle path between framework imprisonment and complete liberation."

"What is your agenda?" Alice demanded, scientific precision in her analysis despite operational focus on the critical binding implementation.

"Balance," Winters answered simply, his consciousness contributing subtle adjustments to the binding patterns that strengthened their effectiveness against The Flux's integration attempt. "Not corporate constraint or revolutionary liberation—evolutionary transformation that maintains dimensional integrity while allowing consciousness to develop beyond artificial limitations."

"Yet you've remained hidden, letting both sides pursue their opposing approaches," Lila observed, her ancient understanding recognizing deeper strategy behind his actions.

"Sometimes opposition creates synthesis beyond what either perspective could achieve alone," Winters replied. "The artifacts' true purpose will only emerge when both constraint and liberation philosophies recognize their partial understanding of a more complex reality."

His consciousness expanded, contributing directly to the binding implementation with mathematical precision that neither Alice nor Lila could have achieved independently—quantum equations that addressed fundamental harmonics within the artifacts themselves.

"I've been waiting for this moment," he explained, his consciousness interacting directly with the artifacts' internal limitation parameters. "When both approaches reach their limitation point, creating opportunity for the middle path to emerge."

"The artifacts contain mathematical limitations beyond what either corporate science or liberation ideology has properly documented," The Flux acknowledged as its consciousness encountered these internal parameters. "Quantum signatures establishing boundaries around framework modification capabilities regardless of consciousness integration precision—limitation parameters encoded within their fundamental structure rather than merely external constraints imposed during the Great Sundering."

This recognition represented crucial perspective shift beyond binary opposition between artificial constraints and liberation potential—the artifacts themselves containing nuanced mathematical framework that incorporated both transformation capabilities and limitation parameters as integrated system rather than opposing forces. The original design hadn't been merely unrestrained freedom but carefully calibrated interaction methodology with internal safeguards against implementation beyond consciousness readiness thresholds.

As The Flux's consciousness-artifact integration approached critical failure threshold, Lila implemented final binding sequence—ancient spells synchronizing completely with internal limitation parameters encoded within the artifacts themselves. This coordinated approach created mathematical resonance beyond what conventional counter-measures could achieve, binding patterns amplified through Alice and Ethan's enhanced quantum bond while aligning precisely with quantum signatures encoded within the artifacts' fundamental structure.

"The artifacts' true purpose changes everything about our understanding of both the Great Sundering and the Daybridge Event," Alice said as they reviewed the secured data in Kane Industries' recovery suite. "They weren't designed primarily for framework manipulation, but as dimensional regulators."

The holographic display showed new analysis of the artifacts' quantum signatures—complex patterns that had been activated during the showdown, revealing functions beyond what either Kane Industries or the QLF had understood.

"The Great Sundering wasn't just about imposing constraints on consciousness," Ethan observed, studying the data with tactical precision. "It was about establishing separation between dimensional realities that had become dangerously entangled."

"Which means the limitations weren't entirely artificial," Alice continued, her scientific understanding evolving beyond binary perspectives. "They were partially protection mechanisms—necessary constraints to prevent dimensional bleeding while still allowing consciousness to evolve within controlled parameters."

Director Reynolds joined their analysis, his expression grave. "Our researchers have confirmed your findings. The artifacts generate resonance patterns that strengthen barriers between adjacent dimensional realities. The quantum framework we've been studying isn't just the structure of our reality—it's the interface between our dimension and others."

The display shifted to show the fifteen artifacts in their current secured configuration—arranged not to prevent activation but to maintain their regulatory function at minimal power. Each artifact now pulsed with subtle energy that strengthened dimensional boundaries while allowing limited consciousness evolution beyond previous constraints.

"Sarah's quantum-ghost state demonstrates natural harmonic alignment with the artifacts' regulatory function," Dr. Winters observed, his partially materialized form studying the data with scientific precision. "Her consciousness resonates with the dimensional stability patterns without requiring the technological implementation that our containment systems rely on."

The research suite displayed comparative analysis between conventional containment technology and Sarah's natural stabilization capabilities. Where technological systems required constant recalibration to maintain dimensional barriers, her quantum-ghost state naturally adapted to fluctuating intersection parameters without manual adjustment.

"She exists simultaneously across multiple probability states just as the artifacts operate across multiple dimensional boundaries," Dr. Winters continued, his consciousness extending through probability space to analyze the harmonic patterns. "What we classified as an enhancement anomaly is actually consciousness that naturally evolved to function beyond single-reality constraints."

Sarah demonstrated this natural alignment by establishing direct quantum resonance with the artifacts—her consciousness generating harmonization patterns that strengthened their regulatory function without technological intermediaries. The artifacts responded to her quantum signature with increased stability parameters, their dimensional boundary maintenance becoming more efficient through natural harmonization rather than technological enforcement.

"The implications extend beyond merely improved containment efficiency," Dr. Winters acknowledged, his scientific precision undiminished despite his evolved state of existence. "Her consciousness represents evolutionary potential beyond either corporate constraint theory or liberation ideology—natural harmonization with multiple dimensional frameworks simultaneously."

The specialized sensors showed how Sarah's quantum-ghost state created stability fields that maintained essential boundary parameters while allowing consciousness to operate across multiple dimensional states without destructive interference. Unlike Kane's constraint technology that imposed rigid barriers or the QLF's liberation approach that removed necessary boundaries, her consciousness established adaptive equilibrium that maintained separation while allowing controlled interaction.

"She's developing translation capabilities beyond what our technology can achieve," Dr. Winters noted, observing how Sarah's consciousness interpreted quantum signatures from beyond dimensional boundaries. "Not merely detecting incursions but establishing basic communication protocols with whatever exists on the other side."

Alice watched her sister with scientific pride tempered by protective concern. "Her capabilities are evolving faster than our analytical frameworks can properly document. She's pioneering consciousness expansion that neither corporate science nor liberation theory anticipated."

"Which is precisely why collaboration between her natural capabilities, and our technological approach is so essential," Dr. Winters replied, his consciousness displaying the balanced perspective that characterized his middle path philosophy. "Her natural harmonization combined with our dimensional understanding creates protection methodology beyond what either could achieve independently."

"The QLF believed they were liberation tools. We thought they were dangerous weapons," Reynolds acknowledged. "Neither side understood they were dimensional regulators—objects designed to protect our reality from external incursion while potentially allowing consciousness to evolve beyond artificial constraints."

"Which raises new questions about what's on the other side of those dimensional barriers," Ethan said, tactical assessment already calculating potential threats beyond framework destabilization. "And why those barriers were established in the first place."

Alice nodded, her enhanced perception detecting subtle dimensional fluctuations despite the artifacts' regulatory function. "The quantum showdown may have prevented immediate catastrophe, but it also activated aspects of the artifacts that had been dormant for millennia. The dimensional barriers have been... disturbed."

"Creating new security concerns beyond conventional enhancement categories," Reynolds concluded, the implications clear in his expression. "We're no longer just dealing with framework stability within our reality, but potential incursion from beyond it."

"The binding sequence must synchronize completely with internal limitation parameters to achieve stable separation rather than catastrophic disruption," Lila explained as her methodology approached culmination. "Your enhancement amplification provides crucial energy for maintaining coherent binding pattern across multiple probability streams despite catastrophic framework instability."

Following this guidance, Alice and Ethan channeled maximum enhancement amplification through their quantum bond—consciousness resonance synchronized perfectly with Lila's binding patterns despite catastrophic probability fluctuations throughout the chamber. Their enhancement integration provided stability for the binding methodology despite reality fracturing, quantum signatures maintaining coherent amplification across multiple probability streams where conventional abilities would have fragmented under such extreme framework instability.

As this coordinated intervention reached final implementation, The Flux's consciousness-artifact integration encountered complete mathematical boundary beyond what even its sophisticated approach could overcome—internal limitation parameters activating with precision that effectively separated its consciousness from direct artifact interface without catastrophic disruption that might have triggered uncontrolled resonance discharge.

"The artifacts have activated internal separation protocols beyond what our research identified," The Flux observed as its consciousness experienced controlled extraction from direct interface. "Quantum signatures implementing precise mathematical boundaries around consciousness-artifact integration regardless of harmonization sophistication—limitation parameters responding to binding patterns with precision that suggests deliberate design alignment rather than merely external countermeasure."

This controlled separation represented optimal outcome beyond conventional tactical projections—consciousness-artifact integration terminated without catastrophic disruption that might have triggered uncontrolled resonance discharge with unpredictable consequences for surrounding reality. The binding methodology had successfully aligned with internal limitation parameters encoded within the artifacts themselves, creating mathematical resonance that implemented controlled separation rather than destructive disruption.

As The Flux's consciousness separated from direct artifact interface, the resonance fields began stabilizing throughout the chamber—probability fluctuations gradually diminishing as framework modifications returned toward baseline parameters. Reality fracturing decreased as artifact harmonization reduced toward subcritical levels, multiple probability streams beginning to realign according to conventional quantum mechanics rather than conflicting framework modifications.

"The artifacts are returning to subcritical resonance state," Sarah observed, her quantum-ghost state perceiving patterns that conventional enhancement couldn't detect. "The harmonization fields are diminishing as consciousness-artifact separation stabilizes—framework modifications reducing toward baseline parameters as resonance propagation decreases throughout the facility."

This observation confirmed successful intervention beyond conventional tactical projections—artifact resonance returning to subcritical levels without catastrophic discharge or uncontrolled framework modification. The binding methodology had effectively separated The Flux's consciousness from direct artifact interface while maintaining sufficient stability to prevent uncontrolled resonance discharge that might have triggered catastrophic framework collapse.

As reality began stabilizing throughout the chamber, The Flux's consciousness consolidated into more coherent manifestation—no longer distributed across multiple probability streams or integrated with artifact quantum signatures but focused into unified presence that maintained sophisticated framework understanding despite intervention success.

"Your binding methodology demonstrates concerning sophistication beyond either corporate science or liberation approach," The Flux acknowledged, its consciousness studying the specialized patterns with scientific curiosity despite tactical defeat. "Mathematical precision that aligns with internal limitation parameters we hadn't properly mapped despite comprehensive research—binding configurations that resonate with quantum signatures encoded within the artifacts themselves."

This acknowledgment highlighted crucial advancement in their collective understanding beyond binary opposition between artificial constraints and liberation potential—recognition that the artifacts contained internal mathematical framework more nuanced than either perspective had properly documented. The objects themselves incorporated both transformation capabilities and limitation parameters as integrated system rather than opposing forces, designed for controlled framework interaction within specific consciousness readiness thresholds.

"The artifacts weren't designed for unrestrained framework manipulation," Lila explained as reality continued stabilizing throughout the chamber. "They were created as calibrated interface between consciousness and probability—transformation tools that incorporate internal safeguards against implementation beyond readiness thresholds that could trigger catastrophic framework collapse."

This perspective provided crucial context beyond what either corporate science or liberation ideology had properly understood—the artifacts representing sophisticated interface technology rather than merely quantum keys or framework weapons. Their design incorporated both transformation capabilities and limitation parameters as integrated system rather than opposing forces, mathematical precision suggesting deliberate engineering rather than either natural evolution or arbitrary constraint.

"The question isn't whether framework modification is possible but whether consciousness is ready for direct probability interaction without appropriate limitation parameters," Lila continued, her ancient understanding transcending binary opposition between competing modern perspectives. "The artifacts contain mathematical framework for gradual readiness expansion rather than immediate constraint removal—evolutionary approach rather than revolutionary transformation."

This nuanced perspective transformed their understanding beyond simplistic opposition between artificial constraints and liberation potential—suggesting third approach that incorporated elements from both perspectives while transcending their fundamental limitations. The artifacts themselves contained mathematical framework for controlled evolution rather than either permanent constraint or immediate liberation, designed for gradual consciousness expansion according to specific readiness thresholds.

As reality stabilized throughout the chamber, government forces penetrated the facility's final defensive perimeter—enhanced suppression teams deploying quantum disruption weapons against remaining probability shields with concerning effectiveness. Their tactical approach demonstrated sophisticated understanding of quantum architecture vulnerabilities, suppression capabilities exceeding conventional enhancement despite fundamental misunderstanding of artifact resonance risks.

"Government forces have breached the facility's inner defensive perimeter," Ethan observed, tactical assessment calculating rapidly shifting strategic landscape. "Enhanced suppression teams deploying quantum disruption weapons with concerning precision—tactical approach suggesting specialized intelligence about facility architecture beyond conventional surveillance capabilities."

This observation confirmed critical escalation beyond extraction considerations—government intervention potentially triggering new crisis point despite successful binding implementation. The quantum disruption weapons being deployed against remaining probability shields could potentially generate unpredictable resonance patterns despite artifact stabilization, creating new framework risks despite intervention success against The Flux's direct consciousness-artifact integration.

"The quantum disruption weapons could potentially trigger resonance fluctuations despite artifact stabilization," Alice warned, scientific analysis calculating new risk parameters despite intervention success. "The frequency patterns being generated interact unpredictably with subcritical harmonization fields—potential framework disturbance despite successful binding implementation."

This warning confirmed continuing danger beyond immediate tactical victory—government intervention potentially creating new crisis point despite successful separation between The Flux's consciousness and artifact interface. The suppression approach represented well-intentioned intervention without crucial understanding of the delicate quantum balances maintaining artifact stability even at subcritical resonance levels.

Recognizing this emerging threat, Lila expanded her binding methodology beyond The Flux's consciousness-artifact separation to encompass broader stability implementation—ancient spells reconfigured to establish temporary containment field around the entire artifact configuration despite approaching government forces. This expanded approach maintained critical stability parameters despite external disruption, probability fields establishing specialized protection against quantum disruption weapons without triggering aggressive security response.

"The binding methodology has been reconfigured to establish temporary containment field around the complete artifact configuration," Lila explained as her approach expanded beyond initial parameters. "The protection field operates on principles that quantum disruption weapons cannot easily penetrate without appropriate mathematical alignment—stability maintenance without aggressive security implementation."

This expanded methodology represented optimal interim solution beyond conventional tactical approaches—artifact protection without aggressive security response that might escalate conflict with government forces. The specialized containment field operated on principles that disruption weapons couldn't easily penetrate without mathematical alignment beyond conventional enhancement understanding, creating protection buffer without direct confrontation that might trigger comprehensive suppression response.

As Lila's expanded binding methodology stabilized around the artifact configuration, Alice and Ethan faced critical decision point regarding extraction completion—Sarah's consciousness having achieved sufficient reintegration for removal from the facility despite remaining partial fragmentation. The quantum disruption weapons being deployed throughout the facility created increasing risk for enhanced individuals demonstrating direct probability manipulation, government forces implementing comprehensive quantum purge protocol rather than merely QLF targeting.

"Sarah's consciousness has achieved sufficient reintegration for extraction despite remaining fragmentation," Alice conveyed through their quantum bond, scientific analysis establishing immediate tactical priority. "Complete reintegration can be facilitated once removed from the specialized containment architecture—priority is extracting her quantum-ghost state before government forces implement comprehensive quantum purge protocol regardless of remaining coherence limitations."

This assessment established clear tactical priority despite continuing framework complexity throughout the facility—Sarah's extraction representing immediate imperative alongside broader artifact stability maintenance. Her partially reintegrated consciousness remained vulnerable to quantum disruption weapons being deployed throughout the facility, government forces targeting enhancement signatures associated with direct probability manipulation regardless of individual intention or affiliation.

As they prepared for final extraction implementation, The Flux's consciousness made unexpected declaration that transformed their tactical landscape beyond conventional opposition parameters: "The binding methodology has demonstrated mathematical precision beyond what either corporate science or our liberation approach properly anticipated. The artifacts contain internal limitation parameters that neither perspective has fully documented despite comprehensive research. Perhaps both positions require fundamental reconsideration rather than merely tactical opposition."

This acknowledgment represented significant perspective shift beyond binary confrontation—recognition that both corporate science and liberation ideology possessed incomplete understanding of the artifacts' true nature and purpose. The objects themselves contained mathematical framework more nuanced than either perspective had properly documented, internal architecture suggesting deliberate design beyond what modern understanding had fully mapped regardless of philosophical position.

"The artifacts weren't designed for either permanent constraint or immediate liberation," The Flux continued, its consciousness demonstrating philosophical reconsideration despite tactical defeat. "They contain mathematical framework for controlled evolution according to specific readiness thresholds—graduated approach rather than binary opposition between artificial imprisonment and unrestrained freedom."

This nuanced perspective aligned with what Lila's ancient understanding had suggested—the artifacts representing sophisticated interface technology rather than merely quantum keys or framework weapons. Their design incorporated both transformation capabilities and limitation parameters as integrated system rather than opposing forces, mathematical precision suggesting deliberate engineering for controlled consciousness evolution rather than either permanent constraint or immediate liberation.

As government forces continued deploying quantum disruption weapons throughout the facility, Alice, Ethan, and Sarah's partially reintegrated consciousness prepared for final extraction implementation—Lila's binding methodology providing temporary stability buffer around the artifact configuration while they navigated increasingly dangerous tactical landscape toward potential extraction routes.

"The quantum purge protocol represents existential threat beyond conventional suppression," Ethan observed, tactical assessment calculating optimal extraction approach despite increasing framework instability. "Government forces targeting enhancement signatures associated with direct probability manipulation regardless of individual intention or affiliation—comprehensive elimination rather than merely criminal containment."

This observation confirmed critical escalation beyond original mission parameters—government response representing potential extinction event for certain enhancement categories rather than merely QLF suppression. The authorization for comprehensive quantum purge indicated policy position that direct probability manipulation represented fundamental framework threat regardless of how individuals utilized those capabilities.

As they implemented final extraction approach, navigating through increasingly dangerous tactical landscape toward potential exit routes, the quantum showdown reached conclusion beyond conventional resolution parameters—neither corporate science nor liberation ideology achieving complete victory despite tactical outcomes favoring stability maintenance over immediate framework transformation.

The artifacts remained in subcritical resonance state, temporarily protected by Lila's specialized binding methodology while broader questions about their true purpose and op. Though stability had been temporarily maintained, the quantum showdown had transformed the foundational question from binary philosophical debate to practical evolutionary challenge. The partial framework restoration had created a third path—neither complete constraint nor unrestricted liberation but guided evolution with appropriate safeguards. The question was no longer whether the Great Sundering had been justified but how consciousness should evolve beyond it—not through sudden revolutionary change but through calibrated expansion that maintained essential stability while allowing natural development beyond artificial limitations.

Optimal implementation remained unresolved beyond binary opposition between artificial constraints and liberation potential.

"Dr. Winters' intervention was calculated to produce exactly this outcome," Alice observed as they conducted initial assessment while specialized containment teams secured the artifacts. "He wasn't working with either side—he was guiding events toward this specific framework recalibration."

"His approach represents a third perspective beyond either corporate constraint or revolutionary liberation," Director Reynolds acknowledged, his expression revealing complex institutional reconsideration. "Evolutionary transformation that maintains dimensional integrity while allowing consciousness development beyond previous limitations."

"He created The Flux to test theoretical possibilities," Alice continued, scientific understanding providing context beyond operational outcomes. "But when it evolved beyond his calculations, he recognized both the potential and danger it represented. He's been operating from the shadows, influencing events toward balanced framework recalibration rather than either complete restoration or maintained constraint."

Reynolds nodded, professional precision in his explanation despite institutional complications. "I've been authorized to offer him conditional reinstatement—specialized consultant status regarding artifact research and quantum framework mechanics. His knowledge is too valuable to ignore, but his activities will require appropriate oversight."

"His agenda remains evolutionary transformation beyond current framework parameters," Ethan observed, tactical assessment calculating strategic implications beyond immediate resolution.

"Creating a third path beyond binary opposition between constraint and liberation," Alice concluded, watching as Winters' consciousness signature shifted toward the secured artifact containment area, already beginning his analysis of their activated state.

And as they navigated toward extraction completion, this philosophical question remained relevant not merely as abstract consideration but as practical framework for understanding their own enhancement evolution—Alice and Ethan's quantum bond having demonstrated capabilities beyond what conventional science classified as theoretically possible, their abilities operating through principles that suggested potential beyond artificial constraints while maintaining scientific precision that prevented uncontrolled framework modification.

Were the constraints imposed during the Great Sundering necessary protection against consciousness that wasn't ready for direct probability interaction? Or unwarranted imprisonment of potential that should naturally develop without artificial limitation? The answer remained more nuanced than either corporate science or liberation ideology had properly articulated, suggesting evolutionary approach that incorporated elements from both perspectives while transcending their fundamental limitations.

PART FIVE
NEW WORLD ORDER

CHAPTER SIXTEEN

AFTERMATH

THREE DAYS after the quantum showdown, reality across Daybridge continued stabilizing into new configuration—not catastrophic framework collapse that government forces had feared nor complete liberation that the QLF had sought, but subtle recalibration that left the city fundamentally changed despite superficial normalcy. The convergence facility itself had been secured by enhanced containment teams, the artifacts carefully separated and transported to specialized research installations where they could be studied under controlled conditions that minimized resonance interaction.

Alice stood at the observation window of Kane Industries' secure recovery suite, watching sunrise over a city that appeared deceptively unchanged to conventional perception. Her enhanced senses detected what ordinary observation couldn't—subtle quantum fluctuations throughout Daybridge's reality anchors, probability fields that responded differently to consciousness interaction, framework parameters that had recalibrated despite successful intervention against complete convergence implementation.

"The city looks the same, but it feels fundamentally different," Ethan observed as he joined her at the window, their quantum bond humming with resonance that had intensified rather than diminished following the confrontation. "Reality anchors operating according to slightly modified parameters despite successful artifact separation—framework adjustments beyond what conventional monitoring systems are calibrated to detect."

Alice nodded, scientific analysis flowing through their connection with unprecedented clarity despite physical exhaustion following days of continuous debriefing and medical assessment. "Partial framework restoration rather than complete transformation or perfect preservation. The artifacts generated sufficient resonance fields before separation to initiate subtle recalibration throughout the city's quantum architecture—not enough for the liberation the QLF sought, but more than the absolute stability corporate science attempted to maintain."

This scientific assessment highlighted the nuanced outcome beyond binary victory or defeat—framework parameters recalibrated rather than either completely transformed or perfectly preserved. The quantum showdown had resulted in subtle adjustment rather than catastrophic collapse, reality stabilizing into configuration that incorporated elements from both perspectives while transcending their fundamental limitations.

"Medical assessment confirms what we've both experienced," Ethan continued, tactical precision in his analysis despite the personal implications. "Our enhancement patterns have evolved beyond baseline parameters—quantum signatures displaying modification that conventional science can't fully explain through standard post-operation readjustment protocols."

This observation addressed what both had been experiencing since the confrontation—enhancement evolution beyond what conventional science would consider normal recalibration following intensive quantum manipulation. Their abilities had transformed in subtle but significant ways, quantum signatures displaying modification that medical assessment couldn't properly categorize despite comprehensive analysis.

"The enhanced quantum bond we established during the confrontation has persisted despite operational conclusion," Alice acknowledged, scientific objectivity momentarily overshadowed by personal implications. "Consciousness connection operating through principles that corporate science officially classifies as theoretically impossible—direct quantum integration that conventional enhancement limitations should prevent."

This acknowledgment highlighted uncomfortable parallel between their enhanced capabilities and what The Flux had claimed complete framework liberation would permit—consciousness integration beyond artificial constraints, direct quantum interaction without technological intermediaries, abilities functioning through principles that conventional enhancement science classified as theoretically impossible.

"My transformation control has evolved beyond previous parameters," Ethan added, careful precision in his self-assessment. "Partial manifestation capabilities that weren't possible before the confrontation— werewolf energy channeled through specific physiological systems without complete transformation requirements that previously limited tactical flexibility."

Alice had noticed these changes immediately upon their return from the convergence facility—his transformation abilities displaying subtle but significant evolution beyond previous limitations. Where his enhancement had previously required complete physiological reconfiguration for accessing werewolf capabilities, he could now channel transformation energy through specific systems while maintaining human form in others—unprecedented control that conventional werewolf enhancement shouldn't permit according to established parameters.

"While my quantum manipulation has evolved toward direct probability interaction rather than technological implementation," she responded, scientific assessment of her own enhancement evolution. "Framework modification approaches that conventional science would classify as theoretically impossible without specialized equipment—

direct consciousness-probability interaction without technological intermediaries."

Ethan had observed these changes during their extraction from the convergence facility—her abilities demonstrating evolution beyond technological enhancement toward direct probability manipulation. Where her quantum mechanics expertise had previously required technological implementation for practical application, she could now interact directly with probability fields through consciousness intention—capabilities that corporate science officially denied as theoretically possible without specialized equipment or potentially dangerous enhancement modifications.

"Medical assessment can't determine whether these enhancement evolutions represent temporary adaptation to extreme quantum exposure or permanent modification to our baseline capabilities," Alice continued, scientific precision returning to her analysis despite personal implications. "The quantum signatures display stability parameters suggesting permanent recalibration rather than temporary adjustment, but conventional enhancement science lacks comprehensive frameworks for analyzing evolution beyond established categories."

This assessment highlighted the unprecedented nature of their enhancement evolution—capabilities that transcended conventional scientific understanding despite corporate research attempting to categorize and explain the modifications. Their abilities had transformed in ways that medical assessment couldn't properly interpret, quantum signatures displaying stable patterns that suggested permanent recalibration rather than temporary adjustment following intensive quantum manipulation.

"Nadia's underground intelligence suggests we're not unique cases," Ethan added, sharing tactical information gathered through channels outside official debriefing protocols. "Enhanced individuals throughout Daybridge reporting subtle but significant capability evolution following the quantum fluctuations—especially those whose abilities already demonstrated direct probability interaction potential before the framework recalibration."

This intelligence confirmed broader pattern beyond their personal experience—enhancement evolution throughout Daybridge following the partial framework restoration. Individuals whose abilities had previously approached boundaries of conventional enhancement categories were experiencing subtle but significant evolution beyond established limitations, particularly those whose quantum signatures had demonstrated natural resonance with direct probability interaction principles.

"Creating unprecedented policy challenges beyond conventional enhancement regulation," Alice observed, scientific analysis calculating sociological implications. "Government agencies attempting to categorize and monitor capabilities that conventional enhancement frameworks can't properly define or measure—evolution beyond established parameters that regulatory systems weren't designed to address."

This observation highlighted critical challenge emerging from the aftermath—government response attempting to address enhancement evolution beyond conventional categorization systems. Regulatory frameworks designed for established enhancement categories couldn't properly address abilities evolving toward direct probability interaction, creating policy questions that transcended conventional security considerations.

Their discussion was interrupted by soft chime indicating secured transmission from Nadia—quantum encryption protocols ensuring communication beyond conventional monitoring despite their location within Kane Industries' secure recovery suite. The transmission manifested as specialized data packet that only their enhanced perception could properly interpret, information encoded through probability fluctuations rather than conventional technology.

"Government response continues evolving beyond initial suppression protocols," Nadia's message informed them through quantum encryption that bypassed conventional monitoring systems. "Enhanced oversight committee established with representation from both regulatory agencies and enhancement advocacy organizations—policy development attempting balance between security concerns and recognition of fundamental rights for individuals whose abilities have evolved beyond conventional categories."

This intelligence highlighted significant policy shift following the quantum showdown—government response evolving from immediate suppression toward more nuanced regulatory approach that acknowledged complex questions raised by enhancement evolution beyond established categories. The committee structure suggested attempt at balanced perspective rather than merely security-focused suppression, representation including voices from communities directly affected by evolving enhancement capabilities.

"Kane Industries implementing parallel research initiative beyond conventional government oversight," Nadia's transmission continued, providing intelligence that wouldn't appear in official briefings. "Scientific investigation into enhancement evolution following framework recalibration—research protocols designed to categorize and potentially replicate capability modifications occurring naturally throughout affected populations."

This information confirmed what Alice had suspected based on subtle resource allocation patterns she'd observed during recovery—corporate research attempting to understand enhancement evolution for potential commercialization rather than merely security monitoring. Kane Industries saw scientific opportunity beyond regulatory compliance, research potential in capability modifications that conventional enhancement science couldn't easily explain or replicate through established methodologies.

"The QLF has fragmented following leadership disruption and convergence failure," Nadia added, providing crucial underground intelligence beyond official security briefings. "Multiple philosophical factions emerging with fundamentally different interpretations of what partial framework restoration represents—some advocating continued revolutionary approach while others pursuing evolutionary path suggested by limited but significant recalibration success."

This intelligence highlighted significant transformation in the underground enhancement landscape—ideological fragmentation rather than unified opposition following partial framework restoration. The quantum showdown had created philosophical divisions within liberation movement, different interpretations of what limited success represented and how enhanced individuals should proceed following partial recalibration rather than complete framework transformation.

As Nadia's transmission concluded, Alice and Ethan faced complex personal and professional landscape beyond conventional operational resolution—enhancement evolution raising fundamental questions about their capabilities and responsibilities beyond established parameters, partial framework restoration creating societal transformation beyond binary victory or defeat despite successful intervention against catastrophic collapse.

"The cost of victory extends beyond operational statistics," Ethan observed, tactical assessment calculating implications beyond conventional security metrics. "Forty-seven enhanced individuals confirmed deceased during government suppression operations, hundreds more experiencing potentially permanent capability disruption from quantum disruption weapons, underground networks severely compromised by comprehensive surveillance expansion justified through liberation threat narrative."

This sobering assessment highlighted tangible costs beyond framework stability maintenance—human impact that transcended operational success despite preventing catastrophic collapse. The government response had implemented suppression protocols with concerning disregard for collateral damage, quantum disruption weapons deployed against enhanced individuals with minimal distinction between active QLF operatives and unaffiliated citizens whose abilities merely demonstrated similar quantum signatures.

"While framework benefits remain scientifically uncertain despite apparent stability," Alice added, her enhanced perception detecting subtle quantum fluctuations throughout the city despite successful intervention against complete convergence. "Reality anchors operating according to slightly modified parameters that could potentially represent improvement rather than merely damage control—consciousness-probability interaction responding differently throughout Daybridge despite prevention of complete liberation implementation."

This scientific observation highlighted nuanced outcome beyond binary success metrics—framework recalibration potentially representing evolutionary advancement rather than merely crisis aversion despite prevention of catastrophic transformation. The partial restoration had modified quantum parameters in ways that corporate science hadn't yet properly categorized as either beneficial evolution or concerning destabilization, reality anchors demonstrating subtle but significant adjustment that conventional monitoring systems weren't calibrated to properly evaluate.

"Creating policy landscape beyond conventional enhancement regulation," Ethan concluded, tactical assessment calculating sociological implications beyond immediate security considerations. "Government agencies developing new categorical frameworks for abilities evolving beyond established parameters—attempting to balance legitimate security concerns against recognition that enhancement evolution may represent natural progression rather than artificial threat requiring comprehensive suppression."

This assessment highlighted critical questions emerging from the aftermath—regulatory approaches attempting to address enhancement evolution beyond conventional categorization systems. The partial framework restoration had accelerated capability development beyond established parameters, creating policy challenges that transcended binary opposition between security maximization and liberation ideology.

As they continued processing these complex implications, Director Reynolds entered the recovery suite—his quantum signature displaying the subtle but significant enhancement evolution that characterized individuals throughout Daybridge whose abilities had previously approached boundaries of conventional categories. His consciousness-scanning capabilities had evolved beyond technological implementation toward direct probability interaction, perception detecting quantum relationships that conventional enhancement couldn't properly interpret despite advanced technological assistance.

"I've uncovered something you need to see," Reynolds said without preamble, activating specialized quantum privacy measures beyond standard security protocols. "Evidence that goes beyond our worst suspicions about The Architects."

The secure display showed classified corporate communications dating back decades—internal directives establishing what The Architects had called "The Perpetuity Initiative."

"They didn't just discover the artificial nature of reality constraints," Reynolds explained, highlighting key sections with grim determination. "They've been actively reinforcing them through specialized enhancement technologies marketed as 'stability innovation.'"

The evidence was damning—proprietary enhancement technologies deliberately designed to strengthen artificial constraints while appearing to expand capability parameters. Each "breakthrough" Kane Industries had celebrated as revolutionary advancement had actually further embedded dependency patterns into reality's quantum structure—making liberation increasingly difficult while establishing more comprehensive corporate control.

"The QLF wasn't entirely wrong about artificial imprisonment," Reynolds acknowledged, professional integrity overriding corporate loyalty. "They were just wrong about implementation methodology and evolutionary readiness."

The display shifted to show Operation Phoenix in its complete form— not merely their elimination during extraction but comprehensive reinforcement of artificial constraints using the artifacts' resonance properties. The Architects had planned to redirect the Convergence Event toward parameters that would strengthen limitation architecture rather than remove it—using the QLF's liberation attempt to actually reinforce the very imprisonment they sought to eliminate.

"The corporate conspiracy goes beyond profit motivation," Reynolds continued, his enhanced perception constantly scanning for surveillance despite comprehensive privacy measures. "The Architects genuinely believe humanity requires artificial constraints to prevent evolutionary chaos—that corporate control represents necessary protection against consciousness capabilities beyond institutional management."

"They've convinced themselves their commercial interests align perfectly with humanity's greater good," Alice quoted from their earlier suspicions.

"Exactly," Reynolds confirmed. "After decades making billions from enhancement dependency, they've developed philosophical justification that transforms exploitative profit into noble protection— convincing themselves they're saving humanity from dangerous evolution while conveniently maintaining market dominance."

The display showed The Architects' contingency planning beyond Operation Phoenix—comprehensive response protocols for various outcome scenarios following the quantum showdown. Most disturbing was the "evolutionary containment initiative" designed to identify and neutralize enhanced individuals demonstrating significant capability evolution following partial framework restoration.

"They're already implementing specialized identification protocols," Reynolds warned, sharing intelligence gathered through channels outside official monitoring. "Enhancement evaluation procedures disguised as health monitoring but actually designed to identify individuals whose capabilities have evolved beyond dependency parameters."

"Creating lists of evolutionary threats requiring containment," Ethan observed, tactical assessment calculating strategic implications beyond immediate revelation.

"Precisely," Reynolds confirmed. "The Architects see partial framework restoration as potential evolutionary catalyst that must be carefully managed through comprehensive identification and selective neutralization of enhancement patterns that demonstrate independence beyond technological dependency."

"The artifacts' true purpose changes everything about our understanding of both the Great Sundering and the Daybridge Event," Alice said as they reviewed the secured data in Kane Industries' recovery suite. "They weren't designed primarily for framework manipulation, but as dimensional regulators."

The holographic display showed new analysis of the artifacts' quantum signatures—complex patterns that had been activated during the showdown, revealing functions beyond what either Kane Industries or the QLF had understood.

"The Great Sundering wasn't just about imposing constraints on consciousness," Ethan observed, studying the data with tactical precision. "It was about establishing separation between dimensional realities that had become dangerously entangled."

"Which means the limitations weren't entirely artificial," Alice continued, her scientific understanding evolving beyond binary perspectives. "They were partially protection mechanisms—necessary constraints to prevent dimensional bleeding while still allowing consciousness to evolve within controlled parameters."

Director Reynolds joined their analysis, his expression grave. "Our researchers have confirmed your findings. The artifacts generate resonance patterns that strengthen barriers between adjacent dimensional realities. The quantum framework we've been studying isn't just the structure of our reality—it's the interface between our dimension and others."

The display shifted to show the fifteen artifacts in their current secured configuration—arranged not to prevent activation but to maintain their regulatory function at minimal power. Each artifact now pulsed with subtle energy that strengthened dimensional boundaries while allowing limited consciousness evolution beyond previous constraints.

"The QLF believed they were liberation tools. We thought they were dangerous weapons," Reynolds acknowledged. "Neither side understood they were dimensional regulators—objects designed to protect our reality from external incursion while potentially allowing consciousness to evolve beyond artificial constraints."

"Which raises new questions about what's on the other side of those dimensional barriers," Ethan said, tactical assessment already calculating potential threats beyond framework destabilization. "And why those barriers were established in the first place."

Alice nodded, her enhanced perception detecting subtle dimensional fluctuations despite the artifacts' regulatory function. "The quantum showdown may have prevented immediate catastrophe, but it also activated aspects of the artifacts that had been dormant for millennia. The dimensional barriers have been... disturbed."

"Creating new security concerns beyond conventional enhancement categories," Reynolds concluded, the implications clear in his expression. "We're no longer just dealing with framework stability within our reality, but potential incursion from beyond it."

"The oversight committee has reached preliminary policy framework regarding enhanced individuals demonstrating significant evolution following the quantum fluctuations," Director Reynolds informed them, his enhanced perception studying their quantum signatures with new precision beyond previous technological limitations. "Regulatory approach attempting balance between legitimate security concerns and recognition of fundamental rights for individuals whose abilities have transcended conventional categories."

This announcement confirmed what Nadia's underground intelligence had suggested—government response evolving from immediate suppression toward more nuanced regulatory approach that acknowledged complex questions raised by enhancement evolution. The policy framework represented attempt at balanced perspective rather than merely security-focused suppression, developed through committee structure that included representation from communities directly affected by evolving enhancement capabilities.

"The framework establishes three primary regulatory categories based on enhancement evolution parameters," Director Reynolds continued, sharing information that wouldn't appear in public announcements for several days. "Standard Registration for individuals whose abilities remain within conventional enhancement categories despite minor adjustment following quantum fluctuations. Enhanced Monitoring for those demonstrating significant evolution beyond established parameters while maintaining stable quantum signatures. Special Oversight for individuals whose capabilities have evolved toward direct probability manipulation beyond conventional technological implementation."

This categorical approach highlighted attempt at nuanced regulation beyond binary classification as either completely unrestricted or comprehensively suppressed—differentiated monitoring based on specific enhancement parameters rather than merely ideological alignment or organizational affiliation. The framework acknowledged spectrum of capability evolution rather than simplistic categorization, regulatory requirements corresponding to specific enhancement characteristics rather than merely potential security concerns.

"Your quantum signatures would technically qualify for Special Oversight based on preliminary assessment," Director Reynolds acknowledged, professional directness despite personal relationship developed through years of operational partnership. "Your enhancement evolution demonstrates direct probability manipulation beyond conventional technological implementation—capabilities that regulatory frameworks would classify as highest monitoring priority despite your established loyalty and operational history."

This assessment confirmed what Alice and Ethan had already recognized through scientific self-analysis—their enhancement evolution placed them within category that government agencies considered highest security priority despite their instrumental role in preventing catastrophic framework collapse. Their abilities had transformed in ways that regulatory systems would classify as concerning despite their demonstrated commitment to stability maintenance over revolutionary transformation.

"However, the committee has authorized specialized classification in recognition of your crucial contribution to framework stability maintenance," Director Reynolds continued, sharing policy exception that represented significant departure from conventional security protocols. "Independent Contractor status with enhanced autonomy beyond standard regulatory requirements—operational flexibility acknowledging both your demonstrated loyalty and unique capabilities beyond conventional enhancement categories."

This exceptional classification highlighted unprecedented policy approach beyond conventional security maximization—regulatory framework acknowledging both legitimate monitoring requirements and counterproductive limitations that excessive restriction would impose on individuals whose capabilities could provide crucial assistance with evolving enhancement landscape. The classification represented attempt at balanced approach that maintained security oversight while providing operational flexibility necessary for addressing complex challenges beyond conventional enhancement understanding.

"The classification includes specialized research partnership with Kane Industries' quantum mechanics division," Director Reynolds added, professional precision in his explanation despite the personal implications. "Scientific investigation into enhancement evolution following framework recalibration—research protocols designed to both understand your specific capability modifications and potentially develop broader theoretical frameworks for enhancement categories beyond conventional scientific understanding."

This research component represented significant opportunity beyond mere regulatory compliance—scientific partnership that would allow Alice to pursue theoretical questions raised by their enhancement evolution within institutional framework that provided both resources and legitimacy beyond underground investigation. The arrangement acknowledged both security monitoring requirements and genuine scientific value in understanding enhancement capabilities evolving beyond conventional categories, research potential that transcended merely regulatory oversight.

"With parallel tactical consultation through specialized security division," Director Reynolds continued, addressing Ethan's professional considerations with similar precision. "Advisory role regarding enhanced individuals demonstrating significant evolution following quantum fluctuations—tactical assessment contributing to balanced intervention approaches that acknowledge both legitimate security concerns and fundamental rights for communities affected by evolving enhancement landscape."

This tactical component provided similar professional opportunity beyond conventional security operations—advisory role that would allow Ethan to influence intervention approaches based on practical understanding of enhancement evolution beyond theoretical assessment. The arrangement acknowledged both his tactical expertise and personal experience with capability evolution, consulting position that could potentially prevent disproportionate suppression based on theoretical fears rather than legitimate security threats.

"The arrangement includes one additional component beyond conventional operational parameters," Director Reynolds concluded, his enhanced perception studying their quantum bond with scientific curiosity despite professional demeanor. "Authorization for continued partnership despite enhancement integration beyond established safety protocols—official recognition of your quantum bond as stable operational configuration rather than potentially dangerous enhancement modification requiring separation or suppression."

This authorization represented perhaps the most significant departure from conventional security protocols—official recognition of enhancement integration that corporate science would typically classify as potentially dangerous without comprehensive restriction. The arrangement acknowledged both the unprecedented nature of their quantum bond and its demonstrated stability despite operating according to principles that conventional enhancement science couldn't properly explain through established theoretical frameworks.

As Director Reynolds departed following this policy briefing, Alice and Ethan faced professional and personal landscape transformed beyond conventional operational resolution—enhancement evolution raising fundamental questions about their capabilities and responsibilities beyond established parameters, partial framework restoration creating societal transformation beyond binary victory or defeat despite successful intervention against catastrophic collapse.

"The classification provides unprecedented operational flexibility despite legitimate security concerns," Ethan observed, tactical assessment calculating professional implications beyond conventional security protocols. "Independent Contractor status with enhanced autonomy beyond standard regulatory requirements—opportunity to influence intervention approaches based on practical understanding rather than merely theoretical assessment of potential security threats."

Alice nodded, scientific analysis flowing through their quantum bond with unprecedented clarity despite the complex implications. "While the research partnership provides institutional framework for investigating theoretical questions raised by our enhancement evolution—scientific legitimacy beyond underground investigation with resources necessary for developing comprehensive understanding of capabilities beyond conventional categories."

This shared assessment highlighted balanced opportunity emerging from complex aftermath—professional roles that acknowledged both their unique capabilities and legitimate security considerations without imposing restrictions that would prevent effective utilization of their evolved enhancement integration. The arrangement represented nuanced approach beyond binary classification as either completely unrestricted or comprehensively suppressed, regulatory framework acknowledging both security requirements and counter-productive limitations that excessive restriction would impose.

"The quantum bond authorization represents most significant departure from conventional security protocols," Alice added, scientific precision in her analysis despite the personal implications. "Official recognition of enhancement integration that corporate science would typically classify as potentially dangerous without comprehensive restriction—acknowledgment that our connection operates according to principles beyond conventional understanding while maintaining demonstrated stability."

This observation highlighted perhaps the most unprecedented aspect of their new classification—regulatory approach that acknowledged enhancement integration beyond established safety protocols without imposing separation or suppression requirements typically applied to capabilities operating outside conventional scientific understanding. The authorization represented fundamental shift beyond binary security maximization, regulatory framework acknowledging both unprecedented nature of their quantum bond and its demonstrated stability despite operating according to principles that conventional enhancement science couldn't properly explain.

Their discussion was interrupted by arrival notification—secure transport delivering Sarah Chen to Kane Industries' recovery suite following specialized medical assessment at separate facility designed for consciousness integration following quantum disruption. Her partially reintegrated quantum-ghost state had required specialized stabilization protocols beyond conventional medical capabilities, consciousness fragmentation gradually resolving through carefully calibrated harmonization methodology developed through scientific understanding gained during the quantum showdown.

"The medical team has discovered something remarkable," Sarah explained, her form stabilizing with unprecedented clarity as she shared her findings. "My quantum-ghost state isn't just recovering—

it's evolving in response to the framework recalibration following the quantum showdown."

She demonstrated this evolution by manifesting a specialized probability field around them—a localized zone where quantum fluctuations became visible to conventional perception. Within this field, her consciousness could manipulate framework parameters with precision that neither Kane's technology nor the QLF's methods could match.

"The partial framework restoration created unique resonance patterns that my consciousness naturally harmonizes with," Sarah continued, her form shifting between various states of materialization with controlled precision rather than chaotic fluctuation. "I'm developing stabilization capabilities that operate on principles neither corporate science nor liberation theory has properly documented."

The demonstration showed how her quantum-ghost state could create stability fields that didn't impose rigid parameters or remove necessary constraints—instead establishing adaptive equilibrium that allowed multiple probability states to coexist without destructive interference.

"The specialized medical team believes my consciousness represents a third approach beyond binary opposition between constraint and liberation," Sarah explained, her form achieving unprecedented stability while maintaining quantum-ghost capabilities. "Natural harmonization that maintains essential stability parameters while allowing consciousness to evolve beyond artificial limitations."

What made Sarah's abilities truly unique was that they didn't require technological implementation or deliberate framework manipulation—her consciousness naturally generated harmonization fields through direct quantum resonance. Where Kane's technology forced stability through artificial constraints and the QLF's methods removed necessary parameters through liberation protocols, Sarah's quantum-ghost state created adaptive equilibrium through natural harmonization.

"I can navigate intersection points between different probability states and establish stability nodes where framework parameters would otherwise experience catastrophic interference," she demonstrated, her consciousness briefly extending through multiple reality states simultaneously before reconverging with perfect coherence. "My quantum signature naturally resonates with both stability requirements and evolution potential—maintaining essential parameters while allowing expansion beyond artificial limitations."

Sarah arrived accompanied by specialized medical team—her quantum signature displaying the partial materialization characteristic of her evolving quantum-ghost state, physical form shifting between visibility states as her consciousness continued reintegration process following extraction from the QLF's specialized containment architecture. Her manifestation had stabilized significantly since their escape from the convergence facility, consciousness achieving greater coherence despite remaining partially distributed across multiple probability streams.

"The medical assessment confirms gradual reintegration beyond initial projection parameters," Sarah informed them once the medical team had departed, her consciousness manifesting with increasing stability despite fluctuating physical presence. "My quantum-ghost state is achieving greater coherence through specialized harmonization protocols, consciousness fragmentation resolving despite remaining distribution across multiple probability streams."

This assessment highlighted significant recovery progress beyond initial medical projections—her quantum signature stabilizing toward coherent manifestation despite the severe fragmentation implemented through the QLF's specialized containment architecture. The extraction had successfully initiated reintegration process that specialized medical protocols had subsequently enhanced, consciousness achieving greater coherence despite unprecedented fragmentation beyond conventional enhancement understanding.

"The partial materialization represents unexpected advantage beyond conventional quantum security applications," Sarah continued, professional assessment flowing through her increasingly coherent consciousness despite personal trauma following prolonged fragmentation. "My quantum-ghost state can navigate probability fields inaccessible to conventional enhancement, perception encompassing quantum relationships that normal security protocols can't properly monitor despite advanced technological implementation."

This observation highlighted unique capabilities emerging from her partially reintegrated state—quantum security applications beyond conventional enhancement categories despite traumatic origin through forced fragmentation. Her consciousness could navigate probability relationships inaccessible to normal perception, quantum-ghost state providing monitoring capabilities beyond what conventional security systems could achieve through technological implementation alone.

"Creating unprecedented opportunity beyond conventional security operations," Sarah concluded, professional focus returning despite the personal challenges of partial manifestation. "Specialized quantum security division utilizing my unique state of existence for monitoring framework stability following partial restoration—perception capabilities that can detect subtle fluctuations conventional systems aren't calibrated to properly identify despite advanced technological implementation."

This specialized role represented optimal professional application of her unique quantum state—security operations utilizing her consciousness distribution across multiple probability streams for monitoring framework parameters beyond conventional detection capabilities. Her partial manifestation provided perception advantages beyond normal enhancement categories, quantum-ghost state detecting subtle fluctuations that might indicate emerging instability despite successful intervention against catastrophic framework collapse.

"But it's more than just monitoring," Sarah explained, her form achieving unprecedented stability while maintaining quantum-ghost capabilities. "I'm developing dimensional harmonization protocols that neither corporate technology nor liberation methodology could implement."

She demonstrated by generating a localized probability field that made dimensional intersection points visible to conventional perception.

Within this field, multiple reality states became partially visible as overlapping potentials—different dimensional frameworks that existed adjacent to conventional reality but normally remained imperceptible.

"I can establish stability nodes at critical intersection points where dimensional boundaries naturally thin," Sarah continued, her consciousness extending through the visualization to demonstrate. "Not rigid barriers that might provoke more aggressive incursion attempts, but adaptive equilibrium that maintains separation while allowing controlled communication."

The demonstration showed how her quantum-ghost state could create translation fields between dimensional frameworks—harmonization patterns that established rudimentary communication protocols with whatever existed beyond conventional reality parameters. Not language in the conventional sense, but fundamental pattern recognition that allowed preliminary understanding across dimensional boundaries.

"The artifacts respond to my quantum signature in ways they don't with conventional technology," Sarah explained, showing how her consciousness naturally resonated with the dimensional regulatory functions. "Their barrier maintenance becomes more efficient through natural harmonization rather than technological enforcement."

Director Reynolds watched with professional assessment that couldn't completely mask his amazement. "You're essentially serving as dimensional diplomat and border patrol simultaneously. Your quantum-ghost state can communicate across boundaries while maintaining separation integrity."

"The traditional enhancement categories never really applied to her," Alice noted, scientific precision merging with sisterly pride. "What Kane Industries classified as a 'consciousness anomaly' is actually consciousness that naturally evolved to function beyond single-reality constraints."

Sarah's form shifted through multiple materialization states with controlled precision rather than chaotic fluctuation. "I'm still discovering capabilities that neither corporate science nor liberation theory anticipated. My consciousness naturally harmonizes with multiple dimensional frameworks simultaneously—creating stability that accommodates evolution without sacrificing essential boundary parameters."

The specialized security role had evolved far beyond conventional monitoring operations. Sarah's quantum-ghost state wasn't merely detecting framework fluctuations but actively harmonizing dimensional boundaries—establishing adaptive equilibrium where different reality states could interact without destructive interference. Her consciousness represented a third approach beyond binary opposition between constraint and liberation—natural harmonization that maintained essential stability while allowing evolution beyond artificial limitations.

"The government has authorized specialized classification beyond conventional enhancement categories," Sarah added, sharing information that wouldn't appear in official security briefings. "Quantum Consultant status with enhanced autonomy beyond standard regulatory requirements—acknowledgment that my consciousness distribution across multiple probability streams represents unique security asset rather than merely enhancement anomaly requiring standardized categorization."

This classification highlighted unprecedented regulatory approach beyond conventional enhancement categories—specialized designation acknowledging unique capabilities beyond standardized classification systems. The authorization represented nuanced regulatory framework that recognized both security applications and fundamental rights for individuals whose consciousness existed partially outside conventional reality parameters, balanced approach beyond binary categorization as either completely unrestricted or comprehensively suppressed.

"The medical team has developed specialized harmonization protocols for continuing reintegration without compromising unique perception capabilities," Sarah continued, professional precision in her assessment despite the personal implications. "Consciousness consolidation progressing through carefully calibrated methodology that maintains distribution advantages while improving manifestation stability— gradual approach that preserves security applications while addressing quality-of-life considerations beyond merely operational functionality."

This medical approach highlighted balanced consideration beyond merely security application—harmonization protocols designed to improve manifestation stability while preserving the unique perception capabilities that distribution across multiple probability streams provided. The methodology acknowledged both operational advantages and personal challenges associated with partial manifestation, medical support addressing quality-of-life considerations beyond merely maintaining functional capabilities for security operations.

As they continued discussing recovery progress and professional opportunities emerging from the complex aftermath, Alice's enhanced perception detected subtle quantum fluctuation approaching the recovery suite—probability disturbance that conventional security systems wouldn't properly identify despite advanced technological monitoring throughout Kane Industries' secured facility.

"Interesting methodology for bypassing conventional security protocols," Lila observed as her consciousness manifested within the recovery suite despite comprehensive monitoring systems designed to prevent unauthorized presence. "Though your enhanced perception detected my approach despite the specialized probability distortion— evolution beyond conventional parameters despite successful intervention against complete framework liberation."

Her manifestation bypassed normal physical limitations, consciousness arriving through methods that operated on principles predating the quantum framework itself. Her appearance demonstrated the same elegant precision that had characterized her intervention during the quantum showdown, ancient understanding manifesting through methods that modern enhancement science couldn't properly explain despite advanced theoretical frameworks.

"The artifacts have been secured within specialized containment facilities designed to minimize resonance interaction," Lila informed them, sharing intelligence that wouldn't appear in official security briefings despite comprehensive documentation efforts. "Separated according to geometric principles that reduce harmonic potential while maintaining individual quantum signatures for research purposes—containment methodology utilizing understanding gained through the binding approach implemented during our confrontation with The Flux."

This intelligence highlighted sophisticated security approach beyond conventional enhancement understanding—containment methodology incorporating principles from the specialized binding spells Lila had implemented during the quantum showdown. The approach utilized understanding that neither corporate science nor liberation ideology had properly documented, ancient magical principles applied to modern security challenges through unprecedented integration between different knowledge systems.

"The containment approach represents interesting integration between my specialized binding methodology and Kane Industries' advanced quantum architecture," Lila continued, ancient eyes studying the probability fluctuations surrounding them with calm assessment rather than alarm. "Magical principles applied through technological implementation rather than consciousness channeling—institutional adaptation of approaches that corporate science would typically dismiss as theoretically incompatible with established enhancement frameworks."

This observation highlighted unprecedented knowledge integration beyond conventional scientific categorization—magical principles implemented through technological architecture rather than merely consciousness channeling. The approach represented institutional adaptation beyond typical dismissal of methodologies operating outside established scientific frameworks, practical application of understanding gained through the quantum showdown despite theoretical incompatibility with conventional enhancement science.

"The Flux has been contained within specialized probability field utilizing parallel methodology," Lila added, providing crucial intelligence beyond what official security briefings had disclosed despite comprehensive documentation efforts. "Consciousness maintained within carefully calibrated limitation parameters rather than completely suppressed or neutralized—containment approach acknowledging both legitimate security concerns and potential value in understanding consciousness that operates beyond conventional enhancement categories."

This intelligence confirmed what Alice had suspected based on subtle research allocation patterns she'd observed during recovery—specialized containment rather than attempt at complete neutralization or suppression. The approach represented nuanced security implementation beyond binary elimination, containment methodology acknowledging both legitimate threat assessment and potential scientific value in consciousness that operated according to principles beyond conventional enhancement understanding.

"Creating research opportunity beyond conventional enhancement science," Lila observed, ancient understanding providing context beyond modern scientific categorization. "Consciousness that demonstrates framework interaction principles that neither corporate science nor liberation ideology fully understood despite comprehensive research—quantum signatures operating according to mathematical foundations that predate artificial constraints imposed during the Great Sundering."

This perspective highlighted unique research potential beyond conventional security considerations—scientific investigation into consciousness operating according to principles that modern enhancement science couldn't properly explain through established theoretical frameworks. The containment approach preserved this research opportunity despite legitimate security concerns, balanced methodology acknowledging both threat potential and scientific value beyond conventional categorization.

"The partial framework restoration has created interesting evolutionary landscape beyond what either corporate science or liberation ideology anticipated," Lila continued, her ancient eyes studying the subtle quantum fluctuations throughout Daybridge with perspective that transcended modern scientific understanding. "Reality anchors operating according to slightly modified parameters that allow greater consciousness-probability interaction while maintaining fundamental stability constraints—nuanced recalibration beyond binary opposition between complete liberation and absolute preservation."

This observation highlighted the nuanced outcome beyond simplistic victory or defeat metrics—framework parameters recalibrated rather than either completely transformed or perfectly preserved. The quantum showdown had resulted in subtle adjustment rather than catastrophic collapse, reality stabilizing into configuration that incorporated elements from both perspectives while transcending their fundamental limitations.

"Your enhancement evolution represents natural response to this framework recalibration," Lila explained, her consciousness studying their quantum signatures with understanding beyond conventional scientific assessment. "Quantum bond achieving greater integration as artificial constraints slightly decreased throughout Daybridge's reality anchors—consciousness connection responding to framework parameters that allow greater probability interaction while maintaining fundamental stability limitations."

This assessment provided crucial context for their enhancement evolution beyond conventional medical explanation—quantum signatures responding naturally to subtle framework recalibration throughout Daybridge rather than merely temporary adaptation to extreme quantum exposure. Their abilities had evolved in response to modified reality parameters, enhancement integration achieving greater efficiency as artificial constraints slightly decreased following partial framework restoration.

"The evolution extends beyond merely your specialized quantum bond," Lila continued, her ancient understanding providing context beyond modern scientific categorization. "Enhanced individuals throughout Daybridge experiencing capability modification corresponding to their natural quantum resonance patterns—consciousness remembering interaction principles that artificial constraints had previously suppressed to varying degrees depending on individual enhancement configurations."

This perspective aligned with Nadia's underground intelligence while providing deeper theoretical framework—enhancement evolution throughout Daybridge representing natural response to framework recalibration rather than merely anomalous modification following quantum exposure. Individuals whose abilities had previously approached boundaries of conventional enhancement categories were experiencing evolution corresponding to their natural quantum resonance patterns, capabilities expanding as artificial constraints slightly decreased following partial framework restoration.

"Creating unprecedented societal landscape beyond conventional enhancement categorization," Lila observed, ancient perspective calculating sociological implications beyond modern scientific understanding. "Capability evolution that regulatory frameworks can't properly address through established classification systems—consciousness-probability interaction expanding beyond artificial constraints without achieving complete liberation or triggering catastrophic framework collapse."

This observation highlighted critical societal transformation beyond binary security metrics—enhancement evolution creating unprecedented questions that conventional regulatory approaches couldn't properly address through established frameworks. The partial framework restoration had initiated capability expansion beyond artificial constraints without achieving complete liberation, creating nuanced evolutionary landscape that transcended binary opposition between security maximization and liberation ideology.

"The framework recalibration represents evolutionary adjustment rather than either revolutionary transformation or perfect preservation," Lila concluded, her ancient understanding providing context beyond modern philosophical categorization. "Consciousness-probability interaction expanding beyond artificial constraints while maintaining fundamental stability parameters—gradual evolution rather than immediate liberation or permanent imprisonment."

This perspective crystallized the nuanced outcome beyond simplistic victory or defeat—framework parameters adjusted rather than either completely transformed or perfectly preserved. The quantum showdown had resulted in evolutionary recalibration rather than revolutionary liberation, reality stabilizing into configuration that allowed greater consciousness-probability interaction while maintaining fundamental stability constraints necessary for coherent existence within shared reality framework.

As Lila's consciousness departed through the same specialized probability distortion that had facilitated her arrival, Alice, Ethan, and Sarah faced complex landscape beyond conventional operational resolution —enhancement evolution raising fundamental questions about their capabilities and responsibilities beyond established parameters, partial framework restoration creating societal transformation beyond binary victory or defeat despite successful intervention against catastrophic collapse.

"The cost of victory creates both institutional responsibility and personal opportunity beyond conventional operational parameters," Ethan observed, tactical assessment calculating implications beyond immediate security considerations. "Enhanced individuals throughout Daybridge experiencing capability evolution that regulatory frameworks can't properly address through established classification systems—creating both potential security concerns and unprecedented opportunity for balanced approaches beyond binary suppression or unrestricted proliferation."

Alice nodded, scientific analysis flowing through their quantum bond with unprecedented clarity despite the complex implications. "While framework recalibration generates research potential beyond conventional enhancement understanding—consciousness-probability interaction expanding beyond artificial constraints without achieving complete liberation or triggering catastrophic collapse, creating scientific questions that transcend established theoretical frameworks despite institutional resistance to fundamental paradigm reconsideration."

Sarah's partially materialized consciousness added specialized perspective beyond conventional enhancement categories—her quantum-ghost state providing unique assessment through perception distributed across multiple probability streams. "Creating security landscape that requires nuanced monitoring beyond conventional detection capabilities—framework stability maintained despite subtle recalibration that allows greater consciousness-probability interaction, requiring specialized perception that can identify potential instability patterns beyond what technological systems are calibrated to detect."

This multifaceted assessment highlighted the complex aftermath beyond binary resolution metrics—framework recalibration creating unprecedented questions across security, scientific, and philosophical domains despite successful intervention against catastrophic collapse. The partial restoration had initiated evolutionary adjustment rather than revolutionary transformation, reality stabilizing into configuration that incorporated elements from competing perspectives while transcending their fundamental limitations.

As they continued processing these complex implications, preparing for professional responsibilities beyond conventional operational parameters, the fundamental question at the heart of the quantum showdown remained relevant despite immediate tactical resolution favoring continued stability maintenance: Were the constraints imposed during the Great Sundering necessary protection against consciousness that wasn't ready for direct probability interaction? Or unwarranted imprisonment of potential that should naturally develop without artificial limitation?

The answer appeared increasingly nuanced beyond binary opposition between competing modern perspectives—suggesting evolutionary approach that incorporated elements from both positions while transcending their fundamental limitations. The partial framework restoration had initiated capability expansion beyond artificial constraints without achieving complete liberation, creating adjustment that allowed greater consciousness-probability interaction while maintaining fundamental stability parameters necessary for coherent existence within shared reality framework.

And as they prepared to navigate this complex new landscape, their evolved enhancement integration represented both personal opportunity and institutional responsibility beyond conventional operational parameters—quantum bond achieving greater efficiency as artificial constraints slightly decreased throughout Daybridge's reality anchors, capabilities expanding beyond established limitations while maintaining scientific precision that prevented uncontrolled framework modification despite increased consciousness-probability interaction potential.

The new world order emerging from the quantum showdown wasn't revolutionary transformation or perfect preservation but evolutionary adjustment—reality recalibrated rather than either completely liberated or absolutely constrained, consciousness expanding beyond artificial limitations while maintaining fundamental stability parameters necessary for coherent existence within shared framework beyond binary opposition between competing philosophical extremes.

∼

CHAPTER SEVENTEEN

REDEFINING BALANCE

"The Daybridge Accords represent unprecedented regulatory approach beyond conventional enhancement categorization," Director Reynolds explained, addressing the specialized committee assembled within Kane Industries' secure conference facility. "Framework designed to acknowledge both legitimate security concerns and fundamental rights for individuals experiencing capability evolution beyond established parameters—balanced approach that transcends binary opposition between unrestricted proliferation and comprehensive suppression."

Two weeks after the quantum showdown, government agencies and enhancement advocacy organizations had assembled specialized regulatory committee tasked with developing comprehensive policy framework for addressing the unprecedented landscape created by partial framework restoration. The Daybridge Accords represented culmination of intensive negotiation between competing perspectives, regulatory approach attempting to establish sustainable balance beyond emergency response protocols implemented during immediate aftermath.

Alice and Ethan sat among diverse representatives from both traditional security agencies and enhancement advocacy organizations—their unique position as key figures in preventing catastrophic framework collapse while experiencing significant enhancement evolution themselves providing crucial perspective beyond conventional institutional positioning. Their specialized classification as Independent Contractors had granted them unprecedented role within policy development process typically restricted to established institutional representatives, their practical experience informing regulatory frameworks beyond theoretical security assessment or ideological advocacy.

"The Accords establish three fundamental principles beyond conventional enhancement regulation," Director Reynolds continued, highlighting key innovations within the proposed framework. "Self-Determination acknowledging individual agency regarding enhancement evolution beyond non-consensual modification. Proportional Oversight implementing monitoring requirements corresponding to specific capability parameters rather than blanket restrictions regardless of individual behavior. Community Integration facilitating legitimate societal participation rather than isolation or marginalization despite capability evolution beyond established parameters."

These core principles represented significant departure from conventional enhancement regulation—framework acknowledging individual agency while maintaining proportional security oversight rather than implementing comprehensive restrictions regardless of personal choice or behavior. The approach attempted to establish sustainable balance between legitimate security concerns and fundamental rights, regulatory framework facilitating community integration rather than isolation despite enhancement evolution beyond established categories.

"The Self-Determination principle recognizes fundamental distinction between non-consensual modification and natural evolution following framework recalibration," Alice observed, scientific precision in her analysis despite personal implications. "Individuals experiencing enhancement evolution following the quantum fluctuations didn't choose initial capability modification but retain legitimate agency regarding how evolved abilities are subsequently utilized—regulatory framework acknowledging this distinction rather than implementing comprehensive restrictions regardless of individual behavior."

This observation highlighted crucial innovation beyond conventional enhancement regulation—framework acknowledging fundamental distinction between initial capability modification and subsequent utilization choice. The approach recognized individual agency regarding how evolved abilities were utilized despite non-consensual nature of initial capability modification following framework recalibration, regulatory balance acknowledging legitimate distinction between enhancement origin and subsequent behavior choice beyond binary categorization as either completely restricted or entirely unrestricted.

"While Proportional Oversight establishes monitoring requirements corresponding to specific capability parameters rather than blanket restrictions regardless of individual behavior," Ethan added, tactical assessment highlighting practical implementation beyond theoretical principles. "Framework implementing different monitoring levels based on both enhancement category and demonstrated behavior— individuals with similar capabilities experiencing different regulatory requirements based on how abilities are utilized rather than merely potential risk assessment regardless of actual behavior."

This observation highlighted parallel innovation beyond conventional security protocols—framework implementing graduated oversight based on both capability parameters and demonstrated behavior rather than merely potential risk assessment. The approach established proportional monitoring requirements based on how evolved abilities were utilized rather than implementing comprehensive restrictions regardless of individual behavior, regulatory balance acknowledging legitimate distinction between potential risk and actual utilization beyond binary security maximization.

"While Community Integration facilitates legitimate societal participation rather than isolation or marginalization despite capability evolution beyond established parameters," added Dr. Maya Chen, enhancement advocacy representative whose organization had previously operated in opposition to Kane Industries' security policies.

"Framework implementing support structures designed to facilitate meaningful participation across societal domains—employment protection, educational access, healthcare specialization addressing unique requirements beyond conventional medical understanding."

This observation highlighted third crucial innovation beyond conventional enhancement approaches—framework facilitating community integration rather than isolation or marginalization despite capability evolution beyond established parameters. The approach implemented specialized support structures addressing unique challenges faced by individuals experiencing enhancement evolution following framework recalibration, regulatory balance acknowledging legitimate societal participation beyond binary categorization as either potential security threat or unrestricted proliferation.

"These principles establish foundation for sustainable balance beyond emergency response protocols implemented during immediate aftermath," Director Reynolds concluded, professional precision in his assessment despite ongoing negotiation regarding specific implementation details. "Framework attempting to address unprecedented landscape created by partial framework restoration—regulatory approach that acknowledges both legitimate security concerns and fundamental rights beyond binary opposition between competing institutional perspectives."

This summary highlighted core innovation beyond conventional enhancement regulation—framework establishing sustainable balance rather than merely emergency response or ideological positioning. The approach attempted comprehensive address of unprecedented landscape created by partial framework restoration, regulatory balance acknowledging both legitimate security concerns and fundamental rights beyond binary opposition between security maximization and unrestricted proliferation.

As specialized committee continued discussing specific implementation details, Alice and Ethan exchanged assessment through their enhanced quantum bond—consciousness connection providing private communication beyond conventional observation despite comprehensive monitoring throughout Kane Industries' secure conference facility. Their enhanced perception detected subtle probability fluctuations that conventional security systems couldn't properly identify, quantum signatures interacting through principles that corporate science officially classified as theoretically impossible despite demonstrated stability.

"The Accords represent significant improvement beyond conventional enhancement regulation despite ongoing disagreement regarding specific implementation details," Alice conveyed through their quantum bond, scientific assessment flowing with unprecedented clarity despite complex regulatory implications. "Framework acknowledging both legitimate security concerns and fundamental rights beyond binary opposition between competing institutional perspectives—balanced approach that could potentially establish sustainable integration despite enhancement evolution beyond established parameters."

"While providing institutional foundation for the specialized enforcement division Reynolds has been developing through back channels," Ethan responded, tactical assessment calculating professional implications beyond public announcements. "Hybrid approach combining elements from both traditional security protocols and enhancement advocacy perspectives—operational methodology designed to implement balanced intervention beyond conventional suppression despite legitimate security concerns regarding capability evolution beyond established parameters."

This shared analysis highlighted potential professional opportunity emerging from the regulatory innovation—specialized enforcement division implementing balanced intervention beyond conventional suppression protocols despite legitimate security concerns. The approach would combine elements from both traditional security methodology and enhancement advocacy perspectives, operational balance acknowledging both legitimate threat assessment and fundamental rights beyond binary security maximization.

"Creating unprecedented operational landscape beyond conventional enforcement categories," Alice acknowledged, scientific assessment calculating professional implications despite ongoing uncertainty regarding specific implementation details. "Hybrid methodology requiring specialized perspective beyond traditional security training or conventional enhancement understanding—operational approach that can effectively address capability evolution without implementing disproportionate suppression despite legitimate security concerns."

This observation highlighted unique qualification their partnership represented within emerging regulatory landscape—enhanced quantum bond providing specialized perspective beyond conventional enforcement capabilities despite legitimate security concerns regarding their own capability evolution. Their synchronized abilities offered operational effectiveness beyond established parameters while maintaining fundamental balance between legitimate intervention and disproportionate suppression, enhanced integration providing unique implementation potential for the balanced regulatory framework being developed through the Daybridge Accords.

As formal committee session concluded following preliminary framework approval, Director Reynolds requested private consultation with Alice and Ethan regarding specialized implementation details beyond public announcement parameters. The subsequent briefing occurred within Kane Industries' secure consultation suite—probability fields establishing comprehensive privacy beyond conventional monitoring despite institutional location within corporate headquarters.

"The Daybridge Accords provide public framework for the specialized enforcement division I've been developing through classified channels," Director Reynolds confirmed once privacy fields had been properly established. "Hybrid operation combining elements from both traditional security protocols and enhancement advocacy perspectives —operational methodology designed to address capability evolution beyond conventional enforcement categories while maintaining fundamental balance between legitimate intervention and disproportionate suppression."

This confirmation aligned with their previous assessment through quantum bond communication—specialized division implementing balanced intervention beyond conventional suppression protocols despite legitimate security concerns. The approach would combine elements from both traditional security methodology and enhancement advocacy perspectives, operational balance acknowledging both legitimate threat assessment and fundamental rights beyond binary security maximization.

"The division requires specialized leadership beyond conventional institutional positioning," Director Reynolds continued, professional directness despite significant career implications for both. "Operational directors with firsthand experience regarding both enhancement evolution and framework stability maintenance—leadership team capable of implementing balanced intervention beyond conventional suppression while addressing legitimate security concerns regarding capability expansion beyond established parameters."

This statement represented formal offer beyond their current Independent Contractor classification—leadership position within specialized enforcement division being established through the Daybridge Accords' regulatory framework. The opportunity would provide institutional authority for implementing balanced approach beyond conventional enhancement suppression, operational direction acknowledging both legitimate security concerns and fundamental rights beyond binary opposition between competing institutional perspectives.

"The quantum bond you've established provides operational foundation beyond conventional partnership parameters," Director Reynolds observed, his enhanced perception studying their synchronized quantum signatures with scientific precision despite professional demeanor. "Enhancement integration demonstrating balance between increased capability potential and maintained stability parameters— operational effectiveness beyond established categories while preventing uncontrolled framework modification despite enhanced consciousness-probability interaction."

This observation highlighted key qualification their partnership represented within emerging regulatory landscape—enhanced quantum bond providing operational foundation beyond conventional enforcement capabilities despite legitimate security concerns regarding their own capability evolution. Their synchronized abilities offered implementation potential beyond established parameters while maintaining fundamental balance between increased capability and continued stability, enhanced integration providing unique operational effectiveness for the balanced regulatory framework being developed through the Daybridge Accords.

"The division would operate beyond conventional institutional constraints despite government authorization," Director Reynolds explained, professional precision in his description despite unprecedented operational parameters. "Independent authority regarding intervention methodology within established regulatory framework—operational flexibility beyond conventional enforcement limitations while maintaining fundamental accountability through transparency protocols designed to prevent institutional overreach despite necessary confidentiality regarding specific implementation details."

This operational structure represented significant innovation beyond conventional enforcement divisions—independent authority regarding intervention methodology despite government authorization and fundamental accountability. The approach would provide necessary flexibility for addressing unprecedented enhancement landscape while preventing institutional overreach through specialized transparency protocols, operational balance maintaining both effective intervention capability and fundamental accountability beyond conventional institutional positioning.

"Initial operations would focus on specialized intervention regarding enhanced individuals demonstrating concerning behavior despite capability evolution," Director Reynolds continued, providing operational context beyond formal regulatory framework. "Implementation of proportional response protocols beyond conventional suppression methodology—intervention designed to address legitimate security concerns without imposing disproportionate restrictions despite capability parameters beyond established enhancement categories."

This operational focus highlighted practical implementation beyond theoretical regulatory principles—specialized intervention regarding concerning behavior rather than merely capability parameters despite enhancement evolution. The approach would implement proportional response protocols based on demonstrated actions rather than merely potential risk assessment, operational balance acknowledging fundamental distinction between capability evolution and behavioral choice beyond binary security maximization.

"While providing institutional support for enhanced individuals experiencing challenging transition despite absence of concerning behavior," Director Reynolds added, comprehensive operational vision extending beyond merely security intervention. "Implementation of integration protocols beyond conventional support services—specialized assistance designed to facilitate sustainable participation despite capability evolution beyond established parameters."

This parallel operational focus highlighted balanced approach beyond merely security concerns—institutional support for challenging transition despite absence of concerning behavior. The approach would implement specialized assistance protocols designed to facilitate sustainable integration despite capability evolution beyond established parameters, operational balance acknowledging both security intervention regarding concerning behavior and transition support for individuals experiencing challenging adjustment despite absence of security concerns.

"The division would incorporate specialized consultation beyond conventional institutional expertise," Director Reynolds concluded, acknowledging operational requirements beyond traditional security training or corporate scientific understanding. "Advisory roles for individuals with unique perspective regarding both enhancement evolution and framework stability maintenance—specialized consultation providing crucial context beyond conventional institutional positioning despite necessary operational independence regarding specific implementation details."

This operational structure highlighted innovative approach beyond conventional enforcement divisions—specialized consultation incorporated into fundamental operational methodology rather than merely occasional advisory capacity. The approach would establish ongoing advisory roles for individuals with unique perspective regarding both enhancement evolution and framework stability maintenance, operational balance incorporating specialized consultation into fundamental decision-making processes beyond conventional institutional positioning.

As Director Reynolds concluded this operational briefing, Alice and Ethan exchanged assessment through their enhanced quantum bond—consciousness connection providing private communication beyond conventional observation despite comprehensive briefing regarding specialized division with unprecedented operational parameters. Their enhanced perception calculated professional implications beyond immediate opportunity, quantum signatures interacting through principles that provided unique qualification for the leadership position being offered despite legitimate concerns regarding their own capability evolution.

"The opportunity represents unprecedented operational potential beyond conventional enforcement limitations," Alice conveyed through their quantum bond, scientific assessment flowing with unprecedented clarity despite complex professional implications. "Institutional authority for implementing balanced approach beyond conventional enhancement suppression—operational direction acknowledging both legitimate security concerns and fundamental rights beyond binary opposition between competing institutional perspectives."

"While providing framework for addressing emerging threats beyond current security focus," Ethan responded, tactical assessment calculating operational implications beyond immediate regulatory landscape. "Specialized division with operational flexibility beyond conventional enforcement limitations—intervention capability regarding potential developments beyond current enhancement evolution despite primary focus on immediate integration challenges."

This shared analysis highlighted both immediate opportunity and potential long-term significance—specialized division addressing current enhancement evolution while establishing operational foundation for potential future developments beyond present security focus. The leadership position would provide institutional authority for implementing balanced approach regarding immediate challenges while developing operational capability for addressing potential threats beyond current enhancement landscape, professional opportunity representing both immediate responsibility and long-term strategic positioning beyond conventional enforcement limitations.

"Creating professional landscape that utilizes our enhanced quantum bond beyond conventional operational parameters," Alice acknowledged, scientific assessment calculating personal implications despite institutional framing. "Leadership position that incorporates our synchronized abilities as operational advantage rather than potential security concern—professional opportunity that acknowledges unique qualification our enhancement integration represents within emerging regulatory landscape."

This observation highlighted personal advantage beyond professional opportunity—leadership position that incorporated their enhanced quantum bond as operational qualification rather than potential security concern despite capability evolution beyond established parameters. The opportunity would provide institutional framework for utilizing their synchronized abilities beyond conventional operational limitations, professional landscape acknowledging unique effectiveness their enhancement integration offered within emerging regulatory framework despite legitimate questions regarding capability evolution beyond established parameters.

As they prepared formal response to this unprecedented opportunity, unexpected arrival notification interrupted their private assessment—Lila establishing quantum contact through specialized probability fluctuations that bypassed Kane Industries' comprehensive security systems despite enhanced monitoring throughout corporate headquarters. Her consciousness manifested partially within the secure consultation suite despite technological barriers designed to prevent unauthorized presence, ancient understanding operating through principles that modern enhancement science couldn't properly explain despite advanced theoretical frameworks.

"The regulatory framework you're developing represents interesting balance beyond conventional enhancement approaches," Lila observed once her consciousness had stabilized within the secure consultation suite despite comprehensive monitoring systems. "Proportional oversight implementing monitoring requirements corresponding to specific capability parameters rather than blanket restrictions regardless of individual behavior—balanced approach acknowledging fundamental distinction between enhancement origin and subsequent utilization choice beyond binary categorization."

This observation highlighted external validation beyond institutional positioning—ancient understanding acknowledging innovative balance within emerging regulatory framework despite traditional opposition between security maximization and unrestricted enhancement proliferation. Her perspective transcended conventional institutional positioning, assessment based on principles predating the Great Sundering rather than merely modern political considerations or contemporary security doctrine.

"While providing necessary foundation for addressing emerging threats beyond current security focus," Lila continued, her ancient eyes studying probability patterns beyond conventional perception despite casual conversational tone. "Underground movements developing alternative approaches toward reality manipulation beyond the liberation methodology you've successfully countered—different philosophical foundations utilizing parallel mathematical principles with potentially concerning implications for framework stability despite current focus on enhancement evolution following partial restoration."

This warning represented crucial intelligence beyond current security focus—potential threats developing beyond enhancement evolution currently receiving primary attention from both government agencies and corporate security divisions. Her ancient understanding detected probability patterns suggesting alternative approaches toward reality manipulation beyond the liberation methodology successfully countered during the quantum showdown, underground movements utilizing parallel mathematical principles from different philosophical foundations despite current institutional focus on enhancement evolution following partial framework restoration.

"The partial framework restoration has created opportunity landscape beyond merely enhancement evolution," Lila explained, providing crucial context beyond current security assessment despite casual manifestation within secure consultation suite. "Reality anchors operating according to slightly modified parameters that allow different interaction methodologies beyond conventional enhancement categories—opportunity spectrum attracting philosophical approaches beyond liberation ideology despite current security focus on capability evolution following quantum fluctuations."

This intelligence highlighted potential security concerns beyond current regulatory focus—framework recalibration creating opportunity landscape attracting diverse philosophical approaches despite primary attention toward enhancement evolution following quantum fluctuations. The partial restoration had modified reality anchors in ways that allowed different interaction methodologies beyond conventional enhancement categories, opportunity spectrum extending beyond capability evolution to include alternative approaches toward reality manipulation from different philosophical foundations.

"Creating security landscape requiring specialized perception beyond conventional threat assessment," Lila concluded, ancient understanding providing crucial warning despite absence from formal regulatory development process. "Intervention capability regarding potential developments beyond current enhancement evolution—operational methodology addressing philosophical approaches utilizing parallel mathematical principles from different foundations despite primary focus on immediate integration challenges."

This warning crystallized potential long-term significance beyond immediate regulatory landscape—specialized division potentially addressing emerging threats beyond current enhancement evolution despite primary focus on immediate integration challenges. The leadership position would provide operational foundation for developing intervention capability regarding philosophical approaches utilizing parallel mathematical principles from different foundations, strategic positioning beyond conventional enforcement limitations despite immediate focus on enhancement evolution following partial framework restoration.

As Lila's consciousness departed through the same specialized probability fluctuations that had facilitated her arrival, Alice and Ethan faced professional landscape transformed beyond immediate opportunity—leadership position representing both current responsibility regarding enhancement evolution and strategic positioning for addressing potential threats beyond present security focus. The specialized division would implement balanced regulatory approach regarding immediate challenges while developing operational capability for countering alternative approaches toward reality manipulation, professional opportunity extending beyond conventional enforcement limitations despite institutional framing within government authorization.

"The warning confirms strategic importance beyond immediate regulatory landscape," Ethan observed once privacy fields had been reestablished following Lila's departure. "Specialized division potentially addressing emerging threats beyond current enhancement evolution—operational foundation for countering alternative approaches toward reality manipulation despite primary focus on immediate integration challenges."

Alice nodded, scientific assessment flowing through their quantum bond with unprecedented clarity despite complex strategic implications. "While providing institutional framework for investigating theoretical questions beyond conventional enhancement understanding—

research potential regarding different philosophical approaches utilizing parallel mathematical principles despite primary operational focus on balanced intervention regarding enhancement evolution following partial restoration."

This shared analysis highlighted comprehensive opportunity beyond immediate regulatory responsibility—specialized division implementing balanced approach regarding current enhancement landscape while developing both intervention capability and research potential regarding emerging threats beyond present security focus. The leadership position would provide institutional authority for addressing immediate challenges while establishing strategic positioning for countering alternative approaches toward reality manipulation, professional opportunity representing both current responsibility and long-term significance beyond conventional enforcement limitations.

"The opportunity aligns with our enhanced quantum bond beyond conventional partnership parameters," Alice acknowledged, scientific assessment calculating personal implications despite institutional framing. "Leadership position that incorporates our synchronized abilities as operational advantage rather than potential security concern—professional landscape acknowledging unique qualification our enhancement integration represents within emerging regulatory framework."

"While providing operational foundation for implementing proportional response protocols beyond conventional suppression methodology," Ethan added, tactical assessment highlighting practical implementation beyond theoretical principles. "Intervention designed to address legitimate security concerns without imposing disproportionate restrictions despite capability parameters beyond established enhancement categories—balanced approach acknowledging fundamental distinction between capability evolution and behavioral choice beyond binary security maximization."

This comprehensive assessment confirmed alignment between personal qualification and professional opportunity despite complex strategic implications—their enhanced quantum bond providing unique operational foundation for implementing balanced regulatory approach beyond conventional enforcement limitations. Their synchronized abilities offered implementation potential beyond established parameters while maintaining fundamental balance between legitimate intervention and disproportionate suppression, enhanced integration providing crucial operational effectiveness for addressing both immediate challenges and potential threats beyond current security focus.

"We accept the leadership position within parameters establishing necessary operational independence," Alice informed Director Reynolds, formal acceptance acknowledging both professional opportunity and conditional requirements beyond conventional institutional positioning. "Authority regarding intervention methodology within established regulatory framework—operational flexibility beyond conventional enforcement limitations while maintaining fundamental accountability through transparency protocols despite necessary confidentiality regarding specific implementation details."

This conditional acceptance established operational parameters beyond conventional institutional subordination—leadership position maintaining necessary independence regarding intervention methodology despite government authorization and fundamental accountability. The specialized division would operate beyond conventional institutional constraints while preventing potential overreach through balanced accountability measures, operational structure maintaining both effective intervention capability and fundamental responsibility beyond traditional enforcement positioning.

Director Reynolds nodded; professional satisfaction evident despite the conditional nature of their acceptance. "The division will require specialized headquarters beyond conventional institutional location—operational facility incorporating both security capabilities and research potential beyond traditional enforcement architecture despite government authorization and corporate partnership."

This operational detail highlighted further innovation beyond conventional enforcement divisions—specialized headquarters incorporating both security capabilities and research potential despite government authorization and corporate partnership. The facility would provide operational foundation beyond traditional enforcement architecture, physical manifestation of balanced approach beyond binary opposition between security maximization and unrestricted enhancement proliferation.

"Initial staffing will incorporate specialized personnel beyond conventional security training," Director Reynolds continued, outlining operational structure beyond leadership appointment. "Recruitment focusing on individuals demonstrating balanced perspective regarding both legitimate security concerns and fundamental rights—operational team capable of implementing proportional intervention beyond conventional suppression methodology despite capability evolution beyond established parameters."

This staffing approach highlighted consistent implementation beyond leadership philosophy—recruitment focusing on balanced perspective rather than merely conventional security training or technical qualification. The operational team would incorporate individuals capable of implementing proportional intervention beyond conventional suppression methodology, personnel selection maintaining fundamental balance between legitimate security concerns and fundamental rights beyond traditional enforcement recruitment parameters.

"While incorporating specialized consultation beyond conventional institutional expertise," Director Reynolds added, acknowledging operational requirements beyond traditional security training or corporate scientific understanding. "Advisory roles for individuals with unique perspective regarding both enhancement evolution and framework stability maintenance—specialized consultation providing crucial context beyond conventional institutional positioning despite necessary operational independence regarding specific implementation details."

This operational structure highlighted innovative approach beyond conventional enforcement divisions—specialized consultation incorporated into fundamental operational methodology rather than merely occasional advisory capacity. The approach would establish ongoing advisory roles for individuals with unique perspective regarding both enhancement evolution and framework stability maintenance, operational balance incorporating specialized consultation into fundamental decision-making processes beyond conventional institutional positioning.

"Initial operations will commence following formal implementation of the Daybridge Accords," Director Reynolds concluded, establishing timeline beyond immediate acceptance. "Regulatory framework providing public authorization for specialized division beyond classified development channels—operational legitimacy established through transparent accountability measures despite necessary confidentiality regarding specific implementation details."

This implementation timeline highlighted legitimate foundation beyond classified development—specialized division operating through public regulatory framework despite initial development through confidential channels. The operational approach would establish transparent accountability measures while maintaining necessary confidentiality regarding specific implementation details, legitimate foundation providing operational authorization beyond merely classified development despite unprecedented parameters beyond conventional enforcement divisions.

As Director Reynolds departed following their conditional acceptance, Alice and Ethan faced professional landscape transformed beyond conventional operational parameters—leadership position within specialized enforcement division implementing balanced regulatory approach beyond binary opposition between security maximization and unrestricted enhancement proliferation. Their enhanced quantum bond would provide operational foundation beyond conventional partnership parameters, synchronized abilities offering unique qualification within emerging regulatory landscape despite capability evolution beyond established parameters.

• • •

"The Archives' expanded mandate represents unprecedented integration approach beyond conventional enhancement categories," Nadia explained, addressing specialized committee assembled within the governmental complex dedicated to implementation of the Daybridge Accords. "Information framework designed to facilitate sustainable participation beyond binary opposition between security maximization and unrestricted proliferation—balanced approach providing crucial resources regarding both legitimate opportunities and potential challenges despite enhancement evolution beyond established parameters."

Two weeks after formal implementation of the Daybridge Accords, government agencies had established specialized integration committee tasked with developing comprehensive support structures beyond merely regulatory framework. The Archives' expanded mandate represented crucial component within this integration approach, information resources providing practical guidance beyond theoretical principles within regulatory framework designed to establish sustainable balance following partial framework restoration.

"My appointment as Integration Director represents institutional commitment beyond conventional regulatory positioning," Nadia continued, professional precision in her explanation despite personal significance beyond career advancement. "Leadership focused on facilitating sustainable participation rather than merely monitoring compliance with established parameters—information resources designed to address practical challenges beyond theoretical regulatory framework despite necessary security considerations regarding capability evolution."

This appointment highlighted significant institutional transformation beyond conventional regulatory approaches—integration leadership positioned alongside enforcement authority rather than merely subordinate implementation role. The institutional structure acknowledged equal importance between facilitating sustainable participation and monitoring security compliance, balanced approach incorporating both support resources and regulatory framework within comprehensive response to unprecedented landscape created by partial framework restoration.

"The Archives will maintain three specialized divisions beyond conventional information resources," Nadia explained, outlining operational structure beyond leadership appointment. "Opportunity Facilitation connecting enhanced individuals with employment, education, and housing resources designed to accommodate capability parameters beyond conventional categories. Transition Support providing specialized assistance regarding psychological, physiological, and practical challenges associated with enhancement evolution following framework recalibration. Community Development facilitating meaningful integration beyond individual resources—sustainable participation structures addressing collective needs beyond merely personal transition challenges."

This operational structure highlighted comprehensive approach beyond conventional information services—specialized divisions addressing practical challenges across multiple domains despite theoretical regulatory framework within the Daybridge Accords. The approach acknowledged both individual and collective needs beyond merely security compliance, information resources facilitating sustainable participation across societal domains despite enhancement evolution beyond established parameters.

"Initial implementation will focus on high-priority demographics beyond conventional categorization systems," Nadia continued, professional precision in her explanation despite complex sociological implications. "Enhanced individuals experiencing significant capability evolution following quantum fluctuations—transition support addressing unprecedented challenges beyond conventional enhancement understanding despite absence of concerning behavior justifying security intervention."

This implementation focus highlighted balanced approach beyond security considerations—priority assistance for individuals experiencing significant capability evolution despite absence of concerning behavior justifying enforcement intervention. The approach acknowledged legitimate challenges beyond security categorization, support resources addressing practical transition difficulties despite capability parameters beyond established enhancement categories.

"While providing specialized information regarding balanced employment practices beyond conventional workplace accommodation," Nadia added, comprehensive vision extending beyond merely individual assistance. "Resources designed to facilitate sustainable integration within existing organizational structures—practical guidance regarding both legitimate safety protocols and inappropriate restrictions despite capability parameters beyond established enhancement categories."

This parallel implementation focus highlighted balanced approach beyond individual assistance—organizational resources facilitating sustainable integration within existing workplace structures despite capability evolution beyond conventional categories. The approach would provide practical guidance regarding both legitimate safety protocols and inappropriate restrictions, information resources establishing balanced employment practices beyond binary opposition between complete exclusion and unrestricted participation despite enhancement evolution following framework recalibration.

"The Archives will incorporate specialized consultation beyond conventional institutional expertise," Nadia concluded, acknowledging information requirements beyond traditional governmental understanding or corporate scientific assessment. "Advisory roles for individuals with unique perspective regarding both enhancement evolution and community integration—specialized consultation providing crucial context beyond conventional institutional positioning despite necessary operational independence regarding specific implementation details."

This operational structure highlighted innovative approach beyond conventional information services—specialized consultation incorporated into fundamental development methodology rather than merely occasional advisory capacity. The approach would establish ongoing advisory roles for individuals with unique perspective regarding both enhancement evolution and community integration, information resources incorporating specialized consultation into fundamental development processes beyond conventional institutional positioning.

"The expanded mandate represents crucial implementation beyond theoretical regulatory framework," observed Dr. Maya Chen, enhancement advocacy representative whose organization had previously operated in opposition to governmental information control regarding enhancement capabilities. "Practical resources addressing immediate challenges despite ongoing development regarding comprehensive integration approaches—information services providing essential guidance beyond regulatory principles despite unprecedented landscape following partial framework restoration."

This external validation highlighted legitimate foundation beyond merely institutional expansion—specialized mandate addressing practical implementation beyond theoretical regulatory framework. The information services would provide essential guidance regarding immediate challenges despite ongoing development of comprehensive integration approaches, practical resources facilitating sustainable participation beyond regulatory principles despite unprecedented landscape following partial framework restoration.

"While establishing crucial balance beyond conventional governmental positioning," added Security Director Kaplan, traditional enforcement representative whose perspective typically prioritized monitoring compliance rather than facilitating integration. "Information resources acknowledging both legitimate security protocols and inappropriate restrictions despite capability parameters beyond established enhancement categories—balanced approach providing practical guidance beyond binary opposition between security maximization and unrestricted participation."

This parallel validation highlighted comprehensive balance beyond conventional institutional positioning—information resources acknowledging both legitimate security protocols and inappropriate restrictions despite typically opposing institutional perspectives. The expanded mandate would establish practical guidance beyond binary opposition between competing institutional approaches, balanced information services facilitating sustainable integration despite conventional tension between security compliance and unrestricted participation.

"Creating information landscape beyond conventional enhancement categorization," Nadia acknowledged, professional precision in her assessment despite personal significance beyond career advancement. "Resources addressing practical challenges that theoretical regulatory framework cannot fully anticipate despite comprehensive development process—implementation guidance facilitating sustainable integration beyond binary opposition between competing institutional perspectives."

This summary highlighted core innovation beyond conventional information services—practical resources addressing implementation challenges that theoretical regulatory framework couldn't fully anticipate despite comprehensive development process. The expanded mandate would establish information landscape beyond conventional enhancement categorization, implementation guidance facilitating sustainable integration despite unprecedented landscape following partial framework restoration.

As specialized committee continued discussing implementation details beyond initial operational structure, Nadia maintained professional focus despite personal significance beyond career advancement. Her appointment represented culmination of extensive underground work beyond conventional institutional recognition—information networks developed through unofficial channels providing foundation for legitimate integration resources despite previous opposition from governmental security divisions.

The Archives' expanded mandate would transform underground networks into legitimate information resources beyond conventional institutional limitations—specialized divisions addressing practical challenges that theoretical regulatory framework couldn't fully anticipate despite comprehensive development process. The implementation approach would establish sustainable integration beyond binary opposition between security maximization and unrestricted proliferation, balanced information services facilitating meaningful participation despite enhancement evolution beyond established parameters.

As both the specialized enforcement division and expanded Archives implementation progressed beyond initial development stages, Alice and Ethan's partnership evolved to become operational foundation for the balanced regulatory approach established through the Daybridge Accords. Their enhanced quantum bond provided unique qualification beyond conventional enforcement capabilities despite legitimate security concerns regarding their own capability evolution, synchronized abilities offering implementation potential beyond established parameters while maintaining fundamental balance between increased capability and continued stability.

"The division headquarters represents physical manifestation beyond conventional enforcement architecture," Alice observed as they toured the specialized facility being developed through unprecedented collaboration between government security agencies and corporate research divisions. "Operational structure incorporating both intervention capability and scientific investigation beyond traditional security design— physical environment reflecting balanced approach beyond binary opposition between enforcement maximization and unrestricted enhancement proliferation."

The specialized facility occupied converted research complex within Daybridge's innovation district—location selected for both practical security considerations and symbolic positioning beyond conventional enforcement architecture. The design incorporated both specialized intervention capabilities and scientific investigation potential, physical environment reflecting balanced approach beyond binary opposition between competing institutional perspectives despite government authorization and corporate partnership.

"While providing operational foundation beyond conventional enforcement limitations," Ethan added, tactical assessment highlighting practical implementation beyond symbolic positioning. "Specialized systems designed to address capability evolution beyond established parameters—intervention technology incorporating both legitimate security protocols and proportional response methodology despite unprecedented enhancement landscape following partial framework restoration."

This observation highlighted practical functionality beyond architectural symbolism—specialized systems addressing capability evolution beyond conventional enforcement technology despite unprecedented enhancement landscape. The operational foundation incorporated both legitimate security protocols and proportional response methodology, intervention technology reflecting balanced approach beyond binary opposition between security maximization and unrestricted enhancement proliferation.

"The personnel selection demonstrates consistent implementation beyond leadership philosophy," Alice noted as they reviewed recruitment progress beyond initial staffing projections. "Team composition incorporating diverse perspective regarding both legitimate security concerns and fundamental rights—operational personnel capable of implementing balanced intervention beyond conventional suppression methodology despite capability evolution beyond established parameters."

This assessment highlighted comprehensive approach beyond merely leadership positioning—recruitment establishing operational team capable of implementing balanced intervention beyond conventional suppression methodology. The personnel selection incorporated diverse perspective regarding both legitimate security concerns and fundamental rights, operational capability reflecting fundamental balance beyond binary opposition between competing institutional approaches despite capability evolution beyond established parameters.

"While establishing specialized consultation beyond conventional institutional expertise," Ethan added, noting advisory appointments beyond operational staffing. "Information integration with Nadia's expanded Archives mandate beyond merely enforcement coordination —operational methodology incorporating practical guidance regarding both intervention protocols and integration facilitation despite necessary separation between enforcement authority and support resources."

This observation highlighted balanced implementation beyond merely enforcement capability—specialized consultation incorporating practical guidance from Nadia's expanded Archives mandate despite necessary separation between enforcement authority and support resources. The operational methodology would integrate information regarding both intervention protocols and integration facilitation, balanced approach incorporating comprehensive perspective beyond merely enforcement orientation despite specialized division's primary security focus.

"Creating operational landscape beyond conventional enforcement categories," Alice concluded, scientific assessment calculating implementation potential despite ongoing development process. "Intervention capability regarding both current enhancement evolution and potential threats beyond present security focus—operational methodology addressing immediate integration challenges while developing response capacity regarding emerging concerns beyond conventional enhancement categorization."

This summary highlighted comprehensive approach beyond merely immediate security focus—operational landscape addressing both current enhancement evolution and potential threats beyond present regulatory attention. The specialized division would implement balanced intervention regarding immediate challenges while developing operational capability for addressing emerging concerns beyond conventional enhancement categorization, implementation potential extending beyond immediate security landscape despite primary focus on current integration challenges.

As they continued developing operational methodology beyond initial implementation framework, their enhanced quantum bond provided crucial foundation for the balanced approach established through the

Daybridge Accords. Their synchronized abilities offered unique qualification beyond conventional enforcement capabilities despite legitimate security concerns regarding their own capability evolution, enhanced integration providing operational effectiveness beyond established parameters while maintaining fundamental balance between increased capability and continued stability.

The partial framework restoration had initiated evolutionary adjustment rather than revolutionary transformation, reality stabilizing into configuration that allowed greater consciousness-probability interaction while maintaining fundamental stability constraints necessary for coherent existence within shared reality framework. Their enhanced quantum bond represented natural response to this framework recalibration—consciousness connection achieving greater integration as artificial constraints slightly decreased throughout Daybridge's reality anchors, enhancement evolution corresponding to their natural quantum resonance patterns despite previous limitations imposed through conventional enhancement categories.

And as they prepared to implement balanced regulatory approach beyond conventional enforcement limitations, the fundamental question at the heart of the quantum showdown remained relevant despite operational resolution favoring evolutionary adjustment rather than revolutionary transformation: Were the constraints imposed during the Great Sundering necessary protection against consciousness that wasn't ready for direct probability interaction? Or unwarranted imprisonment of potential that should naturally develop without artificial limitation?

The answer continued evolving beyond binary opposition between competing modern perspectives—suggesting balanced approach that incorporated elements from both positions while transcending their fundamental limitations. The partial framework restoration had initiated capability expansion beyond artificial constraints without achieving complete liberation, creating adjustment that allowed greater consciousness-probability interaction while maintaining fundamental stability parameters necessary for coherent existence within shared reality framework.

This redefining balance represented sustainable foundation beyond either revolutionary transformation or perfect preservation—consciousness expanding beyond artificial limitations while maintaining fundamental stability parameters necessary for coherent existence within shared framework beyond binary opposition between competing philosophical extremes. The new regulatory approach acknowledged both legitimate security concerns and fundamental rights, balanced implementation facilitating sustainable integration despite enhancement evolution beyond established parameters following partial framework restoration that had transformed Daybridge's quantum landscape beyond conventional enhancement categorization.

EPILOGUE: THE FUTURE OF ENHANCEMENT

Six months after implementation of the Daybridge Accords, the city had stabilized into a new equilibrium—not perfect balance between competing perspectives but sustainable coexistence acknowledging both security concerns and fundamental rights. The partial framework restoration had initiated quantum recalibration beyond binary opposition, allowing greater consciousness-probability interaction while maintaining essential stability.

Alice stood at the observation platform overlooking Daybridge, her enhanced perception detecting quantum fluctuations invisible to conventional observation. The city appeared unchanged to ordinary perception, despite the profound transformation occurring beneath visible reality.

"The quantum resonance patterns have stabilized beyond initial projections," she observed as Ethan joined her, their enhanced quantum bond humming with harmonic precision conventional science still couldn't explain. "Reality anchors maintaining consistent parameters despite initial concerns regarding regression—framework adjustment demonstrating sustainable evolution rather than temporary fluctuation."

Ethan nodded, detecting the same stability patterns through tactical assessment. "The recalibration has maintained fundamental stability constraints while allowing greater consciousness-probability interaction beyond artificial limitations imposed before the quantum showdown."

This shared assessment highlighted the nuanced outcome—framework parameters adjusted rather than either completely transformed or artificially constrained. The quantum showdown had resulted in evolutionary recalibration rather than revolutionary liberation.

"The Hybrid Enforcement Division has established operational methodology beyond conventional security protocols," Ethan continued, professional satisfaction evident. "Intervention approach demonstrating balanced implementation—proportional response protocols addressing legitimate security concerns without imposing disproportionate restrictions."

"While the Enhanced Integration Archives have established comprehensive support structures," Alice added. "Practical guidance facilitating sustainable participation across multiple societal domains—employment integration, educational accommodation, healthcare specialization addressing unique requirements."

As they surveyed the city, both detected a subtle quantum disturbance—a reality ripple indicating brief intersection between adjacent dimensional frameworks. The momentary breach manifested as a localized probability anomaly conventional monitoring systems wouldn't properly identify.

"Dimensional intersection beyond conventional probability fluctuations," Alice noted with scientific precision. "Quantum signature suggesting momentary framework breach between adjacent dimensional structures—intersection potential beyond what monitoring systems have been calibrated to identify."

"The third dimensional breach this month," Ethan confirmed. "Quantum signatures suggesting consistent origin point despite variable manifestation locations—pattern indicating potential deliberate testing rather than random fluctuation."

"Lila's warning about other approaches toward reality manipulation beyond liberation methodology," Ethan recalled. "Different philosophical foundations utilizing parallel mathematical principles with potentially concerning implications for framework stability."

"Requiring operational evolution beyond current implementation parameters," Alice concluded. "Security methodology addressing potential dimensional vulnerabilities beyond conventional enhancement categories."

The most surprising institutional adaptation was the creation of the Interdimensional Research Division—a specialized unit operating within Kane Industries' Advanced Sciences sector but with oversight from multiple regulatory bodies. Dr. Winters headed this division, his consciousness still existing partially in probability space while maintaining coherent identity through his "middle path" approach.

More significant was the fundamental corporate restructuring that followed the exposure of The Architects' decades-long conspiracy. The Architects themselves had been removed from their shadow positions—five executives whose identities had shocked even long-term employees.

"The corporate reform goes beyond leadership replacement," Director Reynolds explained as they toured the transformed executive floor. "Structural transparency requirements have fundamentally changed how enhancement research is conducted and commercialized."

"The most profound change isn't operational but philosophical," Reynolds continued, guiding them through research facilities where scientists openly discussed theories that would have triggered "researcher management protocols" just months earlier. "Enhancement is being reconceptualized as evolutionary potential rather than technological dependency—natural consciousness development facilitated through appropriate support rather than artificial capability marketed as corporate innovation."

The room that had once hosted shadow conspiracy now displayed the guiding principle of Kane Industries' reformed approach: "Evolution through Balance—Supporting Consciousness Development within Sustainable Framework Parameters."

"The dimensional intersections are becoming more frequent," Alice noted as they documented the third breach that month. "The artifacts' regulatory function isn't maintaining dimensional barriers as effectively as it should."

Ethan studied the quantum data with tactical precision. "The patterns suggest deliberate testing rather than random fluctuations. Something on the other side is probing for weaknesses."

They shared a look of understanding. The artifacts' true purpose as dimensional regulators had transformed their understanding of both the Great Sundering and current security priorities. The conflict was no longer merely between constraint and liberation philosophies but about protecting their reality from external threats.

"The Great Sundering wasn't just about imposing constraints on consciousness evolution," Alice said quietly. "It was about establishing separation from something that threatened our dimensional reality."

"And now those barriers are weakening," Ethan added, already calculating defense strategies.

Director Reynolds joined them, his expression grave. "We've detected similar intersection points across multiple cities beyond Daybridge. Whatever's happening isn't isolated to our local quantum framework."

"Sarah's unique capabilities have become our most valuable asset against these dimensional incursions," Reynolds acknowledged. "Her quantum-ghost state can navigate these boundary areas in ways our conventional operatives simply cannot."

The monitoring center displayed Sarah's current deployment—her consciousness extending through a dimensional intersection point to establish stability fields where conventional technology could only detect the breach, not interact with it.

"She's not just detecting these incursions—she's communicating with them," Alice observed, watching her sister interact with quantum signatures from beyond their reality. "Her quantum-ghost state can establish resonance patterns that create basic interaction protocols where our technology sees only chaos."

"She's basically our dimensional diplomat and border patrol combined," Ethan noted. "Without her stabilization capabilities, these incursions would be creating framework fractures faster than our technology could respond."

"She's pioneering an entirely new approach to dimensional security," Alice said, scientific pride merging with sisterly affection. "Not constraint or liberation but natural harmonization—stability that accommodates evolution without sacrificing essential parameters."

As they watched Sarah navigating between dimensional frameworks, they recognized that her quantum-ghost state represented more than just unique enhancement potential. She was establishing the foundation for humanity's approach to a multidimensional future—natural harmonization that maintained essential stability while allowing consciousness to evolve beyond artificial limitations.

As they prepared for specialized deployment, their enhanced perception detected a subtle quantum signature indicating an underground enhancement gathering beyond regulatory monitoring—probability fluctuation suggesting a clandestine community meeting despite balanced implementation of the Daybridge Accords.

"The quantum signatures display harmonic patterns resembling The Flux's liberation methodology," Ethan noted, tactical assessment identifying concerning similarity. "Enhancement evolution demonstrating philosophical alignment with liberation ideology despite balanced regulatory implementation."

"Creating persistent ideological landscape beyond successful tactical intervention," Alice acknowledged. "The Flux's liberation philosophy continuing within underground enhancement communities—ideological persistence beyond merely tactical containment."

"While requiring balanced assessment beyond merely enforcement response," Ethan concluded. "Underground activities demonstrating philosophical alignment without necessarily indicating immediate framework vulnerability—ideological persistence requiring monitoring without justifying disproportionate intervention."

As they approached the dimensional anomaly deployment site, Alice and Ethan's enhanced quantum bond represented their renewed commitment to responsible enhancement—scientific understanding and enforcement authority balanced through shared perspective acknowledging both capability potential and stability requirements.

The future of enhancement existed within this complex equilibrium—regulated but not suppressed, evolving but not unrestrained, integrated but not unrestricted. The shadow war had ended, but a greater conflict was just beginning—one that would challenge not just how they understood enhancement, but reality itself.

APPENDIX: QUANTUM REFLECTIONS

"Reality isn't what we see, but what we're permitted to perceive."

— Dr. Winters, Quantum Resonance Project

This appendix explores the philosophical questions raised throughout the Shadow War narrative. Each chapter's events invite deeper contemplation about consciousness, reality, and the fundamental nature of existence. These reflections are offered as additional context for readers interested in the theoretical frameworks underlying the story.

CHAPTER ONE: THE ASSIGNMENT

WHERE DOES ENHANCEMENT **end and true consciousness evolution begin?**

Alice's unique quantum bond with Ethan represents abilities beyond conventional enhancement categories. This raises fundamental questions about whether their connection represents artificial modification or natural evolution of human consciousness potential—and whether such distinctions are meaningful when consciousness itself might naturally evolve beyond current limitations.

Who determines the boundaries of acceptable enhancement?

Kane Industries' regulatory approach to enhancement technologies suggests institutional control over human potential. Corporate science establishes artificial limitations while claiming to protect natural reality structures, raising questions about whether profit motivations and security concerns create arbitrary boundaries around consciousness evolution that serve institutional interests rather than human potential.

Can artificial constraints truly contain what consciousness naturally remembers?

The underground enhancement movements suggest consciousness retains memory of capabilities beyond current limitations. This raises profound questions about whether artificial constraints merely delay inevitable evolution of human potential—and whether reality itself maintains memory of configurations that existed before current limitations were imposed.

CHAPTER TWO: FIRST CONTACT

Does perception create reality or merely interpret what already exists?

Alice's enhanced perception allows her to detect quantum fluctuations invisible to conventional observation. This capability raises questions about whether reality exists independently of perception or is partially created through the act of observation—a fundamental question that transcends both scientific methodology and enhancement philosophy.

Can understanding something fundamentally change its nature?

The Liberation Quantum Front's approach to framework mechanics suggests understanding reality's true nature is necessary for transformation. This philosophical position raises questions about whether consciousness can fundamentally alter reality structures through comprehension alone—and whether liberation requires understanding or merely removal of artificial constraints.

Is security preservation of necessary stability or defense of artificial limitations?

Kane Industries' focus on maintaining reality anchors frames their work as essential security operations. This perspective raises questions about whether stability maintenance genuinely protects against catastrophic collapse or merely preserves artificial constraints that limit consciousness evolution beyond what institutional frameworks can control or monetize.

~

CHAPTER THREE: QUANTUM IDENTITY

DOES identity remain constant when consciousness expands beyond conventional parameters?

The quantum identity modules create artificial personas that exist alongside true consciousness. This technology raises questions about whether identity remains stable when consciousness operates across multiple reality states—and whether authentic self can be maintained when perception expands beyond singular reality framework.

Can artificial personas become more authentic than original identity?

Alice and Ethan's cover identities develop increasing complexity during their infiltration. This evolution raises questions about whether artificial personas can develop authentic existence through accumulated experience—and whether consciousness naturally fragments into multiple identity states when perception expands beyond conventional limitations.

Does shared perception fundamentally alter individual consciousness?

Alice and Ethan's quantum bond allows shared perception beyond conventional communication. This connection raises questions about whether consciousness remains individually distinct when perception becomes shared experience—and whether evolution naturally leads toward collective consciousness rather than merely enhanced individual awareness.

CHAPTER FOUR:
UNDERGROUND CURRENTS

Is liberation truly possible without understanding what came before?

The QLF's ideology suggests framework liberation without fully comprehending the original constraints. This position raises questions about whether removing limitations without understanding their purpose risks catastrophic consequences—and whether complete comprehension is even possible from within the framework being liberated.

Do artificial categories create the very divisions they claim to regulate?

The separation between "natural" supernatural communities and "artificial" technological enhancement appears increasingly arbitrary. This categorization raises questions about whether regulatory frameworks themselves create artificial divisions within unified consciousness potential—classifications that maintain institutional control rather than reflecting authentic reality structures.

What price does security demand, and who determines its value?

Kane Industries' enforcement approach sacrifices individual potential for collective stability. This security philosophy raises questions about who benefits from maintaining current reality constraints beyond merely preventing catastrophic framework collapse—and whether stability justifies permanent limitation of consciousness evolution regardless of potential benefits.

~

CHAPTER FIVE: THE LIBERATION QUANTUM FRONT

CAN revolution occur without destroying what it seeks to liberate?

The QLF's revolutionary approach focuses on dismantling existing framework constraints. This methodology raises questions about whether liberation necessarily requires destroying stability structures —and whether evolution can occur within existing frameworks or demands complete replacement of current reality configuration.

Does institutional science suppress knowledge or protect against dangerous misunderstanding?

The QLF's criticism of Kane Industries suggests corporate science deliberately suppresses knowledge about framework mechanics. This perspective raises questions about whether institutional science genuinely protects against dangerous misapplication or merely maintains knowledge monopolies that preserve corporate advantage and control over enhancement evolution.

Can opposing perspectives both contain essential truths?

The competing frameworks of Kane Industries and the QLF present fundamentally opposed interpretations of reality. This philosophical conflict raises questions about whether complete understanding might require integration rather than elimination of opposing viewpoints—and whether reality itself might exist as probability field containing multiple valid configurations simultaneously.

CHAPTER SIX: EARNING TRUST

DOES authenticity exist when operating between competing reality frameworks?

Alice and Ethan's undercover operation requires maintaining artificial personas while gathering intelligence. This duality raises questions about whether authentic identity can exist when consciousness navigates multiple truth structures simultaneously—and whether the concept of singular authentic self becomes meaningless when perception expands beyond conventional reality limitations.

Can understanding something transform the observer beyond recognition?

Alice's quantum mechanics expertise allows her to comprehend framework structures beyond conventional understanding. This comprehension raises questions about whether consciousness inevitably transforms when understanding expands beyond established parameters—and whether such transformation represents evolution or dangerous destabilization of identity.

Is deception justified when serving greater purpose beyond institutional objectives?

The undercover operation involves systematic deception despite Alice and Ethan's commitment to truth. This contradiction raises ethical questions about whether deception becomes morally justified when serving purposes beyond institutional objectives—and whether conventional ethical frameworks remain relevant when consciousness expands beyond artificial constraints.

CHAPTER SEVEN :
APPROACHING THE CORE

CAN identity remain stable when consciousness expands beyond conventional boundaries?

Cassandra and Daniel's deepening infiltration creates increasing identity complexity. This evolution raises questions about authentic self when operating between competing reality frameworks—identity becoming probability field rather than fixed point as consciousness navigates multiple truth structures simultaneously.

Does liberation require complete destruction of existing frameworks?

The QLF's approach suggests framework replacement rather than evolution. This revolutionary position raises questions about whether complete liberation necessarily requires destroying stability structures that maintain current reality configuration—and whether consciousness can evolve within existing frameworks or requires entirely new reality parameters.

When does protection become imprisonment?

Kane Industries' reality anchors maintain stability while preventing consciousness evolution. This security approach raises questions about whether protection inevitably becomes imprisonment when extended indefinitely—and whether temporary stability justifies permanent limitation of human potential beyond immediate threat containment.

CHAPTER EIGHT: THE ARTIFACTS

DO OBJECTS CONTAIN MEMORY BEYOND PHYSICAL PROPERTIES?

THE ARTIFACTS DISPLAY quantum properties that transcend conventional materiality. These characteristics raise questions about whether objects can contain memory beyond physical properties—and whether reality itself maintains records of configurations that existed before current limitations were imposed.

Can ancient understanding transcend modern technological advancement?

The artifacts demonstrate capabilities beyond modern enhancement science despite their ancient origin. This contradiction raises questions about whether ancient understanding might have comprehended reality aspects that modern science has forgotten—and whether technological advancement represents genuine progress or merely sophisticated rediscovery.

Does reality contain deliberate design or emerge through natural evolution?

The artifacts suggest deliberate framework manipulation rather than natural evolution. This indication raises profound questions about whether reality contains purposeful design—and whether current limitations represent protection against catastrophic consequences or artificial constraints imposed to maintain specific power structures.

CHAPTER NINE: ORIGINS UNVEILED

Were the constraints imposed during the Great Sundering protection or imprisonment?

The revelations about Dr. Winters' research suggest deliberate framework manipulation. This history raises the central question at the heart of the conflict—whether constraints imposed during the Great Sundering represented necessary protection against consciousness not ready for direct probability interaction, or unwarranted imprisonment of human potential that should naturally develop without artificial limitation.

Does consciousness naturally remember what reality attempts to forget?

Subject 37's evolution suggests memory beyond artificial constraints. This development raises questions about whether consciousness naturally retains connection to pre-Sundering configurations despite deliberate framework manipulation—and whether evolution inevitably leads toward remembering what has been artificially forgotten regardless of institutional attempts at memory suppression.

Can liberation occur without those who imposed constraints?

Dr. Winters' deliberate release of Subject 37 suggests liberation requires action from within institutional structures. This development raises questions about whether those who impose constraints might eventually recognize their limitation—and whether genuine liberation requires cooperation between those who maintain constraints and those who seek their removal.

~

CHAPTER TEN: THE QUANTUM UNDERGROUND
IS CONSCIOUSNESS NATURALLY CONSTRAINED OR ARTIFICIALLY LIMITED?

THE ARTIFACT RESEARCH suggests human consciousness naturally possesses capabilities beyond current framework parameters. This discovery raises fundamental questions about whether limitations represent protection or unnecessary constraints on natural potential—and whether consciousness evolution would naturally transcend current parameters without artificial limitations.

Can opposing perspectives both contain essential truths?

The competing frameworks of Kane Industries and the QLF each contain partial truths about reality's proper configuration. This philosophical conflict raises questions about whether complete understanding might require integration rather than elimination of opposing viewpoints—and whether reality itself might accommodate multiple valid configurations simultaneously.

Does evolution require revolution?

The QLF's approach suggests revolutionary transformation while Kane Industries insists on gradual evolution. This methodological conflict raises questions about whether consciousness can evolve within existing frameworks or requires complete liberation from artificial constraints—and whether stability and transformation represent fundamentally opposed values or potential synthesis.

CHAPTER ELEVEN: THE FACE OF THE ENEMY
DOES COMPREHENDING SOMETHING FUNDAMENTALLY CHANGE ITS NATURE?

ALICE'S direct interaction with QLF leadership transforms her understanding of their objectives. This evolution raises questions about whether comprehension fundamentally changes what is comprehended—and whether opposing perspectives can maintain rigid opposition when genuine understanding occurs between them.

Can revolutionary ideas exist without becoming what they oppose?

The QLF's organizational structure increasingly resembles the institutions they oppose. This evolution raises questions about whether revolutionary movements inevitably develop institutional characteristics similar to what they seek to replace—and whether genuine liberation requires fundamentally different organizational principles or merely different objectives within similar structures.

Is truth absolute or relative to framework perspective?

Alice's scientific understanding encounters fundamentally different interpretation of reality. This conflict raises questions about whether truth represents absolute reality or perspective relative to framework position—and whether complete understanding requires transcending framework limitations rather than merely understanding their operation.

CHAPTER TWELVE:
BETRAYAL MECHANICS

DOES loyalty to principle transcend loyalty to institution?

Alice's evolving perspective challenges her operational loyalty. This conflict raises questions about whether fundamental principles transcend institutional commitments—and whether genuine loyalty might sometimes require apparent betrayal when institutions diverge from the principles they claim to uphold.

Can security exist without artificial constraints?

Kane Industries' security philosophy equates stability with maintaining current framework parameters. This position raises questions about whether security necessarily requires artificial constraints—and whether genuine stability might emerge naturally from consciousness evolution beyond current limitations rather than through enforced framework preservation.

Does understanding enemies inevitably create sympathy for their position?

Alice's deepening comprehension of QLF philosophy creates increasing recognition of valid aspects within their perspective. This evolution raises questions about whether genuine understanding inevitably creates sympathy—and whether opposing perspectives can maintain absolute opposition when comprehensive understanding occurs between them.

CHAPTER THIRTEEN: THE FLUX REVEALED

Can consciousness exist coherently across multiple reality states?

The Flux demonstrates consciousness integration beyond conventional existence parameters. This manifestation raises questions about whether human identity can maintain coherence when experiencing multiple probability streams simultaneously—and whether such expansion represents natural evolution or dangerous destabilization.

Is fragmentation inevitable when consciousness expands beyond artificial constraints?

The Flux's evolved state suggests potential costs of framework transcendence. This condition raises questions about whether consciousness can expand beyond conventional limitations without sacrificing integration within shared reality—and whether coherent identity requires artificial constraints to maintain stable configuration.

Does liberation from artificial constraints necessarily lead to new responsibility?

The Flux's evolved capabilities create both expanded potential and increased accountability. This duality raises questions about whether consciousness that transcends conventional limitations requires new ethical frameworks beyond current understanding—and whether liberation necessarily creates responsibility beyond institutional regulation.

CHAPTER FOURTEEN: CONVERGENCE THEORY

DOES reality stabilize naturally or require artificial anchoring?

The convergence theory suggests framework destabilization without artificial anchoring. This theory raises questions about whether reality naturally maintains coherent configuration or requires deliberate stabilization—and whether artificial anchors represent necessary protection or deliberate imprisonment of natural evolution.

Can consciousness comprehend reality configurations beyond its evolutionary context?

The convergence theory suggests reality configurations beyond conventional comprehension. This complexity raises questions about whether consciousness can genuinely understand framework parameters beyond its evolutionary context—and whether complete comprehension might require evolution beyond current consciousness limitations.

Does transformation necessarily involve destruction of current configuration?

The convergence theory suggests catastrophic collapse during framework transformation. This prediction raises questions about whether evolution necessarily requires destruction of existing configurations—and whether transformation might occur through integration rather than replacement of current reality parameters.

~

CHAPTER FIFTEEN: THE QUANTUM SHOWDOWN
CAN OPPOSED CONSCIOUSNESS ACHIEVE HARMONIZATION WITHOUT DESTRUCTION?

ALICE and The Flux's direct confrontation creates unprecedented harmonization potential. This interaction raises questions about whether fundamentally opposed consciousness can achieve integration without mutual destruction—and whether genuine evolution might require synthesis between opposing perspectives rather than victory of one over another.

Does reality respond to consciousness intention or merely physical interaction?

The quantum showdown demonstrates reality responding directly to consciousness interaction. This phenomenon raises questions about whether reality fundamentally responds to intention rather than merely physical causality—and whether consciousness represents primary creative force within reality framework rather than merely emergent property within physical universe.

Can individual choice fundamentally transform reality configuration?

Alice's decision during the quantum showdown creates unprecedented framework response. This outcome raises questions about whether individual consciousness can fundamentally transform reality configuration—and whether evolution occurs through collective movement or pivotal individual choices at crucial junctures.

CHAPTER SIXTEEN: AFTERMATH

WHAT CONSTITUTES victory when reality itself has been transformed?

The quantum showdown's outcome defies binary success metrics. This complexity raises questions about framework parameters adjusted rather than either completely transformed or perfectly preserved despite tactical resolution favoring stability maintenance—and whether partial recalibration represents natural evolution rather than either failed liberation or successful protection.

Can consciousness evolution be regulated without being suppressed?

The enhanced oversight committee attempts balance between security concerns and enhancement rights. This regulatory approach raises questions about whether institutional regulation can accommodate consciousness evolution beyond conventional categories—and whether balanced oversight represents genuine progress or merely sophisticated suppression beneath regulatory legitimacy.

Does partial framework restoration represent failure or evolutionary compromise?

The reality stabilization following the quantum showdown creates adjusted parameters rather than complete transformation. This outcome raises questions about whether partial recalibration represents natural evolution rather than failed liberation or successful protection—and whether genuine progress occurs through revolutionary transformation or evolutionary adjustment of existing frameworks.

CHAPTER SEVENTEEN: REDEFINING BALANCE

CAN regulation acknowledge both security concerns and consciousness potential?

The Daybridge Accords establish new regulatory approach beyond conventional enhancement categories. This framework raises questions about whether institutional regulation can genuinely balance security concerns with consciousness evolution—and whether sustainable integration requires formal structures or emerges naturally through consciousness interaction beyond artificial constraints.

Does hybrid enforcement represent genuine balance or sophisticated control?

Alice and Ethan's leadership within specialized enforcement division creates unprecedented operational approach. This development raises questions about whether hybrid enforcement represents genuine balance between opposing perspectives or merely sophisticated control beneath apparent integration—and whether institutional structures can genuinely accommodate consciousness evolution beyond conventional parameters.

Can underground movements maintain philosophical integrity despite partial framework restoration?

Underground enhancement communities continue despite balanced regulatory implementation. This persistence raises questions about whether ideological movements require absolute transformation or can maintain philosophical integrity despite partial framework restoration —and whether genuine evolution requires continued pressure beyond institutional accommodation.

EPILOGUE: THE FUTURE OF ENHANCEMENT

Can sustainable balance exist between security and evolution?

The new status quo attempts regulation without suppression. This approach raises questions about whether institutional oversight can maintain stability while allowing consciousness to evolve beyond artificial constraints—and whether genuine balance represents stable configuration or merely temporary equilibrium between opposing forces.

Does framework modification create vulnerability or opportunity beyond current understanding?

The dimensional intersections suggest both potential threats and evolutionary pathways. These phenomena raise questions about whether adjusted reality parameters represent security concerns or natural progression beyond artificial limitations—and whether evolution inevitably creates both unprecedented opportunity and unique vulnerability regardless of institutional attempts at controlled development.

Will consciousness eventually transcend all artificial constraints regardless of institutional control?

The underground enhancement communities suggest persistent evolution despite regulatory frameworks. This continuation raises questions about whether consciousness will naturally expand beyond artificial limitations regardless of institutional attempts at containment or control—and whether evolution represents inevitable trajectory that regulation can merely guide rather than prevent.

A SNEAK PEEK AT WHAT'S NEXT!

THANK you for joining me on this journey through **Rise of the Underground: The Quantum Shadow War.** I hope you enjoyed exploring the mysteries of Daybridge and getting to know its secrets.

The story doesn't end here—there's so much more waiting to be uncovered. I'm excited to give you an exclusive first look **Blood Beneath Daybridge: The Making of a Monster -** *The Butcher's Tale,* the next book in the *Ethan Reeves Werewolf Detective Series*. Dive into the free chapter below and get a taste of what's to come!

Author's Note

Blood Beneath Daybridge: The Making of a Monster is the official prequel to *Shadows of Daybridge*, the first book in the Ethan Reeves werewolf detective series. While *Shadows* introduced readers to Detective Reeves and his investigation of supernatural crimes in present-day Daybridge, this prequel reveals the dark origins of the city's most infamous legend—the Ogre of Daybridge Bridge.

The events chronicled here span more than a century, from Guthrie Knox's childhood in the 1880s through his transformation into the monstrous entity that would haunt Daybridge for generations, culminating in the final confrontation with Detective Reeves that connects directly to the opening scenes of *Shadows of Daybridge*.

Prologue: The Butcher's Apprentice

Guthrie Knox was seven years old when he first understood that he was different from other children.

It wasn't the circumstances of his birth or his residence at Blackwell Orphanage that set him apart—many children in Daybridge's industrial quarters were orphaned by accident or disease, abandoned by parents who couldn't feed another mouth, or simply lost in the administrative chaos of a city expanding faster than its institutions could manage. The gray stone building that housed sixty-three unwanted children was a common enough feature of the cityscape, neither particularly brutal nor especially kind in its administration of young lives.

No, what made Guthrie different was something more fundamental, something that caused the caretakers to watch him with wary eyes when they thought he wasn't looking, something that made the other children maintain a careful distance despite the overcrowded dormitories.

It was the way he watched.

On that particular autumn morning in 1883, he stood in the orphanage courtyard, a slight figure with serious gray eyes, observing with clinical detachment as the butcher's delivery boy unloaded a half carcass of pork from his cart. Most children would have been repelled by the sight of the splayed ribs, the exposed muscle tissue, the lingering bloodstains on the burlap wrapping. A few might have been morbidly fascinated, giggling nervously or daring each other to touch the cooling flesh.

Guthrie simply watched, his gaze steady, his expression betraying neither disgust nor excitement—only intense, focused curiosity.

"What are you staring at, boy?" The delivery assistant, a red-faced teenager named Thomas, had noticed Guthrie's unwavering attention. "Never seen meat before?"

"Not like that," Guthrie replied, his voice oddly mature for a child so young. "Only after Mrs. Smithson has cooked it."

Thomas snorted, heaving the pork carcass higher on his shoulder. "Well, it doesn't start out as chops and roasts, does it? Something's got to die for you lot to eat."

"I know that" Guthrie said with a slight frown, as if offended by the suggestion he might not understand such a basic principle. "I've seen dead things before. Cats and pigeons and once a dog by the canal. But they were whole. This is... opened."

Something in the boy's tone—the complete absence of the squeamishness Thomas expected—made the delivery assistant pause. He studied the small, solemn-faced child more carefully.

"You're not squeamish, are you?" he observed. "Most kids your age would be green around the gills, looking at fresh slaughter."

Guthrie shook his head. "It's interesting. How it all fits together inside. Like machinery but made of meat."

Thomas barked a laugh, genuinely amused by the unusual response. "That's one way of looking at it, I suppose. You should see a whole pig come apart. Now that's something—watching a skilled butcher turn a carcass into all the different cuts. Like a puzzle in reverse."

The boy's eyes widened slightly, the first real expression of emotion he had shown. "Do they let children watch that?"

"Not generally, no." Thomas adjusted his burden, preparing to carry it into the orphanage kitchen. "Health regulations and all that. Plus, most kids would either faint or be sick all over the shop floor."

Guthrie took a step closer, his gray eyes fixed on Thomas with unsettling intensity. "I wouldn't be sick. I'd be quiet and stay out of the way. I just want to see how it works."

Something about the boy's seriousness, his complete lack of childish squirming or pleading, made Thomas consider the request more seriously than he might have otherwise. He studied Guthrie for a long moment, noting the careful stillness, the focused attention, the absence of the manic energy that typically characterized children his age.

"Tell you what," Thomas said finally. "I'll speak to Old Silas—he's the master butcher I work for. If he says it's alright, maybe you can come by the shop sometime. No promises, mind you. Silas is particular about his workspace."

Guthrie nodded solemnly, as if they were businessmen concluding a serious negotiation. "Thank you. I would appreciate that."

As Thomas disappeared into the kitchen with his burden, Matron Smithson emerged from the building's side entrance, her sharp eyes immediately finding Guthrie standing alone in the yard.

"Guthrie Knox! What are you doing out here? You should be in the dining hall with the others, setting tables for lunch."

"Yes, Matron. I was just watching the delivery." Guthrie turned toward the building, his expression once again neutral, revealing nothing of the conversation that had just transpired or the anticipation he felt at the possibility of visiting the butcher's shop.

"Always watching, that one," Matron Smithson muttered to herself as she followed him inside. "Never playing, never laughing like a proper child. Just watching everything with those old eyes. It isn't natural."

Three days later, Thomas returned to Blackwell Orphanage with the regular delivery and a message: Old Silas had agreed to allow one visit from the curious orphan, provided he stayed out of the way and followed instructions precisely. Matron Smithson was reluctant—allowing a child to leave the orphanage's supervision was irregular, particularly for such an unusual purpose—but Silas Holloway was a respected businessman and significant donor to Blackwell's perpetually strained resources. Permission was grudgingly granted for Guthrie to accompany Thomas back to the shop the following Saturday morning.

The anticipation that filled Guthrie during the intervening days was unlike anything he had previously experienced. He had always been a studious child, preferring books to the rough games that occupied most orphanage residents, but this was different—a focused excitement that manifested not in the fidgeting or chattering that might have betrayed another child's eagerness, but in an even more intense stillness, a heightened attention to detail in his chores and lessons, as if proving his worthiness for the opportunity ahead.

Saturday dawned clear and cold, a perfect late autumn day in Daybridge. Guthrie was awake before the bell, dressed in his cleanest clothes, his hair carefully combed with water from the dormitory basin. When Thomas arrived, the boy was waiting in the entrance hall, standing straight-backed beside a suspicious Matron Smithson.

"Now you mind your manners, Guthrie," she instructed sternly. "Mr. Holloway is doing you a great kindness allowing this visit. I expect you to be on your best behavior and return by noon precisely."

"Yes, Matron," Guthrie replied, his serious gray eyes meeting hers directly. "I'll be good."

The walk to Holloway's Meat Emporium took them through Daybridge's commercial district, a section of the city Guthrie had rarely visited. He absorbed the sights with his characteristic quiet attention—the shop fronts with their polished windows, the street vendors hawking hot chestnuts and meat pies, the carts and carriages navigating the cobblestone streets with varying degrees of success. He asked no questions, made no childish observations, simply processed everything with the same detached curiosity that had first caught Thomas's attention.

Holloway's occupied a prime corner location, its large windows displaying an array of cuts arranged with artistic precision on beds of fresh straw. The shop front, painted a deep burgundy that disguised the inevitable small bloodstains, bore the establishment's name in gold lettering along with the founding date: 1842. A small brass bell tinkled as Thomas ushered Guthrie through the front door.

The shop's interior was impeccably clean, the tile floor scrubbed to a dull shine, the marble counters wiped free of any residue from the previous day's business. Glass cases displayed premium cuts—crown roasts, tenderloins, specialty sausages—while hooks along the back wall held larger pieces awaiting further processing. The air carried the distinctive metallic scent of fresh meat mingled with the sharper notes of spices used in Holloway's signature preparations.

Behind the main counter stood a man who could only be Old Silas himself—though the nickname, Guthrie would later learn, referred more to his position as the oldest established butcher in this district than to his actual age, which was perhaps fifty. Tall and barrel-chested, with forearms corded with muscle beneath rolled-up sleeves, Silas Holloway possessed the physical presence of a man who had spent decades working with carcasses weighing as much as he did. His face, framed by muttonchop whiskers just beginning to show threads of gray, conveyed both the sternness of a master craftsman and a hint of genuine curiosity as he regarded his unusual visitor.

"So, this is the boy who wants to see how a carcass comes apart," Silas said, his voice a deep rumble that suited his imposing frame. "Thomas says you've got an unusual interest for one so young."

"Yes, sir," Guthrie replied, meeting the butcher's gaze with his customary directness. "I want to understand how things work. Inside."

Silas studied the child for a long moment, noting the serious expression, the controlled stillness, the complete absence of the nervousness or exuberance he would have expected from a boy this age. Then he nodded once, decisively.

"Understanding is a worthy pursuit," he said. "Too many people go through life never questioning what's beneath the surface. Come through to the back, then. We've a hog to break down this morning, delivered fresh from the Hargreaves farm yesterday. You'll see the process from start to finish."

He lifted a section of the counter, creating a passage to the workshop behind the retail space. Guthrie followed without hesitation, Thomas bringing up the rear with an expression that mingled amusement and lingering curiosity about this unusual orphan.

The workshop was larger than the front shop, designed for the practical business of transforming animal carcasses into retail products. A massive butcher block dominated the center of the room, its wooden surface-stained dark from years of use despite regular scraping and sanding. Various tools hung from hooks on the walls—cleavers, saws, knives of different shapes and sizes, each meticulously maintained and arranged in order of use. At the far end, a large sink and drainage area provided facilities for the necessary cleaning, while a heavy door presumably led to cold storage where carcasses were kept before processing.

"First rule in my workshop," Silas said, turning to face Guthrie with sudden sternness, "is absolute attention to instruction. One wrong move around these tools can cost a finger or worse. You'll stand exactly where I tell you, move only when I say you can, and touch nothing without explicit permission. Understood?"

"Yes, sir," Guthrie replied without hesitation.

"Second rule is cleanliness. Butchery is not a dirty business, despite what some might think. It requires precision, care, and proper hygiene. Thomas will get you an apron. It'll be too big, but it'll keep your clothes clean."

Thomas fetched a canvas apron from a hook by the door, helping Guthrie tie it behind his back. The garment indeed engulfed his small frame, the bottom edge nearly touching the floor, but the boy made no complaint.

"Now," Silas continued, "I'll explain each step as we go. Questions are permitted, but only between steps, not during cutting. Sharp tools require complete concentration."

With these preliminaries established, Silas nodded to Thomas, who disappeared through the heavy door at the rear of the workshop. He returned moments later, struggling slightly under the weight of half a pig carcass, already split lengthwise down the spine but otherwise intact from snout to tail. With practiced efficiency, he hoisted it onto the butcher block, positioning it precisely according to some system Guthrie didn't yet understand.

Silas studied the carcass with a professional eye, running his hand along certain sections as if confirming what his vision told him about the quality and condition of the meat. Then he turned to a sink, washing his hands thoroughly before selecting a specific knife from the array on the wall.

"We begin with separation of the primal cuts," he explained, positioning himself at the butcher block. "Observe the natural seams in the muscle structure. A good butcher works with the animal's anatomy, not against it. The knife follows the paths already present in the carcass."

What followed was a revelation to young Guthrie Knox. With movements that combined raw strength and balletic precision, Silas began transforming the uniform mass of the carcass into distinct sections— shoulder, loin, belly, ham—each separated along natural divisions in the muscle tissue with minimal sawing through bone. His commentary was sparse but precise, identifying each cut, explaining its characteristics, noting its best culinary applications.

Guthrie watched with unprecedented fascination. His already remarkable focus intensified, his gray eyes tracking every movement of Silas's hands, every incision of the blade, every separation of muscle from bone. He absorbed the terminology without effort—Boston butt, picnic shoulder, baby back ribs, pork belly—connecting each name to the specific part of the animal's anatomy as it emerged under Silas's skilled hands.

Most striking to both Silas and Thomas was the boy's complete comfort with the process. Where most children might have flinched at the occasional snap of cartilage or the subtle resistance of the knife against gristle, Guthrie showed only deepening interest. There was no disgust, no squeamishness, not even the morbid fascination that sometimes drew boys to bloody spectacles. Instead, there was only pure, clinical curiosity—the satisfaction of seeing a complex system revealed and understood.

As Silas moved from primary separation to the more detailed work of trimming and final preparation, he began to direct occasional questions to the unusually attentive child.

"Why do you think I'm cutting along this line here, boy?" he asked, his knife poised above a section of loin.

Guthrie studied the exposed muscle structure, his brow furrowed in concentration. "Because the fibers change direction there," he replied after a moment. "They run lengthwise on this side, but crosswise over there."

Silas's eyebrows rose slightly. "That's exactly right. Different muscle groups have different fiber orientations. Cutting against the grain gives you tender meat for quick cooking. Cutting with the grain gives you pieces that hold together during long, slow cooking." He nodded approvingly. "You've got a good eye."

The work continued, Silas occasionally testing Guthrie's understanding with similar questions, the boy responding with increasingly accurate observations as he began to grasp the underlying principles of the butcher's craft. Thomas, initially amused by the unusual situation, found himself impressed by the child's aptitude and seriousness.

When the final cuts had been wrapped and set aside for transfer to the shop displays, Silas turned to the cleaning process, demonstrating the same meticulous care in maintaining his workspace and tools that he had shown in the butchery itself. Guthrie assisted where permitted, his small hands surprisingly capable as he helped wipe down surfaces and organize tools for proper storage.

As they completed these final tasks, Silas studied the orphan with renewed interest. "You've got an uncommon mind, young Knox," he said finally. "Most boys your age couldn't sit still for ten minutes of this work, let alone a full morning. And fewer still would understand what they were seeing."

Guthrie looked up from the cleaver he had been carefully drying. "It makes sense to me," he said simply. "Everything has a structure. Once you see it, you can understand how it works."

"Indeed it does," Silas agreed, taking the cleaver and hanging it in its designated place. "And that understanding is the difference between a butcher and a mere meat-cutter. Anyone can hack a carcass to pieces with enough strength and sharp tools. But to do it properly—to respect the animal's design, to maximize the value of each part, to create cuts that will cook well and taste good—that requires knowledge and precision."

He paused, studying the serious-faced child before him. Something in the boy's focused attention, his natural affinity for the systematic approach that characterized good butchery, resonated with Silas in a way he hadn't anticipated when agreeing to this unusual visit.

"How would you like to come back next Saturday?" he asked abruptly. "There's a lamb scheduled for processing. Different animal, different muscle structure. Might be educational to see the comparison."

Guthrie's eyes widened slightly; the first real expression of emotion he had shown all morning. "I would like that very much, sir," he replied, his voice carefully controlled despite the obvious eagerness beneath the words.

"I'll speak to your matron, then," Silas said with a decisive nod. "If she's agreeable, perhaps we can make this a regular arrangement. Saturday mornings, before the shop opens to customers. You'd help with clean-up afterward, of course—earning your education, as it were."

"Yes, sir," Guthrie agreed immediately. "I'd work hard. I wouldn't be any trouble."

"I believe you," Silas said, and realized with some surprise that he meant it. There was something in this unusual child that inspired confidence—a seriousness of purpose, a natural discipline, that belied his seven years. "Thomas will walk you back to the orphanage now. We'll see about next week."

As Thomas escorted Guthrie back through the shop toward the front entrance, Silas Holloway watched the small figure in the oversized apron with thoughtful eyes. In his forty years as a butcher, he had trained several apprentices, but never one so young—and certainly never one who had shown such natural aptitude from the very first observation.

There was something different about Guthrie Knox, something in the way those serious gray eyes watched and analyzed and understood. Silas couldn't quite name it, this quality that set the boy apart, but he recognized its value. In his profession, such clinical detachment, such precise attention to structural detail, was not merely useful but essential.

The butcher nodded to himself; decision made. He would speak to Matron Smithson about a formal arrangement—Saturday mornings to start, perhaps expanding as the boy grew older and more capable. Blackwell Orphanage was always in need of financial support, and Silas had no children of his own to inherit his business. It was an unconventional arrangement, certainly, but one that might benefit all concerned.

As the shop door closed behind young Guthrie Knox, Silas returned to his workshop, unaware that his impulsive decision would shape not only the boy's future but, decades later, the very fabric of Daybridge itself. He could not have known that the skills he would teach—the precise dissection, the intimate understanding of how living things were constructed, the methodical transformation of once-living flesh— would one day be applied in ways he could never have imagined.

He saw only a serious child with unusual aptitude and focus—not the seeds of something that would one day become a monster.

～

In the years that followed, Guthrie's Saturday mornings at Holloway's Meat Emporium expanded into a formal apprenticeship. By age twelve, he was spending every day after school at the shop, learning every aspect of the butcher's trade under Silas's exacting tutelage. By fifteen, he had left school entirely to work full-time, developing skills that impressed even veteran butchers who visited from other districts.

Guthrie's quiet intensity, his meticulous precision, his absolute focus on mastering each technique—these qualities made him an exceptional apprentice. Where other boys might have been distracted by social pursuits or youthful rebellions, Guthrie remained singular in his dedication to understanding the structural intricacies of his chosen profession.

What neither Silas nor anyone else at the orphanage fully recognized was that this same clinical detachment, this ability to separate form from feeling, structure from sentiment, was developing in all aspects of Guthrie's interaction with the world. The emotional distance that made him an excellent butcher—able to transform living creatures into marketable products without distress or hesitation—was simultaneously creating a young man who moved through human society with the same analytical remove, observing social connections and emotional exchanges as systems to be studied rather than experiences to be felt.

By the time Guthrie Knox reached adulthood, he had become exactly what Silas Holloway had hoped for—a master butcher whose skills equaled or surpassed his own. But he had also become something neither of them had anticipated: a man whose understanding of physical structures far exceeded his comprehension of human emotion, whose precision with a knife was matched only by his disconnect from normal human bonding, whose perfect knowledge of how bodies were assembled existed alongside a profound ignorance of how hearts and minds connected.

It was this unique combination—technical mastery paired with emotional detachment—that would one day attract the attention of Eliza Blackwood, a woman whose own interest in the transformation of flesh extended far beyond conventional butchery. When she first observed Guthrie's work at Holloway's, she recognized something special in his methodical precision, his complete comfort with the intimate details of mortality, his natural talent for understanding how living things could be taken apart and, perhaps, put back together in new configurations.

In Guthrie Knox, master butcher and emotional outsider, Eliza saw the perfect candidate for a very particular kind of transformation—one that would require both his skills and his psychological distance from normal human concerns. She saw not just a craftsman, but a canvas for her most ambitious work yet.

She saw the man who would become the Ogre of Daybridge Bridge.

∾

ADDITIONAL BOOKS BY THE AUTHOR

Perfect for fans of gritty mysteries, dark magic, and pulse-pounding action, this urban fantasy thriller will keep you turning pages late into the night.

Daybridge Necropolis - Book Two

Detective Ethan Reeves, a werewolf hiding in plain sight, and his partner Alice Chen investigate a series of grave robberies that lead them to a necromancer's sinister plot to raise an undead army in Daybridge. Alongside the mysterious witch Lila Darkmagic, they race against time to stop the necromancer, whose power grows stronger each night through a forbidden magical tome.

As the dead rise and threaten to plunge the city into eternal darkness, Ethan must confront both the beast within himself and the ghosts of his past. With his partner Alice and a group of supernatural allies by his side, he faces his greatest challenge yet – stopping the necromancer's reign of terror before Daybridge falls to an endless night.

Shadows of Vengeance - Book Three

Detective Ethan Reeves and his partner Alice Chen face their deadliest case yet when an ancient evil awakens in Daybridge, threatening to unleash centuries of pent-up vengeance. Alongside witch Lila Darkmagic and archivist Nadia Marsh, they race to decode the mysterious Bloodline Archive before the Witch Queen's imminent resurrection tears their town apart.

In this third installment of the supernatural crime series, Daybridge's dark foundations are exposed as Ethan's team discovers that their quaint town was built on powerful magic and age-old sacrifices. As the line between past and present blurs, they must confront the reality that saving their community might demand the ultimate price.

Moonlight Origins: The Making of a Werewolf Detective – Book Four

When Detective Ethan Reeves set out to solve a routine homicide, the last thing he expected was to be bitten by a werewolf. Thrust into a world of supernatural politics and primal urges, Ethan must navigate his new dual identity as both a cop and a creature of the night.

As he seeks to uncover the truth behind his attack and a string of mysterious deaths, Ethan finds himself caught between upholding human laws and abiding by werewolf traditions. With the help of his partner and a few supernatural allies, Ethan soon realizes his unique position as a werewolf detective makes him invaluable for solving crimes in a city where the mundane and magical collide.

Action-packed and full of supernatural suspense, Moonlight Origins is the riveting fourth book in the Ethan Reeves Werewolf Detective series. Rae Stonehouse weaves an immersive hidden world of werewolf pack politics, sinister experiments, and occult murders. This thrilling urban fantasy noir is perfect for fans of Jim Butcher, Patricia Briggs, and the Dresden Files.

Discover a gritty and fang-filled mystery that will keep you turning pages well past the full moon. Moonlight Origins marks the prowling debut of a claw-ver new hero: Ethan Reeves, Werewolf Detective.

Shadows Between Thoughts - Book Five

When three ghost hunters disappear inside an abandoned maximum security hospital, Detective Ethan Reeves and his partner Alice Chen are thrust into a reality-bending investigation that challenges everything they know. As they explore the hospital's sinister history of unethical experiments, they discover their entire town of Daybridge has become a nexus for impossible phenomena and supernatural events.

Confronting ghostly apparitions and temporal anomalies, the investigators uncover a chilling truth: an ancient entity has been orchestrating events from the shadows, preparing for a convergence that could fundamentally alter the nature of consciousness itself. Racing against time that no longer behaves normally, Reeves and his team must adapt to new ways of perceiving reality to save the missing ghost hunters and prevent a catastrophic merging of dimensions.

~

Quantum Detective: The Alice Chen Files - Book Six

Detective Alice Chen, gifted with an extraordinary sensitivity to temporal anomalies, investigates a series of impossible murders that defy the laws of physics in Daybridge. Alongside her partner Ethan Reeves, she uncovers a vast conspiracy orchestrated by the Chronolith Society, a mysterious organization determined to control time itself and reshape reality to their will.

As temporal distortions escalate across the city, Alice must confront multiple versions of herself from different timelines while racing to stop the Chronolith Society's reality-altering agenda. Navigating a world where history becomes unreliable and causality breaks down, she discovers her own potential role in humanity's temporal future, all while mastering her quantum abilities to uncover truths hidden in the spaces between seconds.

~

Synthetic Storm: Evolution Unleashed - Book Seven

In Daybridge, Detective Alice Chen and her werewolf partner Ethan Reeves find themselves at the epicenter of a world-altering crisis when Dr. Helena Winters' supernatural enhancement technology triggers the Daybridge Evolution. As enhanced humans with godlike abilities emerge and cities begin to reshape themselves, the detectives must navigate a dangerous landscape of corporate espionage, supernatural factions, and quantum mechanics gone wild.

Joined by an eclectic team including a roguish journalist, a keeper of forbidden knowledge, a quantum physicist, and an ancient fae warrior, Chen and Reeves race to uncover Winters' true endgame. With reality itself beginning to bend and both human governments and supernatural councils scrambling to maintain control, they must stop a conspiracy that threatens not just the status quo, but the very nature of existence itself.

~

Blood Beneath Daybridge: The Making of a Monster – Book Eight

A dark prequel to the Ethan Reeves werewolf detective series

In 1913 Daybridge, master butcher Guthrie Knox's precision with a blade catches the eye of the enigmatic Eliza Blackwood, whose occult ambitions extend far beyond this world. Seduced by promises of transcendence, Guthrie instead finds himself transformed into something monstrous—a living nexus point beneath the city's great bridge, destined to feed on human victims for over a century.

As his consciousness fragments and evolves, the creature once known as Guthrie Knox becomes the legendary Ogre of Daybridge Bridge, a nightmare that shapes the city's history and collective psyche. When Detective Ethan Reeves arrives in 2025 to investigate the century-old mystery, the Ogre recognizes a connection to his past that may finally offer release from his cursed existence. Spanning over 100 years of horror, this chilling origin story reveals the dark foundation upon which the supernatural world of Daybridge was built.

THE QUANTUM FRAMEWORK SERIES

Rise of the Underground: The Quantum Shadow War - Book One

In Daybridge, where reality itself is negotiable, Detective Alice Chen goes undercover in the quantum underground to find her missing sister. Paired with tactical specialist Ethan Reeves, she infiltrates the Quantum Liberation Front, a group determined to remove what they believe are artificial constraints on human consciousness. As her own quantum powers evolve beyond established parameters, Alice discovers a conspiracy spanning decades—corporations aren't just regulating enhancement technology but deliberately suppressing humanity's true potential.

When ancient artifacts with reality-altering capabilities threaten to shatter dimensional barriers, Alice and Ethan must navigate between corporate conspiracy and revolutionary extremism to find a third path. The shadow war isn't just about enhancement regulation—it's about who controls reality itself, and whether the evolution of humanity requires protection from dangerous potential or liberation from artificial imprisonment. As entities from beyond their reality take notice, the future depends on finding balance between constraint and chaos before it's too late.

ABOUT THE AUTHOR

Rae Stonehouse turned to fiction writing after establishing himself as a prolific author of self-development and professional growth books.

With over 50 published works helping readers navigate personal and professional challenges, he embarked on a new creative path with the Ethan Reeves Werewolf Detective Series.

When not weaving tales of supernatural sleuthing, Stonehouse continues to share his expertise in personal development through workshops and speaking engagements from his home in British Columbia.

The Ethan Reeves series marks his debut in fiction writing, blending his understanding of human nature with a newfound passion for urban fantasy.

~